Regency Surrender

CHRISTINE MERILL — Wicked Deception
August 2018

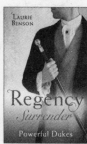
LAURIE BENSON — Powerful Dukes
September 2018

JANICE PRESTON — Scandalous Return
October 2018

ELIZABETH BEACON — Forbidden Pasts
November 2018

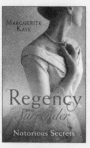
MARGUERITE KAYE — Notorious Secrets
December 2018

SARAH MALLORY — Infamous Reputations
January 2019

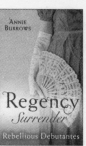
ANNIE BURROWS — Rebellious Debutantes
February 2019

ANNIE HERRIES — Defiant Lords
March 2019

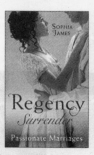
SOPHIA JAMES — Passionate Marriages
April 2019

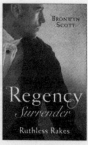
BRONWYN SCOTT — Ruthless Rakes
May 2019

GEORGIE LEE — Debts Reclaimed
June 2019

LOUISE ALLEN — Sinful Conquests
July 2019

Regency Surrender: Infamous Reputations

SARAH MALLORY

MILLS & BOON

First Published in Great Britain 2019
By Mills & Boon, an imprint of HarperCollinsPublishers
1 London Bridge Street, London, SE1 9GF

REGENCY SURRENDER: INFAMOUS REPUTATIONS © 2019 Harlequin Books S.A.

The Chaperon's Seduction © 2015 Sarah Mallory
Temptation of a Governess © 2015 Sarah Mallory

ISBN: 978-0-263-26792-1

52-0119

MIX
Paper from
responsible sources

FSC
www.fsc.org

FSC™ C007454

This book is produced from independently certified FSC™ paper to ensure responsible forest management.

For more information visit: www.harpercollins.co.uk/green

Printed and bound in Great Britain
by CPI Group (UK) Ltd. Croydon, CR0 4YY

THE CHAPERON'S
SEDUCTION

To my wonderful family, who make life so much fun.

Chapter One

Richard Arrandale had been in Bath for less than two weeks and was already regretting his promise to stay. It was not just that Bath in August was hot and dusty, it was exceedingly dull for one used to a hectic social round. He thought of the numerous invitations lining the mantelshelf of his rooms in London, including one from a dashing matron who had been putting out lures for some time. She wanted him to spend September with her at a house party in Leicestershire, where she promised him the hunting would be excellent and the evening entertainments more to his taste than anything he would find in staid and respectable Bath.

He did not doubt it, but he had given his word to his great-aunt Sophia, the Dowager Marchioness Hune, that he would remain in Bath until she was feeling better, even if that took him into the autumn, and he would not break his promise. Sophia had been the only one to support him in his darkest hour, when the rest of the world had seemed to be against him, and now that she needed him he would not walk away.

And it was not as if she expected him to dance attendance upon her at all times; she was quite content to see

him every morning before she went off to the hot baths
with her nurse, and for the occasional dinner at Royal
Crescent. Apart from that he was free to amuse himself.
Which was why he was now whiling away the evening
playing hazard in a small and select gaming hell. From
the outside, there was nothing to distinguish the narrow
house in Union Street from its fellows. The ground floor
was a tobacconist's shop but the curtains on the upper
floors were rarely drawn back, the proprietor, one Mr
Elias Burton, being determined not to distract his clientele by giving them any clue of the time of day.

Richard finished his wine before casting the dice on
to the green baize.

'Seven,' called Henry Fullingham, leaning closer to
peer short-sightedly at the ivory cubes. 'Trust Arrandale
to cast a main with his first throw.'

'Well, I am not going to wager against him matching it,' laughed George Cromby. 'His luck's in tonight.'

Richard said nothing, merely picked up his glass,
which had been replenished by a hovering waiter the
moment he had put it down.

'I won't bet against him either,' grumbled a thin, sour-
faced gentleman in a green coat. 'Luck, d'ye call it? His
throwing is too consistent by half.'

At his words a tense silence fell over the table. Richard scooped up the dice and weighed them in his hand,
fixing his gaze upon the speaker.

'What are you trying to say, Tesford?' he asked, his
voice dangerously quiet.

Fullingham gave a nervous laugh. 'Oh, he doesn't
mean anything, Arrandale. It's just the drink talking.'

Richard glanced around. They had been playing for
some hours with the wine flowing freely. Tesford's face
was flushed and his eyes fever-bright. He was glaring

belligerently across the table and for a moment Richard considered pressing the man, forcing a confrontation. After all, the fellow was questioning his honour. And a duel might alleviate his current *ennui*.

'Well, I ain't afraid to place a bet,' declared Fullingham cheerfully. 'Come along, Arrandale, throw again, we're all waiting!'

The murmur of assent went around the table. Wagers were being placed and Richard shrugged. Everyone was drinking heavily and it would be bad form to call out Tesford when it was clear he was in his cups. He cast the dice again.

'Deuce!' Fullingham laughed, a measure of relief in his voice. 'He's thrown out.'

Richard smiled and signalled to the hovering servant to fill his glass once more. Hazard was a game for those who could calculate the odds and he was good at that, but it was inevitable that sometimes the dice would fall against him. He did not like losing, but he was philosophical about it.

However, after another hour's play he was considerably richer than when he had arrived.

He was a gambler, but he knew when to stop and he was just gathering up his winnings when a noisy group of young bucks burst into the room. At their centre was a fashionably dressed gentleman, slightly older than his companions, whom Richard recognised as Sir Charles Urmston.

'They'll have come from the Assembly Rooms,' observed Cromby, looking round. He raised his hand and hailed the party. 'What news, my lads? I see young Peterson isn't with you, has he breached the defences of the fair Lady Heston?'

'Aye,' replied Sir Charles. 'He is escorting her home.'

'We won't be seeing him again before dawn then.' Cromby chuckled.

'And there's more news,' declared a red-faced young man coming closer to the table. 'A new heiress is coming to Bath!'

'And are you looking to this heiress to restore your fortunes, Naismith?' drawled Sir Charles. 'I doubt she would even look at you.'

Young Mr Naismith's face flushed an even deeper crimson.

'At least I'd make her an honest husband, Urmston,' he retorted. 'Everyone knows you played your late wife false.'

There was general laughter at that, but Richard saw the shadow of annoyance flicker across the older man's face.

'So who is this new heiress?' demanded Fullingham. 'Is she young, old, a beauty?'

'Young, definitely, but as for looks no one knows,' responded Mr Naismith. 'She is the daughter of the late Sir Evelyn Tatham and she is coming to live with her stepmama, Lady Phyllida Tatham, until her come-out next year.'

'A virgin, fresh from the schoolroom,' murmured Sir Charles. 'A plum, ripe for the plucking.'

Cromby frowned, drumming his fingers on the table. 'I remember old Tatham,' he said. 'He was a nabob, bought his knighthood after he made his fortune in India.'

Mr Naismith waved one hand dismissively. 'No one cares about that now. The thing is, Miss Tatham is his only child and she inherits everything!'

'Then she may look like old Tom's prize sow and

she would still attract suitors,' put in Tesford, draining his glass.

Sir Charles called to the waiter to bring them more wine.

'It seems a pity to have such a prize in Bath without making some attempt to win it,' he drawled.

Cromby grinned. 'Aye, by Gad. If I were not a married man I think I'd be making a push myself.'

'If the girl is so rich she will be well protected,' said Fullingham. 'Her guardians will be looking out for fortune-hunters.'

'There are ways to persuade a guardian,' put in Sir Charles, polishing his eyeglass. 'If the heiress was to lose her virtue, for example...'

'Of course,' exclaimed young Naismith. 'They'd want her married with all speed if that were to happen.'

'So shall we have a little wager as to which one of us will marry the heiress?'

Cromby banged on the table, looking up with a bleary eye. 'No, no, Urmston, that is unfair on those of us who are already leg-shackled.'

Sir Charles spread his hands.

'Very well, if you all want to have a touch, let us say instead, who will be first to *seduce* her.'

'Much better,' agreed Cromby, laughing immoderately. 'Then we can all have a pop at the heiress.'

Fullingham raised his hand. 'There must be witnesses, mind—a trustworthy servant or some such to confirm the prize is won.'

'Naturally.' Urmston smiled. 'Waiter, tell Burton to bring the betting book and we will write this down.' His hooded eyes surveyed the company. 'But there is one here who has not yet agreed to join us, one whose reputation as a devil with the ladies is well known in London. What say you, Arrandale? I should have thought you eager for this little adventure.'

Richard did not allow his distaste to show.

'Seducing innocents has never appealed to me. I prefer women of experience.'

'Ha, other men's wives.'

'Not necessarily, just as long as they don't expect me to marry 'em.'

There was general laughter at his careless response.

'What, man?' exclaimed George Cromby. 'Do you mean you have not left a string of broken hearts behind you in London?'

'Not to my knowledge.'

'Best leave him out of it,' cried Fullingham gaily. 'He is such a handsome dog the ladies can't resist him. The rest of us would stand no chance!'

'Certainly I have not heard of Arrandale being involved in any liaisons since he has been in Bath,' murmured Sir Charles, swinging his eyeglass back and forth. 'Mayhap you are a reformed character, Arrandale,'

'Mayhap I am,' returned Richard, unperturbed.

'Or perhaps, in this instance, you are afraid of losing out to the better man.'

Richard's lip curled. 'Hardly that.'

'So why won't you join us?' demanded Fullingham. 'You are single, if the chit took a fancy to you there is no reason why you shouldn't marry her. Don't tell me a rich bride wouldn't be an advantage to you.'

Richard sat back in his chair, saying nothing. As a second son he had been expected to find a rich bride, but his brother's disastrous marriage had made him shy away from wedlock and he was determined to remain a bachelor as long as possible.

He was fortunate to have inherited Brookthorn Manor

from his godfather. It was a neat property in Hampshire that included a home farm and substantial estate. Without its income he would have been obliged to seek some form of employment by now. As it was, Brookthorn gave him independence, but he knew it could not support his lifestyle for much longer. It needed careful management, but when had the Arrandales ever been good at that? Their name was synonymous with scandal and disaster.

Sir Charles was standing over Richard, a faint, sneering smile on his face. He said quietly, 'A thousand pounds says I can secure the heiress before you, Arrandale.'

Surprised, Richard looked up. 'A private wager, Urmston? I think not.'

'Very well.' Sir Charles looked at the men gathered around the table. 'There are eleven of us here.' He gestured to the hovering proprietor to put the betting book, pen and ink down on the table. 'How much shall we say? A monkey from each of us?'

'What had you in mind, Urmston?' demanded Tesford.

'We will each stake five hundred pounds that we will be the first to seduce Miss Tatham. Burton shall hold the money until one of us is successful.'

'Capital! But we should set a date on it, Urmston,' cried Henry Fullingham, his words slurring a little. 'Can't have this going on indef—indefinitely.'

'Very well,' Urmston looked around the room. 'Shall we say the next Quarter Day?'

'Michaelmas,' nodded George Cromby. 'Just over a month. That should be sufficient time for one of us to succeed.'

'Very well. Five thousand pounds to whoever can seduce the heiress by September the twenty-ninth. And of course the added prize, the possibility of marriage for those of us who are single.'

Cromby laughed. 'And if I should be successful…'

'The way would be open for one of us bachelors to snap her up,' Tesford finished for him. 'And her family would be grateful for it, too. By Jove that is an excellent suggestion. I'm not averse to spoiled goods, if they come with a fortune.'

'Quite.' Urmston placed the book upon the table and quickly wrote down the terms.

'Well, Arrandale, what do you say, does five thousand pounds hold no appeal? Or perhaps you prefer to run away, like your brother.'

A sudden hush fell over the table. Not by the flicker of an eyelid did Richard show how that remark angered him. There was a mocking smile around Urmston's mouth, challenging him to refuse. Richard looked at the pile of coins before him on the table. A thousand pounds. He had been planning to use some of it for vital maintenance on Brookthorn Manor, but now, dash it, he would show Urmston who was the better man! He pushed his winnings back to the centre of the table.

'Let's double it.'

The tense silence was broken by gasps and smothered exclamations. One or two men shook their heads, but no one walked away.

'Very well, a thousand pounds each.' Urmston corrected the terms and held the pen out to Richard. 'That's a prize of ten thousand pounds, Arrandale.'

Richard took the pen, dipped it in the ink and added his name to the others.

'Ten thousand,' he repeated. 'Winner takes it all.'

'There.'

Lady Phyllida Tatham placed the little vase of flowers on the mantelshelf and stepped back to look around the room. She had only signed the lease on the house at the beginning of the month and had been busy decorating it to her liking ever since, finally ending with this bedroom overlooking the street. Despite the open window there was still a faint smell of paint in the air but she hoped it would not be too noticeable. The room had been transformed from a rather austere chamber to a very pretty apartment by using cream paint on the panelling and ceiling and adding fresh hangings in a yellow floral chintz around the bed and the window. The dressing table and its mirror had been draped with cream muslin and new rugs covered the floor. Phyllida dusted her hands and smiled, pleased with the results of her handiwork.

It was just such a room as she would have liked when she had been on the verge of her come-out, and she hoped it would appeal in the same way to her stepdaughter. Ellen was even now on her way from the exclusive seminary in Kent to live in Bath with Phyllida. Doubts on the wisdom of this arrangement had been expressed by relatives on both sides of the family. Phyllida's sister had merely mentioned her concern in a letter, questioning if Phyllida had considered fully the work involved in being chaperon to a lively girl only seven years her junior. Her late husband's brother, Walter, was much more forthright and had even posted to Bath to remonstrate with Phyllida.

'My dear sister, you have no idea what you are taking on,' he had told her in his pompous way. 'My niece has always been flighty, but now at seventeen she is far too hot at hand. The tales Bridget and I have heard of her behaviour at the seminary are quite shocking!'

'She is spirited, certainly—'

'Spirited!' he interrupted her, his thin face almost contorting with disapproval. 'She even ran away!'

'No, no, you have been misinformed,' she corrected him soothingly. 'Ellen and her friends slipped off to see the May fair and they were back before midnight.'

'But it is well known who instigated the adventure! Surely you do not condone her gallivanting around town in the middle of the night?'

'Not at all, but thankfully she came to no harm, as Mrs Ackroyd was quick to point out.'

'She was also quick to inform you that she could no longer allow Ellen to remain in her establishment.'

'Only because the squire had developed an…an unquenchable passion for Ellen and had taken to calling at the most unreasonable hours.'

'And Ellen encouraged him!'

'No, she wrote to assure me she had done no more than allow him to escort her back from church.'

'From Evensong. At dusk, without even a servant in attendance.'

Phyllida frowned. 'How on earth can you know all this? Ah, of course,' she said, her brow clearing. 'Bridget's bosom bow, Lady Lingford, has a daughter at Mrs Ackroyd's Academy, does she not? Bernice.' She nodded. 'I recall Ellen telling me about her when she came home to Tatham Park for Christmas. An odious talebearer, she called her.'

'How I came by the information is neither here nor there,' replied Walter stiffly. 'The truth is that if Mrs Ackroyd, an experienced schoolmistress, cannot keep the girl safely contained then what chance do you have? I am sorry to speak bluntly, my dear sister, but my brother kept you too protected from the real world.

You are far too innocent and naïve to be my niece's guardian.'

'I am very sorry you think that, Walter, but Sir Evelyn left Ellen in my sole charge and I am going to have her live with me until next year, when she will make her come-out under my sister's aegis. You need not worry, I am quite capable of looking after her.'

When she had spoken those words to her brother-in-law Phyllida had felt quite confident but now, with Ellen's arrival so imminent, she felt a moment's doubt. Had she been foolish in bringing Ellen to live with her? Since Sir Evelyn's death a year ago Phyllida had been very lonely, living retired and out of the way with only an aged relative for company. More than that, she had been bored. She had not realised how much she would miss the life she had enjoyed as the wife of Sir Evelyn Tatham. She had entered the marriage with some trepidation and few expectations, but Sir Evelyn had shown her a kindness and consideration she had never known at home. She had enjoyed running his household and there was even some comfort to be found in his bed, although there was never the heart-searing elation she had read about in novels or poetry. That, she knew, needed love and she had come to think that such love, the sort that sent one into ecstasy or deep despair, must be very rare indeed. But it did not matter, she filled her days with her new family and friends. It had been enough, and she had felt its lack during those twelve long months of mourning. She also knew from her stepdaughter's letters that Ellen was growing increasingly frustrated at her school. She wanted to be out in the world, to try her wings. When Mrs Ackroyd had written, saying that it was with the utmost reluctance she must request Lady

Phyllida to remove her stepdaughter from her establishment, hiring a house in Bath for herself and Ellen had seemed the perfect solution.

The sounds of a carriage below the window recalled her wandering attention. She looked out to see her own elegant travelling chaise at the door and her smile widened. She said to the empty room, 'She's here!'

Phyllida hurried down the stairs, removing her linen apron as she went. By the time she reached the hall it was bustling with activity as the footmen carried in trunks and portmanteaux under the direction of a stern-faced woman in an iron-grey pelisse and matching bonnet. Her appearance was in stark contrast to the other female in the hall, a lively young lady of seventeen with an excellent figure displayed to advantage by a walking dress of the palest-blue velvet and with a frivolous cap upon her fair head. Phyllida's heart swelled with pride and affection as she regarded her pretty stepdaughter. Ellen was chatting merrily to Hirst, the elderly butler whom Phyllida had brought with her to Bath, but when she saw Phyllida she broke off and rushed across to throw herself into her stepmother's open arms.

'Philly! At last.' Ellen hugged her ruthlessly. 'I am so pleased to be with you!'

'And I am pleased to have you here, my love. Goodness, how you have grown, I would hardly have recognised you,' declared Phyllida, laughing as she returned the girl's eager embrace. 'Was it a horrid journey?'

'Not at all, your carriage is so comfortable and everyone we met on the journey was very kind. When we stopped for the night at the Stag we thought we should have to eat in the coffee room because a large party had taken over most of the inn, but when they heard of our predicament they were generous enough to vacate one of their parlours for us, and then last night, at the Red Lion, a very kind gentleman gave up his room to us, because ours overlooked the main highway and was terribly noisy.'

'Thank goodness you were only two nights on the road, then, or heaven knows what might have happened next,' exclaimed Phyllida. 'Perhaps I should have come to fetch you, only I wanted to make sure the house was ready.'

'And you knew I would be perfectly safe with dear Matty to look after me.'

Hearing her name, the woman in the grey pelisse looked up.

'Aye, but who has looked after my lady while I've been away?' she demanded.

'The new girl we hired, Jane, has done very well,' responded Phyllida calmly. 'I think she will suit me perfectly.'

'Do you mean Matty will no longer be your maid?' asked Ellen, wide-eyed.

'No, love, Miss Matlock would much prefer to look after you. After all, she was your nurse until you went off to school.'

'What my lady means is that I am aware of all your hoydenish tricks, Miss Ellen,' put in Matlock, not mincing matters.

'I have no hoydenish tricks,' exclaimed Ellen indignantly.

'No of course not,' Phyllida replied, hiding a smile and recognising a little of the old Ellen beneath that new and stylish exterior. 'Now let us leave Matlock to see to all your bags and we will go into the morning room. I have lemonade and cakes waiting for you.'

Thus distracted, Ellen followed Phyllida across the hall.

'Oh, it is so *good* to be with you again, Philly,' she said as soon as they were alone. 'Apart from those two weeks at Christmas I have not seen you for a whole year.'

'You know we agreed it was important that you finish your schooling, and you would have found it very dull at Tatham Park this past twelve months.'

'I suppose you are right. But I was afraid, with Papa gone, I should have to live with Uncle Walter and his family until my come-out.'

'Now why should you think that, when you know your father made me your guardian?'

'Because I know how much you dislike fuss, and with everyone saying you were far too young to be my stepmama—'

'When I first married your father, perhaps, but I am four-and-twenty now!' protested Phyllida, laughing.

'*I* know that, but you look far younger and I thought they would bully you into submission.'

Phyllida put her hands on Ellen's shoulders and looked into her face.

'I know I was very shy and, and *compliant* when I married your papa,' she said seriously, 'But I have changed a great deal since then, my love. I made my come-out fresh from the schoolroom and I knew nothing of society, which is a great disadvantage. I was determined you should not suffer the same way, which is why I thought a few months in Bath would be most beneficial to you.'

'And so it will be.' Ellen enveloped Phyllida in another embrace. 'We shall have such *fun* together, you and I.'

'Well, yes, I hope so,' said Phyllida. 'The past year, living on my own, has made me heartily sick of my own company. Now,' she said, leading Ellen to the table. 'Come and try some of the lemonade Mrs Hirst has made especially for you.'

* * *

The evening passed in non-stop chatter and by the time she went to bed Phyllida realised how much she had missed her stepdaughter's company. Phyllida had been just eighteen when she had married Sir Evelyn and she had made great efforts to befriend his eleven-year-old daughter. Even though Ellen had been packed off to school soon after the marriage they had remained close, much more like sisters than mother and daughter. Phyllida had always felt that to be an advantage, but as she blew out her candle she was aware that the tiny worm of anxiety was still gnawing away at her comfort.

At seventeen Phyllida had been painfully shy. She had been educated at home with her sister and had experienced nothing beyond the confines of the small village where they lived. Ellen was not shy. The select seminary in Kent where she had spent the past five years might have given her an excellent education but from her artless conversation it was clear that she had enjoyed far more licence than Phyllida had known at her age. It was doubtful she would feel any of the mortification Phyllida had experienced during her one London Season.

Phyllida had stood firm against every argument the family had put forward but now she wondered if she had been selfish to insist upon bringing Ellen to Bath. The recent elopement of the late Marquess of Hune's daughter with a penniless adventurer showed that danger lurked, even in Bath. What did she, Phyllida, know about playing chaperon to a young girl, and an heiress at that? With a sigh of exasperation she punched her pillow to make it more comfortable.

'Ellen will have me and Matty to look after her, she cannot possibly come to any harm,' she told herself as she settled down again. 'I shall not let doubts and anxieties spoil my pleasure at having Ellen with me. We shall have a wonderful time!'

Chapter Two

'Good morning, sir. Her ladyship's compliments, she hopes you will be able to break your fast with her this morning.'

Richard groaned at his valet's determinedly cheerful greeting. It was not that Fritt had woken him, nor a sore head that caused him to mutter an invective as he sat up in bed, but the memory of last night's events. Had he really signed his name to that foolish wager? He had obviously been more drunk than he realised because he had allowed his dislike of Sir Charles Urmston to get the better of him. It was too late to cry off now, it was against his code of honour to renege on a bet. Damn the man, even the memory of Urmston's self-satisfied smile had Richard fuming. The valet gave a little cough.

'As time is pressing, sir, I have brought your shaving water. I thought we might make a start…'

'Surely it can't be that pressing,' retorted Richard. 'Where is my coffee?'

'Beside your bed, sir, but her ladyship is always in the breakfast room by nine and it is nearly eight o'clock now…'

'For Gad this is an unholy hour,' grumbled Richard. 'What time did I get to bed?'

'I think it must have been about four, sir. Would you like me to inform her ladyship that you are indisposed?'

'You know that's impossible. She doesn't ask much of me, so I must do this for her.' Richard swallowed his coffee in one gulp. 'Very well, let us get on with it.'

He jumped out of bed, yawning but determined. He owed this much to Sophia. She had stood by him when the rest of the family had wanted him to disown his brother and he would never forget it.

'Hypocrites, the lot of 'em,' she had told him when the scandal broke. 'The Arrandales have always had skeletons in their cupboards. Why should they object so much to yours? My door is always open to you Richard. Remember that.'

He had been just seventeen at the time and grateful for her support. She had neither judged nor censured his conduct, even when he left Oxford and took London by storm, embarking upon a frantic round of drinking, gambling and women. No, she had not tried to stem his outrageous behaviour; it was in his blood, his father had told him as much. Everyone knew the Arrandales spread scandal and mayhem wherever they went. He plunged his head into the bowl of warm water on the washstand. He would stay in Bath just as long as Sophia needed him.

An hour later Richard walked into the breakfast room, washed, shaved and dressed in his morning coat of blue superfine. His great-aunt was already sitting at the table.

'Good morning, Sophia.' He kissed her cheek. 'You are looking very well this morning.'

'Which is more than can be said for you,' she retorted. 'I'm surprised that man of yours let you out of your room dressed in that fashion.'

Richard laughed.

'Are my shirt points not high enough for you?'

The Dowager Marchioness of Hune gave an unlady-like snort.

'They are more than high enough. I can't abide the fashion for collars so high and stiff men can't move their heads, they look like blinkered horses! No, 'tis your neckcloth. Too plain. Not a scrap of lace. Your father wore nothing but the finest Mechlin at his neck and wrists.'

Richard sat down at the table.

'Well, you will have to put up with me as I am,' he replied, unperturbed by her strictures. 'It shows my affection for you that I am out of bed at this dashed unfashionable hour.'

'If you did not stay up so late you would find this a very reasonable hour to be up and about.'

'If you say so, ma'am.'

She gave him a darkling look. 'Don't think I don't know how you spend your evenings.'

'Gambling, I admit it.' He grinned. 'It could be worse. I am avoiding the muslin company.'

'I should think so, after that latest scandal in town. From what I hear you were not only involved with the wife of a government minister, but with his mistress, too.'

'Yes, that was a little complicated, I admit. So, in Bath I will stick to the gaming tables. But you may be easy, ma'am, I never gamble more than I can afford.'

He decided not to mention last night's little wager. A mistake, that. He had no intention of joining the pack; they would be sniffing around the heiress like dogs around a bitch on heat. He hid a little grimace of distaste. He would rather lose his thousand pounds, write it off to experience. An expensive lesson and one he could ill afford, but he would not sink to that level.

'And what are your plans for today?'

Lady Hune's question surprised him. Generally she left him to his own devices until dinner time.

'Why, I have none.'

'Good. Duffy has the toothache and I am packing her off to the dentist this morning. I shall forgo my visit to the hot baths but I hoped you would accompany me to the Pump Room.'

'With pleasure, ma'am. Shall you take the carriage?'

'Damn your eyes, boy, I am not an invalid yet! If you give me your arm I shall manage, thank you.'

Richard quickly begged pardon, pleased that his great-aunt had recovered much of her old spirit in the two weeks he had been staying with her. When she had sent for him the tone of her letter had caused him concern and he had set out for Bath immediately. He had found the dowager marchioness prostrate on a day-bed, smelling salts clutched in one hand, but his arrival had greatly relieved her distress and she had soon been able to explain to him the cause of it. She had handed him a letter.

'Read this,' she commanded him. 'It is from that ungrateful baggage, my granddaughter.'

'Cassandra?'

'The very same. She has turned out to be a viper in my bosom. I took her in when her parents died, gave her the best education, petted and spoiled her and this is how she repays me, by running away with a nobody.'

Richard scanned the letter quickly.

'The signature is blotched,' he observed, 'As if tears were shed in the writing. Oh, damn the girl, I never thought Cassie would treat you in this way.'

'She thinks she is in love.'

He looked up. 'This is dated the end of July. Two weeks since!'

'I thought at first Cassie might think better of it and come back. When she did not and my health deteriorated, Dr Whingate suggested I should have someone to bear me company, which is why I wrote to you.' She gave a sharp crack of laughter. 'Whingate expected me to summon poor Cousin Julia, but she is such a lachrymose female I couldn't face the thought of having her with me.'

'I can think of nothing worse,' he agreed, with feeling. 'Well, Sophia, what do you want me to do?' he asked her. 'Shall I go after them? I drove to Bath in my curricle but doubtless you have a travelling chaise I might use.'

The old lady shook her head.

'No, they fled to the border, you know, and were married there. She is now Mrs Gerald Witney.'

His breath hissed out. 'If you had sent for me immediately I might have caught up with them.' He lifted one brow. 'I could still find them, if you wish it, and bring her back a widow.'

'And have her hate me for ever more? Not to mention the additional scandal. No, no, if she loves him let her go. Witney is a fool but I do not believe there is any harm in him. To bring her back would only cause more gossip. It was a seven-day wonder here in Bath of course, everyone was talking of it at first, but that has died down now.' She sighed. 'Her last letter said they were taking advantage of the peace to go to Paris. Cassie always wanted to travel, so I hope she is happy with her nobody.'

'I take it you forbade the banns?'

'Of course I did. As soon as I saw which way the wind was blowing I made enquiries, told her Witney was a penniless wastrel but she would not listen, she had already lost her heart. I did my best to confound them, with Duffy's help, but she slipped away in the night. Laid a false trail, too, sent us careering in the wrong direction. By the time we discovered the truth they had already reached Gretna and were married.' She scowled. 'I have no doubt that was all Cassie's idea, too. She is by far the more intelligent of the pair and not afraid to cause outrage!'

'She is a true Arrandale, then.' Richard gave a wry smile. 'It's in the blood, ma'am. There ain't one of us that hasn't caused a scandal of some sort. Why, if what they say is true, you yourself ran off with Hune.'

'But at least he was a marquess, and rich, to boot! No, I told Cassie I would not countenance her marriage to Witney. His birth is acceptable but he has no fortune, no expectations. Not that that bothered Cassie, she fell for his handsome face. Oh, he is pretty enough, I'll grant you, and amiable, too, but he has not a feather to fly with.'

'Then how will they manage?'

'She took all her jewels. She must sell them and live on that until she gains her majority next year. Then she will have a pretty penny to her name, enough to dispel any lingering gossip. They will be rich enough to be accepted everywhere. 'Tis the way of the world.'

The dowager had shed a few uncharacteristic tears then, and Richard had made his promise to stay.

Cassandra's elopement had not been mentioned since, but it was clear that Sophia had been badly shaken by the incident and Richard was too fond of his great-aunt to abandon her until her health and spirits were fully returned. Thus it was that shortly after noon on a sunny day in late August Richard escorted Lady Hune to the famous Pump Room.

Their progress was slow, for Lady Hune was well known in Bath and they encountered many of her acquaintances, all of whom wished to stop and enquire after her health. They were distantly polite to Richard, making it very clear that he was only tolerated because of his connection to the dowager marchioness. He expected nothing else, given his reputation. After all, he was an Arrandale: they lived hard, played hard and devil take the hindmost.

The Pump Room was busy and noisy, echoing with chattering voices.

'I know now why I have not been here since I arrived in Bath,' muttered Richard as he led his great-aunt through the crowd. 'The great and the good—and the not so good—gather here to gossip about and pass judgement upon their acquaintances. By George how they stare!'

'Most likely they are wondering who my handsome escort can be.' Sophia chuckled.

'Oh, I know most of 'em,' he replied bitterly. 'It is more likely they think no son of the shamed house of Arrandale should be allowed to sully these hallowed portals, especially one whose brother was branded a murderer.'

Sophia tapped his arm with her fan. 'Enough of that nonsense, Richard. You forget that I, too, am an Arrandale.'

'But you married your wealthy marquess, ma'am. That lifts you out of the mire surrounding the family's name. Look at them all. They smile now, but when trouble descends they will not hesitate to tear one apart, like hounds scenting blood, as I know only too well.'

'Not all of them. The Wakefields, for example, are charming people. I see Lady Wakefield is here today, would you like me to introduce you?'

'No need, I am acquainted with the son and I agree, they set no store by my wicked reputation. But they are the exception. The rest live for gossip. You told me how they all gloated over Cassie's elopement, how can you bear to be polite to them now?'

'Easily,' she replied. 'We nod and smile and return each other's greetings with equal insincerity. Hush now, Lady Catespin is approaching.'

'My dear Lady Hune!' A gushing matron bore down upon them, her generous proportions swathed in yellow sarcenet and a feathered bonnet perched on her improbably black curls. Richard was forcibly reminded of a galleon in full sail and was obliged to hide a grin as his great-aunt responded to the lady's fulsome greeting.

'And Mr Arrandale, too, what a pleasure to see you here, sir. I heard you were in Bath, but our paths have not crossed since we met in town—when was it—Lady Whitton's rout, I believe?'

He bowed. 'I believe you are right, ma'am.'

The matron turned back to Lady Hune, saying with blatant insincerity, 'It must be such a comfort to you, ma'am, to have Mr Arrandale staying with you in Royal Crescent. The house must feel so empty with poor Lady Cassandra gone.'

Sophia's claw-like fingers dug into Richard's arm and he covered her hand with his own, giving it a little squeeze of support.

'Yes, Lady Cassandra has married her beau,' he said easily. 'We received a letter from her only the other day, did we not, Aunt? She is ecstatically happy.'

Lady Catespin blinked, her look of spurious sympathy replaced by one of surprise.

'Oh. You…you *approve* of the match?'

'We do not challenge it,' put in Lady Hune, every inch a marchioness. 'I might have preferred a different husband for her, but one cannot always regulate one's affections. My granddaughter is lawfully married now, there is nothing more to be said.'

'Ah, of course. I see.' The wind might have been taken out of Lady Catespin's sails, but she was not yet becalmed. 'And you are here to support your great-aunt, Mr Arrandale. Your family is no stranger to tribulation, is it, sir, what with your brother...?' She gave a gusty sigh and turned her eyes back to Lady Hune. 'I am sure your great-nephew will know just how best to comfort you, my lady.'

'He would, if I needed comfort,' retorted Sophia, losing patience. 'What I *do* need is his arm to push through the crush of gossiping busybodies one finds in the Pump Room these days!'

Lady Catespin drew back at that, flushing beetroot.

'That's spiked her guns,' murmured Richard as they walked away from the speechless matron. 'I thought you said we should merely smile and ignore their barbs?'

'I forgot myself. Bad enough that she should goad me about Cassie, but to bring up something that happened years ago was more than flesh and blood can bear!'

Richard shrugged. 'You have no need to rush to my defence. I have grown used to the censure, even from my own family. Everyone except you thought I was wrong to stand by my brother, ma'am.'

'I really do not know why they were all so quick to condemn Wolfgang. Nothing was ever proved.'

'But Father was convinced he murdered his wife. Convinced enough to try to break the entail.'

Lady Hune waved one dismissive hand. 'Whatever Wolfgang has done he is still your brother. The world is too quick to censure, in my opinion, and in Bath they are more self-righteous than anywhere else.'

'Dash it, Sophia, if that is the case why do you stay?'

'For my health.' She added with a wicked glance, 'And the fact that I enjoy gossip as much as anyone. There is very little else to do when one is my age!'

They had reached the pump and waited silently while a bewigged-and-liveried footman dispensed a beaker of the warm water to Lady Sophia. She sipped it with obvious distaste while Richard stood patiently beside her. Glancing around the crowded room, he nodded to a few acquaintances, including a couple of gentlemen from the gambling hell. He was just wondering how much longer his great-aunt would want to remain when he heard her exclaim.

'Ah, I was wondering if she would make an appearance today.'

'Who, ma'am?' He was at that moment observing a rather handsome brunette who was casting roguish looks in his direction and so did not look round.

'Phyllida Tatham. And she has brought her stepdaughter with her.'

The heiress. Richard's interest sharpened immediately. The dashing brunette was forgotten and his eyes moved to the door, where two ladies were hesitating on the threshold. They were both fashionably attired but his eyes were immediately drawn to the dainty blonde dressed in a cream-muslin gown with a blue spencer fastened over it. A straw bonnet rested on her golden curls, held in place by a blue ribbon, tied at a jaunty angle beneath one ear. This enhanced the startling perfection of her heart-shaped face with its straight little nose and huge, cornflower-blue eyes. Her companion was slightly taller and far less striking in a simple walking dress the colour of rose leaves with a matching cap pinned to her neat brown hair. At least, he considered her less striking until she spotted Lady Hune and a sudden, wide smile transformed her countenance. He was reminded of the sun breaking through on a cloudy day.

'Ah, good. She's seen me and is coming over.'

Richard stifled an exclamation. '*That* is Lady Phyllida? Why, she is scarcely older than her stepdaughter.'

'Tatham married her almost out of the schoolroom,' Sophia told him. 'Nice gel, never a hint of scandal to *her* name, although there was no end of talk at first, because Sir Evelyn was almost in his dotage.'

'Lady Hune.' The widow came up and sank into a graceful curtsy before the marchioness. 'I am very glad to find you here, for I would like to present my stepdaughter to you.'

So this was the heiress. Richard surveyed Miss Ellen Tatham with a coolly professional eye. She was certainly a beauty, from her guinea-gold curls to the dainty feet peeping out beneath the hem of her embroidered muslin. Her figure was good, her tone lively without being strident and she bore herself well, greeting Sophia with a pretty deference that he knew would please. Great heaven, even without a fortune every red-blooded male in Bath would be falling over themselves to court her!

'…my great-nephew, Richard Arrandale.'

Sophia was presenting him to Lady Phyllida. He dragged his attention back, summoning up a careless smile as he reached for the lady's hand. Her eyes widened, dilating as he grasped her fingers. What the devil? Richard concealed his surprise: he had not said or done anything to frighten her. She must know of his reputation, he thought as he kissed her hand and felt it tremble, but she replied calmly enough to him and stepped back to introduce her stepdaughter.

Surely the young widow could not have sole responsibility for this piece of perfection? But it appeared to be so, for even as he addressed Miss Tatham, Lady Phyllida was explaining as much to Sophia.

'Ellen is going to live with me in Bath until the spring,' she was saying in her soft, musical voice. 'Then we go to London, to my sister, Lady Olivia Hapton, who is to bring Ellen out.'

'And will you return to Bath afterwards, Lady Phyllida?' asked Sophia.

'Perhaps, I have not considered. I moved here so that I might have Ellen with me. I thought we could enjoy a little society while she continued her education through the winter.'

'Philly—that is,' Ellen corrected herself with a mischievous look, '*Stepmama* has kindly organised lessons for me in singing, dancing and Italian. Of course I learned all those things at school, but one can always improve.'

'Indeed, it is never too late to improve oneself,' agreed Sophia. Richard felt rather than saw the look she cast at him. 'No doubt you will be attending the balls and concerts, too?'

'Oh, yes, ma'am. That is all part of my education, ready for my come-out in London next year.'

'A very pretty-behaved child,' opined Sophia when Lady Phyllida led her stepdaughter away a short while later. 'Pretty face, too.'

'Exceptional,' agreed Richard. 'A veritable diamond.'

'She has everything,' continued Sophia slowly. 'She is handsome, of good birth and has a considerable fortune, just like—'

She broke off as an elderly gentleman approached and Richard stood back, lost in thought as they conversed. He guessed what she had been about to say.

Just like Cassandra.

Sophia was clearly on good terms with the widow and inclined to approve of her stepdaughter. Thank heaven she did not know about the wager!

'So you have stolen the march on us already with the heiress.'

A soft, drawling voice intruded upon Richard's reverie and he turned to find Sir Charles Urmston at his shoulder.

'Quite a piece of perfection, isn't she?' Urmston continued, raising his glass to study Miss Tatham, who was now on the far side of the room talking with the Wakefields. 'I had thought Miss Julia Wakefield the most attractive girl in the room, but her prettiness is quite eclipsed by Miss Tatham's golden beauty. A fortune is always worth pursuing, but when it comes so deliciously packaged, how can one resist?'

Richard frowned. The idea of Urmston pursuing Ellen Tatham did not please him. Sir Charles was a cousin of Richard's late sister-in-law and they had met upon occasion, but Richard had not felt any inclination to pursue the acquaintance following his sister-in-law's premature demise eight years ago. Richard sensed a cruel and predatory nature behind Urmston's ready smile and urbane manners. He had met his sort before, a charming man about town, befriending eager young bucks and helping them to spend their—or rather their family's—fortune. He did not condemn Urmston for his way of life, after all a man must live.

It was no secret Urmston had bullied his wife, who had died in childbirth a year ago, along with their unborn baby. The idea of any innocent young girl being cruelly tricked into marriage and treated badly was not something Richard could condone, yet he had signed up to the wager, along with the others. His frown deepened as he considered the men who had put their signatures in the book. There was no doubt that any one of them would cold-bloodedly ruin the girl in order to win the prize money. That thought proved equally distasteful, though he knew seductions such as this were common practice. And it was not only Ellen Tatham who would suffer. A sudden vision of Lady Phyllida's distress disturbed him and he quickly pushed it away. Good God, when had he become so fastidious? He must be getting old.

Suddenly the idea of making a play for the heiress himself seemed almost sensible. He would be doing the girl a kindness if he married her, not to mention the fact that her fortune would prove very useful. If reports were true it was sufficient for him to maintain Arrandale and still keep his own family in luxury. He had not come to Bath looking for a wife but it was expected that he would settle down one day, and if Wolf should not return it would clearly be his duty to carry on the line. Perhaps he should not let this chance slip by. He glanced across the room to where Lady Phyllida was presenting her stepdaughter to Lady Wakefield. From this distance they might have been sisters.

It would be an easy seduction. The stepmother was no dragon and he had no doubt he would easily gain her approval. After that, it would be a simple matter to win the hand and the heart of the beautiful Miss Tatham. It was of little consequence whether *his* heart was engaged. He would treat her well and she would be better off with him than any of the other men who would be vying for her attentions. He had no doubt he would win, by fair means or foul. After all he was a rake, wasn't he? One of the infamous Arrandale family. And rake hell was what they did.

So now he smiled at Urmston. 'As you say, Sir Charles, how can one resist such a beauty? I give you fair warning, this is one wager I mean to win!'

Phyllida kept her smile in place as she progressed around the Pump Room, making Ellen known to her many acquaintances, but inside her heart was racing, as were the chaotic thoughts that flew around her head until she felt quite giddy. Richard Arrandale was the last man she had expected to meet in Bath. Since marrying Sir Evelyn their paths had not crossed, but seeing him again had brought it all back, that night at Almack's, seven years ago, when he had danced with her.

She remembered it all so clearly. He had been the most handsome young man she had ever seen, with his brown hair gleaming in the candlelight, and that laughing twinkle in his blue eyes. He was only a year or so older than Phyllida but already he had been a confident man about town, whereas she had been a tongue-tied young girl, fresh from the schoolroom and dressed in an unbecoming pink gown that her mother had thought the appropriate colour for a débutante. Her first and only Season had been a tortuous round of parties and dances, where she had been too shy and plain to attract the attention of any young man. She had spent long evenings sitting at the side of the room while the other young girls danced and laughed and enchanted their partners. Even those gentlemen who were persuaded to stand up with her quickly made their exit when they found that she was too shy to do more than blush and return monosyllabic answers to their attempts at conversation. She had told herself it did not matter, that she cared for none of them, and that was true, until she had danced with Richard Arrandale.

Phyllida had known his reputation—everyone in London was aware of it—but in her silly schoolgirl mind she had thought that she could tame him, that if only he could see past her rather plain looks he would be captivated by her goodness and would repent his wild ways.

How he must have despised her for her awkwardness, even though he had laughed and made light of it when she had moved the wrong way in the dance and collided with him. He had responded to her mistake by giving her his whole attention, smiling at her, putting her at her ease. He had looked at her, really *looked*, as if she was the only lady in the room. As if she mattered. At that point she had lost her heart completely. In her foolishness she had dreamed of him making her an offer, going down on one knee and declaring that he was reformed, for her sake.

All nonsense, of course. A handsome gentleman like Richard Arrandale would never be interested in a gauche schoolroom miss with mousy hair and nondescript greygreen eyes. As her newly married sister had said, when Phyllida had returned starry-eyed from Almack's that night; 'Men like Arrandale can turn on the charm whenever they wish. He will not even remember you tomorrow.'

And Olivia had been right. The next time Phyllida had seen Richard Arrandale in Bond Street he had not even noticed her. It had been a salutary lesson and when, a few days later Papa had told her she was to wed Sir Evelyn Tatham, she had buried her girlish dreams for ever.

Phyllida knew she had been right to do so. While she had concentrated on being a good wife to Sir Evelyn, Richard Arrandale had blazed a trail through London society like a shooting star, his outrageous behaviour discussed, condemned and dissected in the society pages of the newspapers. His name was linked with all the most dashing matrons, he attended the most riotous house parties and was thought to have lost more than one fortune at the gaming tables.

Everyone said it was only to be expected, for it was well known that his older brother had killed his wife and run away with the family jewels. Nothing had been proven, the matter had been hushed up as was the way with rich, powerful families, but everyone knew it all the same. Bad blood, they said, and Phyllida knew she should be grateful not to have attracted the notice of such a notorious rake as Richard Arrandale. But sometimes as she lay in her bed with her kind, worthy husband snoring beside her, Richard's image would return and she could not help sighing for what might have been.

Too late had Phyllida recognised the tall figure standing beside Lady Hune in the Pump Room and recalled that the dowager marchioness was an Arrandale by birth. She was already committed to approaching, but when Richard had taken her hand and kissed it the years had fallen away and she was once again the awkward girl in her first Season, being saluted by a man who was the embodiment of her dreams.

Only, Richard Arrandale was not the heroic figure of her girlhood fantasies. She knew that only too well and looking up into his face she had seen the faint lines of dissipation about his mouth and eyes. There hung about him a world-weariness that made him seem older than his years, for he could not possibly be more than five- or six-and-twenty. Richard Arrandale was a rake and it was only his connection with Sophia, Dowager Marchioness of Hune, that made her acknowledge him and introduce him to her stepdaughter.

Phyllida took Ellen on a full circuit of the room but afterwards she could never recall just whom they had met, nor what was said. All she could remember was Richard Arrandale's laughing eyes and the touch of his lips against her gloved hand. As she and Ellen left the Pump Room arm in arm she risked a last look back. He was still watching them, or, more correctly, he was watching Ellen.

'What is wrong, Philly?' Ellen stopped in the doorway and turned an anxious gaze upon her. 'You are shivering, but it is not at all cold. Are you unwell?'

'What? Oh, no, my love, no, not at all.' She shook off her uneasy thoughts and summoned up a smile. 'We elderly ladies are prone to sudden chills, you know.'

Ellen gave a little trill of laughter.

'Very well, my aged Stepmama! I shall take you home, tuck you up in a shawl and feed you gruel.'

'That will certainly do the trick.'

'I hope so, because you promised we could go shopping today.'

'Very well, let us do so immediately. It will be infinitely preferable to eating gruel,' said Phyllida, laughing.

The sun came out at the moment and her spirits lifted. She was foolish to allow an old memory to make her so fanciful. She squeezed Ellen's arm, quickened her step and set off for Milsom Street to indulge in a few hours of frivolous expenditure.

Chapter Three

Having decided to pursue the heiress, Richard lost no time in making his plans. The Bath season did not start until October, but he was determined not to wait until then to advance his acquaintance with Miss Ellen Tatham. At breakfast the following morning he made his first move.

'Do you wish me to come to the Pump Room with you again today, Sophia?'

'Thank you, no. Duffy had the offending tooth removed yesterday and is quite recovered now. You must have more entertaining things to do than attend an old lady.'

'It is always a pleasure to escort you, ma'am. And I was heartened to find that not all those attending the Pump Room are valetudinarians. Lady Phyllida, for example.'

'Yes. She's a quiet gel, but very sensible, and makes a good partner at whist. I have always liked her.'

This was very encouraging. He said, 'You knew her before she came to Bath?'

'We have mutual acquaintances in Derbyshire, near Tatham Park. I met her there often when Sir Evelyn was alive. Glad to see she is out of mourning now and back in the world where she belongs.'

'What's her background?' Lady Hune shot him a swift, suspicious glance and he added quickly, 'Lady Phyllida looks familiar, and I would judge her age to be similar to my own. I thought perhaps I might know her.'

'She is possibly twelve months your junior. One of the Earl of Swanleigh's two girls. The elder married Lord Hapton and Swanleigh wanted a similar success for Phyllida. She was presented in…let me see…'ninety-six and caught the eye of Sir Evelyn, who was then a widower and looking for a new wife to give him an heir. They were married within the year. Of course there was a lot of talk, but those who prophesied disaster were only half right. The hoped-for heir never materialised but the marriage seemed happy enough. When Tatham died last year it was assumed Lady Phyllida would go to live with her sister or with Tatham's brother and dwindle into mediocrity as some sort of live-in companion, little more than a glorified servant. But give the girl her due, she refused to relinquish her independence. She retired to her house in Derbyshire for her period of mourning.'

'And now she is in Bath.'

'Yes. She has taken a house in Charles Street for herself and her stepdaughter.' Sophia shook her head, adding darkly, 'How *that* will work out I don't know.'

'Ninety-six.' Richard's brow creased in thought. 'Hmm, seven years ago. I had left Oxford and was in town then.'

'Aye, you were, and already kicking up a dust!'

'I must have danced with her. Trouble is, ma'am, I danced with a deuced lot of young ladies in those days.'

'It's no wonder if you don't remember her. Her looks were never out of the ordinary, nothing to attract you. Tatham, however, was desperate for an heir. I think he would have taken anyone.' She looked up, saying sternly, 'She is a fine young woman, Richard, and I count her a friend. I would not have you doing anything to upset her.'

He looked pained.

'I promise you I have no intention of upsetting her.'

No, he had no intention of upsetting anyone, he thought, as he presented himself at the freshly painted front door in Charles Street later that day. He was shown into the drawing room, where Lady Phyllida received him with cool politeness.

He bowed. 'I was pleased, yesterday, to renew my acquaintance with you, my lady.' Her brows went up and he continued smoothly, 'We met in town did we not, at your come-out. We danced together at Almack's.'

This was a chance shot but he thought it had hit its mark. An added flush of colour painted her cheeks, but she spread her hands and gave him an apologetic smile.

'I vow I cannot recall. I know my mother bullied every gentleman present to stand up with me, however reluctantly.'

'There was no reluctance upon my part, ma'am, I assure you.'

'But after, what is it…five years, six?…I am flattered that you should remember.'

She doesn't believe me.

Richard kept his smile in place as he met her gaze. He had thought yesterday her eyes were grey but he saw now that they were flecked with green and her look was surprisingly direct. He had a sudden urge to tell the truth and confess that he didn't remember her at all. Impossible, of course. He must hold his nerve.

She invited him to sit down.

'How are you enjoying Bath?' he asked her as he lowered himself into a chair opposite her own.

'Very much. After the isolation of Tatham Park, Bath seems very busy.'

'And will you put your name down in the book when the subscription opens later this month? That is necessary, I believe, if you wish to attend balls in the Upper Rooms?'

'I shall indeed.'

'But there is still dancing to be had, even now,' he persisted. 'There is a ridotto on Monday night, did you know of it?'

'Yes, I am taking Ellen.'

'Then we will be able to dance together again.'

The tell-tale rosiness deepened on her cheek.

'I am going as Ellen's chaperon, Mr Arrandale. I shall not dance.'

There was a wistful note in her voice. Faint, but he detected it.

'Is it in the rules that widows are prohibited from dancing? I have never heard of it.'

Now why the devil had he said that? It was not the widow he wanted to dance with.

Phyllida's nerves fluttered. Had she been mistaken? Had he really remembered standing up with her at Almack's? She stole another look at him. He was being perfectly charming. Perhaps the lines that creased his lean cheeks might be caused by laughter rather than dissipation and wild living, despite the gossip. She did not think they detracted from his charm, either. If anything she thought him more attractive than ever, especially when he smiled at one in just that way...

She started guiltily when the door opened and Ellen

came in, chattering even as she untied the ribbons of her bonnet.

'There you are, Philly! *Such* fun we have had, I wish you had been there to share—oh, I beg your pardon. Hirst did not tell me you had company, but then, I did not give him time!' She came forward, greeting their guest with her sunny smile and no hint of shyness. 'Mr Arrandale, good day to you.'

He had jumped up when Ellen appeared and Phyllida watched him greet her, his charming smile and nicely judged bow perfectly civil. Too perfect, she thought, her earlier suspicions rising again.

'How do you do, Miss Tatham. Have you been shopping, perhaps?'

'No, sir, I have been to Sydney Gardens with Miss Desborough and her mama. Do you know the Desboroughs, Mr Arrandale?'

'I'm afraid not, I have not been in Bath that long myself.'

'Oh, I see. Well, we were introduced yesterday and Penelope and I found ourselves in such accord that Mrs Desborough invited me to join them in a walk to Sydney Gardens today. Oh, I wish you had come with us, Philly, it was quite delightful. The Ride that runs around the perimeter of the gardens is very well laid, so one can keep one's shoes and feet dry even if the weather has been very inclement. And there is a labyrinth, too, but there was no time to go in and Mrs Desborough says we should buy a plan before we attempt it.'

'Then we shall do so, when we visit.' Phyllida smiled.

'Perhaps I might escort you.'

Phyllida acknowledged Richard's offer with a slight inclination of her head but she did not encourage him. Unperturbed he returned his attention to Ellen.

'I understand you are attending the ridotto on Monday, Miss Tatham. I hope you will stand up with me. If your stepmama allows it, of course.'

'I should be delighted, sir—and you will consent, will you not, Philly?'

Phyllida was tempted to refuse, but Ellen would be sure to demand the reason and she was not at all sure of the answer.

'Of course,' she said at last. 'There can be no harm in you dancing with a gentleman.' Would he notice the slight stress she put on the last word? 'After all, the reason for bringing you to Bath was to accustom you to a larger society.'

'And I have any number of acquaintances in Bath now,' declared Ellen happily. 'Not just Penelope Desborough and Julia Wakefield, who are my especial friends. Mrs Desborough was good enough to present *several* gentlemen to me today when we were in the gardens.'

'Did she?' murmured Phyllida, slightly startled by this revelation.

Ellen threw her a mischievous glance. 'I have no doubt some of them will be seeking you out soon, Philly, for they, too, mentioned the ridotto. However I made it very clear I could not dance with any of them unless they had your approval.'

'I am glad to hear it.'

'And you *will* approve them, will you not, *dearest* Stepmama?'

For once Phyllida did not feel any inclination to laugh at Ellen's sauciness. She was aware of Richard watching her and, disconcerted, she responded rather more tartly that she had intended.

'Since I have approved Mr Arrandale, I doubt I will have any choice with the rest!'

'But they are all very respectable, Philly, or Mrs Desborough would not have introduced them to me.'

Ellen was gazing at her, puzzled, and Phyllida pulled herself together.

'No, of course she would not. I am sure they are all pillars of Bath society.'

A scratching at the door diverted her attention and she looked up as Matlock entered the room.

'Signor Piangi has arrived, my lady. I have put him in the morning room.'

'Oh, is it time for my Italian lesson already?' cried Ellen. 'I will come with you directly, Matty. If you will excuse me, Mr Arrandale.'

He bowed.

'Until Monday, Miss Tatham.'

Phyllida watched Ellen skip out of the room. Matlock hovered by the door, as if unwilling to leave them alone, but Phyllida waved her away.

'Go with her, Matty. You will remain in the morning room until the *signor* leaves.' Richard was watching her and she added, as the door closed upon them, 'It is important to me that no hint of impropriety should touch my stepdaughter while she is in Bath.'

He inclined his head. She thought for a moment he would resume his seat but instead he picked up his hat and gloves from the table.

'I have an appointment I must keep.' He hesitated. 'If you and Miss Tatham would like to visit Sydney Gardens on Sunday, I should be very happy to escort you there.'

'Thank you, sir, but, no. We are, um, otherwise engaged.'

It was not true, and she prayed he would not ask what that engagement might be.

'Of course. Until Monday, then.'

He bowed and was gone.

Phyllida sank back into her chair, her spirits strangely depressed. She would like to believe that Richard Arrandale had merely come to pay his respects to her, that he had truly remembered dancing with her all those years ago, but she doubted it. After all, she had never been rich enough or pretty enough to attract much attention in her one and only Season. Who wanted a soft well-modulated voice when they could enjoy Miss Anston's trilling laugh, or Miss Rollinson's lively tones? The more direct of the mothers with daughters to wed had called her thin and unattractive.

Phyllida gave herself a little shake. That was all in the past. She had lost her girlish ranginess, her glass told her that her willowy form and firm, full breasts showed to advantage in the high-waisted, low-cut gowns that were so fashionable. Yet, for all that, she paled to insignificance when compared to her lovely stepdaughter and she would be a fool to think otherwise.

Richard Arrandale had clearly set his sights upon Ellen. She remembered how he had been watching her in the Pump Room. She might ask Lady Hune to warn him off, but although she was very fond of the indomitable marchioness she could not imagine that Sophia would have much influence over her rakish great-nephew.

No. Phyllida knew it would be up to her to keep Ellen safe.

Richard strode away down Charles Street, well pleased with his first day's work. The widow was cautious, which was as it should be, but Ellen was friendly enough. Very young, of course, but a taking little thing. He frowned when he recalled how she had spoken of the fellows in Sydney Gardens clamouring for an introduction. He had no doubt that some—if not all—of them were involved in the wager, but he had the advantage and he intended that it should stay that way. However, he knew better than to rush his fences. He would dance with the chit on Monday night. None of the others were likely to steal her heart before then.

By the time Phyllida went to bed that night she had made a decision. Jane was waiting to braid her hair and help her to undress, but as soon as she had donned her nightgown Phyllida threw on her silk wrap and went to Ellen's room.

'May I come in?'

She peeped around the door. Ellen was already in her bed, propped up against a billowing mass of pillows, reading by the light of a branched candlestick that was burning perilously close to the bed-hangings. As the door opened she jumped and attempted to hide the book under the bedcovers, but when she saw it was Phyllida she heaved a sigh of relief.

'Oh, it is you. I thought it was Matty.'

'What are you reading? Is it so very bad?'

Ellen nodded, her eyes shining.

'Ambrosia, or the Monk,' she announced with relish. 'It is quite shocking. When I told Matty she promised to burn it if she found it.'

'I am not at all surprised. How did you get a copy?

'Oh, it has been circulating at school for months, but I did not have the opportunity to read it so I brought it with me. You need not worry, Philly, it is the later version, where Mr Lewis has removed the most salacious passages. Although I would dearly like to know what they were, because the story is still quite horrid in places!'

'Then you should not be reading it.'

Phyllida lunged for the book but Ellen was too quick and thrust it under her pillows, saying loftily, 'You know Papa decreed that ignorance was the worst of all sins. He always said I could read whatever I wished, as long as I discussed with him or you anything I did not understand.'

With a sigh Phyllida curled up on the end of the bed, unequal to the task of physically struggling with Ellen.

'Unfortunately I have a lowering suspicion that there is much in Mr Lewis's Gothic tale that I would not understand,' she admitted. 'I am wondering if I have done you a grave disservice in bringing you to Bath, Ellen.'

'No, how could that be?' Ellen frowned suddenly. 'Has Uncle Walter been complaining to you again? Aunt Bridget wrote and invited me to go and stay with them, but I know the only reason she did so is because they do not approve of my coming to live with you.'

'No, it is nothing like that, but—' Phyllida stopped, considering her words carefully. 'There are…dangers in society, Ellen.'

'What sort of dangers?'

'Gentlemen will sometimes prey upon innocent young women, especially if they are…'

'If they are rich,' finished Ellen, nodding sagely. 'I am well aware of that. Mrs Ackroyd was at pains to make sure we all knew the risks that gentlemen posed.' Again that mischievous light twinkled in her blue eyes. 'She prepared us very well, I think. I may even know more than you, Philly.'

'That is very possible,' replied Phyllida, sighing. 'You have had a very good education and I am sure the teachers told you much about the world, but it is very easy to have one's head turned and succumb to the attentions of a personable gentleman.' Phyllida saw the speculative look in Ellen's eye and added quickly, 'At least I believe it is so, although I have never experienced it myself.'

'Poor Philly. Did Papa snabble you up before you could fall in love with anyone?'

'Yes—no! Ellen, that is not the point.'

Ellen laughed.

'I think it is very much the point, my love. You were very young and innocent when you became my step-mama, were you not? Seventeen, in fact. As I am now.'

'Quite. And I was very shy and retiring.'

'Which I am not, so you may rest easy, my love.'

Phyllida shook her head at her. 'You may think you know the ways of the world, Ellen, but there are gentle-men in Bath who may seem very pleasant and respect-able, yet they are not to be trusted.'

'Do you mean rakes?' asked Ellen. 'There were sev-eral residing near the school, hoping one of us would be foolish enough to run off with them. Mrs Ackroyd pointed them out to us.'

'Heavens, I knew nothing of this!'

'No, well, I could hardly write and tell you about it, you would have wanted to fetch me away immediately. In fact we had to sit on that sneak Bernice Lingford to stop her from gabbing about the whole. It's a pity she doesn't have a fortune, because without some incentive no one will ever want to run off with her.'

'Ellen!'

'Well, it is true,' replied Ellen. 'She is a spiteful, greedy cat, so no man could like her, even if she wasn't buck-toothed and fusby-faced.'

'Let us hope she will grow out of it,' replied Phyl-lida, trying to be charitable. 'However, we are straying from the point—'

'The point is, Stepmother dear, that we were all perfectly safe at school. That was why Papa chose Mrs Ackroyd's institution for me, because she is accustomed to having the daughters of the very rich in her care.' Ellen drew up her knees and wrapped her arms about them. 'She is very progressive, though, and thinks that education is the best preparation for any young lady making her come-out. She taught us what to expect from a husband, too, because she says mothers invariably make a hash of it. '

Phyllida blinked, momentarily silenced by her stepdaughter's matter-of-fact statement.

'I am very glad of it,' she said at last. 'But I would still urge you to be cautious. It is very easy for a young lady to lose her heart to a rake.'

'But you said *you* never had done so,' objected Ellen.

Phyllida was about to correct her but thought better of it.

Ellen continued thoughtfully, 'It is not too late, though. We might well find you a husband in Bath.'

'I do not want a husband! That is not why I came here.'

'But you said yourself you were lonely at Tatham Park.'

'That is true, Ellen, but only because I was missing your father. And you. I am very much looking forward to our time here together.'

'But once I have made my come-out, what then? I have no intention of settling upon a husband too soon but I suppose I must marry at some point and then you will be alone again.'

Phyllida felt the conversation was getting away from her. She said crisply, 'I am glad you do not intend to rush into marriage with the first young man who takes your fancy, so I need not contemplate my future for a long time yet.' She slid off the bed. 'Now, I have said what I wanted to say, although it would seem Mrs Ackroyd has already prepared you for the perils of the world, so I shall leave you to sleep.' She leaned close to kiss Ellen's cheek and felt the girl's arms wind about her neck.

'Goodnight, my darling stepmama. We shall have such fun in Bath together.'

Phyllida gave Ellen a final hug and made her way back to her own room. The discussion had not gone quite as she had imagined and she was beginning to suspect that looking after Ellen would be far more challenging that she had anticipated.

The next few days were filled with shopping and visitors. None of the gentlemen Ellen had met in the park were brave enough to call at Charles Street uninvited but when Phyllida took her stepdaughter to the morning service at the Abbey on Sunday it seemed that every one of her acquaintances wished to perform an introduction to Mr This or Sir That. Ellen behaved impeccably, but Phyllida found herself scrutinising every gentleman who came up to her, watching for signs that they might be trying to fix their interest with Ellen. There were several married gentlemen amongst their number, such as Mr Cromby whose jovial, avuncular style was not to her taste. Neither did she warm to the fashionably dressed widower, Sir Charles Urmston, although he appeared to be a favourite of Mrs Desborough, who made the introduction.

Phyllida noticed Lady Hune coming out of the Abbey on the arm of her great-nephew. The dowager looked magnificent, as always, in black and silver but Phyllida's eyes were drawn to Richard's lean upright figure. She thought how well the simple lines of the dark coat and light-coloured pantaloons suited him. When he removed his hat to bow to an acquaintance, his short brown hair glinted with gold in the sunlight. He looked like the epitome of a gentleman and she stifled a sigh. How deceptive appearances could be. The marchioness was moving through the crowd towards her carriage, but when she saw Phyllida she stopped and beckoned to her. Ellen was deep in conversation with Julia Wakefield and Phyllida did not call her away, preferring not to bring her into Mr Arrandale's orbit more than necessary.

Lady Hune greeted Phyllida cordially and invited her to take tea with her later, a singular honour that Phyllida had no hesitation in accepting on behalf of herself and her stepdaughter. Too late did she recall that she had told Richard they were not free. She saw the laughter in his eyes and felt the heat rising to her face.

'Your previous engagement today has been cancelled, perhaps?' he murmured.

'You are promised elsewhere?' said Lady Hune, overhearing. 'My dear, you must not break your engagement on my account.'

Phyllida shook her head, saying hastily, 'I had mistaken the day. We should be delighted to join you, ma'am.'

Richard Arrandale was in no wise discomposed by the fulminating glance she threw at him, merely casting a grin in her direction before he turned aside to greet another acquaintance.

'I am glad you can come.' Lady Hune nodded. 'You will be able to tell me how your charming stepdaughter goes on in Bath. Very well, if appearances are anything to go by.'

Phyllida followed the dowager's eyes to where Ellen was now part of a lively crowd of young people.

'She has already made new friends of her own age, Lady Hune.'

'Which is as it should be—' The dowager broke off as Ellen and Julia Wakefield ran up, their faces alight with excitement that could barely be contained while they made their curtsies. The old lady's eyes gleamed with amusement.

'You are clearly big with news,' she observed solemnly. 'You had best get it out before you burst.'

Julia giggled and Ellen, after a blushing smile towards Lady Hune, turned her expressive eyes towards Phyllida.

'Lady Wakefield says there are the most romantic Gothic ruins just a few miles from Bath at Farleigh Castle. We are on fire to see them and Lady Wakefield says she will set up a riding party, if only you will give your permission, Philly. Dearest, do say I may go. Lord and Lady Wakefield will be accompanying us and Julia has a spare pony that I may ride—'

Laughing, Phyllida put up a hand to stop her.

'Of course you may go, and there is no need to borrow a horse, for Parfett is even now bringing our own horses from Tatham Park. I thought we might like to ride out occasionally before the weather closes in.'

'Will you come, too, Lady Phyllida?' asked Julia in a breathless whisper, 'It will be delightful if you can, I am sure—' She broke off, blushing scarlet when she realised her company. 'And Lady Hune, of course,' she added hurriedly.

'My riding days are over,' replied the dowager, choosing to be amused by Julia's artlessness.

'If Lady Wakefield is going with you then you do not

need me to come,' said Phyllida, not wishing to put herself forward. Besides, she had made up her mind not to be a clinging chaperon. 'You may go off and enjoy yourself with my goodwill.'

Lady Hune turned to Julia.

'Does your mama know the family at Farleigh House?' When the girl shook her head the dowager continued. 'Tell her to write to the housekeeper there, mention my name and I have no doubt she will receive you.'

'Th-thank you, ma'am,' stuttered Julia, wide-eyed.

'Well, off you go and tell your mother to arrange the whole,' Lady Hune dismissed her impatiently.

Ellen looked to Phyllida and, receiving a nod, she curtsied and ran off after her new friend.

Lady Hune tutted. 'She will keep you busy, Phyllida.'

'I think she will, ma'am, but I shall enjoy the distraction, after spending so long alone.'

'I am glad you are come to Bath. You were too young to be incarcerated at Tatham Park.' The dowager tapped Phyllida's arm with one be-ringed finger, saying urgently, 'Find yourself a husband, Phyllida. You are still young and Tatham left you well provided for, so you need not regard the money. This time you can marry to please yourself.'

Phyllida blushed hotly. 'I assure you, my lady, I was perfectly happy—'

'Aye, but no need to tell me it wasn't a love-match.'

'Perhaps not, but Sir Evelyn was a kind husband, and I have a duty to his daughter.'

'Of course, and I know you well enough to be sure you will do your best for the gel, but do not sacrifice your own happiness, Phyllida.' She looked up as her great-nephew came up.

'There is a chill wind getting up, ma'am. Shall I escort you to your carriage?'

'Very well, although I am not so frail that I cannot withstand a little breeze.' She looked back at Phyllida, a decided twinkle in her faded eyes. 'You see how I am bullied?'

'I dare anyone to try and bully you, ma'am.' Phyllida laughed and without thinking she looked at Richard Arrandale, knowing he would share her amusement. The noise and bustle around them ceased to exist as he drew her in with a smile of genuine warmth. The moment felt special, as if they were the only two people in the world. Phyllida's heart leapt to her throat before settling back again, thudding so hard against her ribs that she found it difficult to breathe.

Lady Hune's sharp voice broke the spell. 'You can take me home now, Richard. I shall expect you later, Lady Phyllida!'

Phyllida did not move as they walked away. Suddenly the sun did not seem as bright and she became aware of the cold wind that Richard had mentioned. That was the trouble with the man, she thought, putting her hand up to make sure her spencer was buttoned up. He made her forget to be sensible. She supposed it must be so with all rakes, for how else could they wreak such havoc with ladies' hearts?

Her thoughts went back to the dowager's suggestion that she should find a husband. She did not know whether to be amused or indignant. Lady Hune meant well, she knew that, and perhaps she might consider marrying again at some stage, but for now her mind was fully occupied with looking after her stepdaughter and keeping her safe from men like Richard Arrandale.

* * *

Taking tea with the Dowager Marchioness of Hune was a protracted affair and full of ceremony. Richard decided he would make himself scarce until towards the end, when he would offer to escort Miss Tatham and her stepmother back to Charles Street. Sophia would approve of his civility and his absence for most of the afternoon might prevent her from guessing his intentions towards the heiress.

His plan worked perfectly. He walked in just as Sophia was refilling the tea pot. He accepted a cup from his great-aunt and since Lady Phyllida was sitting next to the dowager he took a seat beside Miss Tatham and engaged her in conversation. He had soon put her at her ease and she chatted away to him in the friendliest manner. Well aware that they were in company and every word could be overheard, Richard said nothing untoward and made no attempt to flirt with Ellen, but since she was well educated as well as quick-witted they were soon getting on famously, so much so that when Lady Phyllida rose to take her leave and he suggested he should escort them home, Ellen was quick to support him.

Lady Phyllida smiled and shook her head. 'I am obliged to you, sir, but I think not. You have only just come in. I am sure Lady Hune would like to have you to herself for a while.'

He laughed. 'But it is only a step. I shall be back again in a matter of minutes.'

'As you say, Mr Arrandale. It is only a step, so Ellen and I will manage perfectly well, but I am grateful for your offer.'

Lady Phyllida smiled but her grey-green eyes held a steely look. It surprised him, for he had thought her a meek, biddable creature. However, he said nothing, merely inclined his head in acquiescence as the visitors went on their way.

'Well, that was much more enjoyable than I anticipated,' declared Ellen as they turned into Chapel Row on their way to Charles Street. 'And *not* just because Mr Arrandale spent a good twenty minutes talking to me! I thought Lady Hune might treat me as a child but she was very pleasant, was she not?'

'That is because she likes you,' returned Phyllida. 'And she is accustomed to having young people about her. Until recently she had her granddaughter living with her.'

Ellen stopped and turned her wide-eyed gaze upon Phyllida. 'Of course. Lady Cassandra! It was in the newspapers that Lady C—had eloped from Bath, but I had not connected her with the marchioness.'

'Yes, that was her granddaughter. The elopement took place just before I came to Bath but I know Lady Hune was distraught, and not only did she have the worry of what had happened to Lady Cassandra, she had to endure Bath's gossipmongers. I believe it has taken a great deal of fortitude.'

'How dreadful for her,' said Ellen, shocked.

'It was,' agreed Phyllida as they began to walk on. 'The gossip has died down now in Bath but it is still mentioned occasionally, even though Lady Cassandra is married and gone out of the country.'

'I had not thought of it before,' said Ellen slowly, 'but as exciting as an elopement is for the couple involved, there must be a great deal of horrid scandal to be endured by the family left behind.'

'I am glad you realise that, my love.'

Ellen slipped her arm through Phyllida's and gave it a quick squeeze.

'Do not sound so serious, Philly, I have no intention of eloping.' She added, with a mischievous gurgle of laughter in her voice, 'And woe betide any man who tries to persuade me to it!'

Chapter Four

The dancing had already started when Richard arrived at the Upper Rooms on Monday night. Miss Tatham was going down the dance with Henry Fullingham and he had leisure to admire her golden beauty, which was in no way dimmed by the simplicity of her embroidered muslin. As he stood waiting for the music to end he wondered if he had been wise to leave his arrival so late. The other gentlemen present would not waste any time in securing a dance with such a diamond. But his doubt was only momentary, and when Ellen's partner escorted her back to Lady Phyllida, Richard made his way through the crowd towards them.

Ellen greeted him with a smile of unaffected delight and an assurance that she had saved a dance for him. The widow, he noted, had looked composed, even serene, until she saw him approaching and then a slight frown creased her brow. He must try to reassure her.

'I hope you do not object, my lady?

'Not at all, Mr Arrandale.'

The frown was put to flight by a smile and he thought how well it became her, warming her eyes and turning them a soft green. Or perhaps that was merely the reflec-

tion from her gown of sage-coloured silk. It was fash-
ioned in the Greek style, falling in soft folds from the
high waistline. Her hair was piled up and held in place
by bands of matching green ribbon with a single glossy
ringlet allowed to fall to her shoulder. It attracted his
gaze to the flawless skin exposed by the low neckline
of her gown.

A single teardrop diamond was suspended on a gold
chain around her neck, drawing his attention to the
shadowed valley between the softly rounded breasts.
His thoughts strayed. In his imagination he was slowly
untying the ribbons of the gown and pushing it aside
while he laid a trail of kisses down the slender column
of her neck and into that same valley...

'Mr Arrandale?'

He started as Phyllida interrupted his reverie.

'The sets are forming for the next dance.'

'What? Oh, yes.'

His eyes searched her face. Could she have read his
thoughts? The hint of a smile in her own and the direct
way she met his gaze made him hopeful she had not.

'Ellen is waiting, Mr Arrandale.'

The gentle reproof in her voice finally recalled his
wandering attention. He took Ellen's hand and led her to
the dance floor, but for all the perfection of his dancing
partner, Richard could not quite shake off the image of
Lady Phyllida's softly twinkling eyes. She was not con-
ventionally pretty, but there was something very striking about Lady Phyllida Tatham that made it impossible
to forget her.

Phyllida retreated to the benches against the wall to
watch the dancing. There was no denying that Ellen and
Richard Arrandale made a handsome couple. She noted

that Mr Fullingham was still hovering nearby, clearly hoping to secure another dance with Ellen, but there were several other young gentlemen who had not yet stood up with her, and Phyllida would not allow any man more than two dances with her stepdaughter.

By the time the music was suspended for the interval, Phyllida knew that Ellen was a success. Not that she had ever doubted it, for her stepdaughter had beauty, poise and elegance, not to mention the fortune she would inherit when she reached one-and-twenty. She had danced every dance and there were still gentlemen waiting for the opportunity to stand up with her. Ellen's present partner was Sir Charles Urmston, who accompanied them to the tea room, where supper was set out on sideboards. Phyllida was pleased to note that Ellen did not appear to favour the gentleman over any of her other admirers. She chatted away quite happily, but showed no sign of discontent when he left them.

'Are you enjoying yourself, my love?'

'Oh, immensely,' declared Ellen, her eyes shining. 'Everyone is so kind and the Upper Rooms are so grand, compared to the George, which is where we attended the assemblies with Mrs Ackroyd. And the company is superior, too. So many gentlemen, when we were used to dance mainly with the local farmers and their sons. But Mrs Ackroyd maintained that it was very good practice and she was right, for I was not at all nervous when I stepped on to the dance floor here tonight.'

'Did you expect to be?'

Ellen's brow wrinkled. 'I am not sure—yes, I suppose I did, for I had never attended a real grown-up ball before, but it is the most tremendous fun. Oh, Philly! How can you bear to sit and watch? I know you love to dance!'

Phyllida had indeed felt a little pang of envy as she had watched her stepdaughter skipping around the floor, but now she said lightly, 'I am your chaperon, Ellen. How can I look after you if I am enjoying myself on the dance floor?'

'Oh, I do not need looking after,' came the cheerful reply. 'I am very well able to look after myself. So if we come again, Philly, promise me you will dance. I hate to see you sitting on the benches like an old lady.'

'As to that, my love, we shall see. I do not want the mortification of having no one ask me to stand up with them.'

'Oh, that won't happen,' replied Ellen. 'I shall refuse to stand up with any gentleman unless he has danced with you first!'

When the music started up again Ellen's hand was claimed by Mr Cromby. Phyllida watched the pair closely, not sure how Ellen would deal with the elderly roué. He was clearly paying her the most fulsome compliments whenever the movement of the dance allowed it, but her mind was greatly relieved when Ellen passed close by and threw her a look brimming with mischief.

It was not far from the Assembly Rooms to Charles Street, but Phyllida had arranged for her carriage to collect them. It was an extravagance, but she deemed it worthwhile, since they need not accept any of the numerous offers to escort them home. As they settled themselves into the carriage she asked Ellen how she had enjoyed her first ridotto.

'Oh, I liked it very much,' came the enthusiastic reply. 'I do not think I missed a single dance.'

'I can vouch for the fact!' declared Phyllida. She

asked, trying not to show concern, 'And was there a favourite amongst your partners?'

Ellen was quiet for a moment as she considered the question.

'Everyone was most kind. Sir Charles Urmston was very charming, was he not? You will recall he was the gentleman who escorted us to tea. And Adrian Wakefield, Julia's brother.' Ellen laughed. 'The poor boy was so afraid of missing his steps he barely spoke two words to me.'

'It was most likely his first grown-up entertainment, too.'

'Yes, I think so. But, of all the gentlemen who were present tonight, I think I liked Mr Arrandale the best, do you not agree?'

Phyllida's heart sank. She replied with forced lightness, 'Why I hardly know, how can one tell from so short an acquaintance?'

'Unfair, Philly! After all, you asked me if I had a favourite.'

'So I did.' Hastily she begged pardon.

'Which of them do you think would make the best husband?'

'Why none of them. You are far too young to be thinking of such things.'

Ellen laughed. 'You are quite right, but I thought it a question that would never be far from a mother's mind. Even a stepmother.'

This was so true that Phyllida did not know how to respond and she was relieved that the carriage had arrived at their door, where she was spared the necessity of answering. She followed Ellen into the house and sent her upstairs with Matlock, who was waiting to hear all about her young mistress's success in the ballroom.

* * *

The following day saw several calling cards left at Charles Street as well as a couple of bouquets. There was nothing, however, from Richard Arrandale. Phyllida wondered if the omission was deliberate, intended to pique Ellen's interest, but perhaps she was becoming far too cynical. Putting aside such thoughts, Phyllida suggested they should walk to Sydney Gardens, and since Lord and Lady Wakefield lived in Laura Place, which was on their way, they might call and ask if Julia would like to go with them. Ellen agreed eagerly and as soon as they had breakfasted the pair set off.

By happy chance Lady Wakefield and her children were just preparing to walk to the gardens themselves and they were only too pleased to make up a party. The ridotto had cemented the young people's friendship and even Mr Adrian Wakefield had overcome his shyness enough to offer Ellen his arm as they set off along the Ride, the main route around the gardens. The three young people were soon chattering away together, leaving Phyllida to walk behind with Lady Wakefield. The two ladies were soon on friendly terms, but they had not gone far when Ellen's voice alerted Phyllida to danger.

'Oh, look. It is Mr Arrandale!'

Phyllida saw Richard's familiar figure approaching from one of the narrower side paths. His eyes were fixed upon Ellen and it was easy to envisage what would happen next. He would have no difficulty in separating Ellen from the others and once he had her on his arm she would feel the full force of his attraction. Quickly Phyllida stepped on to the path, blocking his way and holding out her hand to him.

'Mr Arrandale, good day to you, sir. Have you come to take pity upon us? You will see that the younger members of our party have left Lady Wakefield and me without an escort. We feel shamefully neglected.'

He stopped, looking faintly surprised but to his credit he covered it well.

'That is easily resolved,' he said with his ready smile. 'I shall escort you.'

Julia looked a little disappointed and Ellen intrigued, but Phyllida kept her smile in place as she laid her fingers on the gentleman's sleeve. She avoided the questioning look Lady Wakefield threw at her. She had never put herself forward in such a way before. She felt dreadfully *fast*.

'We are going to the labyrinth,' Ellen informed him. 'Have you been there, sir?'

'Why, yes, I have,' Richard replied. 'However I believe it is very crowded today. It must be an apprentices' holiday or some such thing.'

'Indeed?' uttered Lady Wakefield, dismay in her voice. 'It will be dreadfully noisy, then.'

'They can be a little boisterous, too,' he added. 'Especially if they have visited the ale house.'

'Then let us leave the labyrinth for another day,' suggested Julia, looking nervous.

'Yes, I think that might be best, especially since it is so hot,' agreed Phyllida, thinking of how easy it would be for Richard to be alone with Ellen in a maze. She raised her hand and pointed. 'That path winds through the trees. It looks very picturesque and has the advantage of being quiet *and* shady. But you have just come that way, Mr Arrandale. We must not ask you to retrace your steps.'

He was not so easily dismissed and replied with a bland smile, 'Not at all, ma'am. I am only too delighted to escort you.'

The party set off again, the younger ones leading

the way, Lady Wakefield and Phyllida on either side of
Mr Arrandale. Phyllida was still trying to recover from
her own forwardness. She had never before accosted a
gentleman so brazenly and for a while she was unable
to make conversation. Thankfully Lady Wakefield was
not similarly disabled. It was clear from their conversation that Mr Arrandale was on friendly terms with
Adrian Wakefield and had thus earned the approval of
that young man's fond mama and they were soon discussing the pleasures of Bath. Phyllida was happy to let
them continue, until she heard Lady Wakefield mention
the forthcoming ride to Farleigh Castle.

'My great-aunt is related to the owners of Farleigh
House, you know,' he said.

'Yes, Lady Hune has kindly given us an introduction.
The housekeeper is to provide refreshments for us at the
house,' replied Lady Wakefield. 'I am very glad the family is not at home, for I should feel awkward imposing
upon them, but now we can be easy. We are all looking
forward to it. Julia has been reading about the castle in
a book of local antiquities.'

'It sounds a delightful party, ma'am. I believe Farleigh Castle is well worth a visit. Indeed I should like
to see it myself.'

'Then why do you not join us, Mr Arrandale?' Lady
Wakefield gave a little laugh. 'We are planning to go a
week on Monday. We should be pleased to have you with
us in any case, but since you are related to Lady Hune
that would make your presence even more welcome.'

Phyllida held her breath, hoping he would refuse.
Hoping he might even be planning to leave Bath before then.

'How kind of you, Lady Wakefield. I can think of
nothing I should like more.'

'Excellent. Do you hear that, Julia?' Lady Wakefield raised her voice and the three young people stopped obligingly. 'Mr Arrandale is joining us on our trip to Farleigh.'

'That is wonderful news,' cried Ellen.

Her obvious delight in this addition to the party dismayed Phyllida. It prompted her to say gaily, 'I must admit the idea of the Gothic ruin intrigues me. Would you object if I made one of your party, too, ma'am?'

'Not at all, my dear, I am very pleased that you have decided to join us.'

They had now reached a section of the gravel path that had become seriously overgrown and was only wide enough for them to pass one at a time. Phyllida stood back to allow Lady Wakefield to precede her, but as she picked her way along the narrow path her spine tingled with the knowledge that Richard Arrandale was at her back. She heard his voice close behind.

'So you did not originally intend to join the party to Farleigh Castle,' he said. 'What made you change your mind?'

'It sounds too delightful to be missed.'

'I wondered if you were having second thoughts about allowing Miss Tatham to go without you.'

'Oh, heavens, no. Ellen is very sensible. I would have no worries about her riding out with the Wakefields.'

At least, I would not if you were not one of the party.

Phyllida walked on quickly. Would there come a time when she would have to tell Richard that he must stay away from her stepdaughter? A quiet voice said she should hint him away now, before Ellen lost her heart, but she was very much afraid that hints would not work with Richard Arrandale, not if he had set his heart upon winning the heiress. She must be direct, then. Her mind shied away from such an action, it was not in her nature to confront anyone. She comforted herself by remembering Ellen's assurances that she had no intention of rushing into marriage, but hard upon the memory came the thought that falling in love was not something one could command. Phyllida mentally braced herself. She would do whatever was necessary to protect Ellen.

The winding path widened and Richard resumed his place between the ladies. They came up with the younger members of their party at the park gates, where Julia and her brother were arguing about who was the best rider. They called upon their mother to adjudicate and the three of them walked ahead into Great Pulteney Street, deep in conversation.

Richard smiled. 'That leaves me to escort you, ladies. If you will permit?'

Ellen immediately took his proffered arm and Phyllida was obliged to fall in on the other side. She listened with growing unease as Ellen chattered away as if she had known Richard Arrandale for years. The man was so charming and attentive it would be no wonder if he turned Ellen's head. As soon as there was a break in the conversation Phyllida addressed him.

'How long are you planning to stay in Bath, Mr Arrandale?'

'That depends rather upon my great-aunt. She has not been well, you know.'

'I do know it, but when we took tea on Sunday she assured me she is much recovered now. And with the season here about to begin I feel sure there will be distractions enough to amuse her. However I have no doubt you would find them a little tame, sir.'

'Why do you say that, Philly?' cried Ellen. 'It sounds almost as if you wish Mr Arrandale to leave Bath.'

'Not at all,' she replied coolly. 'I am merely saying that the coming season will provide Lady Hune with more diversions, and she has many friends here, too, so you must not think that she will be without company, Mr Arrandale.'

'I do not see that anyone would want to leave Bath,' remarked Ellen. 'Why, there are concerts and balls, and the shops—the finest outside London, I dare say!'

Richard laughed. 'When you put it like that, Miss Tatham, I am tempted to remain here all winter.'

No! The idea was intolerable.

Phyllida said quickly, 'But you have estates of your own, do you not, sir? They must require a great deal of your time.'

'I have Brookthorn Manor, in Hampshire, but there is nothing there that cannot wait.' Amusement rippled through his voice. 'Why, Lady Phyllida, is Miss Tatham correct, *are* you trying to get rid of me?'

She managed a lighthearted laugh. 'Not at all, sir.'

'No, of course she isn't,' declared Ellen. 'Why should she wish to do that?'

'Why indeed?' he murmured.

Phyllida risked glancing up and read such amusement in his eyes that she quickly looked away again, her face flaming. Angrily she told herself not to be so foolish. If he knew she was aware of his intentions then so much the better.

Richard's lips twitched. Really, Lady Phyllida looked quite delightful when she was blushing and the urge to tease her was almost irresistible. He also felt unusually protective. She was far too young and inexperienced in the ways of the world: how could she hope to protect her stepdaughter from the wolves that were hunting her, himself included? True, she had managed to keep him from having Ellen to himself on this occasion, but she would not always be able to keep him at bay.

The problem was, neither would she be able to keep the other fellows away. And knowing the prize at stake, some of them might prove much more unscrupulous than he. Today Richard had been fortunate. A few coins had elicited the information from her footman that Lady Phyllida was going to Sydney Gardens, and when he had seen Fullingham on his way to Charles Street he had been able to save him the trouble of calling by informing him that Lady Phyllida was not at home.

Remembering Ellen's wish to see the labyrinth, he had made his way directly to this popular spot only to find Tesford and Cromby were there before him. From their brief conversation he realised that they had also bribed Lady Phyllida's footman. Devil take it, the fellow would be able to retire from service at the end of the season if this continued! Luckily Richard had intercepted the ladies and persuaded them to take another route away from the labyrinth. Things had gone his way, but he would have to remain vigilant if he was to win the wager and the heiress for himself.

They had reached Laura Place, where the Wakefields stopped to take their leave. Richard turned to Phyllida.

'Perhaps, ma'am, you will allow me to escort you and Miss Tatham to Charles Street?'

'That is very kind of you, Mr Arrandale, but we are not going directly home. I promised Ellen that we would do a little shopping in Milsom Street. To buy ribbons.'

Richard was not surprised at the lady's response. She suspected his motives and it would be as well if he did not press his suit any further today. He was about to bow and take his leave when he noticed Sir Charles Urmston strolling towards them. He was coming from the direction of Pulteney Bridge but Richard did not doubt that he would turn back to escort the ladies to Milsom Street, given the chance. Richard had no intention of allowing him the opportunity, if he could help it.

He smiled. 'Then allow me to escort you there. I am very good at choosing ribbons.'

'Thank you.' Phyllida shook her head. 'However, we could not impose upon you any longer today.'

'Oh, I am sure it could not be an imposition,' put in Lady Wakefield, who overheard this exchange and had clearly fallen under Richard Arrandale's spell. 'I am old-fashioned enough to think it a good thing to have a gentleman's escort when one walks about town, even in Bath.'

'Oh, yes, pray do come with us, Mr Arrandale,' said Ellen, just as Phyllida was about to make a firm denial. 'I have seen a bonnet that I should like to buy. The milliner told me it is in the latest London fashion but I am not so sure, and I would value your opinion.'

'Then I shall be happy to give it,' he responded promptly.

'There you are then,' declared Lady Wakefield, smiling. 'We shall bid you good day, Lady Phyllida.'

Phyllida pressed her lips together, trying to hide her dismay as Lady Wakefield went off with Julia and Adrian. Richard held out his arms.

'Well, ladies, shall we go on?'

His laughing glance made Phyllida grind her teeth but she had no choice, she must accept gracefully. The alternative would be to face questions from Ellen, questions which she had no intention of answering with Richard Arrandale standing by. Such was her distraction that when they passed Sir Charles Urmston in Argyle Street, her response to his pleasant greeting was no more than a distant nod.

Phyllida said little as they made their way to Milsom Street, allowing Ellen to chatter on. When they reached the milliners Richard accompanied them inside to inspect the bonnet that had caught Ellen's eye. It was a ruched bronze-satin creation decorated with an over-abundance of flowers and tassels. Phyllida declared she thought it far from tasteful, but it was the doubtful look on Richard's face that made Ellen change her mind and decide the bonnet was not for her after all. Phyllida was relieved, but perturbed by the thought that she should be grateful to Richard Arrandale.

They went on to the haberdashers, where Ellen browsed the rainbow of coloured ribbons that the assistant spread out for her inspection. There was barely room for two people to stand together at the counter and Phyllida hesitated before stepping back to let Richard move in and advise Ellen on her choice. Let that be his reward for dissuading her from buying the unsuitable bonnet.

Phyllida stood out of the way by a side door until Ellen had made her purchase, then she accompanied them out of the shop.

'Well…' She smiled. 'Which ribbon did you decide upon?'

'This one.' Ellen opened the package to show Phyllida. 'I could not decide between this and the primrose but in the end I chose the cornflower blue. Is it not a lovely colour?' She added in an innocent voice, 'Mr Arrandale said this matches my eyes.'

Ellen's laughing glance was somewhat reassuring. Phyllida knew her stepdaughter was not taken in by such compliments. Not yet.

'And he is right,' she agreed, keeping her tone cool. 'Shall we go on?'

They had not gone many yards down Milsom Street when Ellen gave a loud sigh.

'Is it not always the same? Now that I have left the shop I am sure I should have bought the primrose ribbon as well as the blue.'

'Well, it is too late to return now,' said Phyllida. 'I think it is going to rain. 'Let us get on now, we can always come back tomorrow.'

Richard stopped.

'I have an errand of my own to run,' he said. 'If you would like to continue with your shopping, I shall catch you up.'

He strode away before they had time to argue. Ellen giggled.

'I do believe he is going back to buy the primrose ribbon for me.'

'Oh, I hope not,' said Phyllida. 'I really do not wish to be beholden to Mr Arrandale.'

'For a few pennies' worth of ribbon?' declared Ellen. 'What harm can there be in that?'

'He is not related to us, Ellen.'

'But he is related to Lady Hune, who is a great friend of yours,' argued Ellen.

They walked on, gazing into shop windows, marvelling at the variety of goods available in Bath and before too long Richard caught up with them.

'Here we are.' He handed Ellen a small packet. 'Your primrose ribbons, Miss Tatham. And for you, ma'am,' He handed a second even smaller package to Phyllida.

Peeping inside she saw a neatly rolled length of dark-green ribbon.

'I thought of the gown you were wearing the first

time I saw you,' he murmured. 'The colour became you so well.' She raised her brows and he quickly corrected himself. 'The first time I saw you in Bath, I mean.'

'Oh?' Ellen was immediately attentive. 'I did not know you were already acquainted.'

'Oh, yes,' Richard nodded. 'I knew your stepmama at her come-out. We danced together at Almack's.'

His blue eyes bored into Phyllida, challenging her to contradict him, but in truth she could not speak, for his look heated her blood and sent her imagination skittering towards secret trysts and stolen kisses. Outrageous thoughts that had no place in a chaperon's mind.

'Oh, that is famous!' cried Ellen, 'Phyllida, why did you not *tell* me? If that is so I am sure there can be no objection at all to accepting Mr Arrandale's gifts. I am very grateful for my ribbons, thank you, sir. Philly? Are you not going to thank Mr Arrandale?'

'Well, Lady Phyllida?'

His eyes continued to hold her gaze, saying so much more than words. In their blue depths gleamed a mixture of amusement and understanding, an invitation for her to share the joke, to accept his friendship. Perhaps even more than that. All of it lies, of course. She had to believe that, or she was lost.

Richard waited for her answer. It would not have surprised him if she had handed the ribbon back but in the end she thanked him, albeit grudgingly, and they continued on their way. He escorted the ladies to Charles Street, left them at the door and turned to make his way back to Queen Square, well satisfied with his progress.

As soon as they were indoors, Phyllida dashed off to her bedchamber, saying there were letters she must write. She knew Ellen would want know about her acquaintance with Richard Arrandale and she needed to prepare her answers. She kept to her room and was thus able to avoid saying anything at all until after dinner.

When they were alone in the drawing room, Ellen placed a footstool before Phyllida's chair and sat down upon it.

'Now,' she said, taking Phyllida's hands, 'why did you not tell me you and Mr Arrandale were old friends?'

'We are not,' Phyllida replied. 'We are acquaintances, merely.'

'But he says you danced together. Did you know him before you met Papa?'

'I met them at the same time. It was my come-out. One dances with a lot of gentlemen in one's first Season, as you will discover when we go to town next year.'

Ellen was not to be distracted. 'And was Mr Arrandale as handsome as he is now?'

Phyllida had been managing rather well to stay calm and matter of fact, but this question caught her off guard. Her cheeks burned. She had not blushed for years, but these days she could not stop!

'I—I suppose he must have been. I really cannot remember.'

But she could. She recalled every painful, tongue-tied moment she had spent with him. He had been charmingly polite, while she had been unable to do more than utter one or two stilted sentences.

'I knew it!' Ellen clapped her hands. 'You fell in love with him!'

'I did not!'

'Then why are you blushing?'

Phyllida managed to laugh. 'I was remembering what a gauche, awkward creature I was in those days.' That much at least was true. 'Now, Ellen, it is most improper for you to quiz me on this. As I told you, a girl in her first Season meets a lot of gentlemen but once she is married she forgets them all. I was very happy with your father, and I hope he was happy with me.'

'But it was not a love match, was it?' Ellen persisted. 'I was only twelve years old at the time but I remember people saying so.'

'Not everyone marries for love, Ellen, and not every family is as happy as we were at Tatham Park.'

Phyllida thought back to her own childhood. She was a younger daughter and not particularly pretty. She had also been painfully shy and constantly afraid of incurring her parents' displeasure. It had been a relief when Sir Evelyn had offered for her and by the time her parents died two years later she was happily settled with Sir Evelyn. At his coaxing she had left off the pale pinks and blues her mother had chosen for her and given up the nightly ritual of tying up her hair in rags to produce a mass of unbecoming ringlets. Now she wore her hair swept up smoothly with only a few soft curls falling on to her neck. Sir Evelyn had given her a great deal, including confidence.

She said now, 'Be assured that I was much more comfortable with your father than I had ever been at home.'

'That is because they bullied you,' replied Ellen. 'Did they force you to marry Papa?'

'Not at all, but I was expected to marry well.'

'Well, that is quite, quite *Gothic*,' declared Ellen. 'I shall not allow anyone to force me into marriage.'

She looked so absurdly young that Phyllida smiled. She squeezed her hands.

'I hope when the time comes you will fall in love, Ellen, but I also hope you will not be in too much of a hurry to do so.'

'Oh, no. I am enjoying myself far too much to think of such things yet.'

Phyllida was relieved to hear this, but she did not say so and turned Ellen's thoughts by asking her what she intended to wear to the Italian concert the following evening.

To Phyllida's secret pride, Ellen was proving to be universally popular. The house in Cháarles Street was besieged by visitors and there were entertainments every day. It was becoming clear that several gentlemen were vying for Ellen's attention, including Richard Arrandale, and Phyllida was relieved, if a little surprised, that the other young ladies of Bath were not more jealous of her success. However, she was perturbed to see how much attention the gentlemen lavished upon Ellen and could only be glad that her stepdaughter appeared to take it all in her stride.

Phyllida insisted that Ellen should be chaperoned at all times. When the party comprised young people under the aegis of careful mamas like Mrs Desborough or Lady Wakefield Phyllida was happy to allow Ellen to go unattended, but at the public breakfasts and dances Phyllida was always there to ensure no gentleman stepped out of line. As an heiress, Phyllida had always known Ellen would attract attention, but there were a number of married men amongst her admirers, and that was a puzzle.

Her puzzlement turned to concern when they attended the recital at the Assembly Rooms the evening follow-

ing their walk in Sydney Gardens and Phyllida returned
from a break for refreshments to find her stepdaughter
in an antechamber with Mr Cromby. The gentleman was
holding Ellen's hand and paying her the most fulsome
compliments. Phyllida lost no time in carrying Ellen
away, but when she remonstrated with Ellen later she
merely laughed.

'We were only a step away from the main room,
Philly. You really did not need to worry. We had gentle-
men far older than Mr Cromby flirting with us at Mrs
Ackroyd's Academy.'

'That is not the point,' objected Phyllida, despairing.
'Bath is a hotbed of gossip and you will do your reputation no good at all if people think you fast.'

In no wise chastened, Ellen threw her arms about
Phyllida and hugged her.

'Very well, I will try to behave, for your sake, darling Stepmama. But I do enjoy being the centre of so
much attention!'

There was no doubt that Ellen was indeed in demand.
The parties and entertainments, together with Ellen's
dancing, singing and Italian lessons, gave Phyllida little time for leisure. Ellen thrived upon the activity and
Phyllida made sure she was always accompanied whenever she stepped out of the door. However, she soon discovered that even the presence of Ellen's maid did not
keep Richard Arrandale away. She was in the morning
room waiting for Ellen to return from her dancing lesson when she saw him pass the window with Ellen on
his arm. He left Ellen at the door but Phyllida watched
in growing alarm as he raised Ellen's fingers to his lips
before striding away.

Phyllida was dismayed at her reaction to this gesture

but she was honest enough to admit that the emotion uppermost in her was envy. She stifled it immediately, composing herself as Ellen burst into the morning room with her sunny smile quite undimmed.

'Did I see Mr Arrandale at the door with you?' Phyllida kept her voice light, determined not to show undue anxiety.

'Yes. We met in Wood Street and he insisted upon escorting me home. Was that not kind of him?'

'Yes, very.'

She said no more at the time, but as the conversation moved on Phyllida knew she must speak to Matlock about the matter.

However, when she did so Matty's response was typically blunt.

'What would you have me do, my lady? Miss Ellen greeted him like a friend and I could hardly forbid him to walk with us. And even if it had been in my power I would not have done so, for nothing is more certain to make a spirited girl want something than to tell her she can't have it.'

Phyllida nodded. 'I am well aware of that, Matlock. And Miss Ellen is definitely spirited.'

'But nothing untoward happened,' added the maid. 'I can assure you of that, ma'am. In fact, I was pleasantly surprised in Mr Arrandale, after all I had heard about the man.'

'Oh, Matty, pray do not tell me you are falling under his spell, too.'

The older woman gave a grim little smile.

'No, no, I'm too long in the tooth to be taken in by a handsome face, my lady, but credit where 'tis due, the gentleman never said anything out o' place while he was escorting Miss Ellen. And he made no attempt to lower his voice to avoid my hearing it, either.'

'Well, perhaps there is some good in the man, after all,' murmured Phyllida, but she added, her suspicions not completely allayed, 'Or perhaps he is playing a deep game.'

Chapter Five

Phyllida had still not made up her mind about Richard Arrandale by the time they rode to Farleigh the following Monday. Her groom Parfett brought the horses around from the livery stables, warning that they were very lively since they had not been ridden for some time. Phyllida was soon in control of Sultan, her own rangy chestnut gelding, but she watched anxiously as Ellen's spirited grey mare pranced and sidestepped playfully.

'No need to worry about Miss Ellen,' said Parfett, observing Phyllida's frown. 'You know there wasn't a horse in her father's stable she couldn't master. She's at home to a peg.'

As if to prove him correct, the mare quickly grew quiet under Ellen's confident handling and they set off to meet up with the rest of the party at Laura Place, where they found the Wakefields already mounted and waiting for them.

'Our little riding party has grown to nine, Lady Phyllida,' Lady Wakefield greeted her with a cheerful smile. She waved her hand towards the pretty brunette talking with Julia and Adrian. 'Mrs Desborough has allowed Penelope to join us, and Mr Henry Fullingham came up to me just yesterday and begged to be allowed to join us. Here he comes now, with Mr Arrandale.'

Phyllida looked back to see the two gentlemen approaching. Surely it was not merely her fancy that of the two men, Richard had the advantage? It was not only his superior height, nor the way his blue riding coat moulded to his form. He looked relaxed and at home in the saddle, completely in control of the powerful black hunter he was riding. She thought it could not be a livery-stable horse, and this was soon confirmed when Mr Arrandale rode up to Lady Wakefield as the party prepared to set off.

'I do not know the country,' he said. 'Will we be able to give the horses their heads? I was going to hire a hack, but in the end I sent for my hunter. He has been eating his head off at Brookthorn Manor and could do with the exercise.'

'There are a couple of places one can gallop, although Wakefield and I will not do so,' replied the lady. 'And I should warn you that Miss Desborough and Julia are rather nervous riders, so I pray you will not encourage them to join you.'

Phyllida knew Ellen was anything but nervous and would undoubtedly wish to gallop across the country with the gentlemen. She made up her mind that if Lord and Lady Wakefield would not accompany them, then it would be up to her to do so. She patted Sultan's glossy neck, reflecting that neither she nor her mount would consider it a penance to career across the countryside.

They rode out of Bath at a sedate pace. Mr Fullingham and Mr Arrandale both looked as if they would like to ride with Ellen but she remained happily between Phyllida and Penelope Desborough. Phyllida considered the picture they must make. Penelope's plum-coloured habit was sober enough, but Ellen's sky-blue velvet with its matching hat was quite eye-catching, and there was no doubt that the colour accentuated her flawless complexion and shining curls. Phyllida thought her own dove-grey habit must look very dull by comparison and was obliged to stifle a pang of regret. She felt a little envious, then scolded herself for such nonsense. As a girl she would never have been confident enough to choose bright colours, even if Mama had allowed it. She glanced again at her kerseymere skirts. She was out of mourning now, there was no reason why she shouldn't order a new riding habit. Something a little more…showy.

What on earth am I thinking? I am Ellen's chaperon. I do not wish to draw attention to myself.

But at that moment her gaze fell upon Richard Arrandale and she knew that she was not being quite honest. Phyllida glanced again at her stepdaughter. Ellen was looking particularly lovely today, her eyes sparkling, her countenance so animated that Phyllida thought no man would be able to resist the attraction. She would have to keep her under close scrutiny. She passed the gentlemen in the party under quick review. Lord Wakefield and his son posed no threat, she decided, but Messrs Fullingham and Arrandale were a different matter. They were both fashionable men with considerable address and Phyllida had no intention of allowing either of them to spend time alone with Ellen.

This was not a problem until they reached the first stretch of open ground where Lord Wakefield indicated it would be safe to gallop.

'Our route lies along the road here,' explained Lady Wakefield, 'so those of us who do not wish to race may walk on at a respectable pace. The rest of you may gallop over to that copse yonder and back again.'

'But there will be no racing,' Lord Wakefield reminded them.

'Actually I think I will remain on the road,' said his son, drawing closer to Penelope Desborough.

Lord Wakefield turned his attention to the other two gentlemen. 'We have a long way to go,' he barked. 'I do not want to be turning back because one of you young dogs has broken his neck.'

He frowned so direfully at Mr Fullingham that the young man flushed.

'No, no, sir. Wouldn't dream of it.' His glance flickered towards Ellen who was trotting up. 'Especially when we will have ladies with us.'

'Oh, do not hold back for me, I want no special treatment,' replied Ellen, laughing.

'Your stepmama may not agree with you,' said Lord Wakefield.

Ellen looked around, her brows rising when she saw Phyllida approaching. 'Oh, are you coming with us Philly?'

The surprise in her tone irked Phyllida and roused a tiny spurt of rebellion.

'Coming with you?' She kicked her horse on. 'Catch me if you can!'

Sultan was fresh and leapt forward without a second bidding. Phyllida heard the cry of delight from Ellen and a startled call from Lady Wakefield for her to take care but she ignored them both. She felt suddenly, gloriously free as the gelding flew across the turf. She glanced behind. Three riders were following, Ellen's grey mare galloping beside Mr Fullingham's bay but in front of them and closing fast upon her was Richard Arrandale on the black hunter. Phyllida turned back, crouching lower over Sultan's neck, urging the horse on. She could hear the hunter thundering up behind her. The copse was approaching all too quickly, but she did not want to rein in Sultan. Her only relief during her year of mourning and self-imposed exile at Tatham Park had been her early morning gallops. She had missed them when she had come to Bath and now she wanted the feeling of excitement to go on for ever.

'Don't pull up,' Richard shouted. 'We'll go on to the barn yonder!'

It was madness. She was setting a poor example to Ellen, but with the wind in her face and the exhilaration of the ride firing her blood, Phyllida could not resist prolonging the race. She touched her whip to Sultan's flank and they shot past the copse and on towards the barn in the distance. Above the thud of Sultan's hoofs she was aware of the hunter closing up. The black nose was at her shoulder. She pushed Sultan on, urging him to make one last effort and they thundered past the barn neck and neck.

The horses slowed and Phyllida straightened in the saddle, unable to hold back a laugh of sheer delight.

'Impressive, Lady Phyllida.' Richard had brought his hunter alongside and was grinning at her. 'And unexpected.'

She met his eyes, still exhilarated by the race. The glowing, soaring elation intensified when she saw the admiration in his glance. She could not stop smiling at him. They were very close, his muscled thigh encased in tight buckskin was so near that she might reach out to touch it. Phyllida was startled to realise how much she wanted to do so. How much she wanted *him*.

The urge to smile disappeared. In a panic she dragged her gaze away and stared determinedly between Sultan's ears.

She said remorsefully, 'It was very bad of me. Lord Wakefield expressly forbade us to race. And then to extend it here, out of sight of the road.' The pleasure of the moment had subsided and she bit her lip, suddenly mortified at her lack of decorum.

'Console yourself with the fact that the others did not follow us,' said Richard. 'They are obediently waiting at the copse even now. Shall we go back?'

'I suppose we must.'

His look was searching as they turned about and Phyllida realised she had sounded quite regretful. Heavens, she hoped he did not misunderstand her and think she wanted to keep him by her side. She rushed into an explanation.

'It is a long time since Sultan has raced against another horse. When Sir Evelyn died the family thought it would be best to sell all the horses except Sultan and Ellen's mare.'

'Surely that was your decision?'

'Yes. Yes, of course.'

And it *had* been her decision, but she could acknowledge now the pressure that had been brought to bear, while she was still coming to terms with her loss. It was not just from Sir Evelyn's family, but her own, too. She had been brought up to believe that a man must be head of the family and his word was law, that she should always bow to his will, but marriage had changed her. She had enjoyed being mistress of her own house and had grown more confident under Sir Evelyn's benevolent protection. He had encouraged her to think for herself.

Her parents had died by the time Phyllida became a widow, but her family had descended upon her, discussing with Sir Evelyn's relatives what would be best for her and it had taken all her newfound strength to stand out against them. Thank goodness she had not allowed them to persuade her to give up Sultan, or to sell Tatham Park.

Richard was silent, watching the play of emotion on Lady Phyllida's countenance. The excited glow died from her eyes and her cheeks lost their hectic flush. He thought there was a shadow of sadness about her. She was thinking back to her dead husband, perhaps. Did she miss him? Had she loved him?

Richard shifted in the saddle, uncomfortable with the thought. A sudden and unfamiliar feeling swept through him. He wanted to protect her, to keep her safe. To make her happy.

The others were waiting for them at the copse, keeping their horses in the shade of the trees. As Phyllida and Richard approached Ellen called out, 'Philly, are you all right? When I saw you racing on I wanted to follow but Mr Fullingham thought we should wait here, since this is where we agreed to stop.'

'We were afraid Sultan had bolted with you,' added Mr Fullingham.

'No such thing,' said Richard. 'We were enjoying the race and decided to go on.' He glanced at Phyllida. 'It was my fault, and I beg your pardon.'

'I knew you were in no danger, Philly,' said Ellen comfortably. 'You were always a clipping rider, I had forgotten just how good you are!'

Phyllida chuckled and shook her head. 'It was most irresponsible of me, but I cannot deny that I enjoyed it.'

Ellen looked back towards the road. 'I think we should be getting back to the others. I am not sure how much they will have seen...'

'Not the race to the barn,' said Richard. 'That would have been screened by the copse.'

Ellen giggled. 'Then we shall not tell them how reprehensibly you both behaved.'

'Thank you,' said Phyllida meekly.

'And it has done you good, Philly,' Ellen continued. 'I have never seen you looking better.'

Richard grinned. He had to agree, Lady Phyllida was looking radiant. She had surprised him and he thought that perhaps she was not such a mouse after all. He fell in with the others, but as he did so he caught Henry Fullingham's eye and the fellow winked at him. Richard's jaw tightened and he cursed inwardly. By allowing himself to gallop off with the widow he had left the field free for Fullingham to advance his cause with Ellen Tatham. And if that smug expression was anything to go by, he had taken full advantage of it.

Richard hoped for an opportunity to draw Ellen away as they continued towards Farleigh but she fell in beside her stepmother. Phyllida's unexpected escapade had clearly impressed her and the two ladies rode together, laughing and chattering. Watching them, and listening to them reminisce about past rides and excursions, Richard was again struck by Phyllida's youthfulness. She could only have been about Ellen's age when Sir Evelyn had married her. She and Ellen were obviously good friends and he wondered if that had been a comfort to the young bride in the early days of her marriage.

The question was still in his head when he finally managed to ride beside Ellen, and instead of taking the opportunity to engage her in a gentle flirtation he remarked that she appeared to be on very good terms with her stepmother.

'Yes. Philly has always been much more like an older sister than a mama to me.'

She turned her head and regarded him for a moment with unwonted seriousness. 'I would do nothing to hurt her, Mr Arrandale.'

'I am sure you would not.' He added, surprising himself, 'I hope that will always be the case, because it might well prevent you from getting into any serious scrapes.'

She thought about this for a moment.

'Sometimes I think I am much more worldly-wise than Philly. In fact, I have decided to promote her happiness.'

His lips twitched. 'And how do you propose to do that, Miss Tatham?'

The solemn look fled and she shook her head, eyes gleaming with mischief.

'I shall not tell you. It is always best to play one's cards close to one's chest, is it not?'

He frowned. 'Now where did you learn that expression?'

'From my teacher, Mrs Ackroyd. She explained to us about games of chance. Cards, and dice and the like.'

'Ah, I did not think you would have heard Lady Phyllida say such a thing.'

'Goodness, no. Sometimes I think Philly needs me to look after her, not the other way round.'

Before he could respond, a call from Lord Wakefield informed them that they had reached Farleigh and the party reorganised itself to ride up the drive to the house. They were met at the door by the housekeeper, who confirmed that the family were not at home but that refreshments were waiting for them, if they would care to step inside for a little while before they inspected what was left of the castle and the chapel.

Phyllida moved closer to Ellen. She had observed her talking to Richard during the ride, seen the looks, brimful with laughter, that Ellen had thrown at him and she had been conscious of a strong feeling of desolation. It had formed itself into a hard, unhappy knot deep inside. Phyllida wanted to snatch Ellen away but that would do no good at all. She was Ellen's chaperon, not her gaoler, and would never prevent her merely talking to a gentleman. So she entered the house beside Lady Wakefield and left the younger ones to chatter together while they enjoyed the cold collation that had been set out for their delectation.

Afterwards, when they went off to look at the ruins of the castle, she made no attempt to keep Ellen at her side, but watched her scamper off with the other girls. Adrian, Mr Fullingham and Richard Arrandale accompanied the group to help them over the uneven ground while Phyllida followed a short distance behind with Lord Wakefield and his lady.

'Oh, dear,' murmured Lady Wakefield when the breeze brought snatches of the young people's conversation floating back to them, 'Adrian is recounting the castle's gruesome history. Should we tell him to stop? I would not wish him to give the girls nightmares.'

'Do not silence him on Ellen's account,' replied Phyllida, thinking of the copy of *The Monk* currently secreted in her stepdaughter's bedchamber, 'She will enjoy the horrid stories immensely.'

'As will Julia and Penelope,' added Lord Wakefield, with a complacent chuckle. 'Do not worry, ladies, the children will not come to any harm here.'

Phyllida wondered if that were true, but she soon saw that the young ladies were much more interested in clambering over the ruins and listening to Adrian Wakefield's blood-curdling tales than in dalliance with any of the gentlemen.

There was little to see of the castle except the gatehouse and what remained of the thick walls. The rest was merely piles of rubble, much of it overgrown, but this did not prevent the younger members of the party from scrambling around like excited children.

'Which is what they are,' remarked Lady Wakefield, watching them with smiling indulgence. 'The girls are barely out of the schoolroom and Adrian is only a couple of years their senior. I wish I had their energy! The ride and then the refreshments have left me feeling quite languid, so Wakefield and I are going to find a convenient stone block to sit upon, Lady Phyllida, if you would like to stay with us?'

Phyllida declined gracefully. She was not at all fatigued by the ride and glad to have some time to herself. She wandered off, enjoying the solitude. She loved Ellen dearly, but having responsibility for such a pretty girl, and an heiress at that, was proving more arduous than she had thought. Having spent the past year living on her own at Tatham Park she had thought having Ellen to live with her would provide her with the companionship she had lacked since Sir Evelyn's death, and it did, but Phyllida knew now that it was not enough. Ellen was not a kindred spirit, they could not converse upon equal terms, because Phyllida could never forget that Ellen was her responsibility.

She did not regret taking Ellen to live with her and she would devote herself now to looking after her. But later, when Ellen was married and she could look to her own happiness, what then? Perhaps she should marry again. Sir Evelyn had proved himself a kind and considerate husband but Phyllida knew that only the deepest love would make her give up her independence now, and ladies who had reached the advanced age of four-and-twenty did not readily fall in love, did they? The question hovered and impatiently she closed her mind to it. The future must look after itself. She was comfortably situated and had sufficient funds to do whatever she wished.

Such as wandering around ruined castles all alone?

Yes, she told herself firmly, and set off to prove it was possible.

The area adjoining the gatehouse was now a farm-yard so Phyllida made her way in the opposite direction, where trees and bushes obscured what was left of the thick curtain wall. Stones from the ancient building were scattered around, making the ground uneven and she gathered up her voluminous skirts to avoid snagging them on the rampant vegetation.

'Exploring, Lady Phyllida?'

Richard Arrandale was coming towards her. She quickly dropped her skirts, but not before she was sure he had glimpsed her stockings and half-boots.

And what of it? No doubt he has seen scores of ladies' ankles in his career.

She told him, 'I wanted, if I could, to discover something of the size of the castle.'

'It is quite extensive. Here, take my hand and let me help you over these stones. We may find the path a little easier further on.'

'Perhaps I should be getting back. Ellen—'

'Miss Tatham is safely under the eye of the Wakefields,' he replied. 'And Fullingham has taken himself off to smoke a cigar.' He said solemnly, 'You are at liberty to enjoy yourself, Lady Phyllida.'

Tentatively she put out her hand. As his fingers closed around her glove she felt his thumb moving over the soft leather. The slow sensual strokes made her want to purr and she had to struggle to ignore it. He led her on through the ruins, pointing out portions of carved stone amongst the rubble and the outline of walls that were now no more than ridges in the ground.

'You are very well informed, Mr Arrandale.' She cast a suspicious look up at him. 'When Lady Wakefield told you of this excursion you gave the impression you had not been here before.'

'Did I?'

She stopped. His expression was innocent enough but there was laughter in his eyes. She said severely, 'You know very well you did.'

He laughed.

'Very well, I admit it. My great-aunt brought me here several times when I was younger. I explored the ruins then.'

'Oh? Did all your family visit here?'

'Good God, no. My father would have thought this place beneath him. He and my mother were too busy enjoying themselves in town to bother with their children.'

She tried to ignore the bitterness in his response.

'Did your brother come here too?'

'No. By the time I visited here Wolf was at Oxford, causing mayhem.'

'Ah.' She smiled. 'The Scandalous Arrandales.'

'Quite. However, unlike me, he wasn't sent down. He saved his disgrace for something far more serious.'

He looked so grim that she could not prevent herself from squeezing his hand.

'I am very sorry.'

'You need not be.'

He spoke roughly and she knew he wanted to pull away from her. It was an almost imperceptible movement but she was aware of it and immediately she released him. He took a couple of paces towards one of the low stretches of wall rising up through the grass and rested one booted foot upon the stones.

He said with feigned carelessness, 'It gives one a certain…standing, don't you know, to have a murderer for a brother. I attracted all the choicest spirits at Oxford, most of 'em older, all of them ripe for mischief. I did not last a year before they kicked me out.'

'Why, what did you do?' The question was voiced before she could prevent it.

'Gambling, drinking. Women. Then I moved on to London, where I found even more of the same pleasures to be enjoyed.' His mouth twisted. 'After all, I had to maintain the family reputation. Although *I* stopped short of murder.'

Her heart went out to him.

'I do not believe the Arrandales are as black as they are painted. As for your brother—it was a long time ago but I know the whispers, the rumours, continue.' She tried to smile. 'They are probably much worse than what actually happened.'

'I doubt it.'

'Would you like to tell me?'

She spoke the words softly and wondered if he had heard them for he ignored her, idly swiping at a thistle with his riding crop. Phyllida waited and eventually her patient silence was rewarded.

'I am no better informed than you about how my sister-in-law died. I was spending that winter with my great-aunt at Shrewton and my parents decided it would be best if I remained in ignorance of what had happened. Of course that state of affairs could not last, Sophia's acquaintances soon informed her of the situation and she took me back to Arrandale but by then it was too late. Florence, my sister-in-law, had been dead three months and my brother was gone.'

He turned and began to stroll on. She fell in beside him.

'How did she die?'

'Fell down the stairs. Florence was pregnant at the time and the fall brought on the birth. The child survived but Florence died that night. Everyone thought Wolf had killed her. Oh, the death was recorded as an accident, my father saw to that. After all he'd had plenty of practice covering up his own transgressions.' His lip curled. 'I come from a family of wrongdoers, Lady Phyllida. My family history is littered with murder, abduction and thievery, the stories of Farleigh Castle pale in comparison. Wolf was merely following the family tradition.'

She shook her head, but did not contradict him, merely asked what had happened to his brother.

'My father sent Wolf abroad immediately after the tragedy. Then Florence's parents demanded the return of a diamond necklace. It was a family treasure, apparently, to be passed to the heir, in this case Florence's twin, but she had borrowed it for her wedding and had kept it to wear on grand occasions. Only it wasn't there. It would seem that Wolf took it to pay his way abroad.'

'And do you believe that?'

His scornful glance scorched her.

'Does it matter what I believe? My father refused to talk of it. I was sent back to Shrewton Lodge with a tutor to finish my schooling, then I was packed off to Oxford and by the following spring my parents were dead. Officially it was scarlet fever, there had been a particularly bad outbreak at Arrandale, but I think it was more likely the shame of it all that overcame them, at least for my mother.'

'Or the heartbreak,' she murmured sadly, thinking of how the tragedy must have ripped apart the family. 'What happened to the baby?'

'It was a girl. When my parents died she was sent to live with a distant cousin, the Earl of Davenport.' A wry smile broke through for a moment. 'Another Arrandale, but James is as sober as the rest of us are dissolute and he was thought the best guardian for the girl. He has a daughter of the same age, so it was deemed the best thing to do with the child.'

'And Wolfgang? Where is your brother now?'

He spread his hands. 'We never heard from him again. I made enquiries, hired men to search for him, sent letters.' A muscle worked in his jaw. 'It may be that he did not want to be found. Or he may well have been drowned on the crossing to France, there were some exceptionally vicious storms that winter.'

'How sad, that he never had a chance to explain himself.'

Richard stopped.

'I desperately want him to be innocent,' he burst out. 'Wolf is seven years my senior and I always looked up to him. Oh, I know he was hot tempered and rash, but he was never unkind, not intentionally. And I really cannot believe—'

He broke off. Phyllida saw the muscle working in his cheek. He was wrestling with profound grief and she wanted only to comfort him.

'You really should believe he is innocent, Mr Arrandale, until it is proven otherwise.'

He did not answer. He did not appear to have heard her but remained staring at nothing, his thoughts clearly elsewhere. Unhappiness wrapped about him like a cloak and there was nothing she could do to relieve it. A small cloud momentarily blocked out the sun and Phyllida shivered. The faint movement recalled his wandering attention. He was once again his usual, urbane self.

'You have not yet seen the chapel, Lady Phyllida. Perhaps we should go back there now, if you have seen enough?'

He extended his arm.

'Yes, please.' She slipped her hand on to his sleeve. 'These broken walls have lost their charm for me.'

As they made their way back across the ruins she noted that Lord and Lady Wakefield were still sitting on their stone seat. Ellen, Penelope and the two younger Wakefields were exploring what was left of the gatehouse. She eased her conscience with the thought that she was keeping Richard Arrandale away from Ellen. Wasn't she?

The little chapel was built within the curtain wall of the castle and had been restored sufficiently for visitors to go inside. Richard stood back for Phyllida to pass before him into the narrow building. Odd that he had told her about Wolf. He had never said as much to anyone before. After all, what was the point? Everyone believed Wolf was guilty, he was just another in the long line of scandalous Arrandales. So why had he spoken so freely to Phyllida? Was it because she had seemed genuinely interested, prepared to think something other than the worst of an Arrandale?

Richard followed her into the centre of the chapel. Her soft boots made no sound on the stone flags, her skirts floated out as she moved, a silent figure in pale grey. She looked so ethereal that he could not help himself. He reached out and touched her shoulder. She turned and he found himself subjected to her enquiring gaze.

'I beg your pardon,' he said. 'I needed to reassure myself that you were real.'

'Of course I am real.' Her mouth curved into a smile. 'Did you think me a ghost?'

'No, an angel.'

An angel sent to redeem him.

She was surprised into a laugh. The warm, delicious sound echoed around them, breaking the sepulchral calm of the stone building. Quickly she put a hand over her mouth but her eyes still gleamed with merriment, green as emeralds. His blood quickened. She no longer looked ethereal, she was a living, breathing woman and he wanted to pull her into his arms and kiss her.

He was aware of the change immediately and he knew she had read his thoughts. Her eyes were no longer alight with laughter but something else, an instinctive response to him. He felt the connection, the sizzle of excitement that held them immobile. They were less than an arm's length apart, beneath her mannish jacket and white shirt her breast rose and fell as she took a deep, ragged breath. When she lowered her hand he reached for it, felt the quiver of excitement as their fingers touched, not in the least dulled by the soft kid of their gloves. They were caught in a bubble that tightened around them, moving them slowly but inexorably together.

The air shimmered with anticipation. He saw the tip of her tongue flicker nervously over her lips, as if she knew that they would kiss, that it was inevitable and there was nothing she could do to prevent it. Looking into her eyes, he saw a shy smile there and he knew with startling clarity that she did not *wish* to prevent it. He was holding her hand, drawing her closer. They were breast to breast, he had only to lower his head now for the sweetness of a first kiss from those full, inviting lips.

Laughter, the chatter of familiar voices intruded upon the silence, breaking the spell. Phyllida jumped back, shaken. She felt very much as she did when she dreamed of falling and awoke with a start. What was she doing, standing so close to this man, wanting him to kiss her? She forced herself to turn away, to face the door where the Wakefields now appeared, the others crowding in behind them. Thankfully they all stopped in the doorway, blinking as their eyes grew accustomed to the dim light and that gave her the opportunity to recover herself and school her face into a semblance of calm.

'Why, Lady Phyllida, you are here before us. We thought you were still wandering through the ruins.'

She forced herself to acknowledge Lady Wakefield's cheerful greeting, to smile and make a suitable reply. The moment was gone, the small chapel was now full of people and noise. Phyllida linked her arm with Ellen's and accompanied her around the small church, admiring the ancient tomb and the arched window with its elegant tracery. She did not look back at Richard. She could hear his voice, cool and steady with just a hint of amusement, but in her mind's eye she recalled his face when they had stood alone in the chapel. The blaze of passion that had set her heart racing and then something quite different when they were interrupted. The look of shock, of horror, at what had almost occurred.

They did not tarry in the chapel and soon the party made its way back to the stables to collect the horses. Henry Fullingham was waiting for them, sitting on a mounting block and chatting with Parfett and Lady Wakefield's groom. Phyllida blinked. She had not even noticed he was not with the others. To be honest she had noticed very little since that moment alone with Richard in the chapel. She heard Lady Wakefield murmur to her husband as they followed Phyllida into the stable yard.

'If you were to ask me, Mr Fullingham is not at all interested in the romantic ruins.'

'I quite agree, my dear,' chuckled Lord Wakefield. 'He lounged off in a sulk when it was clear the girls preferred Adrian's ghoulish tales to his flirting. And look now, if he was hoping to help any young lady on to her horse he is foiled again, for the grooms are there before him!'

Lady Wakefield turned to Phyllida, saying as they watched the younger ones mounting up, 'Well, ma'am, are you glad you came?'

'I have enjoyed it very much, ma'am. I am grateful to you for arranging it.'

'Thanks, too, should go to Lady Hune for her introduction,' put in Lord Wakefield. 'Without it I doubt our reception would have been quite so hospitable. The refreshments were truly exceptional. Pray, Mr Arrandale, tell Lady Hune we are obliged to her, when you get back to Royal Crescent.'

Phyllida had been lost in her own thoughts and had

not realised Richard was so close. He had filled her thoughts and now the unexpected sight of him at her shoulder caught her unawares. The erratic beat of her heart disturbed her breathing. She was obliged to concentrate very hard to prevent herself from simpering and blushing like a schoolgirl when he asked if he might help her into the saddle.

She accepted in as dignified a manner as she could manage, trying not to think how strong he must be to throw her up so effortlessly. She forced herself to appear calm and unruffled while he checked the girth and adjusted her stirrup but her nerves were still on edge. She could not prevent her thoughts from racing ahead. What if he helped her down when they reached Charles Street? She would slide into his arms. They would envelop her, of course, and hold her close while he smiled down at her. His eyes would be gleaming with tender amusement and that would draw from her an answering smile before he bent his head and…and…

'We must behave ourselves on the return journey, Lady Phyllida.'

Richard's quiet words made her jump guiltily. He was standing beside Sultan, one hand resting on the gelding's neck and only inches from her knee. She looked down at him, dazed, and saw just such laughter in his eyes as she had imagined. It stirred something deep inside her, something that disturbed and excited her in equal measure.

From across the yard Ellen called out with mock severity, 'Indeed you must, Stepmama. Such a bad example you would be setting us!'

Phyllida was at a loss to answer her. She knew Ellen was referring to the madcap race across the turf, but she was aware that in the chapel she had come perilously close to being discovered locked in an embrace with Richard Arrandale. The look of smiling understanding in that gentleman's eyes compounded her confusion. There was such warmth, such friendship in his glance that she could not resist smiling back at him, but as they set off on the long ride back she regained command of her senses and forced herself to face the depressing reality of the situation. Richard Arrandale had no interest in her, he was merely trying to put her at her ease in order to advance his pursuit of Ellen.

Chapter Six

The afternoon was well advanced by the time they rode into Bath and the party broke up in Laura Place.

'What a delightful day,' exclaimed Ellen. 'Thank you so much for inviting me, Lady Wakefield.'

'It was a pleasure to have you with us, my dear.' Lady Wakefield's smile encompassed everyone. 'I think we all enjoyed it.'

'Well, Lady Phyllida?' Richard brought his horse alongside Sultan. '*Did* you enjoy yourself?'

She had had time to regain her composure and now answered cautiously, 'The castle was well worth seeing.'

'But originally you did not intend joining the party. Why did you change your mind?'

'Does there have to be a reason?' she parried lightly.

'Well, I am very glad you *did* come,' he said. 'I have enjoyed renewing our acquaintance, my lady.'

Her brows went up.

'Trying to turn me up sweet, Mr Arrandale?'

He grinned. 'Could I do so?'

'Never.' She was in control of herself now, and felt confident enough to add, 'I am no longer a shy *ingénue*, sir, to be impressed by your blandishments.'

She inclined her head, dismissing him, and walked

Sultan across to where Ellen was taking her leave of Julia and her family. A brief word with Lady Wakefield and she drew her stepdaughter away, saying it was time they went home.

'Oh,' said Ellen. 'Perhaps Mr Arrandale and Mr Fullingham would like to—'

'No, I think not. We have imposed upon them quite long enough today. Good day, gentlemen.' Phyllida's voice was firm, she would brook no argument.

Richard touched his hat as they rode past him and once he had taken his leave of the Wakefields he was left with only Henry Fullingham for company. They turned their horses and made their way together towards Pulteney Bridge. Fullingham chuckled.

'Well, I am indebted to you today, Arrandale. In trying to ingratiate yourself with the mother you left the field clear for me to cut you out with the heiress.'

'Perhaps that was my intention,' drawled Richard. 'I knew she would soon grow weary of your inane chatter.'

'Not a bit of it. Miss Tatham was as friendly as can be.'

'Not when we were at the castle,' Richard pointed out.

Fullingham scowled at him.

'Not *then*, perhaps, but on the ride there and back she was clearly delighted with my company. Urmston's right, she is a ripe plum, ready for plucking.'

'Do not be too sure. There is a sharp intelligence behind Miss Tatham's pretty face. She'll not easily fall for your charms, Fullingham.'

'Pho, Arrandale, that is sour grapes.' He laughed. 'Admit it, man, you have caught cold on this one. The widow has your measure. She'll be spending her time keeping you away from her precious daughter and won't spare a thought for the rest of us!'

They had reached the junction and Fullingham went

on his way, still laughing. Richard rode slowly to the stables behind Royal Crescent. He couldn't help thinking that the fellow was right, Phyllida might well be blind to the danger posed by the other men. She might even welcome their attentions towards Ellen, even those of Sir Charles Urmston. There was no doubt the fellow could be very charming, but underneath he was a villain. Richard's mouth tightened. He meant to win this wager. When it came to women he had never yet lost out to a rival, and he had no intention of starting now.

And what of Phyllida?

Richard's hand tightened on the reins. That incident in the chapel should never have happened. He had felt curiously lightheaded, probably from the wine they had been served at the house. It could certainly not have been anything else; he was not one to lose his head over any woman, especially one who was only tolerably pretty.

Although she did have particularly fine eyes.

And her smile. When she smiled she illuminated a whole room—

No! His only interest in Lady Phyllida was as Ellen Tatham's guardian and as a friend of his great-aunt. If she were to confide her worries to the dowager that would make life difficult. Not impossible, but he should not like to fall out with Sophia. A bitter, humourless smile twisted his mouth. Phyllida had told him she did not believe the Arrandales were really so scandalous. This little adventure would show her how wrong she was.

For the next few days he concentrated upon fixing his interest with Miss Tatham. He paid morning calls in Charles Street, and when Ellen hinted they were going shopping he tarried in Milsom Street until they arrived, or he sought them out at the Pump Room and curtailed his own visit to walk them home. Lady Phyllida was cool, even a little reserved, but not overtly hostile and when Ellen informed him innocently that she and Lady Phyllida would be taking a stroll in Sydney Gardens with Julia Wakefield the following morning he made sure he was there, just in case he needed to head off any of his rivals.

'Mr Arrandale, what a surprise to find you here,' declared Ellen when she saw him approaching, not long after they had entered the gardens.

'Yes, isn't it,' muttered Phyllida.

'We are going to the labyrinth,' explained Julia Wakefield.

'Then I will walk with you, if I may.'

'But we are going in the opposite direction to you, Mr Arrandale,' Lady Phyllida pointed out. 'Are you sure you have time?'

He ignored the challenge in her eyes and replied with a smile as false as her own, 'All the time in the world, ma'am.'

He turned to walk with Ellen but Phyllida stepped between them.

'Then that is very civil of you, Mr Arrandale.'

She proceeded to converse with him as they strolled along the wide path. Occasionally they were obliged to move aside to allow a carriage to pass, but every time they recommenced their walk she was there, at his side, and engaging him in conversation.

He wondered briefly if she was trying to fix his interest, following their time together at Farleigh Castle but he soon dismissed the thought. Then she had been open and relaxed with him. Now her cool friendliness did not ring true. She was on her guard and he thought it much more likely that she was suspicious of his motives. Clearly she did not intend to allow him a chance to converse with either of the young ladies and he knew better than to attempt it. When they arrived at the labyrinth he thought it politic not to offer to accompany them inside, and prepared to take his leave.

'Oh, but you must stay and keep Phyllida company,' Ellen protested. 'She does not like the maze and means to wait for us outside.'

'No, Ellen, that will not be necessary. I am sure Mr Arrandale has better things to do with his time.'

Lady Phyllida's answer was delivered firmly. Clearly it was designed to dismiss him. He knew he should retire with good grace but his particular devil prompted him to stay.

'I should be delighted to wait for you, Miss Tatham.' He patted his pocket. 'And I have a plan of the labyrinth, so if you get lost you only need to call out and I shall come to your aid.'

Phyllida's eyes sparkled with indignation, but Ellen was duly admiring.

'How gallant, and enterprising,' she remarked. 'Come along, Julia. Phyllida, pray you, wait on that bench for us—we will not be too long.'

The girls ran off, leaving Phyllida with Richard Arrandale. It was the first time they had been alone together since the chapel at Farleigh, when she had come close to making a complete fool of herself. It had not been mentioned, of course, and since then she had been careful to keep a distance between them. Until today, when she had put herself in his way and kept him talking. She had not been comfortable about it, but she was determined that he should not be allowed to give his arm to Ellen or Julia Wakefield.

She had to admit that he had taken it in good part and had behaved like the perfect gentleman, conversing with her as if there was nothing he would rather do. He had a knack of setting her at her ease, of making her feel important. Cherished. That was what made it so difficult to dislike him.

Yet it did not mean she should encourage him. She moved towards a bench.

'I must not take up any more of your time, Mr Arrandale, so I will bid you good day.'

'I assure you, Lady Phyllida, I am at your disposal.'

She sat down, saying with finality, 'Really, Mr Arrandale, it is not at all necessary for you to wait with me.'

'But I have a plan of the labyrinth.'

It gave her no little satisfaction to respond, tapping her reticule. 'So, too, have I.'

'Ah.'

It was then she made the mistake of peeping up at him. She saw his rueful look and burst out laughing.

'Admit it, sir, you have been brought to the *point non plus*. There is no reason to stay now.'

'Would you have me be so unchivalrous as to agree with you?' he said, sitting down on the bench beside her. 'It has never been my practice to abandon a lady when she is on her own.'

'But I shall not be on my own once the girls return.'

'Then I shall keep you company until then.'

His cool response flustered her.

'But I do not wish for your company.'

He shifted to the far end of the bench and twisted in his seat to look at her, resting one hand negligently along the backrest. Phyllida remained rigidly upright, staring straight ahead. He really was the most infuriating man. Well, she hoped he appreciated her profile.

'We could converse,' he said at last.

'We have already done so, on the way here.'

'But there must be something we have not yet talked about.'

'No.'

She could feel the warmth of his gaze upon her. It sent little shards of excitement to pierce the armour of cool civility with which she had surrounded herself. If only he would go away! She recalled reading somewhere that the best form of defence was attack and she turned to face him.

'Yes, there is something. Why do you remain in Bath, Mr Arrandale?'

'I enjoy spending time with my great-aunt.'

'Is that truly the reason?' She subjected him to a searching look.

'Yes, truly. She was laid very low when Cassandra eloped, and I know how cruel the gossipmongers can be. None better.' He raised his brows. 'You look sceptical, Lady Phyllida. Do you not believe me?'

She pursed her lips.

'I can believe you came to Lady Hune's assistance when she wrote to you, but she is much better now and the image of you playing companion to an elderly lady does not quite fit with your reputation.'

'Perhaps you should not put too much store by all you hear of me, ma'am. I am extremely fond of Lady Hune. When I was younger she was the only one of my family who had any faith in me and while she needs me I shall remain in Bath.'

'But it is hardly London, is it? Do you not find it dull here? After all, Lady Hune demands very little of your time.'

'True, but there are gambling hells, if one knows where to look, and—'

'And heiresses to chase.'

'That is not what I was going to say.'

'No, I thought I would save you the trouble.'

'There is sufficient society in Bath to entertain me for a few weeks, Lady Phyllida. I am not so very exacting.'

Oh, heavens, he was smiling at her, just as he had done in the chapel at Farleigh. She could feel the tug of attraction building again. It must not, could not happen. With relief she heard Ellen and Julia's girlish laughter near at hand. It gave her the strength to look away and she observed the girls running towards her.

'We lost all track of the time, Lady Phyllida,' said Julia guiltily. 'I do hope we were not gone too long.'

Phyllida rose to her feet and replied with determined cheerfulness, 'Not at all. I am glad I did not have to resort to my map to find you and bring you out. However, we had best be getting back now.' She turned to Richard. 'We can trespass on your time no longer, sir. I am going to escort Miss Julia home now.'

'Too soon, Lady Phyllida. My way lies with you. It would look very odd if I were to follow you all the way to Laura Place, would it not?'

'It would indeed.' Ellen giggled.

She showed no desire to release Julia's arm in favour of Richard Arrandale's, which relieved Phyllida's mind of its greatest worry, but the gentleman was in no way discomposed and merely fell into step beside Phyllida, which threw up quite a different anxiety.

She felt such conflicting emotions about this man. She knew he was a rake and even though she suspected— nay, she was sure—he was pursuing Ellen, she could not dislike him. Just having him at her side set her pulse jumping. She thought it would be easier if she cut the acquaintance altogether, but that might well precipitate the thing she was most anxious to avoid. Phyllida knew Ellen liked Richard Arrandale, but at present it was no more than that. If Phyllida was to forbid Ellen to have anything more to do with him she was very much afraid it would invest Richard with an air of danger and illicit excitement that a spirited young girl would find irresistible.

Her companion showed no desire to talk, so Phyllida was able to consider her dilemma in peace, until she realised they had traversed almost the length of Great Pulteney Street in silence. Even worse, Ellen and Julia were nowhere in sight.

'They hurried on ahead and are by now at Lady Wakefield's house,' Richard told her, as if aware of her alarm.

He kept up with her easily as she quickened her step and they reached the Wakefields' door just as the two girls emerged and Julia very prettily requested that Ellen might join them for dinner.

'I have asked Mama,' she added, 'and she says she will send Ellen home in the carriage, if you will allow it, Lady Phyllida.'

Ellen clasped her hands and subjected Phyllida to a beseeching look.

'Please tell me I may stay, *darling* Stepmama. And I am sure Mr Arrandale will accompany you, so you need have no worry about walking back to Charles Street unattended.'

'I should be delighted to escort Lady Phyllida,' he responded promptly.

Ellen beamed at him.

'Then it is all settled to everyone's satisfaction!' Ellen reached up and gave Phyllida a hasty kiss on the cheek, then ran indoors with Julia.

Speechless, Phyllida watched them go. This was not at all to her satisfaction. Richard held out his arm to her and silently she placed her fingers on his sleeve. They began to walk.

'Are you going to tell me that you are quite capable of walking back to Charles Street unattended?'

'I should not say anything so uncivil,' she replied loftily.

'That's put me in my place.'

She caught herself up on a laugh.

'You are quite shameless, you know.'

'I fear you are right. And I am going to prove it by asking you why you married Tatham.'

It was an impertinent question and Richard wondered if he had gone too far. She had every right to protest. She might even snatch her arm away and refuse to walk further with him. Instead she answered him quietly.

'Because he offered for me. I didn't *take*, you see, amongst the *ton*, but I had very little to recommend me. If you really do remember then you will know how gauche and awkward I was then.'

'So Sir Evelyn proposed.'

'Yes. He was rich, but he was also kind, much kinder to me than my parents were. To them I was nothing more than a commodity, to be used to the family's best advantage.'

Richard's jaw clenched tight. Knowing his world he was well aware of what might have happened to her, sold to the highest bidder.

'And was it a good marriage?'

'I think so. I believe I made Sir Evelyn happy, even though I failed to give him the heir he wanted.'

'I am not interested in Tatham,' he said roughly. 'What about *you*, were you happy?'

She smiled. 'Why, yes, why should I not be?'

'Did you love him?'

The little hand resting on his sleeve trembled.

'I did not dislike him, and that is very important.'

Her cool, reasonable response angered him. Smothering a curse he stopped and pulled her round to face him.

'How old are you, Lady Phyllida?'

She blinked. 'I am four-and-twenty, not that it is any concern of yours!'

'No, but it concerns me that you should be dwindling into widowhood before you have even lived.'

'Mr Arrandale, I assure you I am not at all unhappy with my lot.'

He shook his head at her.

'I saw your face when we raced the horses the other day. How often have you felt like that? When was the last time you really enjoyed yourself, dancing 'til dawn, walking in the moonlight, being kissed senseless—?'

Her eyes widened at that and she drew away from him.

'You should not be talking to me in this way.' She looked around. 'We—we are at Charles Street. Thank you for your escort. Forgive me if I do not ask you to come in.'

With that she left him, almost running the last few yards to her door, where she was soon lost to sight.

Damn, damn, damn! What was he thinking of? Richard turned on his heel and strode away. He was supposed to be making a friend of her, preparing the ground so that she would support him when he made Ellen an offer. Instead he was saying all the wrong things.

What in hell's name had got into him?

* * *

September advanced and the invitations continued to flood into Charles Street, including an urgent message one morning from Mrs Desborough, inviting them to take advantage of the continuing good weather to drive out of town and enjoy a picnic that very day. The Wakefields were going, which made Ellen keen to go and even Phyllida found the idea too tempting to resist.

'I always think these things are so much better *impromptu*,' declared Lady Wakefield as they made themselves comfortable on the rugs and cushions spread out upon the grass. 'I am so pleased Mrs Desborough suggested it, and such a pleasant spot, too.'

Phyllida could not deny the spot was indeed delightful, a sloping meadow near the little village of Claverton, but she was not quite so happy with some of the company. Mrs Desborough had laughingly explained that Mr Fullingham had come upon her as they were about to set off.

She continued. 'I had not the heart to say him nay, not when young Mr Wakefield had already asked Mr Arrandale to join us. After all, there is space enough here for everyone, is there not?'

'And you have refreshments enough for an army,' chuckled her fond spouse, eyeing the array of hampers set out before them. 'But it is not only good food she has arranged for us, is that not so, my dear?'

'Well, I did think that afterwards the young people might like to gather blackberries. The hedgerow is positively thick with them.' She chuckled and beckoned to one of the servants who came forward. 'You see I have brought three small baskets for you to fill, and to save you young ladies ruining your gowns there are aprons for you to put on.'

Lady Wakefield laughed. 'Then there can be no objection. You have thought of everything, ma'am!'

They dined well on cold meats and cakes washed down with wine or small beer, but soon the effects of good food and the heat of the day took their toll. The party became less noisy and conversation began to die away to a soft murmur that Phyllida found quite soporific. Her eyelids were beginning to droop when she heard Penelope Desborough's eager voice.

'May we go and collect blackberries now, Mama?'

Mrs Desborough and Lady Wakefield were nodding sleepily, their spouses already snoring gently in the warm sunshine. As the young ladies donned their aprons Phyllida glanced across at the hedgerow. It meandered away for quite some distance and she was suddenly struck with misgiving. Of course, the gentlemen might not go to help, but Mr Fullingham was already on his feet, followed quickly by Adrian Wakefield and Richard Arrandale.

She jumped up, which caused Mrs Desborough to exclaim, 'What's this, Lady Phyllida, do you wish to collect berries too? I made sure you would want to rest a little.'

'No, no, I am not at all tired,' Phyllida assured her.

Mrs Desborough sat upright, looking perturbed.

'But there are only three baskets, and I have no more aprons, ma'am, your gown—'

'Oh, that is of no consequence,' she replied airily.

Ellen laughed. 'I doubt if Matlock will agree with you, Philly! But never mind that. Here, you may have my basket, and I shall share with Penelope.'

The arrangements settled, they moved off towards the hedgerow.

Richard fell into step beside her.

'Three gentlemen, four ladies,' he murmured.

'Even numbers are not required for berry picking, Mr Arrandale.'

'Nor is a chaperon, Lady Phyllida.'

She put up her chin. 'That, sir, depends upon the company.'

Ellen had stopped by the hedge and her voice floated across on the still air.

'Adrian, will you help me and Penelope to fill our basket?'

Mr Fullingham stepped up. 'Allow me, Miss Tatham—'

'Ah, sir, I was hoping you would help Julia, because you see that she cannot quite reach those berries at the very top, there, and they look so delicious...'

He was subjected to a dazzling smile and Phyllida smothered a laugh as the gentleman went off to do as he was bid. She glanced towards Richard and saw that he was grinning at her. Caught off guard, she blushed and looked away, but her confusion increased when she heard Ellen's next words.

'That leaves Mr Arrandale to help Phyllida.'

That could *not* please him any more than it pleased Phyllida. He would surely protest. She waited, but after a brief hesitation he swept a low bow.

'Your wish is my command, Miss Tatham.'

Phyllida glared at him and without another word she hurried away to begin filling her basket.

Mrs Desborough was right, the tall hedgerows were thick with ripe blackberries and Phyllida worked steadily. Her gloves were soon stained with berry juice and she had to take care to prevent herself from becoming caught up on the brambles. Richard Arrandale was only feet away from her. His body and the lush, straggling hedgerow hid the others from her sight although their voices floated to her from time to time. They were distant, unimportant. All that mattered, all that she could think of, was the man beside her. He had removed his gloves to pick the fruit and she found herself watching his long lean fingers as they gently plucked each soft, plump berry.

They worked in silence. Phyllida had placed the basket on the ground between them and was surprised at how companionable it felt. She was aware of the birdsong, of the hum of insects and the warmth of the sun on her back, but more than anything she was aware of Richard at her side. Occasionally he moved closer and pulled down the higher stems for her to collect the soft fruit, or held aside the thick branches so she could reach deep into the heart of the bush.

Clearly, it was her duty to keep Richard Arrandale away from Ellen, but there was no denying that she was enjoying herself, more than she had done in a long time. The thought surprised her and she realised how staid her life had become, not only the twelve months she had spent in mourning at Tatham Park but the years before that. Years spent running a household and looking after an ageing husband.

I became a matron at eighteen, she thought, as she reached between two long branches to pluck a few particularly juicy berries. *I was caught up in the duties of being a wife and mother as soon as I left the schoolroom, with no time for frivolous pastimes.*

'Oh!'

A thorn had penetrated the soft kid of her glove and pierced her finger.

'Keep still.'

Richard was at her side immediately and she found it impossible to remain silent.

'I fear I have no choice but to obey,' she told him. 'The thorns have caught at my sleeve.'

He stepped closer and she was painfully aware of the hard wall of his chest against her back. Her mouth dried, he filled her senses. She breathed in the masculine smell of him, the mix of soap and leather and an indefinable hint of musky spices. Surely she was imagining the thud of his heart against her shoulders, but she could feel his breath on her cheek and she trembled.

'Steady now.'

One hand rested on her shoulder while the other reached past her to lift away the offending thorny tentacle.

'There, you are free.'

Free? How could she be free when her whole body was in thrall to him? When he was so close she could feel the heat of him on her back? Phyllida shook off the thought and carefully withdrew her arm from the briars. When Richard removed his hand from her shoulder she felt it immediately, a yearning chill and an emptiness that was almost a physical pain. She stepped back and turned, only to find that he was close behind her, less than a hand's width away, his broad chest and powerful shoulders filling her view, like a cliff face. She was distracted by detail, the fine stitching of his exquisitely tailored blue coat, the double row of buttons on his pale waistcoat, the snowy folds of linen at his neck. The hammering of her heartbeat thrummed in her ears. Surely he must hear it, see how shaken she was? She tried to speak lightly to divert his attention and her own.

'Thank you, sir. I fear I could not have extricated myself without ruining this gown.'

She stretched her cheeks into a smile and looked up,

confident she could ask him calmly to let her pass, but her gaze locked on to his mouth and the words died in her throat as she studied the firm sculpted lips. She was distracted by imagining how they would feel on her skin. She swallowed, forced her gaze upwards but that proved even more dangerous, for his blue eyes held her transfixed. She was lost, unable to move. She could no longer hear the skylark's distant trill, nor the laughing voices of those picking berries further along the hedgerow. The world had shrunk to just the two of them. Anticipation tremored through her when he ran his hands lightly up her arms and the skin beneath the thin sleeves burned with his touch. His fingers came to rest upon her shoulders, gently pulling her towards him as he lowered his head to kiss her. She made no effort to resist. Instead her chin tilted up and her lips parted instinctively as his mouth came closer.

It was the lightest contact, a slight, tantalising brush of the lips, but Phyllida felt as if a lightning bolt had struck her, shocking her, driving through her body and anchoring her to the spot. She kept her hands at her sides, clenched into fists to prevent them clinging to him like a desperate, drowning creature. She found herself straining upwards, trying to prolong the contact but it was over almost as soon as it had begun and as he raised his head Phyllida felt strangely bereft. The kiss had been the work of a moment, but it had shaken her to the core and she struggled to find a suitable response.

'You, you should not have done that.'

There was a faint crease at one side of his mouth, the merest hint of a smile.

'No one saw us.'

That was not what she meant at all, but it brought her back to reality. The thorny brambles were at her back so she sidestepped, breaking those invisible threads that had held her to him, even though it was like tearing her own flesh to move away from him. Distance gave her the strength to think properly again.

'I did not mean that and you know it. Your behaviour was ungentlemanly, sir.'

'You could have said no. You could have resisted.'

She scooped up the little basket and began to walk away.

'I should not have had to do so.'

He laughed softly as he fell in beside her.

'I believe I deserved some reward for rescuing a damsel in distress.'

She stopped, saying angrily, 'What you deserve, sir—'

'Yes?'

He was smiling down at her, sending her thoughts once more into disorder. Alarms clamoured in her head, it was as much as she could do not to throw herself at him and the glint in his blue eyes told her he knew it. With a hiss of exasperation she walked on.

'You deserve to be shamed publicly for your behaviour.'

'Ah, but the Arrandales have no shame, did you not know that?'

He spoke lightly, but there was something in his tone, a faint hint of bitterness that undermined her indignation. It could have been a ploy, a trick to gain her sympathy, but somehow she did not think so. With a sudden flash of insight she thought he was like a child, behaving badly because it was expected of him.

'Oh, how despicable you are!' she exclaimed. 'I should be scolding you for your outrageous behaviour and instead—' She broke off.

'Yes?' he prompted her gently.

I want to take you in my arms and kiss away your pain.

Phyllida was appalled. She had come very close to saying the words aloud. With a tiny shake of her head she almost ran the last few yards to where Mrs Desborough and Lady Wakefield were sitting under a large parasol.

The two ladies greeted Phyllida cheerfully and although they noted her flushed countenance, they put it down to too much sun and suggested she should come and sit with them in the shade. Mr Desborough, who was now awake and enjoying a glass of claret, invited Richard to join him.

As the ladies admired her basket of blackberries, sympathised with her ruined gloves and uttered up thanks that she had not spoiled her gown, Phyllida recovered her equilibrium. She decided not to say anything about Richard's disgraceful behaviour, especially since it did not reflect well upon her own judgement in allowing him to take such a liberty.

No, she thought, as the others returned and they prepared to make their way back to Bath, she had learned a valuable lesson and she would be sure Richard Arrandale had no opportunity to repeat it, or to try such tricks upon her stepdaughter.

Chapter Seven

The season had not yet started in Bath but the Assembly Rooms were crowded for the latest ball. Lady Wakefield had offered to include Ellen in her party, but Phyllida had decided she should go, too. She was concerned at the number of gentlemen who were vying for Ellen's attention, so much so that she had mentioned it to Lady Hune, when they had met a few days earlier. Ellen was attending her dancing class and Phyllida had taken the opportunity to call upon Lady Hune and enquire after her health, but the dowager's kindness encouraged Phyllida to confide in her.

'I had not thought there would be so many gentlemen in Bath on the lookout for a wife,' she admitted. 'Ellen's inheritance is held in trust until she attains her majority in four years' time but even that knowledge does not seem to deter them.'

'And does Ellen favour any of these gentlemen?'

'No, she doesn't, and that is the most comforting thing, ma'am. She is a minx, and willing to flirt with them, although I make sure she does not go too far, and I allow none of them to be alone with her.' Phyllida stopped, frowning, trying to make sense of her worries. 'I wonder if perhaps I made a mistake in bringing her to Bath. Only, she could no longer remain at the school, and to incarcerate her at Tatham Park would have been too cruel. You see, the families of her close friends have moved away and the society there is somewhat limited now.'

'As you have discovered in the past year.'

She gave a reluctant smile. 'Precisely, ma'am. Oh, I know I was in mourning, but it would have been a comfort to have at least a few families I could call upon, instead of having to entertain my husband's relatives.'

'Is that Walter Tatham?' asked Sophia. 'He was always a pompous slow-top. I never met his wife but I suppose she is the same—you need not say so, my dear, I can tell by your face that it is the case.'

'I do not mean to be unkind, but when one has been the mistress of one's own household for years...'

'They tried to browbeat you, I suppose.' The dowager gave a little huff of exasperation.

'The thing is, they were against my bringing Ellen to live with me, and I...' Phyllida bit her lip '...I wonder now if they were right.'

'Nonsense, it is doing you the world of good to be out in society again. You have regained your glow.'

'You are very kind, ma'am, but it is not about me.'

'From what I know of your stepdaughter she is well able to look after herself,' retorted Sophia. 'She is a very pretty-behaved young lady, confident, yes, and spirited, I always like that in a girl, but she also appears to be quite sensible. She will do very well, as long as none of these fellows steals her heart.' She fell silent and from the shadow of pain that crossed her face Phyllida thought that perhaps she was thinking of Lady Cassandra, her granddaughter. Phyllida waited, not wishing to disturb the old lady's thoughts and after a few moments the dowager gave herself a little shake and resumed, saying briskly, 'Let her enjoy herself, within the bounds of propriety, and she will do very well.'

Sophia had hesitated for a moment, then changed the subject. Looking back, Phyllida wondered if she had been about to ask if Richard Arrandale was one of those paying court to Ellen, but the old lady was sharp enough to know the answer to that. If Lady Hune would warn him off, then all to the good, thought Phyllida now, as she watched Ellen going down the dance with Henry Fullingham.

Phyllida felt a little guilty because her concern over Ellen was not the only reason she had decided to attend the ball. She had given in to the temptation to put on one of her old ball gowns. When she had seen that Phyllida was prepared to dance, Lady Wakefield had immediately found her a partner, and since she had assured her that she was perfectly able to keep an eye on Ellen as well as Julia, Phyllida gave herself up to the enjoyment of the music. She was not quite lost to all sense of her responsibilities, but Ellen appeared to have a partner for every new set, so Phyllida salved her conscience with the thought that the child could come to very little harm while she was dancing.

Richard saw Phyllida as soon as he entered the ballroom. She was on the dance floor, the folds of her peach-coloured gown flowing gracefully around her elegant figure as she moved. She was laughing at something her partner was saying, her face was positively glowing with happiness and his breath caught in his throat. She might not be an accredited beauty but there was an elusive charm about the lady that made her stand out from the crowd.

He dragged his eyes away. This was not why he was

here, his goal was to secure a fortune by winning the hand of Ellen Tatham. The previous evening at Burton's gaming hell he had heard the other fellows complaining that it was impossible to get the heiress alone. She was friendly to a fault, blushed adorably at their compliments, but made no effort to dismiss her maid when they were out together, nor would she allow herself to be separated from her friends. And if she was escorted by her stepmother the two were well-nigh inseparable.

Richard had said nothing but he was faring no better. In fact, whenever he met Ellen and Lady Phyllida the chit seemed to delight in palming him off on her stepmama. No, the only chance of a private word with Miss Ellen Tatham was on the dance floor and he quickly scanned the room for her. She was partnered by young Naismith, who was gazing at her with blatant adoration as they trod the final measure of a lively country dance. The music was ending and Richard saw his chance. He moved forward as Naismith escorted his partner from the floor. Ellen was already smiling but her smile widened when she saw him. Naismith was dismissed even before Richard had begged the honour of leading her out for the next set.

'Mr Arrandale, how delightful!' She tucked her hand in his arm and began to walk away with him. 'I would be very happy to stand up with you, sir, but first you must dance with my stepmama.'

'What?'

His step faltered but the little hand on his sleeve pulled him on. He could see Phyllida standing only feet away. She had just walked off the floor on the arm of an elderly brigadier.

'It is a rule I have made for tonight,' Ellen told him. 'Stepmama, here is your next dance partner!'

The brigadier bowed and walked away. Lady Phyllida looked around, her smile slipping a little when she saw Richard arm in arm with her stepdaughter. Then, as the meaning of Ellen's words sank in she blushed scarlet.

'My dear child, do not be absurd!'

'I told you I would not stand up with any gentleman tonight unless he had first danced with you.'

'Does that include the brigadier?' murmured Richard.

'No, but he pounced on Phyllida without my having to ask him.'

'Ellen, you cannot order people around in this way!' hissed Phyllida, frowning at her.

Richard put up his hand.

'Believe me, ma'am, I should be delighted to stand up with you.'

'Thank you, sir, it is not at all necessary.'

'Yes, it is, Philly, or I shall not be able to dance with Mr Arrandale, and you said yourself he is quite the best dancer in Bath.'

'I said no such thing! Really, Ellen—'

Lady Phyllida was looking very flustered and Richard felt obliged to protest.

'Miss Tatham, I cannot dance with Lady Phyllida if she is averse to it.'

Ellen's face grew suddenly serious. She reached out and took Phyllida's hands.

'I only want you to enjoy yourself, Philly. Do you truly not wish to dance any more tonight?'

Phyllida hesitated. She could lie, and spend the rest of the evening sitting on the benches, watching everyone else enjoying themselves.

'I would, of course, like to dance…'

'There, I knew it.' Ellen was triumphant. She stood

back. 'Off you go now. And, Mr Arrandale, I shall save the next dance for you!'

This was said so much in the manner of granting a child a treat that Phyllida, catching Richard's eye at that moment, burst out laughing. It relieved the tension and he grinned back at her.

'We have been outmanoeuvred, Lady Phyllida.' He took her hand and led her away. 'Your stepdaughter is very persuasive.'

'She is outrageous,' replied Phyllida. 'I do not know what she is thinking of.'

'Your happiness,' said Richard, remembering the conversation he had had with Ellen during the ride to Farleigh.

She shook her head at that and took her place opposite him. The hot blush had cooled to a faint staining of her cheeks. It was very becoming, and in keeping with the smile that curved her lips and glowed in her eyes.

The music started, they saluted one another, stepped up, back, joined hands, moved away. They were in perfect time, thought Richard, their steps matching as if they had always danced together. A memory surfaced, clear as crystal. He suddenly remembered Phyllida at her come-out seven years ago: pale and shy in a room full of strangers. He had been pursuing his latest quarry, a dashing matron who had been throwing out lures to him for weeks, but every time he entered the hallowed walls of Almack's the patronesses seized upon him and he was obliged to dance with any number of débutantes before he was allowed to escape. Some became simpering idiots as soon as a man spoke to them, others were so forward he indulged them in a fast and furious flirtation before disappearing into the crowd.

One night there had been a débutante who neither

simpered nor flirted. She was tall and thin, pale as her gown, pushed forward by her mother and clearly being offered up to anyone looking for a bride. No wonder they called the place the Marriage Mart! Richard had taken pity on the girl, treated her kindly and taken her back to her dragon of a mother when the dance was over. Then he had returned to his dashing matron and forgotten all about the poor little dab of a girl.

Except, he recalled now, how it had felt to dance with her. True, during the first few bars of the music she had made a mistake and cannoned into him, but he had recognised that she was crippled with nerves and he had exerted himself even more to put her at her ease. After that she had danced beautifully, so beautifully he had thought at the time it was like holding hands with an angel.

That same angel was dancing with him now, holding his hand, circling, crossing, skipping around him. How could he have forgotten? All too soon the dance ended. Richard was unprepared for it, he was still confused by his memories. Mechanically he made his bow to his partner. Phyllida was not smiling, she did not meet his eyes and was reluctant to take his hand. In fact, he thought with dismay, she could not wait to get away from him.

Ellen was waiting as they left the dance floor, compliments on their dancing tripping from her tongue.

'Yes, well, now I have done my duty and it is your turn,' Phyllida responded, a shade too brightly, Richard thought, before excusing herself and hurrying away.

He led Ellen out to join the next set but he found it difficult to concentrate. His head was still full of Phyllida, how well they danced together, how he had enjoyed having her tall, graceful figure beside him. The way the candlelight glinted on the golden strands in her hair, the elusive, seductive scent of her. For pity's sake he must stop this sentimental yearning and concentrate upon his partner. After all, Ellen Tatham was the prize he had set himself to win. Never had a dance seemed longer, or less enjoyable, but at last it was over. Richard surrendered Ellen to her new partner and took himself off to the card room, but the games held no allure and after a wasted hour he returned to the ballroom, his eyes immediately seeking and finding Phyllida, who was dancing with Sir Charles Urmston.

Richard frowned. Was that at Ellen's instigation? If she was playing off her tricks on Urmston she might find herself undone. He stationed himself against one wall and watched until the dancers reorganised themselves for the next set and he was relieved to see Ellen stand up with Adrian Wakefield. Phyllida, he noticed, had detached herself from Urmston and was standing on the far side of the room. She looked composed now. Had she enjoyed dancing with Urmston? More so than standing up with himself? The idea annoyed him.

As if aware of his scrutiny she looked across at him and their eyes met, but she looked away again immediately. That annoyed him, too, as did the temptation to cross the room and join her. What was he thinking? A little dalliance was one thing, sufficient to win the lady over, but anything more would not help him to win Miss Tatham's hand and that was his objective. Wasn't it?

He wanted to leave, to clear his head, but Tesford and Cromby were clearly waiting to pounce on Ellen when the dancing ended and he knew he should stay. It was not in his interests to let any of them gain an advantage with the heiress. He glanced at his watch. There would be a break for refreshments next and Richard knew what to do. A quiet word with George Cromby came first, telling him that his wife's bosom friend was looking for him. That sent the fellow scuttling away to the card room. The music faded and young Wakefield was leading Ellen back to Phyllida. Urmston and Tesford were already closing in, determined to escort the ladies into supper. Richard made his move. A judicious nudge sent a waiter's tray flying and claret cascaded over Tesford's white-quilted waistcoat, forcing him to retire. He then intercepted Sir Charles on the pretext of asking him about the mare he was selling. By the time Urmston had shaken him off it was too late for him to do any harm: young Wakefield had carried off Ellen and her stepmother to join his family. Richard sank down on the fast-emptying benches in the ballroom. He needed to think.

Phyllida listened to Ellen chattering away to the Wakefields but the words did not make sense. Nothing had made sense since she had danced with Richard Arrandale. The moves, the touch of hands, the closeness of their bodies when the dance brought them together—it had stirred emotions within her that she had never felt before. The crowd had disappeared; for a while it had been just her and Richard, alone together. Of course it did not last and she was foolish to wish it could. It was just a dance and however much he might smile into her eyes, however much she might read into his look, he was merely being courteous, as he had been all those years ago.

Even worse, she knew his courtesy had an ulterior motive, to gain her approval for his courtship of Ellen. That was out of the question. Ellen would make her come-out next year and Phyllida would ensure she enjoyed at least one Season in town before she decided on a life partner. Ellen herself had declared that it was not her intention to marry too soon, but Phyllida knew that hearts were fickle. A look, a touch was enough to send all sensible plans flying out of the window. Phyllida watched her stepdaughter as she chatted happily to Julia and Adrian Wakefield. She showed no signs of having lost her heart and Phyllida sent up a silent prayer that she would not do so for a long time yet.

Phyllida's head was aching. She longed to go home but the dancing had recommenced and her stepdaughter was once more in great demand. She watched with dismay as Richard Arrandale cut out Henry Fullingham and carried Ellen off for a second time. That was enough. She dared not allow Ellen to stand up with him again. It was not pique or jealousy, she told herself. Tongues would wag if any one admirer became too particular.

'Lady Phyllida, you are looking very pale, are you unwell?' Lady Wakefield's voice interrupted her thoughts.

'No, ma'am. I am a little tired perhaps.'

'Why do you not go home? I can easily convey Ellen to Charles Street later.'

'No, I am her guardian, I must be here to look out for her.'

She shook her head, but that made it ache even more horribly.

Lady Wakefield touched her arm. 'My dear, you look positively white. Do, at least go into the tea room and sit down quietly for a little while.' When Phyllida hesitated she said bluntly, 'You are concerned for Ellen, having seen her stand up again with Mr Arrandale.'

'I know it is only a second dance,' said Phyllida. 'Perhaps I refine upon it too much, but...'

Lady Wakefield patted her hand.

'I shall make sure he does not dance with her again, nor any of the other gentlemen who have had their two dances. There are several young friends of Adrian's who have not yet danced with Ellen and I will make sure they get their turn. Off you go and look after yourself.'

'Ah, you understand,' murmured Phyllida, with a grateful smile. 'I will do as you suggest, ma'am, and find somewhere quiet to sit for a while.'

She slipped away through the door to the Octagon, but this was quite as noisy as the ballroom and she moved on to the tea room, where there were fewer people but their jackdaw-like chatter echoed around the lofty space. Quickly she passed on to the antechamber. It was empty for the moment and she sat down on one of the benches there. After a while the pain in her head subsided, but the hard knot of unhappiness in her chest did not. She closed her eyes as regret, deep and bitter, welled up. For a brief moment she wished that at seventeen she had been as beautiful and confident as Ellen. Then perhaps some young and attractive gentleman might have made her an offer, instead of a man old enough to be her father. Perhaps even Richard might have been tempted.

But there her sensible nature fought back. Richard Arrandale was a rake. If she had been pretty enough to attract his attention then the hard truth was that he would have seduced her. Phyllida sighed. The past was gone, it could not be brought back. Sir Evelyn had been a good husband, and even though they had not been in love they had been happy. He had treated her very well and given her the confidence and the means to stand up to her relatives and choose to live alone. She would always be grateful to him for that. And she would always be grateful for Ellen. She had become very fond of her stepdaughter and would do her best to make sure she was happy.

A familiar, amused drawl interrupted her reverie.

'I wondered where you had gone. Do you consider it safe to let Miss Tatham out of your sight?'

Her eyes flew open. Richard Arrandale was standing before her, looking so devilishly handsome in his close-fitting dark coat that her heart missed a beat and a wave of desire washed over her, so strong she thought she might faint. Afraid he might read her thoughts if she looked into his eyes, Phyllida fixed her gaze upon the single diamond winking from the folds of his snowy neckcloth as she responded.

'She will come to no harm while she is dancing.' Her voice at least was under control. 'Are you leaving?'

'Yes. That should relieve you of one worry, at least.'

'I have no idea what you mean.'

'Do you not?' To her alarm he sat down beside her on the bench. 'I have the distinct feeling you do not trust me. Is that why you are always putting yourself in my way, claiming my attention when we meet?'

'How…how absurd.'

He continued as if he had not heard her faint protest.

'And is that not why you changed your mind and joined the ride to Farleigh Castle, to save Ellen from falling into my clutches?'

'Of course not.'

'No? Then perhaps it was because you have developed a liking for my company.'

'How arrogant you are. And quite mistaken.'

'You did not stop me from kissing you, at the picnic. In fact, I think you enjoyed the experience.'

'Pray do not try to flirt with me, Mr Arrandale. You are wasting your time.'

'Am I? But you blush so adorably.'

His fingers touched her cheek and she jumped up as if she had been burned.

'Quite the contrary.' She took a deep breath. It was time to nip in the bud any pretensions the man might have. 'I think I should tell you, Mr Arrandale, that your reputation is well known to me. Before you came to Bath Lady Hune delighted in recounting your scandalous intrigues. You may be her nephew, she may be very fond of you, but from what the dowager has told me I do not think you are a fit and proper acquaintance for Ellen.'

He had risen too and was looking down at her, a faint crease in his brow.

'That is the word with no bark on it.' He paused a moment, as if weighing his words. 'Lady Phyllida, I did not come to Bath with the intention of pursuing any…er… *scandalous intrigues.*'

'But you had not then seen my beautiful stepdaughter.'

'Madam, I—'

Phyllida drew herself up as tall as possible, but even so her eyes were only level with his mouth. It was a disadvantage, to have to look up to him, but where Ellen was concerned she must be strong.

'Mr Arrandale, I am well aware of the temptation Ellen must be to you, and others of your ilk. She is rich and she is pretty, but she is to be presented at Court next year and *I have no intention* of allowing anything or anyone to interfere with my plans, do you understand me?'

She forced herself to meet and hold his gaze, hoping he would see how determined she was. To her consternation the lines deepened around his eyes and a disturbing glint appeared in their blue depths.

'I might almost take that as a challenge, Lady Phyllida.'

A tiny spark of anger flared. Her chin lifted a fraction higher.

'You may take it any way you wish, Mr Arrandale. I am not afraid of you.'

Richard stared at the slender woman standing before him. Egad, how had he ever thought her mousy? Her honey-brown hair highlighted the creamy perfection of her skin and anger had deepened the colour of her eyes to a rich sea-green. They positively sparkled in the candlelight. With that stubborn tilt to her head she was quite captivating. He admired her spirit, but did she really think she could prevent him, if he wished to seduce Ellen Tatham? A tiny voice in his head urged caution, he should walk away and leave her alone, but for the life of him he could not ignore this woman. When he had seen her sitting alone and forlorn in the antechamber he had stopped to tease her, wanting only to put her sadness to flight. Now she had thrown down the gauntlet and the desire to pick it up proved irresistible. He could not help responding but he grinned to show he was only teasing her.

'Let battle commence, then, my lady.'

Phyllida stared at him. Did he think she was funning? Perhaps a young girl's reputation meant nothing to him, but if he or any other man were to compromise Ellen her life would be ruined. With a final, scorching look and a toss of her head Phyllida turned and walked quickly back to the ballroom. If he wanted battle then she was ready. She would defend Ellen with her life, if necessary!

* * *

Dawn was breaking by the time Richard returned to Royal Crescent, where a sleepy servant let him in. He collected his bedroom candle and made his way slowly and unsteadily up the stairs.

He had just gained the landing when he heard his name.

'Is that you, Richard?' His great-aunt stood in her doorway, a shadow against the lighted room behind her. 'I cannot sleep, my boy. Would you join me for a glass of Madeira?'

He had had a surfeit of the wine already but he could not refuse Sophia's request. With a murmured assent he followed her back into the room, blinking in the light. It was an antechamber to the dowager's bedroom and he frowned when he saw the decanter and glasses standing on a side table.

'Have you been waiting up for me?'

'Devil a bit,' she retorted crudely. 'Can you not see I am in my cap and nightgown? When you get to my age you will realise that sleep does not come so readily. You may pour us both a glass of wine and then sit down. Where have you been tonight?'

'Oh, here and there.' He settled back in his chair. 'I stopped off at Burton's. Playing hazard.'

'And did you win?'

He grinned. 'Of course.'

'Good. And were you at the Assembly Rooms earlier?'

'I looked in.'

'I believe Miss Tatham is attracting a great deal of attention.'

He was on his guard now.

'Is it any wonder? She is a diamond.'

'She is also a babe,' Sophia retorted. 'Not yet eighteen.' She held up her empty glass. Richard eased himself out of his chair and went to the side table to collect the decanter. She continued. 'Rumour has it that there is a wager to see who can be first to seduce the heiress.'

'Where in blazes did you hear that?'

'I have my sources,' she replied darkly. 'Are you aware of the wager?'

'I am.'

As he stood over her, refilling her glass, she said sharply, 'Are you a party to it? Are you making a play for Miss Tatham?'

He did not answer immediately, returning the decanter to its tray and settling down again in his chair before saying lightly, 'I would be a fool not to do so. She is very beautiful, besides being worth a considerable fortune.'

His great-aunt snorted. 'A schoolroom miss who would bore you within a month.'

'She would be better off married to me than to many of the fellows who are chasing her!' He let his breath go in a long sigh and sat forward, rubbing his temples. 'I was at Burton's when the idea was suggested. I went along with it—'

'Of course. When have you ever refused a wager?' She gave a rueful smile. 'You are an Arrandale, after all.'

'I had intended—that is, I thought I might make a push to secure Ellen Tatham for myself. After all, her fortune would prove very useful. Now...' His breath hissed out. 'I have had plenty of affairs, Sophia, you know that, and I've enjoyed them, but I have never yet met any woman I wanted to marry.' He shook his head. 'Pursuing an heiress, seducing an innocent—I have never been in that line. If you want the truth, I don't think I have the heart for it.'

'You relieve my mind.' He heard the rustle of a silk dressing gown as the dowager sat forward in her chair. 'Richard, I have known you all your life. I know you were sent down in disgrace from Oxford. I followed your career in town, all the scandals, the affairs, but I have never believed that was the man you were meant to be.'

He laughed. It was a harsh, humourless sound, even to his own ears.

'I am an Arrandale, madam. Scandal is our destiny. Look at my brother. And your own granddaughter, for that matter!'

'Perhaps it is too late for Wolfgang, and I admit Cassandra's elopement was foolish, yet it was her choice and she must live with it. But you—Richard, there is much goodness in you, it is merely that you have not discovered it yet.' When he lifted his head to look at her she smiled. 'You think at five-and-twenty you know everything there is to know but trust me, I am older and wiser than you and I say you are not a rake.'

He spread his hands. 'Then what am I?'

The question hung in the air, answered only by the soft tick of the ormolu clock on the mantelshelf. Richard gave a shrug and passed one hand across his eyes.

He said wearily, 'I think I am more drunk than I realised. I beg your pardon, Sophia.'

'No matter. It is not the first time I have seen a man in his cups. Go to bed, Richard, but first help me out of this chair.'

He asked, as he pulled her to her feet, 'Shall I ring for your maid?'

'Lord, no, I have only to throw off my wrap and blow

out the candle. I am not so infirm that I cannot do that for myself.'

He kissed her cheek. 'Goodnight, then, Sophia.'

'Sleep well, my boy.' She clung to his hands, her fingers thin as claws. 'In the morning things might seem clearer.'

Her words came back to him the following morning as he lay in bed, hands clasped behind his head, gazing up at the intricately carved tester above him. The night's sleep had confirmed his thoughts, that he was damned uncomfortable hunting a schoolgirl, even if she was an heiress.

He shifted restlessly. Why had he made that foolish remark to Lady Phyllida? He should have realised she was serious, and would think that he was, too. Blast it, he had no wish to fight with her, but she roused in him feelings he had never known before. Feelings that confused him. More than that, they frightened him. He was no longer in control when he was with her, he acted in ways he could not explain and he was very much afraid that it was only a matter of time before he did something they would both regret. What that might be his mind shied away from, and he turned his thoughts once more to the wager.

Richard had committed many sins in his career but he had never deliberately set out to hurt anyone but himself. And his name. He had besmirched that with scandal, but any good that was left to the ancient name of Arrandale had been destroyed when Wolf fled the country. But Richard would not seduce a chit merely for a wager. He would leave that to those whose conscience was less troubled. His own conscience reared up uncomfortably, telling him he could not abandon Phyllida and Ellen to their fate but he beat it down again ruthlessly. He was more a knave than a knight in shining armour, even though Phyllida made him feel like one. Ellen Tatham was none of his concern and Lady Phyllida had shown herself more than capable of defending her ward. After all, it was only until Michaelmas. Three more weeks. And Sophia was in much better spirits now. If she could do without him he would quit Bath, and leave Lady Phyllida and Miss Tatham to their fate.

Having made his decision, Richard rang for Fritt and dressed quickly, hurrying downstairs to join Sophia in the breakfast room.

She said, without looking up from buttering a freshly baked muffin, 'I expected Fritt to bring your apologies this morning. How's your head?'

'Aching damnably.'

'It serves you right. Drinking dubious brandy at that gaming hell, then coming home and keeping me up to all hours and consuming nearly a bottle of my best Madeira.'

Despite the headache Richard grinned.

'You do not appear to be suffering from the night's revels, ma'am.'

'No, I am very well this morning. In fact I think I shall forgo my visit to the hot baths and take myself shopping later in Milsom Street instead.'

'Your spirits are clearly restored, Sophia. I am very glad of it, for I think it is time I left Bath.'

That did make Sophia look up.

'Oh, might one ask why you should suddenly decide to leave me?'

'It is not you, Sophia, but you know it was never my intention to remain here indefinitely.'

'And what about that outrageous wager concerning Ellen Tatham?'

He frowned. 'I told you last night I have no wish to be involved in that.'

'But you *are* involved, Richard.'

He shook his head, which set off a thudding pain inside his skull. He said irritably, 'I shall forfeit my stake, but I want nothing more to do with that damned affair.'

Sophia did not reply, but he knew she would not let the matter rest there. In the ensuing silence he addressed his plate of cold meats. The food and a couple of cups of scalding coffee were beginning to take effect and he began to feel more hopeful. He would convince Sophia that she did not need him and he could be at Brookthorn Manor by the morning.

'So you would leave Ellen Tatham to the mercy of the fortune hunters.'

'She is none of my concern.'

'And Lady Phyllida?'

Let battle commence.

How he regretted those words!

'She is perfectly capable of protecting her own.'

'Is she? Do you really think she can keep her stepdaughter safe from the rogues and libertines who are pursuing her? I do not.'

He put up his hands.

'Even if that is not the case she would not accept my help. She thinks me the villain of the piece. No, ma'am, it is better if I leave Bath.'

'You promised to stay until I was better.'

'You *are* better, Sophia.'

'I do not think so.'

'There is work to be done at Brookthorn. You are always telling me I should not neglect my estate.'

'Brookthorn Manor has been neglected for many years. It will wait a little longer for you.'

'Sophia—'

'Dr Whingate will tell you I am not yet fully recovered.'

'Whingate will say whatever you tell him—'

Sophia dropped her knife with a clatter.

'Must I beg you to stay with me?' she burst out, a slight tremor in her voice that he had never heard before. Immediately he capitulated.

'No, of course not,' he said quietly. 'I shall remain, if that is your wish.'

He thought he saw a flash of triumph in her eyes but it was gone before he could be sure.

'Thank you, Richard.' She sat back. 'And you will do your best to protect the heiress?'

'Now, Sophia—'

'I know, she is nothing to you, but she reminds me of Cassandra, and I would not like any harm to come to her.'

Richard stared at his great-aunt. She had never asked anything of him before, save his company. How could he refuse? The image of Lady Phyllida rose in his mind, indignant, outraged. It would take all his skill to lay her ruffled feathers. A *frisson* of pleasurable anticipation ran through him at the thought of it, but there was alarm, too. Instinct warned him against tangling with Lady Phyllida.

'Very well,' he said at last. 'I will remain in Bath until that sawbones of yours tells me you are well enough to survive without me. And I will do my best to foil any attempts to seduce the heiress, but it won't be easy. Ellen Tatham is as headstrong and spirited as Cassandra, and Lady Phyllida regards me with suspicion.'

She smiled at that.

'A challenge for you, then, my boy. At least you won't be bored!'

Chapter Eight

For Ellen and Phyllida the round of parties, dances and outings continued unabated. Invitations poured in and it was difficult to keep up with them all, but at least Phyllida knew that with so many social engagements Ellen had little time for secret trysts or meetings, even if she were tempted to agree to them. Phyllida was gratified that Ellen was in such demand and the most pleasing aspect of it all was that Ellen's head did not appear to be turned by all the attention. She was as happy to visit the library or the Pump Room with Phyllida as to dance the night away.

Following her confrontation with Richard Arrandale, Phyllida was at pains to keep an even closer eye on her stepdaughter, but although Ellen's suitors were as attentive as ever, Mr Arrandale was not one of them and it was a full week before they met again. Lady Wakefield had arranged a riding party to see the monument on Lansdown but Phyllida's sister was due to arrive in Charles Street on the same day. Phyllida had planned to allow Ellen to ride out under Lady Wakefield's aegis and with Parfett in attendance, knowing that if all else failed the groom was more than capable of quelling the high spirits of a girl he had known from the cradle. However, on the morning of the ride a carefully worded message arrived from Lady Wakefield to say that she had sprained her wrist and that the party would now be chaperoned by her married daughter, who was staying in Laura Place for a few weeks. The message was couched in the friendliest terms, which raised no suspicion in Ellen's mind, when it was read out to her at the breakfast table, but Phyllida knew immediately what must be done.

'I shall come with you.'

'But what about Aunt Hapton? I thought you wished to stay and make sure everything was ready for her?'

'I am sure I can leave that to Mrs Hirst. Besides, Olivia is not due until dinner time, and we shall be back well before then. Now, if you have finished your breakfast, Ellen, perhaps you would send word to Parfett to bring both our horses to the door.'

'I will indeed. I am so glad you will be able to come with us, Philly, Parfett is always much more strict with me when you are not there!'

The party was to congregate in Laura Place, and when Phyllida and Ellen arrived, Julia and Adrian were already mounted and talking to Penelope Desborough. As the young people greeted one another Phyllida moved closer to speak to Lady Wakefield, who was standing at her door.

'How is your wrist, ma'am?'

'Very well, if I do not use it.' The lady stepped on to the pavement. 'A very silly thing. I was playing battledore and shuttlecock with my grandchildren when I slipped and fell.' She looked towards the house, where Phyllida could see two young boys standing in the window. 'There they are, Charles and Edwin, delightful boys, but so lively. They really wanted to come with you but Grace, my daughter, thought that at seven and eight years old they were too young.'

'Perhaps next time.' Phyllida smiled and waved to the little figures.

'I admit I was hoping you would join the ride.' Lady Wakefield dropped her voice a little. 'Grace is the kindest soul but she is far too complaisant to keep a close eye on the younger members of the party.'

'I would not have done so if your son was the only gentleman in attendance, but knowing that was not the case...'

She let the words hang and Lady Wakefield gave her an understanding smile.

'I know how anxious you are to keep Ellen safe, Lady Phyllida. I had hoped to keep it a very private riding party and was not pleased when Adrian told me Mr Arrandale was coming, but then, when Grace met Mr Tesford at the Italian concert last night and invited him to join us, I was most put out! However, it cannot be helped, and to forbid either of the gentlemen to come along would only make them more fascinating to the girls, do you not agree?'

'I am afraid you are right, ma'am.' She glanced around. 'Perhaps they will not come.'

That hope was immediately dashed when Lady Wakefield declared that she could see the gentlemen approaching now.

'Well, you need have no fear,' Phyllida told her. 'I will be vigilant on behalf of the girls.'

'I am sure you will and I am grateful, for I fear Grace will be little help to you on that front. Now, let me present her to you.'

Grace Stapleton was a cheerful young matron a few

years older than Phyllida and with a restless manner. She was constantly looking about her and when the two gentlemen arrived she immediately turned her horse and moved off to greet them. Phyllida let her go and afforded the men no more than a distant nod as the little party set off through the busy streets. She positioned herself close to the three girls, ready to head off any gentleman who tried to talk to them but her caution proved unnecessary. A glance ahead showed her that Mr Tesford was riding with Grace Stapleton while Richard had engaged Adrian Wakefield in conversation. She relaxed, satisfied that for the moment there was no danger.

The open heights of Lansdown were soon reached and with the monument in sight they all cantered across the springy turf towards it. They agreed to leave their horses at a small stand of trees within sight of the monument and by the time Phyllida rode up with the Ellen, Julia and Penelope, the others had dismounted. Two of the gentlemen were already making their way towards the girls and Phyllida quickly requested the grooms to help the young ladies to dismount. Mr Tesford stopped when he saw Parfett run to Ellen's side, but Richard Arrandale strode on and Phyllida warily watched his approach.

He put a hand on her bridle.

'Since your groom is engaged, perhaps you will allow me to help you down.'

She was prepared for Sultan to throw up his head and protest at the strange hand on the reins but instead he stood quietly, unusually obedient.

Traitor.

'Well, my lady?'

Richard was already reaching up to her. There was no choice, and just as she had imagined doing in a dozen restless dreams, Phyllida slid down into his waiting arms.

They tightened fractionally and she wondered if he could feel the frenzied thud of her heart as she was pressed against his chest. How she would love to give in to the temptation to stay there, to close her eyes and rest her head on his shoulder, which was at such a convenient height for a tall lady. If only he had been a gentleman and not a rake. Disappointment seared and she addressed him sharply.

'Thank you sir, I am perfectly able to stand.'

'Of course.'

He let her go and she stepped away from him, concentrating on shaking out her skirts so that he might not see the heat in her cheeks. She did not look up until her groom approached.

'We'll keep the horses here, m'lady, under the trees, until you're all ready to leave.' Parfett took Sultan's reins from her and led the horse away, leaving Phyllida with only Richard Arrandale for company.

'The others are heading for the monument. Will you allow me to escort you?'

She ignored his outstretched arm and set off, saying as he fell into step beside her, 'At least while you are here I need not fear that you are seducing my stepdaughter.'

'I would be very unwise to attempt it here.'

The amusement in his voice struck her on the raw.

'You would be unwise to attempt it anywhere!'

'I think you are right, ma'am.' Her suspicious glance swept over him and he continued. 'Would you believe me if I said I had no intention of seducing Miss Tatham?'

'No, Mr Arrandale, I would not.'

Richard sighed. What else could he expect, when he had teased her so at their last encounter?

'Lady Phyllida, I swear, on my honour, that I have no improper intentions towards your stepdaughter.'

'You *have* no honour.'

'Does it not occur to you that there may be other men who may be a danger to your stepdaughter?'

She waved a hand.

'I am aware of the dangers. I will protect her from them all.'

She spoke with confidence and he admired her spirit, but he was suddenly afraid for her, too.

'Is there no male relative who can help you to look after Ellen?'

She frowned, surprised by his question.

'There are uncles and cousins enough. As you will discover, should you attempt to compromise her.'

'Confound it, woman, I have no intention of compromising her!'

'Oh?' She stopped and turned to look at him. 'What has caused this change of heart? A week since you were only too ready to do battle with me.'

Richard looked down at the defiant figure before him. She was so slender a puff of wind might blow her away, yet here she stood, toe to toe with him. He felt the smile tugging at his mouth. She was at least talking to him. He would be honest.

'You,' he said simply. 'You made me change my mind. I do not want to fight with you, Phyllida.'

Her eyes widened and darkened as she understood his soft words. He saw the varying emotions played out across her countenance, the flash of understanding, then desire, quickly followed by fear and indignation. He was sorry when she began to walk on, keeping her gaze steadfastly ahead. He set off beside her, tempering his long stride to match hers.

'You will not turn me up sweet with your practised arts, Mr Arrandale.'

'I thought we had already agreed I could never do that. But perhaps I should take inspiration from Sir Bevil.'

'I beg your pardon?'

He nodded towards the monument, soaring up into the sky and topped by its proud griffin.

'Sir Bevil Grenville. He was a Royalist commander who fought his way up here and defeated the Parliamentarians, who were holding the high ground. Incredible odds, but he succeeded in opening the way for a Royalist march upon London.'

'Really?' she asked, diverted. 'I knew the monument was something to do with the Civil War but I did not know its significance—there was a battle on this very spot?'

'Yes.' They had reached the monument and he followed her as she walked close to the railings that surrounded it. 'It was erected nearly a century ago by his grandson to commemorate the battle. The griffin on the top holds the Grenville coat of arms.'

'How fascinating.'

He shook his head, pleased but bemused at the sudden change from frosty ice maiden to eager student. She was quite enchanting. Phyllida turned to him, her former animosity forgotten, at least temporarily.

'And what happened to Sir Bevil?'

'Sir Bevil?'

He looked into her eyes and felt something shift, deep inside.

'Yes,' she said. 'What happened to him?'

Richard struggled to think.

'Poleaxed.' Was he talking of Sir Bevil Grenville, or himself? Something had changed within him, but for good or ill Richard did not yet know. He forced his mind back to Sir Bevil. 'He was slain as his men gained the high ground.'

She considered the monument for a moment.

'So the poor man never lived to see his success,' she said slowly. 'And in the end it did not make any difference to the outcome of the war.' She turned back to him and the twinkle in her eyes deepened. 'Courageous, I grant you, but it is not inspiration you should gain from here, sir. Rather, you should take a warning not to attempt the impossible.'

Phyllida walked away, head held high. She was unable to suppress her smile and a delicious feeling of elation. The gentleman had certainly not been the victor of *that* encounter. Perhaps Richard Arrandale was not such a threat, after all.

At least, not to Ellen.

The rest of the party were on the far side of the monument and Phyllida walked around to join them. Adrian Wakefield and Grace were trying to read the poems carved into the stone while the three young ladies were strolling arm in arm with Mr Tesford beside them. When he saw Phyllida approaching he gave a slight bow and moved away. She looked at the girls, her brows raised.

'Have I interrupted something?'

'Not at all,' replied Ellen with feeling. 'He is the most tedious character, always trying to separate us. Thank goodness you came and scowled at him.'

'I did not scowl,' Phyllida protested.

'No, no, of course not,' agreed Penelope. 'But you did look a little serious, and the fact that he retreated so quickly confirms Ellen's suspicion that he is up to no good.'

'Really?' replied Phyllida, startled. 'Has he said or done anything untoward?'

Ellen shook her head.

'Oh, no, he is always very polite, but he does prowl around, watching us.'

'Watching *you*, Ellen,' Julia corrected her. She turned to Phyllida, saying with a giggle, 'Ellen thinks he is trying to make up to her, ma'am. Because of her fortune. And it is true, he threw out the broadest hints for Grace to invite him today. He told her he had always had the liveliest curiosity to see Sir Bevil's monument yet he has scarcely looked at it.'

'I have no doubt Mr Arrandale did much the same with your brother,' Phyllida responded.

'He would not need to do so,' put in Ellen. 'Adrian is friends with Mr Arrandale and he knows that his mama likes him, too, in spite of his wicked reputation. Lady Wakefield says Mr Arrandale has been a model of propriety while he has been in Bath. And I have always found him most entertaining.'

Phyllida was startled by Ellen's fierce defence of Richard and she replied swiftly, 'I believe that is the way with most rakes. They are universally charming and it behoves ladies—young and old!—to beware of them.'

The girls stared at her and Phyllida wondered if she had been wise to respond quite so sternly, then Ellen gave a little trill of laughter.

'Goodness, Philly, that is the nearest you have ever come to lecturing me.' She reached out her free hand. 'Come along, *Stepmama*, if you are so worried for our virtue you had best stay with us until it is time to ride back.'

Before Phyllida could remonstrate with Ellen for

her sauciness Grace Stapleton came up, hanging on her brother's arm.

'Did someone mention going back? I think it is time we did. There is a cold wind blowing and the monument's exposed position means we feel the full force of it.'

'Then if everyone has seen enough, let us return to the horses, by all means,' said Phyllida, wondering, not for the first time, if she was indeed up to the task of taking care of her stepdaughter.

As the little party made their way back to the copse where the grooms were waiting with the horses, Arnold Tesford fell in beside Richard.

'I saw you trying to butter up the widow, Arrandale. You won't succeed. I have tried but she is having none of it. She keeps a close eye on the heiress, too.'

'Are you surprised?'

'No, but I thought the chit might be ripe for a lark. Young women are very keen on secret meetings, that sort of thing. They think it romantic.'

'Perhaps it is your methods that are at fault,' drawled Richard.

'Oh? Have you had more success?'

'None at all, but then, I have decided to withdraw from the lists.'

Tesford subjected him to another searching glance then, having satisfied himself that Richard was sincere, he nodded moodily.

'Aye, thinking of doing so myself. Not that she ain't a little beauty, but she eludes my every attempt to get close. I don't see that I'll ever get her into my bed.' He was silent for a moment. 'I suppose I could try abducting her.'

Richard's blood ran cold, not only for Ellen Tatham

but for the effect such an action would have on Phyllida. He feigned indifference.

'I doubt if she'd go quietly, she looks like a little spit-fire. And even if you compromised her I wouldn't put it past the family to hush it up and forbid the banns.'

'Perhaps, but remember the wager. I should still be ten thousand pounds better off.'

'If you lived to collect it.'

Tesford stopped, his brows raised in surprise, and Richard felt compelled to explain.

'It's true that the widow is the girl's sole guardian, but that doesn't mean she is friendless.'

'You mean there is someone who would call me out?'

'Oh, yes,' said Richard grimly. 'And he's a crack shot, too.'

'The devil!' Tesford went very pale. 'I wonder if the others know that?'

'I have no idea,' said Richard, as they began to walk on again. 'If I were you I'd warn 'em.'

Now what had possessed him to say such a thing? According to Lady Phyllida, Ellen Tatham had plenty of male relations, but he had no idea if any of them would be prepared to fight for her honour. Still, if the thought kept vermin such as Tesford from attempting an assault upon the girl he could not regret it.

Phyllida used the ride back to Bath to think over all Richard had said and done. He had assured her he had no interest in Ellen, and his behaviour today had gone some way to confirm it, but she could not be sure. She had so little experience of men. Of life. She wanted to believe him, she *would* believe him, although she would not trust him, not just yet. She would give him the opportunity to prove himself. That, she thought, was a sensible solution, and one that made her feel just a little happier. When they reached the streets of Bath and the party broke up to go their separate ways, Julia asked shyly if Ellen might be allowed to join them at Laura Place for dinner. Ellen spoke up before Phyllida had time to reply.

'That is very kind of you, Julia, but I really must go home. My Aunt Hapton is arriving today. She is Phyllida's only sister and I should like to be there to greet her. But we shall all meet up again at the Denhams at the end of the week, will we not?'

'Was that not the most wonderful ride out, Philly?' declared Ellen as she rode back to Charles Street with Phyllida. 'So much more interesting when there is a goal to be reached, although I think on balance I preferred the ruins at Farleigh, did not you?'

She chattered on, and when they had left their horses with Parfett and made their way into the house she even went so far as to throw her arms about Phyllida and hug her ruthlessly.

'I am so glad Mrs Ackroyd could no longer keep me in Kent. I thought at first that Bath would be the most boring place, full of invalids and old people, but I am having a most enjoyable time. And Penelope and Julia are quite delightful, so I am not missing my school friends very much at all.'

Phyllida returned her embrace, her heart swelling with pleasure and no little relief. She felt she had made the right choice after all.

'I am very pleased to hear you say so,' she said. 'Now, I think we should go upstairs and change. We must be positively windblown and if your aunt catches us looking like this we shall both be in trouble!'

* * *

They had only just come downstairs again when Lady Olivia was announced. She sailed into the drawing room, full of energy and with an apology tripping from her tongue.

'I have bad news, I am afraid, I can only stay three nights and then must away to London. Hapton is already there, poor lamb, trying to rally the opposition to this disastrous peace that Addington has brokered and he needs me. There are dinners to arrange.'

This was said so much in the manner of a soldier anticipating battle that Phyllida was obliged to smile.

'Oh, well, that is a disappointment but at least we have you for a few days.'

She invited her sister to sit down upon the sofa beside her. Lady Olivia was some four years older than Phyllida and had always been described as the prettier of the two sisters. She was now considered a handsome woman. Since her marriage to Lord Hapton ten years ago she had provided her doting husband with a quiverful of children, including three lusty boys. She ruled her household with a loving tyranny, and supported her husband's political aspirations. She would happily have taken the newly widowed Phyllida under her wing, if her younger sister had permitted it, but Phyllida was no longer the shy and biddable girl who had left the Earl of Swanleigh's household six years ago. Marriage to the kindly baronet had given her the confidence to take control of her own life and she had no wish to give up her independence. However, that did not stop Olivia from expressing her opinions.

When Ellen retired after dinner, leaving the sisters to enjoy a little private conversation, her first act was to take Phyllida by the shoulders and turn her towards the light.

'Hmm, widowhood suits you, Phyllida, you are positively blooming.'

'Olivia!'

She shrugged off her sister's laughing protest and made herself comfortable on a sofa.

'It is true, you look even better than when Tatham was alive.'

'Be careful what you say, Sister,' Phyllida warned her, 'I was very fond of my husband.'

'And so you should have been. He looked after you exceedingly well and you blossomed under his care. You lost the careworn, anxious look you had as a girl. That of someone about to be reprimanded.'

'With good reason,' put in Phyllida, a touch of bitterness entering her voice. 'Nothing I did ever pleased Mama and Papa. Save for marrying Tatham, and even then they made it very plain how fortunate I was to find anyone to offer for me.'

'Yes, well, your lack of looks did not matter to Sir Evelyn. He wanted a good bloodline and I must say he was always very generous, considering you never produced the son he wanted.'

Phyllida flinched at her sister's bluntness, but she could not deny it. Sir Evelyn had married her for an heir, but when their union failed to bear fruit he had accepted the situation with grace, behaving with more forbearance than Phyllida's parents, who considered her failure to conceive a personal slight upon their family and continued to rebuke her for her undutiful behaviour until their deaths some four years ago, when a sudden chill carried them off within weeks of each other.

'No,' continued Olivia, blithely oblivious of her sister's sombre thoughts. 'You are looking very well. Of course, you are tall and your figure shows to advantage in these high-waisted fashions.'

The unaccustomed wistful note in her sister's voice was not lost on Phyllida, who said quickly, 'As the mother of a large family, Olivia, it is no wonder if your figure is not so, er, willowy as it was.'

'That is true. And speaking of children brings me to another thing I meant to say to you, Phyllida. It has taken me only a few hours in Ellen's company to realise that she has lost none of her liveliness! From everything I heard at dinner she is leading you a merry dance, with parties and outings every day.'

'And I am enjoying it immensely,' replied Phyllida, with perfect sincerity. 'I have never been so busy, nor felt so happy. You have said yourself I am looking very well.'

Lady Olivia shook her head, saying ominously, 'She will run you ragged, mark my words.'

'No, no. Ellen is certainly spirited, but she means no harm.'

'But?' Olivia prompted her. 'I can tell from your voice that something is worrying you.'

Phyllida sighed.

'I had not expected her to be so, so *courted*.' She paused, her brow furrowed as she sought to explain. 'I know she is an heiress, but gentlemen are positively falling over themselves to befriend her, and not all of them unmarried, which is not at all what I expected.'

'Men are always susceptible to a pretty face, married or not.'

'And Ellen is undoubtedly very pretty.' Phyllida sighed again. 'I wonder, sometimes...however, Ellen is very good. Her head does not appear to be turned one jot by all the attention she receives. But I confess I had not thought Bath would be so full of dangers. She must be accompanied everywhere.'

'I thought you had brought her maid with you.'

'Matlock? Yes, she is here and I do, often, send her out with Ellen.'

'But you prefer to be with her yourself, is that it? So you have exchanged looking after a husband for caring for his daughter. You should pack her off to her uncle. Tatham would have her, would he not?'

'Yes, but Walter and Bridget are so, so…'

'Stuffy?' suggested Olivia. 'Outmoded? Boring?'

Phyllida laughed. '*Yes*! They would put Ellen in the schoolroom with their own children and that dragon of a governess until her come-out next year, which would be disastrous. I am sure she would run away. No, I am her mama—'

'Her stepmama.'

'Very well, her stepmama, but it is my duty to look after her.'

Olivia snorted. 'You are not old enough to be anyone's mama.'

'I am four-and-twenty.'

'Yes, and you should be enjoying your freedom now that Tatham is dead. A rich widow is a very attractive prospect for a man, you know. Well, there is no point in being coy, Philly,' she continued, when Phyllida made a quiet protest. 'Tatham only married you to get an heir.'

'And I failed him miserably.'

'That is not your fault,' said Olivia robustly. 'Sir Evelyn's health was poor when he married you and you must admit he behaved very handsomely to you. I have no doubt you would find yourself a dozen suitors if you did not have Ellen constantly by your side. I cannot lie to you, Phyllida, she does rather put you in the shade,' said Olivia, crushingly frank. 'If you would but send her to her relatives you could have a very pleasant life.'

'But how could I do that to her? She has never liked her Tatham relatives and having lost her father how could I turn her off?

'Easily. She is not you, Phyllida, she is far more robust and could survive a few months with Walter and Bridget, I am sure. And although I am very fond of Ellen I must say that she is very forward. The sooner she is married off the better.'

'No, not at seventeen,' said Phyllida quickly. 'It is far too young. Why, even Papa—'

She broke off but Olivia finished for her, saying in her blunt fashion, 'Papa waited until you were eighteen before he married you to a man old enough to be your father. But you are not Ellen, that school she attended has made her far more independent than is proper for a gel. I have never been in favour of educating young women but I know her father was adamant about it. No, at eighteen you were far too young to be married, and far too innocent. But then, that is what Tatham wanted, a young bride he could keep to himself, no hint of scandal.'

Phyllida could not deny it. Sir Evelyn had looked after her very well, making it plain to any young buck and even to the married men of his acquaintance that any attempt to dally with his young bride would not be tolerated.

'You have no idea how to keep the rakes at bay,' Olivia told her.

Phyllida put up her chin.

'I am learning,' she said quietly.

Olivia pursed her lips.

'Yes, well, I shall come out and about with you while I

am here and see for myself just how well you go on. It is a pity that Hapton needs me with him next week or I would remain in Bath with you. But if Addington can be made to see that the peace will not hold then I may be able to come back here very soon.'

After that dire warning no more was said on the subject and the two ladies soon retired to their beds, the one with her head full of plans to bring down the government, the other hoping for nothing more than to get through the next few days without mishap.

Lady Olivia might stigmatise Bath as a slow, unfashionable place, but she was not unknown amongst its residents. When they visited the Pump Room the following morning it seemed to Phyllida that her sister was acquainted with almost everyone present, and of the remainder she knew some relative and thus claimed a connection. Consequently, their progress around the room was very slow. Ellen had already gone off to talk to Penelope Desborough, and as Olivia showed a propensity to take over every conversation, Phyllida found herself with little to do. She was happy to stand back and watch, thinking with an inward smile that with her talent for remembering everyone's name and family connections, her sister was the ideal political hostess.

'My dear, I can see that you are very well regarded in Bath,' murmured Olivia, as they moved on from the latest introductions.

'I am glad to have earned your approval, Sister,' Phyllida replied drily. 'I—'

'But that does *not* meet with my approval!' Olivia interrupted her, staring fixedly across the room.

Following her gaze, Phyllida observed that Richard Arrandale was now part of a small group gathered about

Ellen and the Desboroughs. Olivia gripped her arm and began to propel her through the crowds.

'I do not know what brought Arrandale to Bath but he is not the sort of man to be allowed anywhere *near* Ellen. His reputation is most unsavoury.'

'I know all about his reputation,' retorted Phyllida, bridling, 'but I assure you he—'

'Oh.' Olivia's pace slackened as they drew nearer and the whole group came into view. 'So he is here with Lady Hune. I suppose in that case you are obliged to acknowledge the connection.'

There was no time for Phyllida to reply. Mrs Desborough had spotted her and was even now smiling and making room for them to come up. More introductions followed. Olivia might not approve of Mr Richard Arrandale but there was no sign of it in her greeting, and if, in the course of their brief conversation, she gave the impression that Miss Tatham was under her especial protection and would not be allowed to fall into the clutches of a known womaniser, it was done so subtly that no one could take offence.

Phyllida glanced surreptitiously at Ellen, hoping she would not resent her aunt's interference and was relieved to see that she and Penelope Desborough had their heads together and were paying no heed to anyone else. When Olivia claimed Lady Hune's attention Richard had moved to stand beside Phyllida.

'I am impressed,' he murmured. 'I have never been warned off in such an elegant manner before.'

She fought down the urge to apologise.

'Your reputation precedes you, sir. You cannot blame my sister for disliking the acquaintance.'

'I do not blame her. I am impressed by her eloquence.'

'But it is unnecessary, is it not?' She raised her eyes

to his face. 'You have already assured me you have no interest in Ellen.'

The smile in his eyes deepened, drawing her in and rousing the now familiar excitement within her.

'No,' he said softly. 'I have no interest in Ellen.'

For one heart-stopping moment Phyllida thought she might faint. It was as if, suddenly, there was nothing solid beneath her feet. She felt giddy, lightheaded as she gazed up into those blue eyes and read her fate.

'Phyllida, my dear, we should get on. We need to get back for Ellen's Italian lesson.'

Olivia's hand was on her arm, the ground was firm again and she tore her eyes away from Richard's smiling face, trying to muster her thoughts into some sensible, coherent order.

'Yes, of course.' Her vague smile encompassed them all, she did not think she was capable of saying anything more. She put her hand out to Ellen who was looking at her with an arrested look on her face. 'My dear?'

At her gentle prompting Ellen started and with a murmured apology she hurried to join her stepmama and Lady Olivia as they made their way out of the Pump Room.

Phyllida was lost in her own thoughts as they made their way back to Charles Street, but Olivia and Ellen were happily talking and her silence went unnoticed. Her head was full of Richard Arrandale, the few words he had spoken, the look in his eyes that had sent her spirits into such disorder. Had she misunderstood him? How could she believe that he might truly be interested in her? It was too incredible, too much of a fairytale.

'And what do you think of Mr Arrandale?'

Ellen's enquiry brought Phyllida crashing back to reality and it was with inordinate relief that she realised the question was posed to her sister.

'A wastrel.' Olivia did not mince her words. 'He is a gamester and a shocking flirt.'

'Well, I like him,' replied Ellen, equally blunt.

'That is neither here nor there,' retorted Olivia. 'It is common knowledge that he has squandered his own fortune and may well have his eye on yours. Your stepmama would do well to keep you away from such characters.'

'But I will have to meet *such characters* as you call them when I come out next year, so it is as well that I am prepared, do you not think?'

There was no arguing with Ellen's simple logic and Phyllida, seeing her sister for once at a loss for words, burst out laughing.

Phyllida was genuinely sorry when Olivia's short stay in Charles Street drew to a close. It was very pleasant to have her company when they went shopping or enjoyed a walk in Sydney Gardens and she also shared in the task of chaperoning Ellen about Bath. Even on the final morning Olivia insisted upon escorting Ellen to her dancing class.

'Let me do this one last thing for you, Phyllida. It will give me an opportunity to say goodbye to Ellen. I believe Matlock is to escort her to Laura Place with Julia Wakefield afterwards, so we can enjoy a little time together before I set off for London.'

'But surely you would prefer to spend the morning resting,' Phyllida protested. 'Or perhaps you might even wish to set off a little earlier.'

'Why should I need to rest when I will spend the better part of the day sitting in a chaise? And as for leaving earlier, I have bespoke a room at the Castle in Marlborough and have no wish to arrive there much before dinnertime, so my morning is free.'

With that she collected Ellen and went out, leaving Phyllida to spend a couple of hours in the morning room, catching up on overdue correspondence.

Phyllida had just finished the last of her letters and was placing it on a side table when her sister returned.

'Do take a seat, Olivia. I asked Hirst to bring in refreshments just as soon as you returned—' She stopped when she saw the look upon her sister's face. 'My dear, whatever is the matter?'

'I think it is you who had better sit down,' said Olivia, grimly. 'I have just heard the most appalling news.'

The butler's entrance brought a temporary halt to their conversation. Phyllida went to sit in a chair next to her sister and they waited impatiently until Hirst had served them both with a glass of wine and placed a plate of little cakes on the table before them. As soon as he had withdrawn Phyllida put down her glass and turned to her sister.

'Pray, now, tell me what has upset you so.'

Olivia did not reply immediately. She took a sip of her wine, but one foot was tapping impatiently, a sure sign that she was seriously troubled.

'I have heard the most disturbing report, Sister. After I left Ellen at her dance class I thought I might purchase some marzipan as a little gift for Hapton—he has such a sweet tooth—and thus I went to the confectioners in Milsom Street. There I met with Lady Heston—not a particular friend of yours, I know. She is considered a little *fast*, I believe, but we were at school together, and it is never wise to cut a connection. As Hapton always says, one never knows when someone may prove useful.'

'Yes, yes, but what has this to say to anything?' asked Phyllida, bemused.

Olivia's countenance grew darker.

'Lady Heston has a…a gentleman friend. I shall put it no stronger than that, although I have my suspicions.'

'Olivia, will you please get to the point?'

'The point is, dear Sister, that there is a wager between certain gentlemen in Bath, as to which one of them will be the first to seduce Ellen! And there is a prize of ten thousand pounds for the winner.'

Chapter Nine

'Ten thousand!'

'You may well stare,' said Olivia. 'I was truly shocked when I heard of it. Not that I should have been surprised, when I saw the likes of Richard Arrandale and Sir Charles Urmston in Bath.'

'I do not believe Mr Arrandale is a part of it.'

'Then you are a fool. His family is renowned for their outrageous behaviour.'

Phyllida wrapped her arms across her chest. She suddenly felt very cold. Had he lied to her? She could not believe it. Surely the look she had seen in his eyes had been genuine. But she could not think of that now. She must fix her mind upon the bigger problem.

She said, 'It certainly explains why so many gentlemen have been attentive to Ellen.'

'Like bees around a honeypot.' Olivia nodded. 'I think you would be wise to remove Ellen from Bath immediately.'

'Do you think I should tell her?'

'By no means. I do not believe in telling children more than necessary.'

Phyllida was tempted to reply that Ellen was not a

child, but Olivia's experience of the world was so much greater than her own. Surely she must know best.

'Seduction implies that Ellen would be willing, does it not?' she said thoughtfully. 'My stepdaughter is spirited, but I do not believe she has any romantic inclinations. Indeed, she has told me as much.'

'But with such a sum at stake, the inducement for any man to attempt to win her is very high, and by fair means or foul,' said Olivia. 'What are you going to do?'

Phyllida considered.

'I think we should remain in Bath,' she said slowly. 'At least here we are well known, and Ellen is accustomed to being accompanied everywhere. If we removed to Tatham Park it would be much more difficult to keep an eye on her, for she is so used to going out alone there and it would irk her beyond bearing to be shadowed. And if I insisted upon it, she might even begin to slip off on her own.'

'You have allowed that girl far too much freedom, Phyllida. We would never have disobeyed our parents in such a manner.'

'*I* certainly would not have done so, but I recall several occasions when you went off alone to meet a beau.'

'Yes, well never mind that now,' said Olivia, hastily. 'Besides, there was no financial incentive for any man to seduce *me*.'

Silence fell. At length Phyllida turned anxious eyes upon her sister.

'It seems too fantastical. Are you sure it is true?'

Olivia sighed. 'Lady Heston was always prone to exaggeration when she was at school,' she admitted. 'That may not have changed, but I do not think she would have concocted the whole story for my benefit.'

'If there is the slightest chance that such a wager exists then I must be on my guard.'

'But you will not remove from Bath?'

'No, I think not, although I shall hire another man-servant to go about with us.'

Lady Hune had only recently suggested it. Did she, too, suspect Ellen needed extra protection, possibly from her own great-nephew? Phyllida shook her head. 'I have seen no sign that Ellen favours any one of her suitors above the others, so I do not fear an elopement. But there is no saying that if I were to take Ellen away some of these, these *persons* might follow us with a view to staging an abduction. That would be very much more difficult in Bath, where we are surrounded by friends.'

'That is very true.' Olivia struck her hands together and uttered a little cry of frustration. 'Oh, I am tempted to write to Hapton and tell him I must stay here with you. I really do not see how you will cope with this on your own.'

Phyllida put up her chin. 'I will cope. I am not the shy little girl you once knew, Olivia, and where Ellen is concerned I can be a positive lioness, I assure you.'

Despite her brave words Phyllida could not rest and once Olivia had departed she fetched her shawl and told Matty she would meet Ellen from her dancing lesson and accompany her and Miss Wakefield to Laura Place. The walk gave her time to consider what Olivia had told her and she decided to take Lady Wakefield into her confidence.

'Are you sure it can be true?' asked that lady, when Phyllida had explained everything. 'Is it from a reliable source?'

'My sister had it from Lady Heston, ma'am.'

'Well, I do not like to doubt the lady's veracity but

I find it hard to believe such a thing would happen in Bath.'

'Nevertheless I cannot ignore it,' said Phyllida.

'No, of course not.' Lady Wakefield thought for a moment, a tiny crease furrowing her brow. 'It would explain the inordinate amount of interest that some creatures are taking in your stepdaughter. Mr Tesford, for example. And George Cromby. One cannot cut their acquaintance, of course, without solid proof, but I have never liked either man very much.'

'And then there is Sir Charles Urmston, and Mr Arrandale.'

Phyllida held her breath while Lady Wakefield considered the two names, only letting it go when the lady shook her head.

'I cannot think they would be party to such an outrage, but neither of them has a spotless reputation and how do we know what any gentleman is up to at these clubs and gambling hells? Even Wakefield has been known to visit them.' She caught herself up and added hastily, 'Not that I mean he would ever be involved in anything as reprehensible as this, I assure you! Hmm. Have you mentioned it to Ellen? No? Well, I think you are wise. It could damage her confidence.'

That made Phyllida smile, despite her concerns.

'I have no fears for Ellen's *confidence*, ma'am. It is more likely to make her angry, and to wish to punish those concerned.'

'Nevertheless it would do Ellen's reputation no good at all if it got out. I think we would be advised to keep this between ourselves, if we can. You may be sure that I shall take good care of Ellen whenever she is with Julia, and will send my own maid with her in the carriage when I send her home to you this evening.'

Thus reassured, Phyllida left Ellen in Lady Wakefield's care and went back to Charles Street via the registry office, where she set about finding another footman to add to her household.

The next evening was the Denhams' ball. Phyllida was tempted not to go, but what good would that do? If she was to prevent Ellen from attending parties in Bath she might as well remove from the city. A number of nosegays were delivered during the morning, from the tasteful to the absurd and Phyllida found Ellen in the morning room with them all spread out on the table. Normally she would have been amused by her stepdaughter's popularity, but Olivia's revelation prevented her feeling anything but anxiety.

'Goodness,' she said, forcing herself to speak lightly. 'Are you deciding which gentleman to favour?'

'Well, some of them are far too big to pin to my gown,' replied Ellen, surveying the array with a slight frown. 'And I have no wish to raise false hopes.'

'No, indeed,' replied Phyllida solemnly.

'There is a very pretty arrangement from Sir Charles Urmston and—oh, this is not for me at all.' Ellen picked up a small spray of white rosebuds. 'This one is for you, Philly. It is from Mr Arrandale.'

'Indeed?' She felt herself colouring under the speculation in Ellen's eyes. 'How, how ridiculous.'

But how gloriously flattering. And heartening. Surely Richard would not be showing her quite such attention if his target was Ellen. Dare she believe what her heart was telling her?

'I do not think it is ridiculous at all, Philly. Why should he not send you flowers?'

'Because I am far too old for such things. I cannot

wear them, of course, but they are so pretty I shall put them in a vase.'

Taking the nosegay from Ellen she left the room, glad of the excuse to get away from Ellen's bright, enquiring gaze. No man had ever given her flowers before, not even her husband. When she had mentioned it, on the eve of their wedding, Sir Evelyn had laughed and said that once they were at Tatham she could have as many flowers as she desired, all she had to do was order the gardener to send them indoors. Suddenly, she was quite looking forward to the evening. Phyllida had planned to wear her lilac gown with the white overdress. It would mark her out as Ellen's chaperon and preclude her from dancing, but at the last moment she decided instead to put on the peach silk. She had worn it before, but unlike the lilac it had no demi-train, and she would therefore be free to dance.

If anyone should ask her.

The Denhams owned a large property on the outskirts of Bath, but this did not prevent the city's residents from making the journey, for Lady Denham's parties were renowned. Phyllida had offered to take up the Desboroughs, since they kept no carriage in Bath and by the time they arrived at Denham House the dancing was already in progress. A large ballroom had been built at the back of the house with glass doors leading directly on to the gardens, which Ellen had heard would be decorated for the occasion with hundreds of coloured lamps.

Ellen and Penelope went off to find Julia Wakefield while Phyllida took her place with the matrons. There was no doubt the three young ladies made an entrancing picture, Ellen's golden curls showing to advantage against the darker heads of her friends and Phyllida watched the gentlemen beginning to gravitate towards the little group. Ellen was wearing none of the flowers so hopefully sent to her but she needed nothing to augment her sparkling looks as she stepped on to the dance floor with Mr Naismith. Phyllida's eyes roved over the assembly. Sir Charles Urmston was present, as was Arnold Tesford and Henry Fullingham. George Cromby was dancing with his wife, so she hoped he would not be paying Ellen undue attention that evening. She wondered which of the gentlemen were party to the wager.

If indeed such a wager existed. Here, amongst so many friends and acquaintances it seemed too fantastical to believe. After all, Olivia had heard it from only one source, and Lady Wakefield was inclined to dismiss it as mere conjecture. Perhaps it was all gossip. She prayed that might be the case. A sudden flurry of excitement ran through the room and she glanced towards the door, standing on tiptoe to see above the crowd. The Dowager Marchioness of Hune had arrived, escorted by Richard Arrandale. Phyllida's heart skipped a beat when she saw his tall, elegant figure with the black coat stretched across his broad shoulders. His light-brown hair was brushed back and gleamed almost golden in the candlelight. She turned away, trying to ignore the fluttering in her stomach as she tried to concentrate on what Lady Wakefield was saying to her.

Richard could not remember the last time he had felt such anticipation when attending a party. For once he was not seeking out the most dashing matrons with whom to while away the evening. Instead his eyes were roaming the crowd, looking for the willowy figure of Lady Phyllida Tatham. He soon saw her on the far side of the room, standing with Lady Wakefield and Mrs Desborough. Sophia tapped his arm.

'There is a free chair beside Colonel and Mrs Ongar, I shall sit there and you can go off and enjoy yourself.'

He did not argue, and after delivering her to her seat and exchanging a few polite words with the colonel and his lady, Richard made his way across the room to Phyllida. She had her back to him and he had no idea if she was wearing his roses. They would not look amiss against the muted shade of her gown which was the colour of a ripe peach. Then she turned towards him, as if aware of his approach and he saw the low-cut bodice was unadorned. His smile did not falter, but his spirits plummeted like lead, only to rise again when he observed the shy smile of welcome in her eyes.

Lady Wakefield claimed his attention and he spent precious moments talking with her until he could invite Phyllida to stand up with him, but at last he was leading her out. Her hand on his arm and the hectic flush on her cheeks stirred the blood and made his heart pound. She used no arts to attract him yet she moved him far more than any of the ripe beauties he had known. He wanted to sweep her into his arms and carry her away. Perhaps there was a summer house in the gardens where he could whisper endearments to her and steal a kiss, or even more. Deuce take it, he was acting like a moonstruck schoolboy.

'You are laughing, sir. Not at me, I hope.'

Her soft voice interrupted his thoughts. The musicians were striking up but there was still time to talk before the movement of the dance separated them.

'No, ma'am, at myself, for being conceited enough to think you would wear my flowers.' They crossed, turned, but she did not reply and he said anxiously, 'Did they offend you?'

That brought her eyes up to his. The soft glow in them made his heart swell.

'Offend? No, no. But I did not think it right to…' She paused, her cherry lips firmly closed, as if reluctant to speak. She said, just before the dance parted them again, 'I have them in water. On my dressing table.'

The idea of his flowers in such an intimate setting sent his imagination rioting and he almost missed his step. Phyllida moved away and they circled other dancers before coming back together. The dance obliged him to take her hand and pull her close, which suited him perfectly.

'So you will think of me when you go to bed tonight.'

Colour flooded her cheeks and he felt the hot burn of desire in his blood. They separated again. It was a penance to smile at his next partner, to keep in time when he wanted to rush through the dance until he was beside Phyllida once more. When at last he did get back to her she was very composed and her eyes warned him to go carefully. He smiled. It should be as she wished. He would court her as he had never courted a woman before.

Phyllida's heart was singing. She had never enjoyed a country dance more, never known a partner to regard her with just such a look as Richard was bestowing upon her. When he asked her to remain for the next dance her hesitation was brief. A quick glance showed her that Ellen was joining another of the sets so she could relax her duties as chaperon for a little longer and give herself up to the exquisite pleasure of dancing with the partner of her choice. Every look, every touch inflamed her and kept her heart fluttering like a captive bird. If he had taken her in his arms there, on the dance floor, she thought she might well have surrendered to him and thought the world well lost.

'Now *you* are laughing,' he murmured when at last the music ended. 'May I share your amusement?'

'No you may not,' she replied, blushing and smiling at the same time.

'Perhaps I can persuade you—no, I can see Wakefield bearing down upon us, and if I am not mistaken he means to steal you away from me.' He squeezed her fingers briefly. 'Until later, Lady Phyllida.'

She felt a momentary regret when he released her hand and turned to acknowledge Lord Wakefield's cheerful greeting.

'Come along, Arrandale, time for you to give way and allow the rest of us to dance with your charming partner.' He bowed. 'Ma'am, if you would do me the honour?'

'With pleasure, my lord.'

Exhilarated and giddy as a schoolgirl, Phyllida slipped her hand on to Lord Wakefield's arm. Richard Arrandale should see that he was not the only man she would dance with that evening.

Richard watched her walk away, noting the sway of her hips beneath the folds of her silken skirts. His eyes moved up to the creamy skin of her shoulders and the slender column of her neck, kissed by a few honey-coloured curls that had escaped from her swept-up hair. By Jove, how he wanted her, and soon! The garden beckoned him with the promise of the night air to cool his heated thoughts and he made his way towards the open doors. He did not rush, pausing for a word here, a smile there, but he would not be turned from his goal. A few ladies tried in vain to catch his eye and secure him as a partner but he ignored them all and soon gained the terrace. One or two couples were visible in the shadows but he paid them little heed as he ran lightly down the shallow steps into the garden, lit not only by the rising moon but myriad coloured lamps strung beneath and between the trees. The grounds were extensive and he headed away from the immediate lawn, looking for a pavilion or orangery, somewhere he might take Phyllida. He had no doubt he would be able to persuade her to walk outside with him, the glow in her eyes had told him she felt the attraction between them. He wanted—needed—to hold her, to kiss her, to discover if she felt the same overwhelming desire that consumed him. And if she did he would take her in his arms and kiss those soft, inviting lips, feel her body melt against his own—

This pleasant reverie was interrupted when he heard a rustling in the shrubbery. Some couple was taking advantage of the seclusion, no doubt. He would not disturb them.

'Let go of me. Stop it!'

The angry whisper ended in a gasp. Richard stopped. The lady was clearly not willing. He shrugged, it was none of his business, yet he could not move on. There was something familiar about the female's voice. He turned and stepped between the bushes. There, before him, was Ellen Tatham, struggling in the grasp of Henry Fullingham.

'*Brava*, ma'am, you dance very well, it is a pleasure to watch you.'

Lady Wakefield's praise made Phyllida's smile grow even wider as Lord Wakefield carried her back to where his wife was standing. He was puffing from his exertion and she could not help comparing him to Richard, who had danced so effortlessly.

'I quite agree,' said Lady Hune, coming up. 'I am very pleased to see you enjoying yourself, Lady Phyllida.'

'Thank you, ma'am.' Phyllida made her curtsy to the dowager marchioness. 'And may I say how pleased I am to see *you* here tonight? You have kept too much to yourself recently.'

The old lady inclined her head.

'After the scandal of Cassandra's elopement I did not wish to go out, but my scapegrace nephew is determined that I should not dwindle into a recluse.'

Scapegrace. Phyllida smiled. The dowager was referring to Richard, but the term was clearly used with affection. She was beginning to believe he might not be quite so bad, after all.

'He is quite right, ma'am,' declared Lady Wakefield. 'One must get out, and not only to parties such as this. I am a great believer in fresh air.'

'Perhaps Lady Hune would like to join one of your little excursions, my dear,' suggested Lord Wakefield. He beamed at the dowager. 'I know you no longer ride, ma'am, but there is no reason why we should not take an open carriage. Julia is already pestering her mother to arrange another jaunt while the weather holds.' He chuckled. 'My daughter has a taste for the Gothic, and Miss Tatham is quite as bad. They were in raptures over Farleigh Castle.'

'Really?' Lady Hune turned to Phyllida. 'And do you accompany your stepdaughter on these jaunts?'

'Why, yes, ma'am, and I have to confess I enjoy them just as much as the young people.'

'I understand the druidical monuments are quite the rage now,' remarked Lady Hune.

'Indeed they are.' Lady Wakefield nodded. 'Julia has been pressing me to arrange a ride to see the standing stones at Avebury, but I have told her it is quite out of the question. It is too far to ride there and back in a day.'

'What is too far?' asked Julia, coming up at that moment and tucking her hand into her father's arm.

'We are trying to arrange another outing, my love,' said Lord Wakefield, smiling fondly at her.

'Oh, yes, please! And we should go soon, before the season starts and the weather begins to turn.'

'What would you think to Stonehenge?' asked Lady Hune.

'Stonehenge?' cried Julia, 'Oh, how I would love to go there! There is a picture of it in one of Papa's books and I am mad to see it for myself.'

Lady Wakefield shook her head.

'Out of the question, my love. Why, it must be all of sixty miles there and back.'

'If I might offer a suggestion.' Lady Hune waited until all eyes in the group were turned upon her. 'I have a house nearby, at Shrewton, where we might all spend a night or two. That would give you a full day to explore the druidical stones. It is large enough to accommodate everyone, including you, Lady Phyllida. You and your stepdaughter must join us.'

Julia clapped her hands. 'Oh, yes, do say we can go, Papa!'

'Well, well, that is very generous, Lady Hune.' Lord Wakefield beamed, clearly delighted.

'And what of you, Phyllida?' Lady Hune put a hand on her arm. 'I shall not take a refusal from you.'

Phyllida beamed at her.

'I have no intention of refusing, ma'am.'

She dare not ask if Richard would be accompanying them, but she thought it very likely, and the idea lifted her spirits even higher.

Lady Hune nodded, satisfied.

'Very well, I shall send word to have the house put

in readiness. Miss Wakefield is quite right, of course. We should make the outing before the Bath season begins. Shall we say the week after next, the last week in September?'

There was a murmur of assent. Phyllida found herself once more under the dowager's scrutiny and she nodded.

'Ellen and I have no commitments to detain us in Bath that week, my lady.'

Then it is agreed,' declared the dowager. 'We shall go to Stonehenge.'

'Thank you, ma'am,' said Lord Wakefield. 'What a treat that will be for our young ladies.'

Phyllida was unable to suppress a smile. A journey of pleasure, made with friends, would be a treat indeed, not only for Ellen but herself, too, especially if Richard Arrandale was one of the party. She glanced around, hoping she might see him in the crowd. She wanted to stand on tiptoe and search the room for him. More than that, she wanted to find him and spend the rest of the evening at his side. It could not be, of course, however much she desired Richard's company it would be a dreadful example to set before Ellen. She glanced at the press of dancers, wondering if she should seek out her stepdaughter but then she decided against it. Ellen would not quit the ballroom while the music was playing, she was sure of it, so Phyllida felt at liberty to think of her own concerns.

Richard hesitated. Despite his promise to Sophia he had signed his name to the wager, and even though he had decided not to take part, interrupting Henry Fullingham would be considered bad form. But, dash it all, he could not stand by and let the chit be ravished.

Even as the thoughts raced through his head Fullingham gave a yelp of pain and jumped away from Ellen.

'Why, you little—'

'Having trouble, Henry?' Richard's drawling voice stopped the fellow as he was about to advance once more upon Miss Tatham.

'Nothing to concern you, Arrandale.'

'Now there I beg to differ.' Richard kept his tone cheerful. 'Clearly the lady has had enough of your company.'

'Yes, I have,' declared Ellen. 'Go away, Mr Fullingham, now.'

Fullingham was undecided and angry at the interruption. Even in the darkness Richard could see his hands clenching into fists and he said softly, 'Pray do not even consider it, Henry. I should hate to have to mill you down, especially in front of a lady.'

For a tense moment he thought the fellow would not heed him, then with a curt nod he lounged away, leaving Richard alone with Ellen Tatham. He spoke quickly to reassure her.

'No need to worry about me, Miss Tatham. I have no designs upon you.'

'No, I didn't think you had,' she said unexpectedly. 'Thank you for coming to my aid, sir.'

'You are very welcome. We had best get you back to the ballroom.' He followed her through the gap in the bushes and they set off together towards the house.

'I suppose you think I am very foolish, to put myself in such a situation.'

'I admit I was surprised at you, Miss Tatham.'

'It was just that I was being pursued around the ballroom by Mr Tesford, and when Mr Fullingham suggested we step out on to the terrace I thought it would not do any harm, and in any case I was very warm. Then he took my fan—playfully, you see—but he dropped it over the balcony, and we had to go and retrieve it.' She gave a little huff of exasperation. 'I see now that it was all a ruse to get me away from everyone, and I never thought I should fall for such a thing—'

'Do not upset yourself over it, my dear. You are not the first to make such a mistake and you will not be the last.'

'It was very fortunate that you should come along when you did.' She glanced up at him. 'Can I count you my friend, Mr Arrandale?'

'Why, yes, I suppose so.'

'Good. Then I shall call you Richard and you may call me Ellen.'

'I do not think that is appropriate,' he replied, startled. 'I doubt if Lady Phyllida would approve.'

'I do not see why she should object. You are Lady Hune's great-nephew, after all, and I know Philly likes you.'

Richard stopped.

'Miss Tatham,' he said gravely, 'my reputation is such that Lady Phyllida might not consider me a suitable friend for you.'

'Oh, stuff. Most of it is nothing but gossip, I am sure.'

'I regret that it is not merely gossip. Most of it is all too true.'

'You mean you really are a dangerous rake?'

The awe in her voice made him laugh in spite of himself.

'I *was*,' he told her, adding lightly, 'I have decided to reform.'

'I knew it,' she said triumphantly. She slipped her arm through his and gave him a little tug. 'Come along. We must get back to the ballroom before we are missed.'

Richard was thankful that there was no one in sight as they made their way along the lamp-strewn path to the house, where the sounds of the orchestra could be clearly heard from the open windows. When they reached the steps leading to the terrace Ellen stopped.

'I must look terrible, having been, been *mauled* by that man.'

'You have escaped remarkably lightly,' he said, looking her over critically. 'Your hair is no more untidy than it would be from energetic dancing.'

She put her hands on her shoulders.

'But he grabbed at my gown and I think the tie at the back is undone.'

Richard was sufficiently experienced to know she was not being coquettish, but what surprised him was that he felt nothing but a mild exasperation with the chit as she tried to reach around herself.

'Here, let me.'

He turned her about and quickly began to fasten the ribbons. Egad, he must be growing old, he felt positively avuncular.

Phyllida's head was pounding. She was constantly being drawn into conversation when all she wanted to do was think of Richard Arrandale. He caused such a tumult of new and exciting emotions within her that she felt quite confused by it all. She must take care, of course. She still had Ellen to look after and must do nothing that would reflect badly upon her, but surely there could be no harm in allowing Richard to call. To be her friend. The thought was comforting. She had not realised how alone she felt. And he was so well acquainted with the world, he might even be persuaded to advise her, where Ellen was concerned. No, no, she must not assume too much. It was all speculation, he had said nothing to warrant this glow of happiness she felt, but it had been implied in his every look.

With a smile and a murmured, 'Excuse me...' Phyllida moved away from her friends. The music was loud and merry, the noise in the room growing quite raucous, and she wished there was some empty room where she could be alone for a little while and collect her thoughts. Impossible, of course, but there was the garden. She had glimpsed the coloured lamps through the windows, they winked and beckoned to her, inviting her to slip outside. She would do so, just for a few moments.

She stepped out through the nearest window, closing her eyes as the cool air caressed her cheek. Sheer bliss after the stuffy heat of the ballroom. She would not go too far, merely take a short stroll around the lawn. A set of shallow steps led down from the centre of the terrace and it took her but a moment to reach them.

It took her even less time to see who was standing at the bottom of the steps, and to destroy all her happiness.

Chapter Ten

Phyllida took in the scene in an instant. Ellen, her cheeks flushed, hair tousled and Richard standing behind her, fastening her gown. There could be no mistaking what had been going on. While she had been wrapped in a euphoric dream, the rake had been ravishing her stepdaughter.

'How dare you?'

The words were inadequate, but they had an effect.

'Philly!' Ellen looked up guiltily, but Phyllida's eyes were fixed on Richard.

'Go inside, Ellen.'

'Philly, it is not as it seems—'

Phyllida cut her off.

'Do as I say, if you please. Immediately.'

If anything was needed to fuel Phyllida's rage it was the look Ellen cast up at Richard, as if needing his approval before she would leave. He gave a little nod and Ellen hurried away into the ballroom. Pain sliced into Phyllida like a dagger. Was the girl already under his spell?

'I know it is not an original line, but it is not as it seems.' Richard was coming up the steps towards her.

'I found Miss Tatham in the gardens, fending off an admirer and I brought her back.'

'You expect me to believe that?'

'As a matter of fact I do. Phyllida—'

She stepped back quickly as he reached for her.

'I am not that gullible.' She almost spat out the words as her frail, barely acknowledged hopes shattered and pierced her heart.

He shrugged, feigning indifference but she saw by the tightening of his mouth that he was angry.

'It is the truth and Miss Tatham will confirm it.' He continued, observing her hesitation. 'You are very ready to jump to the wrong conclusion, Phyllida. I thought you knew me better than that.'

'I know you for a charming snake,' she flashed. 'I have no doubt that you, too, are a party to this wager, this vile plan to deflower my stepdaughter.'

She watched him carefully, hoping he knew nothing of the wager, that he would disclaim any involvement. Instead she saw the damning understanding in his eyes. The disappointment only fuelled her anger and she wanted to hurt him, as she was hurting.

'But of course you are. What else would one expect of an Arrandale?'

His hands clenched. He gave her one last angry look from narrowed eyes and strode past her into the ballroom.

Phyllida pressed one hand to her mouth, as if to force back the tears. Deep breaths, one, then another. And again. She must go back indoors as calm and serene as she had come out. At least she must appear so. It had all been a lie. Every look, every smile he had bestowed upon her, had been designed to gain her trust, to allow him to get closer to Ellen.

And what did you expect? You were never interesting enough to attract a suitor when you came out, why should that change now, when you do not even have youth on your side?

She could almost hear Olivia saying the words in her blunt, matter-of-fact manner. What a fool she had been! Another steadying breath, a moment to gather her courage and she stepped through the long windows into the light, noise and stifling heat of the ballroom. Ellen was hovering close by and immediately pounced upon her.

'Philly, I am very sorry,' she said contritely. 'It was very foolish of me, I know, and it will not happen again.' She touched Phyllida's arm. 'Did Mr Arrandale tell you what happened?'

'We will not discuss it now, if you please.' The music had stopped but the crowded room rang with laughter and bustling movement. Phyllida looked around her, thankful that there was no one near enough to hear them. Ellen caught her arm.

'Have you fallen out with him? You should not, you know, he was most gallant.'

'I have said we will not discuss it.'

'But we must.' Ellen drew her further into the empty corner. 'Mr Naismith was following me around like a lost puppy, and Mr Tesford was also shadowing me in the most tiresome fashion, so I stepped outside with Henry Fullingham, only *he* proved to be a toad, until Mr Arrandale rescued me from him—'

Phyllida stopped her.

'Do you mean *all* these gentlemen were importuning you?'

'Not Richard.' She added, observing Phyllida's look of shock, 'He is my friend, we are on first-name terms.'

'Oh, no, you are not!' Phyllida drew herself up. 'Ellen, this has gone far enough. I cannot condone your behaviour this evening. It was most improper of you to go off alone into the gardens. I should not have to tell you that. And if you do not mind me then I shall...I shall pack you off to your Uncle Tatham.'

'You would not!'

'Believe me, I *would*. It is for your own safety.'

Phyllida met Ellen's reproachful glance steadily. This was too serious for cajolery, the girl must realise that she was deadly serious. After a moment Ellen sighed.

'I beg your pardon, Philly. Are you very cross with me?'

Phyllida was not immune to the beseeching look in those blue eyes. She said more gently, 'You are very young, Ellen, a mistake now could ruin your whole life. I have to do all I can to avoid that.'

'But it was not your fault. Richard said—'

'*Mr Arrandale*, if you please, Ellen. He is a dangerous character and I have no wish to hear what he said to you. Neither do I wish you to speak to him again this evening.'

For a moment Phyllida thought Ellen would refuse to obey her, but something in her face made the girl pause.

'Very well,' said Ellen at last. 'If that is your wish, but you are very wrong about him, Phyllida. He really did rescue me from Mr Fullingham. If he had not been there I fear it would have been more than my gown that was undone.'

'Ellen!'

'Well, Philly, it does not do to be mealy-mouthed about these things.' Ellen looked past her. 'Oh, Julia and Penelope are waving to me. May I go to them? Please,

Philly, I promise I shall be as good as gold for the rest of the evening.'

Phyllida frowned.

'I should take you straight home,' she said severely.

'Oh, please do not do that, Philly. If you drag me away like a naughty schoolgirl that really would set tongues wagging. I have learned a valuable lesson this evening, I promise you. Let me show you that I can be a model of decorum and respectability.'

Fighting down the desire to insist they leave immediately Phyllida nodded and Ellen went off to join her friends. She was right, if they left so precipitately there would be questions and conjecture, and who knew what gossip might arise. Besides, Phyllida had brought the Desboroughs with her and she could not abandon them. She closed her eyes and rubbed her temples, fearing the next few hours would feel interminable.

'Lady Phyllida, are you unwell?'

She heard the soft voice, warm with concern, and her eyes flew open.

'Lady Denham, I beg your pardon. I have a slight headache, that is all.'

She tried to smile, to alleviate the anxious look upon her hostess's face.

'Ah, 'tis a migraine, I have no doubt. I suffer from them myself.'

'No, no, merely the heat, and the noise. I shall be well again immediately.'

'You will recover more quickly if you have a little peace.' Lady Denham took her arm and led her from the ballroom. 'There, that little door in the corner. It is my own little room and you may sit there quietly, if you wish.' She laughed when Phyllida hesitated. 'You are thinking someone might already be in there? No, you will be quite safe. The room is locked and the key is behind the very ugly vase you see on the console table over there.'

'You are very kind, but I cannot leave Ellen—'

'I will keep watch on Miss Tatham while you are gone, I know how you worry about her.'

Her hostess's kindness almost overset Phyllida. She murmured gratefully, 'Just ten minutes, then.'

Lady Denham patted Phyllida's shoulder. 'As long as you wish, my dear.'

Phyllida let herself into the little room. Candles burned in two of the wall sconces, not enough for sewing or reading, perhaps, but sufficient for Phyllida to make her way to one of the padded armchairs and sink down. The noise from the crowd was muted and she leaned back and closed her eyes. Really, when had she grown so old that parties such as this exhausted her? Honesty compelled her to admit her exhaustion had little to do with the party and everything to do with Ellen and Richard Arrandale. He knew about the wager, he had not denied that, but both he and Ellen denied that he had been flirting with her. Phyllida sighed. Ellen was a minx but she was not deceitful and if Richard had truly rescued her from one of her beaux then she should be grateful for it.

There was a sudden rush of noise. Someone had entered the room. Phyllida opened her eyes and sat up.

'I saw you come in. I thought you might be ill.'

Richard turned to close the door behind him. It was only partly true. He wanted to talk to her. For once in his life he had been acting honourably and he wanted her to believe it. He *needed* her to believe it.

'I am not ill, so you may return to the party and leave me in peace. But you will stay away from my stepdaughter.'

'Blast it, Phyllida, why can you not understand that I am not trying to harm Ellen?'

With a cry of frustration she flew out of the chair.

'Then just what are you trying to do?'

'Damn it all, woman, I am doing my best to protect her!'

He pressed his lips together to prevent a further outburst. He was a man noted for his sang-froid, what was it about Phyllida that made his even temper desert him? She was facing him across the room and even in the dim light he saw her eyes were shadowed with pain. He wanted very much to go to her, take her in his arms and kiss away that troubled look.

Richard opened his mouth to speak but she put up her hand to silence him. She came towards him, her hands clasped across her stomach and when she addressed him the words were slow and delivered with an obvious effort.

'Mr Arrandale, as Ellen's guardian it behoves me to ask you what your intentions are towards my stepdaughter. You say you wish to protect her. Can…can it be that you, that you are *in love* with her?'

Oh, lord.

Richard looked into those soft eyes raised so anxiously to his and the truth hit him like a runaway horse. He was not in love with Ellen. In fact, he had no interest in the girl at all, except that she was Phyllida's stepdaughter and if Phyllida's happiness depended upon Ellen, then his did, too. It was so simple. He was in love with Phyllida Tatham.

The revelation shocked him, robbed him of speech for just a moment too long.

'Of course not.' Phyllida drew back, her lip curling. 'You mean only to amuse yourself, do you not?'

'No! Phyllida, I—'

'You have no permission to use my name!' She cut across him, her eyes flashing. 'You can have nothing more to say to me, or to Ellen.' She drew herself up, shoulders back, almost quivering with fury. 'I shall give orders that you are not to be admitted to my house. We will of course be obliged to meet, since we have some mutual acquaintances in Bath, but believe me, sir, I should prefer to have nothing more to do with you.'

The disdain in her tone lashed him and he retorted without thinking.

'And what of Ellen, will you forbid her to speak to me?'

'No. That would be foolish in the extreme. It would merely push her into imagining herself as a latter-day Juliet.'

'Always so damned reasonable!'

'Yes, I am. I shall be watching you, Mr Arrandale. You shall not play fast and loose with my stepdaughter.' She glared at him. 'If you had any vestige of honour in you at all you would leave Bath now that I have found you out.'

'Found me out?' He shook his head, thinking of Urmston and Tesford and Fullingham. 'Madam, you have it all wrong.'

'Have I?' she said furiously. 'Can you deny you signed up to the despicable plan to ruin my stepdaughter? That you took advantage of my friendship with Lady Hune to effect an introduction with us?'

'We were already acquainted.'

'One dance at Almack's,' she said contemptuously. 'And even that you did not remember.'

'No, not at first, perhaps.' Even as the words left his lips Richard cursed himself for a fool. He saw the flicker of pain in her eyes, brief but unmistakable, then she raised her hand and pointed one shaking finger towards the door.

'Get out. Now.'

The words were quiet and all the more effective for it. Richard's brain was reeling. He knew he was not thinking properly. There was nothing he could say or do to retrieve the situation. In silence he made a stiff little bow, turned on his heel and left.

Phyllida glanced at the clock. She had been in this room for more than the ten minutes she had promised herself. She must get back. She must find Ellen and take her home. A laughing group of merrymakers surged past as she slipped back into the ballroom and she had to flatten herself against the wall to avoid being crushed. Once they had moved on she looked around the room. Lady Wakefield and the dowager had found seats at the far side and Phyllida began to move towards them, wondering how best to explain to Lady Hune that she and Ellen could not go to Stonehenge. By the time she reached the ladies she had realised it was impossible to do so, when only moments ago she had accepted the invitation so eagerly. The dowager would insist on a reason for this sudden change of mind and Phyllida had no answer, without disclosing Ellen's folly and Richard Arrandale's dastardly behaviour to his great-aunt.

Ellen's explanation of events came back to her. Was she perhaps maligning Richard unfairly? Had he behaved honourably on this occasion? It could not be. Everything she knew about the man said he was a rake and he was not wealthy enough to refuse the chance to win ten thousand pounds. She had to face the fact that his behaviour towards her, and towards Ellen, was calculated to win their trust. But it was all a sham.

As if she had conjured it, the restless, shifting throng parted briefly and she saw Richard on the far side of the room. He was standing beside a voluptuous brunette, bending close to murmur something that made her laugh and rap him playfully on the knuckles with her fan. Quickly Phyllida turned away, her fears confirmed. Richard Arrandale was no gentleman, and the only interests he had at heart were his own.

'You are very quiet.'

In the blackness of the carriage Richard felt the tap of Lady Hune's ebony stick against his leg.

'Forgive me, Sophia, I must be fatigued.'

'From flirting so outrageously.'

'That would be it.'

He forced himself to smile, even though he knew she could not see him. He had had to do something for the rest of the infernal evening, after Phyllida had ripped up at him and left his spirits flayed and sore. Lady Heston had been throwing out lures to him all evening. It was a comfort to his bruised self-esteem that someone appreciated him. His great-aunt's voice interrupted his thoughts.

'Do you wish me to drop you off in Union Street, at that hell you frequent?'

'Not tonight.'

He had no interest in gambling. He wished to heaven he had never gone to Burton's. Even more he wished he had refused to get involved in that damnable wager.

'You have not asked about that little matter we discussed,' she said. 'It is all arranged. We go to Shrewton Lodge a week on Monday. The Wakefields, Mr and Mrs Desborough and their daughter, and of course Lady Phyllida and Miss Tatham.'

He turned his head to look at her, but Sophia's face was no more than a pale blur in the darkness.

'Are you sure? When was it agreed?'

'Before you fell out with Phyllida. Do not deny it, I saw you studiously ignoring one another for the last hour. Would you like to tell me what it was about?'

'I was trying to be a gentleman, for once.' He rubbed a hand across his eyes. 'My actions were misconstrued. I think I may have ruined your plans, Sophia. I doubt Lady Phyllida will come to Shrewton now.'

For a while there was silence in the carriage, the only sound the rhythmic clop of the horses' hoofs and the creak of wood and leather. Then he heard Sophia's soft, determined voice.

'She'll come.'

There was little time for private speech once the Desboroughs had been set down at their door, so when they reached Charles Street Phyllida sent Ellen up to bed. She waited until Matlock had gone downstairs before following Ellen to her room.

'Are you come to scold me, Philly?' Ellen eyed her nervously. 'I pray you won't. I was about to blow out my candle, I am too tired even to read tonight.'

'No, I have not come to scold you.' Phyllida perched herself on the edge of the bed. 'I have been thinking that perhaps we should remove from Bath.'

'Oh, pray do not do so on my account, Philly!'

'I thought we might spend a few weeks at Worthing. The weather is so warm, do you not think we would be much more comfortable by the sea?'

'I would prefer to remain here, with all my new friends.' Ellen reached out and caught her hand. 'Please don't take me away,' she begged. 'I have promised to be good. And indeed, I *have* behaved myself since I have been with you. I have not once slipped out of the house alone, or exchanged love letters with anyone, or persuaded any gentleman to sing outside my window—'

'Did you do so at Mrs Ackroyd's?' asked Phyllida, momentarily diverted.

'Oh, yes, several times. It was mostly the very young men, you see, when they had been too *pushing*, but sometimes the older gentlemen could be just as silly, trying to entice me away from my friends to flirt with them, or even to enter their carriage! If I thought they needed a lesson I would tell them how partial I was to hearing a love song outside my window at night. My room was at the back of the house, but Cook slept just above and when they came serenading she would tear into them and threaten to throw the contents of her chamber pot over them if they did not desist.'

Phyllida smothered a laugh.

'I am relieved you have not been playing such tricks here!'

'Oh, no, I have been trying to be so good, and I thought I was succeeding very well, until I allowed myself to fall for Mr Fullingham's silly ruse this evening. But that will not happen again, Philly, and I quite see that I must behave with even greater circumspection in future. I promise you I mean to do whatever you wish, Philly. You may positively hedge me about with guards and chaperons and I shall not utter one word of complaint.'

'That is very good of you, my love, but I am coming to realise that Bath is more fraught with danger for a young lady than I had ever envisaged.'

'What, because a gentleman tried to make love to me?' Ellen laughed at that. 'I have already explained that it was entirely my own fault and I have learned from it.'

'But I think I should remove you to somewhere less dangerous.'

Ellen shook her head.

'Darling Philly, I am as safe in Bath as anywhere—indeed, if you were ever to read *The Monk* you would believe that no one is safe, even in a nunnery! No, to be serious, Mrs Ackroyd always says that most young ladies, even heiresses, are perfectly safe if only they remain on their guard. She says it is their own foolish hearts that so often let them down, but you know I have no interest in any of the gentlemen I have seen in Bath. Indeed, it is a very sad fact that I have never yet found any gentleman who has made me want to throw my cap over the windmill.' A loud sigh filled the darkness. 'I fear I am going to be very hard to please.'

'I am glad to hear it,' replied Phyllida seriously. How was she to make Ellen understand? She tried again. 'I am concerned for your safety, my love. There are—there appear to be—gentlemen in Bath with an eye to your fortune.'

'But that will always be so, will it not? I am an heiress.'

'Yes, but these are unscrupulous men who, who would stop at nothing.'

Ellen's eyes sparkled.

'You mean they would seduce me? Well, I have already told you I shall not allow that, so short of laying hands upon me and performing a physical abduction I am in no danger at all, am I?'

'Perhaps not, but—'

'And another thing,' said Ellen, triumphantly. 'If we

were to go to Worthing, or Brighton, or anywhere, I might meet the gentleman of my dreams who will sweep me off my feet and I will not be able to help myself. So we will be much safer if we remain in Bath, won't we?'

Phyllida retired, momentarily defeated and too exhausted to argue further. When she left Ellen's room she found Matlock on the landing, a pile of clean sheets in her arms.

The maid said in her abrupt way, 'Miss Ellen's right, my lady.' When Phyllida raised her brows she continued, by way of explanation. 'The doors in this house being so ill fitting, l couldn't help overhearing, and if you want my opinion we'd be best keeping Miss Ellen here, where there's a whole army of folks to look out for her, not only myself and Parfett but also the servants from Lady Wakefield's household and others that I've got to know around the town. There isn't one of 'em wouldn't hesitate to come forward if they thought Miss Ellen were in any trouble.'

'Thank you, Matty, that is a comforting thought.'

'Aye, well, I know you're worried about her, my lady. Miss Ellen's always been one to land on her feet, but she can be hot to handle when she's unhappy. I'd rather have her behaving herself here in Bath than misbehaving somewhere else.'

'I believe you are right. Perhaps we would be wise to stay here, where we already have such good and trusted friends.' Phyllida stretched a tired smile. 'Goodnight, Matty. Ellen is lucky to have you to look after her.'

She moved on, but not before she heard the old retainer mutter as she walked away.

'If you asks me, it ain't Miss Ellen who needs looking after.'

* * *

Ellen arrived at the breakfast table the following morning in high good humour. Phyllida had risen from her bed feeling dull and listless and it was an effort even to respond to Ellen's cheerful greeting. The girl was clearly full of energy, and as soon as Hirst had retired and they were alone, Ellen launched into speech, explaining again what had happened in the garden. Knowing it would take more effort to stem the flow than to allow Ellen to talk herself out, Phyllida kept silent.

'So you see, Philly,' said Ellen at last, 'Ri—Mr Arrandale is completely blameless in the whole affair.'

No. He is playing his own game.

Phyllida knew it would be useless to say as much to Ellen.

'Perhaps,' she conceded. 'However, there is no doubt that what happened to you last night could have been very serious. You must understand, Ellen, that a scandal now could ruin your chances of a successful come-out.'

'I do understand, Philly, and I promise I shall be more careful in future.' She put her elbows on the table and rested her chin on her hands. 'It is very unfair, don't you think, that we must behave with such propriety at all times while a man may flirt and behave in the most outrageous fashion and no one will think any the worse of him.'

'That is not quite true. A man may gain a bad reputation, which will make it prudent for respectable people to approach him with caution.'

'You are thinking of Mr Arrandale,' said Ellen. 'He has been very wild, I know, but that is all in the past.' She beamed at Phyllida. 'He is reformed now. He told me so.'

Hollow laughter echoed in Phyllida's head.

That is just what a rake *would* say.

* * *

Richard was relieved, if a little surprised, that rumours of the wager were not more widespread. The appearance of another footman in the Tatham household did not go unnoticed with the gentlemen who frequented Burton's gaming hell in Union Street, and dampened the spirits of at least two of those who had signed up for the wager.

Richard had joined them at the card table, and the conversation naturally turned to the heiress.

'The chit is damnably elusive,' grumbled Tesford. 'She won't make any effort to give her protectors the slip.'

Sir Charles Urmston drained his glass and called for another bottle before inspecting his hand.

'I must say she seems immune to the charms of every gentleman,' he murmured, hesitating over his discard. 'She flirts most deliciously, but cannot be tempted into anything remotely clandestine.'

Richard listened in silence. A glance at Henry Fullingham showed that he was scowling, but he said nothing of his unsuccessful attempt to seduce Ellen in the Denhams' garden.

'And now there's a new footman following her everywhere,' observed Tesford, staring moodily into his glass. 'Big, burly fellow who looks very handy with his fists. I am minded to withdraw.'

'So, too, am I,' agreed Fullingham.

'And lose your thousand pounds without a fight?' Urmston's brows rose a little and both men flushed angrily.

'What have you in mind, to snatch the chit off the street?' retorted Fullingham.

'It's a possibility,' murmured Sir Charles.

'Not for me,' remarked George Cromby, shaking his head. 'A little dalliance with a willing gel is one thing, but abduction—it would be bound to get out and I have my family to consider. Think of the scandal.'

Tesford flicked a sneering look at Richard.

'Scandal has never worried Arrandale, but he has already given up. Told me so himself,' he added, when a murmur of surprise ran around the table.

'He was bamming you, Arnold.' Sir Charles Urmston laughed softly. 'Putting you off the scent to give himself the advantage. Ain't that so, Arrandale?'

Richard did not deny it, but Arnold Tesford gave a short laugh.

'Well, he hasn't done very well so far. His attempts to get the widow on his side have failed dismally, from what I saw at the Denhams'. Tore you off a strip, didn't she, and barred you from calling—my man was drinking with one of the Denhams' footmen in the Running Horse t'other night and the fellow said he, er, overheard it.'

'Really?' murmured Urmston. 'You must be losing your touch, Arrandale.'

Richard smiled, outwardly unmoved by the laughter around the table, but as he made his way back to Royal Crescent he thought morosely that perhaps Sir Charles wasn't so far off the mark.

He awoke the following day to a leaden sky that promised rain, and after a hasty breakfast he announced to Sophia that he would accompany her to the Pump Room.

'This is an honour,' Sophia remarked as they rattled off around the Crescent in her ancient carriage. 'Are you going to drink a cup of the famous waters?'

He smiled a little at that.

'Not quite.'

'Well, perhaps you should try it. You have been quite out of sorts these past few days. You have an umbrella, too.' Her keen eyes searched his face. 'Do I take it you do not mean to return with me?'

'That very much depends.'

'Upon what?'

He grinned. 'Upon whether I find a more attractive prospect.'

'You are fobbing me off. Very well, if you do not wish to tell me your plans so be it. I shall ask you instead about Arrandale. There was a letter for you, was there not, from the steward?'

'Why, yes, he tells me the repairs to the roof are now finished.'

'It is a bad business,' declared Sophia, shaking her head. 'You should not be using your own money to maintain your brother's house.'

'If I did not it would fall into ruin and the staff would have to be turned off. That I will not allow. Why, most of them were there when I was a boy, they are like my family. You know very well that since Father's death the entailed property has been in the hands of the lawyers, and they won't budge without instruction from my brother.' He paused, fighting back his frustration. 'It would be easier if I could manage Arrandale properly, sell some of the land or the timber to raise the funds to maintain the place, but that rascally lawyer of my father's insists that nothing can be done without Wolf's authority.'

'It is almost ten years since your brother fled the country, Richard, and you have heard nothing from him. He may well be dead by now. You could claim the inheritance.'

'No. I would never do that. Not while there is a chance Wolf is alive.'

'So you continue to pour your own money into Arrandale. Money you can ill afford.'

Richard could not deny it. He was trying to achieve the impossible, using the meagre income from Brookthorn to support a much larger estate.

'You are a fool, Richard,' Sophia continued in her sharp, direct way. 'It cannot go on, my boy. And do not look to gambling to restore your fortunes.'

'I do not. Neither do I look to the heiress.'

'Miss Tatham? I never thought you did.' She added, in the casual voice he had come to mistrust, 'I think Lady Phyllida is more your style.'

Richard was about to agree when Sophia continued.

'You could do worse, my boy. Tatham provided well for both his ladies.'

'Really?' Richard frowned. 'There is nothing in her style to suggest it. I thought all the money had been settled on Miss Tatham.'

'Not at all. Phyllida is a very wealthy widow.'

She could not have delivered a more severe blow. He shrugged and replied carelessly, 'Then that is another reason she would never entertain my suit. She would think I was interested only in her fortune.'

Sophia gave a very unladylike snort.

'Sometimes, Richard, for a man with your reputation for pleasing women, you understand very little about them.'

Chapter Eleven

Having decided that they would stay in Bath, despite the dangers, Phyllida was determined that life would go on as normal. Or as normal is it could be. Ellen cheerfully accepted that she must always be accompanied when she went out, and when Phyllida could not go with her she was to take either Matlock or the new footman she had engaged, a brawny Irishman named Patrick who came with glowing references from a respectable family, well known to Lady Wakefield.

'It relieves my mind greatly to know that you can vouch for the family,' Phyllida told her when they met at the Pump Room a few days later. 'I am grown so suspicious of everyone these days.'

'That is not such a bad thing.' Lady Wakefield gave her an understanding smile. 'Are you regretting taking on the responsibility? It must be quite onerous, to have sole charge of your stepdaughter.'

'I know it, ma'am, and I have considered moving Ellen out of Bath.' Phyllida lowered her voice. 'My housekeeper intercepted a note only yesterday. It suggested an assignation and when I told Ellen of it she was quite unsurprised, but she *did* tell me that she had no intention of meeting any gentleman in such a clandestine manner. I am very thankful for it, but I fear if she were to be confined at Tatham, or even worse in the schoolroom with her young cousins, as my brother-in-law has suggested, who knows what her rebellious spirit might cause her to do?'

'Very true. Better that you keep her here, under your eye.'

'That is what I think, ma'am.' Phyllida laughed suddenly. 'And I am becoming most adept at chaperoning! When Sir Charles Urmston *happened upon* us in Milsom Street and invited us to step into the confectioners and try the latest batch of Naples Diavolini I gave him no opportunity to converse privately with Ellen and kept up such a flow of inane chatter while we sampled the delicious chocolate drops that by the end of it I was quite exhausted. And yesterday, when Mr Tesford intercepted us in Sydney Gardens I took up my place between him and Ellen. I am always determinedly cheerful, but any gentlemen, be he potential suitor or would-be seducer, must be shown that I am not to be distracted from my role as chaperon.'

'Good for you,' declared Lady Wakefield approvingly. 'Although, you need not worry over her today. Once she and Julia have finished their dancing class this morning they will return to Laura Place under the watchful eye of Julia's maid. Graveney is very much like your Matlock, she is very protective of her charges. She shall also accompany Ellen in the carriage, when I send her back to you after dinner.'

'Thank you, I know I need not worry about Ellen for the whole day.'

'What will you do with yourself?'

Phyllida laughed. 'I hardly know.'

But in truth she knew only too well. She would busy herself with her accounts and with her household duties, tasks that would occupy her mind, because if she turned to her painting, her books or strolling in Sydney Gardens, then the nagging ache that had been with her since the Denhams' party would intensify and her thoughts would again be filled with Richard Arrandale.

Phyllida had spent the days and nights following the Denhams' party going over the events of the evening and trying to understand Richard's behaviour. Her head told her the man was a rake and that any chivalrous action would be designed to ingratiate himself with Ellen, but her heart did not want to believe it. Ellen was convinced that he was reformed and Phyllida had to admit that in these matters Ellen appeared to be wise beyond her years. Lady Wakefield, too, believed Richard Arrandale to be a reformed character. Even after Phyllida had confided to her all that had occurred on that night she had no hesitation in defending him, or in concluding that he must be truly fond of Ellen. Could she have been wrong? Phyllida wondered. Could Richard really be the honourable man her heart wanted him to be? The trouble was, she thought sadly, if that was so, then she had insulted him most grievously.

Resolving not to waste her free time in fruitless speculation Phyllida took her leave of Lady Wakefield. The clouds that had been gathering all morning had descended even lower and as she reached the Pump Room doorway the first fat spots of rain began to fall.

'Lady Phyllida.'

She tensed as she heard that familiar voice at her shoulder.

'We have nothing to say to one another, Mr Arrandale.'

'Are you going to Charles Street? That is on my way, allow me to escort you.'

'No, thank you,' she responded icily. 'I am perfectly capable of walking alone.'

'But it is raining and you have no umbrella. And I do.' Phyllida knew it was a mistake to look at him but she could not help herself. The corners of his mouth had curved upwards and he was smiling at her in a way that broke through all her resolve. He held out his arm. 'Shall we?'

As if they had a will of their own her fingers slid on to his sleeve. In her own defence, Phyllida told herself that if she refused him he was quite capable of walking behind her all the way to Charles Street.

They stepped out of the Pump Room. Phyllida was obliged to keep close to his side to avoid the rain, which was now falling steadily.

She told him, 'If you expect me to thank you for your gallant behaviour the other evening you will be disappointed.' When he made no reply the guilt that was worming away inside her became unbearable. 'But I do beg your pardon, for what I said to you that night.'

'You admit, then, that I meant no harm to Miss Tatham?'

'She has assured me that was the case.'

The words came out stiffly, but Richard was heartened by them, until she added, 'At least on that occasion.'

He smothered an exclamation.

'Lady Phyllida, there are other, far more dangerous men seeking to undo your stepdaughter.'

'I am aware she is the subject of a wicked gamble, Mr Arrandale, but whether the other participants are more dangerous than you is questionable.'

'You are an innocent, Lady Phyllida. You do not know what these men are capable of.'

'Just because I have lived retired does not mean I am not aware of what men are like.'

'From gossip and discreet whispers!'

'And from novels,' she flashed, stopping to look up at him. 'I have read *Clarissa*.'

'What, *all* of it?'

She put up her chin. 'Yes.'

A grin tugged at his mouth.

'By George, your marriage must have been extremely dull if you had so much time to read.'

Her eyes flashed. Richard laughed. She had withdrawn her hand but he caught it and tucked it on to his arm again, saying as they began to walk on, 'Forgive me for that last remark, ma'am. Will you concede it is a fair trade with the insult you flung at me at the Denhams' party?'

'I shall concede nothing,' she replied with icy dignity but did not pull away. It was progress, of a sort.

They strolled on and Richard exerted himself to draw her out, talking to her of books and art and the theatre. Inwardly he was smiling, thinking how well their steps matched, how similar were their tastes.

How conveniently tall she was, so he would only have to drop his head a little to reach those full red lips. He glanced down at her profile with its straight little nose and determined chin. She was frowning a little as she considered the question he had asked her about the new Theatre Royal in Drury Lane.

'I think it is the fact that it is so large,' she was saying. 'The audience is too distant. Too...'

She looked up at him at that moment, her lips remaining pursed around the word long after the sound had faded. He watched the colour rise in her cheeks, saw her eyes darken as she recognised the attraction between them. Then her head snapped back, she gazed ahead of her and presented her profile to him once more.

'You were saying?' he prompted.

'I seem to have forgotten it. But it is no matter, for we are in Charles Street now. I am home.'

'Yes.' He found himself wishing they had another mile to walk, just for the pleasure of her company. He gave a little bow.

'Then I shall take my leave of you, until next week. Our visit to Shrewton.'

Phyllida drew a deep breath. The decision she had been putting off for so long was now clear.

'We shall not be going,' she said. 'I shall write to Lady Hune today to inform her that Ellen and I will not be able to join her party.'

'May I ask why you have changed your mind?'

'I might have misconstrued your actions at the Denhams', Mr Arrandale, but that does not alter the fact that you are party to a vile conspiracy against Ellen and where she is concerned I dare not trust you.'

Richard's brows rose fractionally, but he said nothing, merely inclined his head and walked away. She watched him go. He had not tried to change her mind, he had not argued, merely accepted her news. She should be glad, for she would have had to resist his persuasions and although she knew she was doing the right thing, it would have been hard. She must keep away from Richard Arrandale, for her own sake as much as Ellen's. How could she allow herself to become fond of a man she would not let near her stepdaughter?

She hurried indoors and went directly to her writing desk. She must write now to Lady Hune and when Ellen returned that evening, she must face the even more difficult task of breaking the news to her.

The note to Lady Hune received a reply by return, inviting, nay, commanding Phyllida to call upon her that very afternoon. Phyllida toyed with the idea of declining, but only for a moment. She had planned to spend the time writing to Olivia but since she had no good news to convey the task was no more welcome than taking tea with the dowager marchioness. She therefore changed her gown and made her way to Royal Crescent.

'Your letter came as no surprise,' said Lady Hune, as soon as they were alone. She poured tea into a cup and handed it to Phyllida. 'My nephew told me to expect it.'

'In truth, ma'am, I should have sent it days ago. I beg your pardon, and hope it will not affect your arrangements overmuch.'

'I take it your reason is that Richard will be one of the party?'

'Yes.' Phyllida saw no reason to prevaricate.

'I suppose it is useless for me to tell you that, despite his reputation, Richard has no designs upon Miss Tatham?'

Phyllida shook her head. She wanted to believe it, part of her *did* believe it, but she no longer trusted her own judgement. How could she, when she knew now that she was in love with Richard Arrandale?

'My mind is made up, Lady Hune. It is best if Ellen and I do not go to Shrewton Lodge.'

'I hope you will forgive me, my dear, but I disagree.'

Phyllida blinked. 'Ma'am?'

'I know of the wager concerning your stepdaughter.'

'And do you know also that your nephew is a party to it?'

Phyllida was unable to keep the bitterness out of her voice.

'Yes. He was foolish to agree to it, but men were ever thus. He assures me now that he has no intention of following it through.'

'He is hardly likely to tell you anything else, ma'am.'

To her surprise Lady Hune smiled.

'He is a rascal, Phyllida, I know, but in this instance I think he is sincere.' She paused for a moment. 'He is not a bad man, my dear. I believe I know him as well as anyone and I assure you he had no wicked intentions to ruin your stepdaughter.'

Phyllida gave a tiny shake of the head. The marchioness was undoubtedly biased.

Lady Hune continued. 'Even if I am wrong, have you considered? The terms of the bet are for one of these so-called gentlemen to seduce Ellen before Michaelmas.'

Phyllida looked up.

'I did not know that,' she said slowly. 'So it will all come to naught once the twenty-ninth is past?'

'Yes, when we are at Shrewton. It was this knowledge that persuaded me to arrange the visit for next week. Think, my dear. You will have Lady Wakefield and myself to help keep an eye on Ellen with you, plus her maid, whom Richard tells me is quite fearsome.'

Phyllida did not notice her last words. She was thinking that even if Richard was planning mischief, she would have only one rake to look out for, rather than several. She looked up to find Lady Hune smiling at her.

'So, Phyllida, will you reconsider?'

'Well, what did she say?'

Richard asked the question as soon as he entered

his great-aunt's drawing room, shortly before the dinner hour.

Sophia nodded. 'She and Miss Tatham are coming to Shrewton.'

Richard let out a sigh of relief, his breath a soft hiss in the quiet room.

'Then we will be able to keep Miss Tatham out of harm's way for the last few days of the wager.'

'You truly think the danger is that great?'

'With ten thousand pounds at stake?' He handed Sophia a glass. 'Men have committed murder for less.' He threw himself down on the sofa. 'I cannot tell you how hard it has been, keeping the wolves at bay.' A wry grin twisted his mouth. 'I never thought turning respectable could be so exhausting.'

'It is good practice for when you become a father.'

The grin disappeared. 'Please, Sophia, spare me that.'

'Why should I? You will want an heir, and Phyllida Tatham is a young woman. '

He scowled. 'I mislike your jest, madam.'

'No jest, Richard. I have seen the way she looks at you.'

'You are mistaken,' he said bleakly. 'She thinks me beyond hope.'

'Then you must show her otherwise.'

'Perhaps, once Michaelmas is passed she might be persuaded to overlook my reputation.'

'A reputation you have done nothing to refute. The face you show the world is that of a devil-may-care rake-hellion, but it is very far from the truth. Who knows, save I, that the better part of your income goes into the upkeep of your brother's house rather than being lost at the gaming tables? And how long is it since you kept a mistress?'

'Faith, my lady, you profess to be very well informed of my affairs!'

'I have my sources. I know full well that very few of those ladies seen hanging on your arm in London find their way into your bed. In my time I have seen many magicians play their tricks, all smoke and mirrors. You have been the same, my boy, hiding behind your reputation as a rake.'

'And why should I do that?'

'Why? To show the world you are equally as bad as your brother. To draw society's disapproval away from Wolfgang and on to yourself.'

He stared at Sophia. She was right, of course. His father had always decreed Richard was no better than his brother and he had done his best to confirm that view. At first it had been boyish pranks, a way to gain his parents' attention, but this had changed after Wolf disappeared. Richard had adored his brother and when he could not defend him he had tried to outdo him in excess. Never murder, if one excluded the duels, but by the time he reached his majority Richard had been notorious for his drinking, his wenching and his deadly ability with pistol and swords.

Had it made him happy? No. There had been a savage satisfaction in being considered the worst of the Arrandales but not happiness, or contentment. That was something he had glimpsed, briefly, here in Bath, but it could never be within his grasp. He pushed aside the thought and raked his fingers through his hair, turning his thoughts back to his brother.

'I cannot believe Wolf is a murderer.'

'Nor I, but unless and until he returns we will not know the truth. One thing I do know, my boy: sacrificing yourself will not help him.'

Richard knew it, but he shied away from discussing it further. He looked around, seeking some other subject to distract his great-aunt. His eyes alighted upon a folded paper on the table at Sophia's elbow.

'I beg your pardon, did I interrupt you reading your letter?'

'It is from Cassandra.' She picked up the letter and handed it to him. 'She is in Paris. She seems happy.'

A shadow crossed her face, she suddenly looked older, more frail and Richard cursed his absent cousin. He opened the letter and quickly scanned it. Cassie addressed her grandmother with love and affection, but no sign of remorse.

'She is a minx to make you suffer like this.'

'The young do not realise the pain they cause.'

He kept his eyes on the sloping writing as he asked casually, 'And have my escapades grieved you, Sophia?'

'Naturally.' She reached out and caught his free hand. 'But I have hopes that that is about to change.'

He squeezed her fingers, touched by her belief in him.

'I shall try not to let you down, love.'

'What a beautiful day for driving to Shrewton.'

Ellen's cheery remark lightened Phyllida's spirits as they left the house. It was a true autumn morning, crisp and bright with a clear blue sky and a slight mist just lifting from the hills. Three carriages were drawn up, Phyllida was to join Lady Sophia in the first, Ellen would travel with Julia and her parents in the second while Matlock rode in the third vehicle with Lady Hune's maid, her butler and Richard's man, Fritt. Mr Adrian Wakefield, they learned, had cried off from the visit, having been invited to join a party of friends in Leicestershire.

Richard, Phyllida noted, was accompanying them on

horseback. At first she was relieved that the gentleman would not be riding in one of the carriages, but as they drew out of Bath and the road widened she changed her mind, for he spent the majority of the day riding beside their carriage, directly in her view. He looked lean and athletic astride the black hunter, straight-backed, his strong legs encased in buckskin and leather. The familiar ache was almost a pain. He was so handsome, everything a young girl would dream of in a hero. If she thought of him thus, how much more susceptible was Ellen? Phyllida closed her eyes, but although she could block him from her sight she could not block him from her mind. She might keep Ellen safe from his machinations now, but what if he should follow them to London when Ellen made her come-out next year? She had promised Ellen she should not be forced into marriage, that she should have the husband of her choice. But what if, *what if* she chose Richard? Phyllida could think of no one more desirable. No one less suitable. But at that point a terrible doubt shook her. Was it jealousy that made her think him the wrong man for Ellen?

Hot tears threatened. They prickled at her eyelids and filled her throat. She would argue against the match, of course, but if Ellen really loved him and Richard proved faithful, she knew she would not stand in their way.

'My dear, is anything the matter?'

Lady Hune's concerned enquiry made Phyllida fight back her unhappiness.

'Nothing, ma'am. I assure you.'

'You looked so sad.'

Phyllida forced a smile. 'I was merely thinking what I shall do once Ellen is married. She is so beautiful I do not expect her to remain single for long after her presentation.'

'Really?' observed Lady Hune. 'She tells me she is in no hurry to take a husband.'

'She has said as much to me, but that may change, when she falls in love. And when she is married she will no longer need me.' She added thoughtfully, 'I think, if the peace holds, I shall go abroad. I have always wanted to travel.'

'You might marry again.'

'No!' The word came out swift and sharp. Phyllida gave Sophia an apologetic glance. 'No,' she repeated, softly this time. 'I have no thoughts of marriage. Not any more.'

Sophia's smile was sceptical and Phyllida turned her eyes again to the window, resolutely staring at the passing landscape rather than the tall rider cantering just ahead of them.

Shrewton Lodge was an old manor set within its own park. The house itself was built of golden stone from Ham Hill and had been much altered, until it was a sprawling mass of gabled wings and tall chimneys.

'It is very beautiful,' declared Phyllida as they bowled along the curling carriageway towards the north front of the house.

'Do you think so?' Lady Hune leaned forward to get a better view. 'It has a certain charm, I suppose. I have spent many happy times here over the years.' She sat back. 'But it is a tiresome mix of styles, with several staircases and labyrinthine corridors. All dark panelling and uneven floors that cause the doors to swing open or shut of their own accord.'

'I am not deceived, ma'am, I can tell you like the house. It is a pity you do not make more use of it.'

The marchioness smiled at her. 'Ah, but when you get

to my age, Bath and its society is far more entertaining than the country.'

They pulled up before the arched entrance where liveried servants were waiting to greet them. Phyllida could only guess at the hard work that had gone into preparing the old house for their visit, but judging from the beaming faces of the staff they were very pleased to welcome their mistress. A diminutive figure ran out to take charge of Richard's horse and Phyllida recognised him as Collins, Richard's groom. She had not seen him on the journey and concluded that he had travelled down in advance. As she followed the others into the house it occurred to her that Lady Hune and her great-nephew had taken a great deal of trouble over this visit.

Once indoors, they found themselves in a large galleried hall, the heavy oak panelling decorated with ancient weapons and hunting trophies. Impatient of unpacking and too young to need a rest after their journey, Ellen and Julia begged to be allowed to explore. Receiving assent from Phyllida and Lady Wakefield, their hostess gave her permission, adding severely, 'But be warned, dinner will be early, and you must present yourselves in good time, washed and dressed as befits young ladies and not a couple of hoydens.'

'We will indeed, ma'am,' laughed Ellen. 'Thank you!'

'If there is one thing I envy young people, it is their energy,' murmured Sophia, smiling after them.

'If they had your wisdom it would make them truly formidable,' remarked Richard, holding out his arm to his aunt. 'Let me escort you to your room, ma'am.'

Phyllida watched them ascend the main staircase while she waited with Lord and Lady Wakefield for

Mrs Hinton, the housekeeper, to come and show them to their rooms.

'There is something very attractive about a reformed rake, I think,' remarked Lady Wakefield, with something very like a sigh.

'I admit I was a little suspicious of him at first, but I have never seen anything of the libertine about him,' replied Lord Wakefield. 'I believe he spends a deal of time gambling at Burton's, but that is true of so many gentlemen. It seems to me his name has been tarnished by gossipmongers with nothing better to do.'

Phyllida said nothing. They had clearly fallen under his spell and without explaining her own encounters with Richard Arrandale it would be impossible to change their opinion of the man. For herself, if he was reformed let him prove it.

In Phyllida's opinion, the rooms allocated to her and Ellen could not have been better. All the guest rooms were reached by a long shadowy corridor on the opposite side of the galleried hall to the family's apartments. The rooms were connected by a dressing room that included a bed for Matlock, who would be acting as maid to them both during their short stay. The windows looked over the drive rather than the prettier formal gardens of the south front but Phyllida did not mind that. They were as far away from Richard Arrandale as possible, and that was all that was required.

Dinner was an ordeal. Really, thought Phyllida, it was very kind of Sophia to place Richard beside her and keep him away from Ellen, but the marchioness did not realise how unsettling she found his proximity. He behaved with perfect propriety but she was painfully aware of him, his thigh, encased in the tight knee breeches, just inches from her own. She was conscious of every look, every word he bestowed upon her.

'You are not hungry?' he asked, his voice low and concerned as he watched her push her food around the plate.

'Y-yes, of course. It is all quite delicious.'

Richard felt a warm smile spreading inside him as he watched the hectic flush mantle her cheek. She might deny it but she felt the attraction just as much as he. If they were not in company he would kiss her, here and now. Instead he tempted her appetite with succulent slices of chicken and a little of the fricassee of mushrooms. She was wearing lilac, as if to remind everyone that she was a widow, yet the lacy white overdress shimmered in the late afternoon sunlight, giving her an ephemeral grace. Like an angel. He found it difficult to drag his eyes away from her, to respond when anyone else spoke to him. He wanted to dine with her alone, to kiss her while her lips tasted of the honey and Rhenish cream she was currently enjoying, before savouring every inch of her body as he slowly removed the fine silk that clung to each delicious curve.

He shifted on his seat, his body hot and aroused by the very thought of it. Enough. If she suspected his thoughts she would shy away from him like a frightened colt. She might be a widow, but she was so delightfully innocent.

All too soon the ladies withdrew and Richard was left alone with Lord Wakefield to enjoy their brandy. He had never found it so hard to converse, to contain his impatience to see Phyllida again, but thankfully Sophia had given him an excuse not to linger. She was clearly fatigued by the journey and had announced that she would retire immediately after dinner, but she ordered Richard to show their guests the gardens before the sun went down. He therefore allowed Lord Wakefield no more than one glass of brandy before he escorted him to the drawing room.

The ladies were gathered around the pianoforte, where Phyllida was playing a lively sonata. Richard started towards the little group but he was intercepted by Ellen Tatham.

'Richard, I must speak to you privately.'

He glanced quickly at Phyllida. She was engrossed in her music but he would not risk her thinking he was behaving with any impropriety, so he moved to the window, in full view of the others but where they would not be overheard.

'Well, Miss Tatham, what is so urgent?'

'Did you know that I am the subject of a…a wager?'

'How on earth did you learn of that?'

'I have my sources.'

He laughed. 'That sounds so much like my great-aunt! Very well, yes, I do know of it, but you are not to let it worry you.'

'Oh, no, of course not. When I was at school the gentlemen in the town were often making such bets. And it is much better for one to be aware of these things, do you not agree? Does Philly know of it? Is that why she has been so concerned for my safety these past weeks?'

He paused a beat before replying.

'It is, and you must behave yourself, and not cause her any more anxiety than she already suffers on your behalf.'

'You are very fond of my stepmama, I think.'

Richard did not attempt to deny it. He said slowly,

'She is very wary of me and will not accept my help to protect you, but be assured, Miss Tatham, I have taken my own measures to keep you safe.'

'Really?' Her eyes widened. 'Have you set another man to spy on me?' When his brows snapped together she continued blithely. 'I know very well that it was you who persuaded Patrick's last employers to send him to us.'

'The devil you do!'

'He let it slip when he was accompanying me to my dancing lesson one day, but you need not worry, I warned Patrick that he is not to speak of it to anyone else.'

'Miss Tatham, you are a minx.'

'Thank you. And if you have set people to watch me, then I am very grateful for it. I just wish I might tell Philly, for I know she worries a great deal about me.'

'No! Ellen, I forbid you to tell Lady Phyllida anything about this.'

'I will not say a word, if you do not want me to, even though I know it is for her sake that you are going to all this trouble for me.'

With another seraphic smile she wandered away, leaving Richard wondering who else knew of his feelings for Lady Phyllida.

Chapter Twelve

'Your great-aunt misled us, Mr Arrandale,' remarked Lady Wakefield as they strolled along the wide paths edged with trimmed box. 'I was expecting a house in holland covers and romantically overgrown gardens.'

'My aunt enjoys her comfort,' he replied. 'She sent an army of servants ahead of her to ensure everything was in order.'

'But not the gardens,' put in Phyllida, looking about her with approval. 'There are no signs of recent cutting or weeding here, everything is in excellent order.'

'The gardener has been here since he was a boy and his father before him. One cannot put a garden under holland covers, Lady Phyllida.'

He was smiling and for the life of her Phyllida could not help but respond. A cry distracted them. Ellen and Julia had run on ahead and now they were calling and beckoning to the others to catch up. The girls disappeared around the house and as Phyllida turned the corner she realised what had excited them. A large statue of Neptune surrounded by dolphins dominated the south-facing gardens and from its centre a large fountain of water frothed high into the air before it tumbled back into the surrounding pond.

'Oh, it is quite delightful,' exclaimed Lady Wakefield. 'But, girls, be careful. You do not want to wet your gowns.'

'Too late, I fear,' laughed Phyllida, watching as the girls sat on the low wall surrounding the fountain, trailing their hands in the water. Lord Wakefield chuckled.

'They look like a couple of water nymphs.' He shot a glance at Richard. 'You will not tell me Lady Hune keeps the fountain playing when she is not here.'

'No, sir, she sent instructions that it should be cleaned and set working for the duration of our visit. What do you think of it, Lady Phyllida?'

'It is enchanting.' She smiled, putting her hands together and pressing her forefingers to her mouth as she watched the water rise up from the central column, cascading back into the pool below, droplets of water sparkling like diamonds in the setting sun.

'Good. I am glad you like it.'

There was something in his voice, a note of quiet satisfaction that made her look at him and she felt a light, fluttering excitement deep inside, a delicious sense of anticipation.

Stop it, Phyllida.

'Come along, girls,' Lady Wakefield called out. 'Come away from the water now. We must see the rest of the gardens before the sun goes down.'

Phyllida stepped up beside Lady Wakefield as they moved on to the west front of the house with its terraced lawns giving views of the extensive park and woods beyond.

'The trees are already beginning to turn,' said Richard. 'In a few weeks more they will be a blaze of red and gold.'

'That must be a magnificent sight,' observed Lord Wakefield.

Phyllida stared at the trees but she knew Richard's eyes were upon her.

'Yes. I wish you could see it.'

He is speaking directly to me.

The tug of attraction between them was so strong it was like a physical thread, pulling them together. A sudden, wild joy rose inside Phyllida as she thought of what he might mean, but she quickly stifled it. She dare not allow herself to think such things were possible, not until he had proved himself, until she could trust him.

And that might take a very long time.

The next day was dominated by their visit to Stonehenge. By the time they set off the rising sun had burnt off the morning mist and they rode in two open carriages, the better to enjoy the excellent views the journey afforded. Julia and Ellen took along their sketchbooks, determined to capture the magnificent druidical monument on paper, for who knew when they might have another chance? Phyllida had seen pictures of the site, but still their first view of the huge stones rearing up on the flat plain made her catch her breath.

The dry weather meant they could drive the carriages across the short turf and stop closer to the monument. As the party alighted a woman in rags came running up, offering to be their guide. They declined, but Phyllida saw Richard slip the woman a few coins before sending her on her way. The day was warm and the party was happy to roam amongst the stones, wondering at their size and speculating about their origin and purpose. After a lively discussion they all agreed to discount myths of giants and gods in favour of Mr Stukeley's book with its arguments for an ancient civilisation and Ellen and Julia wandered off to find a good spot for their sketching. The rest of the party broke up to stroll around as they wished.

Phyllida was happy to wander on her own and when she saw Richard start towards her she quickly changed her own direction and moved away. She was still not ready to trust him, but whenever he was near her she dared not trust herself either. She had decided therefore that it would be best to avoid him. From the corner of her eye she saw him stop and turn back. It was what she had intended, but it did nothing for the heaviness that settled over her spirits as she continued to make her solitary progress. A few minutes later she stepped between two of the towering blocks and saw Sophia resting against one of the fallen stones.

'Are you quite well, Lady Hune?'

'I am a little tired,' the old lady admitted. 'But I would not spoil anyone's pleasure.'

'Let me give you my arm back to the carriage,' said Phyllida. 'We may sit there in comfort while we wait for the others.'

'Are you sure, my dear?'

'Perfectly. I have seen enough here and would like to view the whole edifice from a distance, which I can do perfectly well from the carriage.'

Satisfied, Sophia took Phyllida's arm and they began to stroll back towards the waiting vehicles.

'Did my nephew show you the grounds yesterday, Phyllida? What did you think of them?'

'Quite delightful, ma'am. I hope I shall have the opportunity to explore the park a little tomorrow.'

'Feel free to wander where you choose, my dear.'

'Thank you. You said yesterday you had been happy there, was that with your husband, my lady?'

'Yes, we spent the summer months here when my son was born, and when I was widowed it became my home. Much more comfortable than the dower house at Hune. I brought Cassandra to Shrewton when her parents died and Hune's cousin inherited the marquessate. Richard, too, spent time at the Lodge with me. We were here when the scandal broke about his brother. I believe it has always felt like home to him. It was never part of the Hune estate, you see. It is mine to dispose of as I wish and it will be Richard's eventually. Cassandra's father provided very well for her, so she does not need it. Richard may use it as he will. He may even sell it, since he is foolish enough to spend every penny he has on keeping his brother's property in order.'

Phyllida looked at her, puzzled, and Lady Hune answered her silent question.

'Richard is convinced Wolfgang is still alive, but in his brother's absence he has no access to the Arrandale fortune and he uses his own money to repair and maintain Arrandale House.'

'Oh.' Phyllida bit her lip. 'I am ashamed to say I thought he frittered his money away,' she confessed. 'I thought he spent it on drinking and gambling and, and the like.'

'As does the rest of the world.' Lady Hune sighed. 'It has amused him for years to maintain his rakish reputation, but he is paying for it now, I think.'

Phyllida's head came up. 'But his reputation is not undeserved, ma'am.'

'He *was* very wild, I grant you, but his family and his world expected nothing else. His father was a rogue who showed little affection for his sons. He left them to grow up without the precepts of charity or honour. When Wolfgang's wife died in mysterious circumstances his father immediately shipped the boy off to France and by that very action he as good as admitted his guilt. Richard was a schoolboy at the time. He was adventurous, energetic but no more wayward than any other seventeen-year-old, yet he was considered by his father to be as dissolute as his brother.

Phyllida was moved to exclaim, 'Oh, poor boy!'

'Poor boy indeed. He was expected to behave badly and he did so.'

'So badly that before he reached twenty he was notorious,' said Phyllida, thinking back to her one short Season.

Sophia gripped her arm, saying urgently, 'Show him a little charity, Phyllida. He was never as black as he was painted.'

They had reached the carriage and Phyllida made no reply as they settled themselves on the comfortable seat, but she reflected upon Sophia's words as she looked back towards the monument. She could see Richard standing behind the girls, admiring their sketches. Even as she watched Ellen looked up and laughed at something he had said, completely at ease with him.

How she would like to believe Lady Hune, but there was so much at stake and if she was wrong it would be Ellen's life that was ruined.

However, when the party arrived back at Shrewton Lodge at the end of the day Phyllida allowed Richard to hand her down from the carriage without hesitation. His grip on her fingers was firm and she looked up briefly to meet his eyes, a shy, tentative smile in her own.

Richard's spirits lifted as he followed Phyllida into the house. She was melting, just a little. She had every right to be cautious, but he hoped if all went well that by the time they returned to Bath they might be friends. He felt a wry grin growing inside him. It was an unusual term for Richard to use for a woman, but in Phyllida's case he knew he not only wanted her in his bed, but in his life, too.

Fritt was already filling his bath when Richard went up to his room, and he took particular pains over his dress that evening, laughing to himself as he thought Fritt must think him the veriest coxcomb, changing his coat three times before he was satisfied.

He tried to hide his disappointment when he found himself sitting at the other end of the table to Phyllida at dinner. It did not matter, he would bide his time. He did not wish to rush her. When he and Lord Wakefield joined the ladies after dinner they found Phyllida and Lady Wakefield playing at cards with Julia while Ellen and Sophia were deep in conversation on the far side of the room. He followed Lord Wakefield across to watch the card players.

'Lady Hune and Miss Tatham have had their heads together since we came in,' chuckled Lady Wakefield as they approached.

'I think Miss Tatham reminds my great-aunt of Lady Cassandra,' said Richard.

'Ah, yes, her granddaughter,' murmured Lady Wakefield. 'Poor child.'

Julia looked up. 'Why poor, Mama? She married the man she loves and Lady Hune says she is now happily settled in Paris.'

Lady Wakefield shook her head. 'He stole her away from her family, and may yet turn out to be an unscrupulous rogue.'

'And there are many such men in society,' added Phyllida. 'Even in Bath.'

Richard met her eyes without flinching.

'I agree wholeheartedly, my lady.'

Phyllida quickly returned her attention to the cards. Was he trying to convince her he was not one of them? She did not yet believe he had reformed, even if he had convinced Lady Wakefield and Lady Hune.

The evening passed very quietly which was due, everyone agreed, to a combination of the day's exertions and the unseasonably warm weather. The long windows from the drawing room were thrown wide but the evening air was sultry, though there was little cloud and a bright moon was sailing serenely across the night sky.

But Phyllida did not feel at all serene. She was on edge, nervous. She could not relax. Richard's eyes were on her, she sensed that he was watching her every move. It was unsettling, and strangely arousing. Her lips and her breasts felt full, ripe as the berries they had picked together so recently. When the tea tray was brought in and she carried his cup to him the merest touch of their fingers heated her blood. She turned away quickly but her spine tingled with anticipation.

Ellen and Julia were yawning and as soon as they retired she followed them, glad to be away from Richard's unnerving presence, but she could not forget him. He dominated her thoughts. She went to bed and tried to read, but the flickering candle made the print dance before her eyes and instead of words she saw his face, felt those blue eyes boring into her. Even when she blew out the flame and settled down his image haunted her, achingly handsome in the dark evening coat that clung to his lithe figure and his smile that she found so hard to resist. She pushed the thoughts from her mind at last and drifted to sleep, only to dream of Sir Evelyn, her late husband. They were in the marital bed and she was listening to his breathing, knowing he was not sleeping. But then it was not her kindly husband beside her but Richard. He was turning, reaching for her, wanting her. Her hands clenched on her nightgown and she dragged it up, arching her body, ready to give herself to him.

Phyllida sat up, gasping. She felt hot, dizzy with the tumult of emotions swirling inside. Heavens how she wanted him, so much that he invaded her very dreams. She sank back, willing herself to be calm.

It was then that she heard a noise, the faint click of a door closing and the whisper of hasty footsteps past her room. Quickly she slipped out of bed and threw on her wrap.

'Matty?'

Quietly she opened the connecting door, but the soft regular breathing from the bed told her that the maid was sleeping. She crossed the dressing room and went into Ellen's chamber. A square of moonlit sky at the window offered sufficient light for Phyllida to see that the room was empty.

Alarm shook her. She hurtled out into the corridor, just in time to see a tantalising glimpse of billowing skirts disappearing around the corner. She followed, but when she reached the gallery she could see no one. Something caught her eye and she strained her eyes to peer across to the opposite landing where she thought she saw a figure, a shape, dim and ghostly, fading into the black-shadowed void of the passage. Picking up her skirts, she dashed around the landing and into that far corridor. Above the thundering of her heart she heard a stifled giggle but when she turned the corner the corridor was empty. Phyllida was alone. She bit her lip and looked at the doors. One of these rooms was Richard's, Sophia had told her so, hoping its distance from the guest chambers would reassure her.

Silently Phyllida moved forward, straining her ears to listen. Nothing. Then she noticed the faint line of light beneath the second door. Someone was not asleep. She crept towards the door, a board creaked within the room and then she heard the faint but unmistakable sound of girlish laughter. Ellen's laughter.

She had prayed she was wrong but now rage, dismay and hurt consumed Phyllida. In a fury she grasped the door handle and stormed into the room.

'Ellen, you will leave here this min—'

Her words trailed away. A single candle burned beside the bed, which was empty. Richard was standing by the open window, but there was no sign of Ellen. The door swung shut behind Phyllida but she barely noticed, for her eyes were fixed on Richard.

He was exactly as she would expect a rake to look, his hair a little wild, dark and gleaming in the candle-light, coat and waistcoat removed, his unrestrained shirt flowing in full and sumptuous folds over his powerful torso and unbuttoned to display the dark shadow of hair on his chest. The width of his shoulders and upper body was enhanced by the tight breeches that encased his thighs. He looked tall, powerful, masculine. Irresistible. No wonder Ellen had fallen in love with him.

Phyllida marched forward and looked all around the

bed, expecting to find the girl hiding in the shadows on the floor.

'Where is she?' she demanded angrily. 'Where is Ellen?'

'She is not in here.'

Phyllida glared at him. 'Do not lie to me, I heard her—'

He reached out and caught her arm, pulling her closer. At the same time she heard another stifled giggle.

'There,' he ground out, turning her towards the window. 'There is your precious stepdaughter.'

Phyllida stared. Moonlight flooded the gardens and illuminated two pale figures. Julia and Ellen were dancing in the fountain. Richard's hands tightened on her shoulders.

'If you had walked on a little further you would have seen that there are backstairs at the end of this passage, leading to a garden door.'

'Oh. I thought…I thought…'

'I know exactly what you thought,' he flashed, his words harsh and bitter, 'The very worst of me!'

The shock of relief had not quenched Phyllida's outrage. It surged up, relentless, like fat on a fire, fuelled even more by her own feelings of guilt and remorse. The cool, reasonable façade she had kept up for so long shattered and she turned upon Richard like a wildcat.

'And why not? Have you not given me reason to think the worst of you? "Let battle commence", you said.'

'And have I not shown you since then that I did not mean it?'

She gave a savage laugh. 'A few weeks of good behaviour!'

Impatiently he dragged her away from the window and she found herself pinned against the heavily carved bedpost.

'Hush! Do you want to draw their attention to us? Remember where you are, madam!'

She remembered.

She was in Richard Arrandale's bedroom, something she had dreamed of, wished for, but had thought could never happen. But he had *not* enticed Ellen there and the hot blue fire sparking in his eyes was not only anger, but passion, too. And desire. She saw it, recognised it and felt it stir her already heated blood. He wanted her. She had put her hands against his chest to steady herself. Now she slid them upwards, wound them around his neck as she reached up and kissed him. There was no reasoning, just an overwhelming need to taste him, to blot out the aching loneliness that was life without him.

His response was immediate. He crushed her to him and returned her kiss savagely. She parted her lips, giving him back kiss for kiss, revelling in the hot, sensuous tangling of her tongue with his. He drew back a little and she nipped his lip. He groaned against her mouth, sending her dizzied senses flying still higher. His hands moved to her shoulders and he pushed at their silk covering. Quickly she shrugged it off and the wrap fell to the floor with a whisper. Richard's mouth shifted away from her lips to kiss her jaw, moving on to the tender spot beneath her chin and then down towards her breast, leaving a burning trail in its wake.

The ribbon ties of her nightrail snapped easily beneath his fingers and he cupped one breast in his hand. Phyllida gasped as his thumb circled the hard nub, but the pleasure only increased when his mouth covered its twin. Her head went back and she moaned softly. Her heart was thundering, making it hard to breathe, but just as she thought she might swoon Richard gathered her up, swept her into his arms and laid her gently on the bed.

She cupped his face, feeling the rough stubble against her palms. He kissed her, his hands fumbling with the fastening of his breeches. His urgency excited her. During her marriage the couplings with her husband had been slow, measured and unexciting. Now she felt a breathless, frantic need to have Richard's skin press against her own. She sat up and clutched at his shirt, dragging it up and over his head. She paused to gaze in wonder at his naked chest, the muscled contours shadowed and exaggerated by the single candle's flame. Richard moved away from her to shed his breeches and stockings and impatiently she threw off her nightrail.

Richard stood beside the bed, looking down at Phyllida. She had fallen back against the covers, her creamy breasts rising and falling with every ragged breath. Her naked body lay open and inviting, her eyes dark, molten with desire. He was aroused, taut as a wire and his jaw clenched when she reached out and ran her fingers over his erection. By sheer force of will he held off from throwing himself upon her and sating his lust there and then. He wanted to satisfy the yearning he sensed in her. To bind her to him for ever. He stretched himself beside her, cradled her cheek as he moved closer for another long, lingering kiss. Her body arched against him as he ran his fingers down her side, dipping into the valley of her waist, caressing the swell of her hips, revelling in the silky smoothness of her skin.

Fierce exultation ran through Phyllida. She felt glorious, all-powerful, her body thrummed with wild anticipation. His fingers were moving with slow deliberation over her body and she trembled as they edged towards her core. Then, even as his tongue flickered between her parted lips she felt his fingers slip inside her. Instantly her body reacted, arching, clenching. She felt as if she was flying, soaring high and free. She broke away from his kiss, moaning. The pleasure was almost unbearable, but those gentle fingers continued their inexorable rhythm. Her body was no longer hers to command, it moved against his hand. Her skin tingled, heat flooded her in a shimmering wave yet still he did not stop. The surge that had been mounting inside her suddenly broke. She bucked, cried out. Richard stifled her scream with his mouth and at the same time he moved over her and she felt the ultimate triumph as he entered her, matching her bucking rhythm as he drove her to the edge of oblivion and beyond.

Phyllida opened her eyes. It was still dark but she heard the crow of a cockerel, so dawn must be approaching. The birth of a new day, and she felt reborn, too. She had shared such pleasure with Richard as had only been hinted at in her marriage bed. It was all so new and exciting. Frightening. She needed to think. Silently she slipped from the bed.

Richard stirred and his hand reached out, only to find the bed beside him was empty and cold. He opened his eyes to the grey light of the breaking dawn. Phyllida was standing by the open window, slightly to one side, in the shadows, where she could look out without being seen. Desire surged through him at the sight of her. She had put on her wrap but it did little to disguise the curve of her body, the firm breasts, tiny waist and those long, long legs that had wrapped around him as he drove into her, pleasuring her, he hoped, as much as himself. His body began to stir again and he shifted restlessly. She turned then, as if aware that he was awake, but instead of the serene smile he expected her face was pale, the eyes solemn.

'What is it?' He sat up. 'What is wrong?'

To his relief the shadowed look fled.

'Nothing. That is, Ellen—'

'You need not worry about Ellen. She is safe enough. As soon as I saw her and Julia Wakefield in the gardens last night I sent word to Sophia's dresser. Duffy will have scolded them back indoors when she thought it was time. She is quite used to doing so, you know. She often had to chase after Lady Cassandra.'

Phyllida's smile was a little forced.

'I fear I have not acted as befits a chaperon.'

'You are too young to be a chaperon. I have always thought so.' He put out his hand. 'Come back to bed.'

'I should go.' But she was moving towards him.

'Not yet.' He pulled her on to the bed beside him, wrapping his arms around her. She melted against him, raising her face for his kiss and returning it with a passion. He murmured against her hair, 'It is still early, no one is yet abroad.'

She laughed, a soft, throaty sound that made his heart race, but she struggled in his arms and immediately he let her go.

'The servants will be rising soon and I dare not risk being seen. Think of the scandal.'

He cared nothing for that, but he knew it mattered very much to her.

'Very well,' he said. 'Leave me, if you must.'

She nodded but as she moved away from him he caught her hand, pressing a kiss into the palm. Looking up, he saw the glow in her eyes, the shy smile that curved her lips but still she disengaged herself and glided away from him. He propped himself on one elbow and watched as she slipped out of the door, closing it almost silently behind her.

Richard rolled onto his back and put his hands behind his head, smiling. She had felt so good in his arms, so right. He could not wait to have her there again, to awake that smouldering desire and make her cry out for him once more, but he would not rush her. The trust she had in him was fragile and he must take care not to break it. The feeling of well-being intensified: he could afford to be patient, they had the rest of their lives to enjoy each other. Richard blinked, realising that it was not a brief affair that he envisaged, but a lifelong commitment. Marriage.

It was a shock, but he suddenly knew that he wanted to abandon his wayward life, to forgo the bustle of London and spend more time at Brookthorn, looking after his property. A shaky laugh escaped him.

'By God you are ready to settle down.'

But only if Phyllida was beside him, only if he could wake up every morning to find her in his bed, her hair spread over the pillow in wild abandon and those greeny-grey eyes dark with desire. With love. He needed her to love him as he loved her.

Richard turned and pulled the bedcovers over him, but it was not the cold of the morning air that made him shiver, it was the tiniest whisper of doubt that Phyllida might not accept his proposal. She was no lightskirt, no wanton woman, and their lovemaking last night would have meant a great deal to her, but he could not forget the shadow he had seen in her eyes. She was a woman of principle, and it was just possible that his reputation was too much for her. The thought that he might lose her, even now, chilled him to the bone. He contemplated going after her immediately, asking her now if she would marry him, but already there were faint sounds from below. The house was stirring. He must wait, do the thing properly with no breath of scandal.

He heard a faint scratching at the door and his heart leaped when he thought Phyllida had returned, but the sudden elation evaporated quickly enough as he heard his valet's soft voice asking if he was awake.

'Come in, Fritt.'

'I beg your pardon for disturbing you so early, sir, but Collins has sent word, asking if you could go to the stables.' Immediately Richard was on the alert and he was reaching for his clothes as the valet continued. 'They have apprehended an intruder in the grounds, sir.'

Richard made his way to the stable block, turning without hesitation towards the buildings furthest from the house, where no horses had been kept for many years. Inside he found Collins and two of the men he had hired to patrol the grounds. They were standing watch over a man dressed in rough country garb. He was seated on a stool, his hands bound behind his back.

'Found this fellow prowling in the gardens,' the groom explained. 'He tried telling us he worked on the estate, but we'd made ourselves acquainted with all her ladyship's people soon as we got here, so we knew that weren't the case.'

Richard stared hard at the man.

'Well, who are you and what are you doing here?'

When his question elicited nothing more than a vicious glare Richard shrugged. 'Very well. Collins, take him to the magistrate, and take along a brace of pheasant.'

'I ain't no poacher!'

The groom grunted with satisfaction. 'Then if you don't want to hang you'd better tell us what you was doing prowling around the gardens, my lad.'

The fellow licked his lips and looked nervously from the groom to Richard.

'I ain't done nothing wrong.'

'You are Sir Charles Urmston's man, are you not?' barked Richard.

'What if I am?'

'And what were you doing in the grounds?' Richard's eyes narrowed. 'Would you prefer to take your chances with the magistrate? If you are lucky you may get off with transportation—'

'Sir Charles brought me here.'

The reply was swift, and once he started talking the words came tumbling out.

'We followed you from Bath. He's been dropping me off at the edge of the park each morning. He said I was to look out for a yellow-haired chit. He'd pointed her out to me in Bath, so's I'd know who she was. Sir Charles couldn't come into the grounds himself, you might have recognised him, but he said if anyone saw me I was to say I was one of the dowager's tenants.'

'And what were you to do when you found the lady?'

'I was to take her to him. He's waiting in his carriage on the Salisbury Road.'

Richard strode out across the park, making directly for the point where the main road to Salisbury ran close to the palings. He was relieved Urmston had not set his servant to prowl the grounds during the night. He might well have evaded Richard's guards and come across the girls playing in the fountain, and if Ellen had been snatched away in the dark it would have been almost impossible to find her. His mouth tightened as he thought of Phyllida's distress if that had happened. Well, today was Michaelmas. If he could keep the girl safe until midnight then the damned wager would be over.

Not that that would be the end of it. Ellen Tatham was still an heiress and a beautiful one at that. He had no doubt she would be pursued by any number of men and it would fall to her stepmother to look after her until she could be safely married off. A rueful grin tugged at his mouth. It would seem he was not only prepared to take on a wife, but a full-grown daughter, too. Before he had come to Bath the idea would have appalled him, now he found himself looking forward to it.

His amusement died away as he neared the edge of the park. The trees and bushes grew thickly here, providing for the most part a dense barrier between the grounds and the road, but there was a definite track meandering through the bushes. No doubt this was the point used by the daily staff to make their way to and from the lodge. Soon he could see the highway, and a carriage drawn up at the roadside. Richard approached cautiously. A coachman and guard were sitting up on the box but a caped figure stood behind the carriage, pacing restlessly to and fro. Screened by the bushes, Richard moved along and stepped out into the road just as the man was at the furthest point from the carriage.

'What the—?'

'Good day to you, Sir Charles.'

Urmston's face registered surprise, anger and disappointment before he recollected himself.

'Arrandale. I, um…'

'You are waiting for your henchman to bring Ellen Tatham to you,' suggested Richard.

'How perceptive of you.' Urmston's thin lips curved

into an unpleasant smile. 'I take it you have foiled my little plan.'

'I have. I suspected you might try something like this. Your man is even now on his way to Salisbury in the soil cart. You may collect him from there.'

Urmston's face darkened.

'Devil take you, Arrandale, you have stolen the march on us all.'

'It would seem so,' replied Richard, unmoved.

'You have the heiress here all right and tight and mean to have her for yourself. Very clever, using Lady Hune to befriend the heiress and her stepmother.'

'It was certainly an advantage.'

'You are a cunning devil, Arrandale. I suppose you plan to seduce the wench under Lady Phyllida's nose. Or have you already done so?'

Richard's lip curled. Let him think what he liked, the truth would be out soon enough, but he could not resist one final twist of the knife.

'You shall hear all about it tomorrow when I return to Bath to collect my reward.' He grinned at the thought: not ten thousand pounds, but Phyllida's hand in marriage. Sir Charles was glaring at him, chewing his lip in frustration. Richard laughed. 'Admit yourself beaten, Urmston. Off you go to Salisbury to find your lackey, and leave me to enjoy my victory.'

Sir Charles stood for a moment, undecided, then with a final, vicious, 'Damn you Arrandale!' he turned on his heel and strode to his carriage, barking orders to his coachman.

Richard watched the carriage drive off. Another hurdle overcome, but he would keep his men on the alert, just in case. It would not do to let down his guard now, not when everything was working out so well. Smiling, he turned to retrace his steps, only to find an outraged figure on the road behind him.

'Phyllida!'

Chapter Thirteen

'You—you *rogue*! You scoundrel.'

'Oh, lord, you were not meant to hear any of that.'

'Obviously not.' She was pale and shaking with anger. 'You have been making May game of me.'

'No!' Richard ran after her as she turned on her heel and almost ran back into the park grounds. 'Phyllida, listen to me.'

He touched her arm but she shook him off.

'I have listened to you far too much. Never again.'

'I have no intention of harming Ellen. You know that.'

She stopped and fixed him with a look of burning reproach.

'I know nothing of the kind. You and your...your *sort*, you will stop at nothing for your pleasures, I am well aware of that. I should never have trusted you, but I was weak, and as guilty as you last night.'

'Last night was not planned, but when you came to my room—how could any man resist you?'

Her chin went up. 'Easily.' Her voice trembled. 'I know I am no beauty, I have been told often that I was fortunate to find a husband, let alone such a good one as Sir Evelyn.'

'Stop it!' He caught her arms, frowning. 'You *are* beautiful. And desirable. I have wanted you for weeks now, you know that.'

She tore herself free.

'You want any woman who crosses your path,' she hissed. 'You are a *rake*. That is what they do. But you shall not have Ellen, not for your precious wager, not ever.'

'I do not want Ellen. Phyllida, it is you I want. I love you.' The words were out before he could stop them. So much for caution, for taking his time and earning her trust. He caught her hands and dropped to one knee, saying with a reckless laugh, 'My darling girl, will you marry me?'

Thus the practised rake made his first proposal of marriage. Even to his own ears it sounded awkward and insincere. Phyllida's cheeks, at first red, now turned white with rage.

'How dare you laugh at me?' She snatched her hands away.

'I am not laughing at you. I am very much in earnest. Blister it, I should be in a pickle if I went around proposing to ladies without meaning it. What if one of them accepted me?'

Richard jumped to his feet. Good God, what had happened to his wits? Where was his fabled charm? He was making a bad situation worse! Phyllida was staring at him as if he had run mad.

'You need not be anxious about it on this occasion,' she threw at him. 'Oh, *what* a fool I have been. How easy a conquest. From the start you have tried to win my approval. From the very first time you came to Charles Street, *pretending* to remember that we had danced together at Almack's. You knew it was very likely to have happened, since we were in town at the same time.'

'Yes, it was a lucky guess,' he admitted. 'But I recalled it later.'

You witless fool!

Richard cursed. It was as if he was standing outside his own body, watching himself do everything he could to turn Phyllida against him.

'Oh, I am sure you did.' Her scathing tone told him clearly she did not believe him. 'No doubt you remember every plain, tongue-tied débutante you have been obliged to stand up with.' She started towards the house again, saying bitterly, 'Oh, you were very clever, Mr Arrandale. You knew I was suspicious so you never overtly courted Ellen, instead you made a friend of her and pretended to be concerned for her safety.'

'I *am* concerned for it. I even sent extra men down here knowing that someone was likely to make a final bid to seduce her.'

'You were protecting your investment. No doubt it amused you to keep the wager going to the very last minute, to wait to make your move on Ellen until today, Michaelmas itself.' She stopped again, dashing away a tear. 'And when I presented myself in your room last night, you could not resist the opportunity to add the chaperon to your list of conquests.'

'There is no list!' he retorted. 'Phyllida, I have not looked at another woman since I came to Bath, only you.' He grabbed her shoulders. 'I will show you!'

He dragged her into his arms and kissed her. It was a savage, angry kiss and she stood perfectly still, like a rock against his onslaught. At last he let her go, his breathing ragged and laboured.

Her eyes blazed at him, darts of green fire that accentuated her deathly white face. Slowly she raised her hand and drew the back of it across her lips, as if to wipe away the taste of him.

'What does that show me, except that you are practised in the arts of the libertine.' She uttered the words with a slow, icy deliberation. 'I know your true self now, Richard Arrandale, you shall not beguile me again with your rakish charm.'

She turned on her heel and walked away from him, rigid with fury, head held high, and Richard watched her go.

He had lost her.

As soon as she reached the house Phyllida went in search of her hostess, to inform her that she and Ellen were leaving.

Lady Hune was all concern.

'My dear, will you not wait until tomorrow, then we may all travel back to Bath together.'

'I am very sorry, ma'am, but it is impossible. We cannot stay.'

'Will you not tell me why you must go?' Her sharp eyes were searching. 'It has something to do with Richard, does it not?'

Phyllida fought with her conscience, but she could not lie.

'Forgive me, I do not consider you responsible for your great-nephew's actions, ma'am, I know you hold him in esteem and think him misunderstood, but I do not—cannot—share your opinion of him. He has deceived me most grievously. He contrived this whole visit as an elaborate charade to seduce Ellen.'

'And has he succeeded?'

'No.' Phyllida bit her lip. She could not bring herself

to admit her own weakness. 'But there is still time, if we remain here,' she continued. 'He knows now that I would forbid the banns, but even so, there is ten thousand pounds to be won just for…for ruining my stepdaughter. A man would have to be a saint to forgo such a sum.'

And Richard Arrandale had proved himself to be no saint.

For a long moment Sophia did not speak.

'I find it hard to believe that Richard has deceived me so completely,' she said at last. 'I cannot believe it.'

'I do not ask it of you, ma'am. Just as I would never ask you to choose between a friend—and I do count myself as your friend—and a family member. That is why Ellen and I must leave.'

'Have you told her yet?'

Phyllida sighed. 'No, but I must do so without delay. If you will be good enough to order the carriage, we will pack immediately.'

'Of course. I hope our acquaintance can continue, my dear. I value your friendship.'

'And I yours, Lady Hune, but I fear it will be difficult, while your great-nephew is in Bath.'

'I live in hope that it is all some misunderstanding.'

'Oh, my dear ma'am…' Phyllida tried to blink away the threatening tears '…you do not know how much I wish it could be!'

She left the room quickly and Sophia rang for her butler. She gave him precise instructions for the travelling carriage to be prepared for Lady Phyllida and asked him to send her great-nephew to her. Croft returned in a very few minutes with the news that Mr Arrandale was nowhere to be found.

'His man thinks he might be in the park, my lady,' Croft offered.

Sophia nodded. 'Very well, that will be all. Send Mr Arrandale to me as soon as he comes in.' She added, when the door had closed behind her servant, 'I do not know what he is about, but I fear he has made a mull of it.'

It was not to be expected that Ellen would submit quietly to the news that they were leaving, but Phyllida's clear distress kept her from protesting too much. They returned to Bath in one carriage, which meant that Matlock travelled with them, but even when the maid fell asleep Ellen forbore to press Phyllida for her reasons for leaving Shrewton so suddenly.

Phyllida was thankful for the respite. She knew it was time to tell Ellen the whole story of Richard's perfidious actions, and she was not looking forward to it. She tried to sleep in the carriage, but when she closed her eyes she could not stop the memory of that final kiss from intruding. It had taken every ounce of willpower for her to remain unmoved. Her body had screamed to respond and if he had not released her when he did she thought she might well have surrendered, even though she knew it was wrong, even though she knew he was making a fool of her. It was that knowledge that had given her the strength to walk away from him.

It was raining when they reached Bath and the chill dampness in the air announced that summer was finally over. Hirst was surprised to see them return a day early, but being an excellent servant he soon had the candles burning in the main rooms and a cheerful fire blazing in the drawing room. It was here, after dinner and sitting in the comfortably cushioned chairs flanking the hearth that Ellen finally demanded to know the truth and Phyllida told her everything. Well, nearly everything. She stopped short of revealing that she had spent the night in Richard's bed.

Ellen was remarkably unmoved.

'I knew about the wager,' she told Phyllida. 'I heard a rumour and Richard confirmed it to me, but you have it wrong, Philly. Richard was doing his best to protect me.'

'He was saving you for himself, Ellen.'

'I do not believe it for a moment. We are friends, that is all, and he knows I have no intention of marrying for a long time yet.'

'It is part of his charm that he is so very…likeable,' said Phyllida, pleating the folds of her skirt between her fingers. 'He draws one in, puts one at ease. When you are with him it is as if you are the only person in the world who matters.'

Ellen looked at her closely.

'You are in love with him.'

'I am not!'

Phyllida's cheeks flamed, giving the lie to her words, and Ellen clapped her hands.

'Oh, by all that is famous, I knew it! How I shall tease Richard when I see him.'

'You will not see him. I forbid you to see or speak to Mr Arrandale again. And in fact, we shall not be in Bath much longer. We are going to Tatham Park.'

'But why? The wager is over, there can be no danger now, and the Bath season is about to begin.'

'The idea of coming here was to give you a taste of society. You have had that, even before the season, so we shall return to Tatham. It is only for the winter months. I am sure Bath in the dead of winter cannot be so very entertaining.'

'It will be more so than Tatham,' Ellen retorted. 'You

said yourself you were bored to screaming point when you were there.'

'But that was because I was in deep mourning, and I was there alone. This time we shall have each other, and…and we will be able to dine with our friends there, and attend the local assemblies.'

She expected Ellen to point out that all her particular friends had moved away but instead she merely asked how soon they were leaving Bath.

'It is Friday tomorrow, a day or so to pack up…I think we can be away on Monday.'

'No!' Ellen flew out of her chair and dropped to her knees before Phyllida. 'There are preparations to be made, packing to be done. The house at Tatham will need to be opened and made ready for us.'

'That can all be done in a trice.'

'No, no—' Ellen shook her head vehemently '—we have friends here, we must take leave of them.'

'We may write notes to them. That can be done in a morning. If it were possible I would be away from here before Lady Hune's party returns—'

'That *would* set everyone gossiping. They are bound to discover we left Shrewton a day early and if we fly from Bath in such a hurried manner it will be assumed we have something to hide.'

Phyllida bit her lip. Ellen was right, and the most likely guess would be that Richard had seduced Ellen. Not that she cared a jot for Richard's reputation, of course, but Ellen's good name must not be questioned.

'There is also the sketching party,' Ellen continued, sensing victory. 'Lady Wakefield has invited me to go with them to Beechen Hill next week. On Wednesday, if the weather permits, and I would dearly like a sketch of Bath to remind me of my stay here.' She caught Phyllida's hands and squeezed them. 'Do say we may stay for that, Philly dearest. We would then have time to order some new winter gowns. And to take a proper leave of all our friends.'

Phyllida felt herself weakening. She was relieved by Ellen's acceptance of the situation. She had been braced for tears, even tantrums and even another full week in Bath was a small price to pay to reward her stepdaughter's co-operation.

'Very well, we will delay our departure until Thursday.' A sudden gust of wind sent the rain pattering against the window and she added, 'But if the sketching outing is postponed for inclement weather you must give up the idea. I shall not stay longer.'

'No, of course not, dearest Stepmama.'

Ellen jumped up, smiling. Her blue eyes were glowing as if they had been discussing a special treat rather than their imminent withdrawal to the country. Phyllida frowned, but before she could speak Ellen gave a yawn.

'Goodness, the journey has made me very tired. I think I shall go to bed.' She bent and hugged Phyllida. 'Goodnight, Philly, my love. Sleep well, and do not be too unhappy. Everything will work out for the best, you will see.'

Phyllida returned her embrace and wished her a goodnight, too exhausted to question Ellen's words or her behaviour.

The continuing dank, dismal weather of the next few days mirrored Phyllida's spirits as she made her preparations to leave Bath. She gave strict instructions that Mr Arrandale was on no account to be admitted, should he call at Charles Street. That he was still in Bath she learned from his great-aunt when they met in the Pump

Room a few days later. Phyllida was determined not to mention his name, but Ellen was not so reticent.

'Yes, he is staying with me a little longer,' said Lady Hune, in response to Ellen's direct enquiry. 'Richard has given me his word he will remain until the doctor tells him I am well enough to live alone, and since my doctor is out of town he must kick his heels in Bath a few more days. There is nothing wrong with me,' she added quickly, observing Phyllida's look of concern. 'It is merely that the trip to Shrewton Lodge was more tiring than I anticipated.'

'I am so sorry you had to put yourself to such trouble for us all,' said Phyllida quickly.

'It was merely that I am unused to so much travelling in such a short time. The visit itself was delightful. I am only sorry you felt it necessary to leave so precipitately.'

'Yes, so was I,' put in Ellen. 'Especially when you and I were getting along so famously, ma'am.'

'Ellen!' Phyllida frowned at her stepdaughter's forthright speech.

'Do not scold her, Lady Phyllida, I enjoy Miss Tatham's company, she cheers me up.' The dowager's attention was claimed by another acquaintance and as Lady Wakefield arrived in the Pump Room at that moment, Phyllida carried Ellen off to talk to Julia. They had not met since Phyllida's departure from Shrewton and the girls soon had their heads together. Phyllida took the opportunity to inform Lady Wakefield of her plans to leave Bath.

'We shall be sorry to lose you, of course,' returned that lady. 'But I am not surprised, it is clear something has upset you.' She patted Phyllida's arm. 'Do not worry, my dear, I do not mean to pry, although I can guess that you have had some sort of falling out with Mr Arrandale.'

Phyllida could not prevent herself from saying bitterly, 'I am not convinced he is so innocent as everyone seems to believe.'

'Truly? I know he has a fearsome reputation, but he has been behaving himself in Bath.' A sudden inquisitorial gleam came into Lady Wakefield's eye. 'Or am I mistaken?'

Phyllida felt the betraying blush rising through her body. She said hastily, 'He was involved in the wager to seduce Ellen.'

'That is very bad, of course. I cannot understand why gentlemen must act so reprehensibly. It does make it very hard for those of us with daughters to look after. However, I believe he is regretting his rash behaviour, and we have certainly seen nothing of it. Indeed, Adrian informs me Mr Arrandale has turned over a new leaf.'

Phyllida shook her head. 'I do not believe in repentant rakes,' she muttered darkly.

'How soon do you intend to leave?' asked Lady Wakefield.

'Thursday at the earliest,' said Phyllida. 'Ellen persuaded me to allow her to stay for your sketching party to Beechen Hill on Wednesday.'

'Really? I do not recall setting a day for it, but no doubt the girls have arranged it between themselves.'

Lady Wakefield glanced up, smiling as an elderly matron came up to speak to her and Phyllida moved on. The Pump Room was crowded with her acquaintances and she would use this opportunity to take her leave of them. Ellen remained with Julia, but Phyllida was not concerned for her. Richard Arrandale was not in the Pump Room. In fact none of the gentlemen whose attentions to Ellen had been so marked were in evidence, which convinced Phyllida that they had all been party to that horrid wager. Thankfully Ellen did not appear worried to have lost the majority of her suitors and Phyllida was now happy for her to go off with her friends.

When it was time to leave Phyllida found her step-daughter sitting beside the marchioness. They were deep in conversation but they broke off as she approached.

'Well, now,' she said, forcing a smile, 'what is this talk of bishops, Lady Hune? Is my stepdaughter show-ing a healthy interest in religion?'

'I regret not,' replied Sophia. 'She has an *unhealthy* interest in special licences.'

'I wondered how easy it was to obtain one,' said Ellen. 'One of my friends at Mrs Ackroyd's Academy ran off and was married by special licence.' She laughed. 'Do not look so concerned, Philly, Lady Hune has explained that the marriage would still not be legal without a guard-ian's permission, if the bride is underage. I promise you I am not thinking of one for myself.'

'You should not be thinking of such things at all,' re-torted Phyllida. 'Lady Hune must be shocked by your conversation.'

'Not at all,' Sophia assured her. 'I find Ellen very en-tertaining. I shall miss you both when you have gone to Tatham Park.'

They took their leave, and Phyllida felt a pang of re-gret that her friendship with the marchioness must be suspended, at least for the present.

The mood around the gaming table was very cheerful, which was not surprising, Richard thought. None of them had won the wager to seduce the heiress, and the agreement they had drawn up now meant that each of them would be getting back the majority of his stake. Burton himself had brought the betting book and his cash box and was even now counting out the money and taking a small commission for himself.

Sir Charles Urmston's voice made it heard above the general conversation.

'So Arrandale, the widow outfoxed you in the end.'

Richard instructed a hovering waiter to attend to a guttering candle before replying, 'It would appear so.'

'Miss Ellen Tatham and her reputation are unblemished and I hear the widow is taking her out of Bath at the end of the week.'

'Can you blame her?' declared George Cromby. 'Keeping an heiress out of harm's way must be an exhausting business. To be honest I am glad this damned affair is over. If my wife had got wind of it I should have been in the suds!'

'Nevertheless it grieves me to let a fortune go begging,' muttered Tesford. 'What say you, Urmston?'

'One should know when to admit defeat,' murmured Sir Charles. He shot a malevolent glance towards Richard. Neither man had spoken of their encounter at Shrewton but it was there, between them. It did not worry Richard. Urmston was a bully. He had a sharp tongue, but he was unlikely to cause any more damage.

'The gel is being presented next year,' said Cromby. 'You single gentlemen could go to London and try your luck there. It may prove easier in town.'

'I doubt it,' grumbled Fullingham. 'If Arrandale with all his famous charm couldn't win the chit in Bath I don't see any of us succeeding in London, where a host of more eligible suitors are likely to be pursuing her.'

'And the stepmother has proved herself a veritable

dragon,' drawled Urmston. 'Surprising for one who looks so insignificant.'

It was all that Richard could do to stay in his seat, but if he leapt to Phyllida's defence that would only rouse conjecture. No, he thought as he made his way back to Royal Crescent in the early hours of the morning, he had done enough damage to Phyllida. Best that he should stay well away in future. At least he had the best part of his thousand pounds back. That would go some way to the repairs needed at Brookthorn. If only he could get back there, but Sophia insisted she was not yet well enough for him to leave her. Most likely she was lonely, he concluded, but although he sympathised he knew he could not remain much longer. Bath held too many painful memories for him.

The following morning he tried to persuade his great-aunt again that she could do without him, only to be met with the same story. The journey from Shrewton had taken its toll and she was not yet recovered.

'And Phyllida's decision to quit Bath has overset me,' she continued. 'Do you tell me that has nothing to do with you, Richard?'

'I shall not tell you anything,' he replied, shying away from even thinking about it.

'Have you tried talking to her?'

'Phyllida does not believe in reformed rakes.'

'By heaven, boy, then you must persuade her!'

He put up his hand as if to ward off a blow.

'Sophia, please, do not continue with this. It does not concern you.'

'You are my family, Richard, of course it concerns me.' She stared at him for a moment, until his implacable look convinced her he was not to be moved. She sighed.

'Very well, I will not tease you more with it. But perhaps you will do a little errand for me? I have a book from the circulating library in Milsom Street and wonder if you will return it for me?'

'With pleasure, ma'am, but do you not wish to come with me? It is a fine day for a stroll.'

'Thank you, Richard, but, no. I shall wait here for your return.'

Richard set off immediately, pondering upon his great-aunt's health. Whingate was currently in the country but as soon as the doctor returned he would ask him to call. It was unlike Sophia to be so lacking in energy. It did not take Richard long to reach the library and his task was soon completed. He was turning to leave when he heard someone call his name.

'Miss Tatham!'

She beckoned him towards the shelves where she was standing. She drew a book from the row before her and, pretending to peruse it, said quietly, 'I have been waiting for you.'

Richard kept his distance. He picked up a book.

'This is not wise, Ellen,' he said warily. 'We should not be seen together.'

'Oh, fiddle, I know you have no designs upon me.'

'That is not the point.'

'How long do you stay in Bath?'

'Another week, no more. As soon as Whingate pronounces my great-aunt fit I shall leave.'

'Where will you go?'

'I do not know, and if I did I should not tell you,' he responded bluntly.

She pouted but did not pursue the matter. Instead she

said, 'I saw a man following me yesterday. Is he your creature?'

'Why, yes, although I doubt if there is a need for it now.'

'Oh, pray do not take him away just yet.'

His brows rose a little. That damned wager must have unsettled the girl more than he had realised.

'If you wish I will leave the men in place until you leave for Tatham Park.'

'Thank you. Phyllida would be overcome with grief if anything should happen to me.'

Richard barely noticed the blinding smile she gave him, his thoughts distracted by a stab of jealousy. Would Phyllida grieve if anything happened to him? He doubted it.

'I feel much safer knowing you are looking out for me,' murmured Ellen. She looked around. 'You had best go. I sent Matty off on an errand but she will return any moment and I would not have Phyllida know we had been speaking together.'

He could not help himself.

'How is your stepmama?'

Ellen gave him a thoughtful look.

'She is in very low spirits.'

Her words twisted like a knife, but he forced himself to say cheerfully, 'No doubt she will revive once she is back at Tatham.'

'I think she is more like to go into a decline.'

He said quickly. 'Why do you say that?'

Ellen gave him an innocent look.

'Oh, I do not know, but she has been quite out of spirits since we returned from Shrewton. I wonder why that should be?'

'I have no idea, Miss Tatham.' He lifted his hat. 'Good day to you.'

He hoped Sophia's doctor would give him a good report of her health when he returned at the end of the week. He needed to get out of Bath, whether to lose himself in the distractions of London or immerse himself in the business of restoring Brookthorn he did not care, as long as it helped him to forget Phyllida Tatham.

Phyllida carefully folded another gown and laid it on top of the clothes already packed into the trunk. Tomorrow they would set off for Tatham Park and everything must be in readiness. Matlock had offered to do the packing for her, but Phyllida had instructed her to accompany Ellen to Laura Place to join Lady Wakefield's sketching party. The invitation had included Phyllida but she had used the excuse of their imminent departure to cry off.

In truth she had no spirits for company and she knew Ellen would be perfectly safe with Lady Wakefield, who had assured her that no gentlemen would be accompanying them. It had been impossible to refuse all the invitations that had come in over the past week but Phyllida had accepted only those where she could be certain she would not meet Richard. Her plan had worked, she had not seen him, but he was there, in her mind, ready to fill her thoughts as soon as she let down her guard.

He crept in now as she laid the peach silk in the trunk. It was the gown she had worn to the Denhams' party. How her spirits had soared when she had danced with Richard. Her heart had beat so heavily it had almost drowned out the music, especially when he had smiled at her and she had felt her own smile spreading until it felt as if her whole face was beaming with delight. With an impatient huff she turned away from the trunk. What a simpleton she was and how he must have laughed at his easy conquest. Even then, with ample evidence to the contrary, she had been prepared to believe he was a good man.

But no more. At Shrewton Lodge he had shown his true colours, he had seduced her and shown no remorse. Instead he had laughed at her. Going down on one knee he had ridiculed her with actions that brought back memories of their one dance at Almack's and her foolish daydream that she might reform him. She had felt quite sick then, much as she had done when she was a girl, sitting on the benches while the gentlemen passed her over in favour of those who were prettier, livelier, richer...

Angrily Phyllida dashed away a tear. She was no longer that shy innocent girl but a woman of independent means with a stepdaughter to consider. She had been foolish enough to fall in love with Richard Arrandale, but she would not let that break her. Life would go on and she would survive her mistake. Her hands slid protectively across her stomach. Whatever the consequence of giving into her passion, she would survive.

Through the open door voices floated up from the hall below. Matty had returned and was even now coming upstairs. Quickly Phyllida wiped her cheeks. No one must know her weakness, the constant aching loneliness that filled her waking moments. It would pass. Pray heaven it would pass quickly.

She heard Matty's firm tread on the landing and prepared to greet her, but when the maid appeared she was far too distressed to notice Phyllida's forced cheerfulness. She burst out wildly,

'Oh, my lady, I've lost Miss Ellen!'

Chapter Fourteen

'What do you mean, you have lost her?'

Phyllida stared at Matlock, whose usually severe countenance was wild and ravaged by tears.

'Miss Ellen said she wanted to buy a little present for Miss Julia so we stopped in Milsom Street on the way to Lady Wakefield's, to buy some ribbons. Miss Ellen asked me to wait outside. Well I thought nothing of that, for there was her parasol to hold, and her sketchpad and pencils, and the shop was very crowded. So I waited, and when she didn't come out after ever such a long time I went in, but she wasn't there. The assistant said she thought Miss Ellen might have left by the side door, the one that comes out into the passage. I went on to Laura Place, thinking somehow I had misunderstood her. But she wasn't there, my lady. She had never arrived.'

'Oh, good heavens!' Phyllida put her hands to her cheeks but Matlock hadn't finished.

'The family had already set off for Beechen Hill. Lady Wakefield's butler told me they had received a note from Miss Ellen crying off from the sketching party.' Matty sank down on to a chair and pulled out her handkerchief. She said, between noisy sobs, 'Oh, my lady, I do fear Miss Ellen has run away.'

'I do not believe it,' declared Phyllida, but in her heart there was already a numbing chill when she recalled the fierce hug Ellen had bestowed upon her before setting off that morning. She ran into Ellen's room and her heart shrank into a hard icy block when she saw the note propped against the trinket box on the dressing table. With trembling hands she picked it up.

'Oh, my lady, what does she say?'

Matlock's shaking voice came from the doorway.

'It would seem you are right, Matty, she has run away. Eloped,' Phyllida replied calmly, but inside she was burning up. How had she missed the signs? Ellen had shown no preference for any of the gentlemen who clustered about her. Who had stolen her heart? Phyllida knew that only the deepest passion would have persuaded Ellen to take such a rash step. She closed her eyes.

Please, please let it not be Richard....

'I beg your pardon, ma'am, but Mr Arrandale is below, and insists upon speaking to you.' The butler's voice was like the answer to her silent prayer. 'I am very sorry, my lady, but I couldn't keep him out, leastways not without an unseemly scuffle on the doorstep, so I've put him in the morning room. If you like, I could fetch Patrick and the scullery boy to try to eject him...'

'No. Thank you, Hirst, I will go down to him.'

Pulling herself together, Phyllida followed the butler to the morning room, where she found Richard pacing the floor. Almost before Hirst had closed the door upon them he spoke.

'Did you know Ellen was going out of town today?'

She shook her head.

'She was engaged to join the Wakefields for a sketching party to Beechen Hill. Her maid has just returned to say Ellen gave her the slip in Milsom Street.'

His brow darkened still further.

'My man tells me he saw Ellen climbing into a travelling carriage at the White Hart. The blinds were drawn down so he could not see who else was in the carriage, but there was a quantity of luggage on the roof.'

Phyllida swayed. She put a hand out and gripped a chair back.

'So it is true. She has eloped.'

'This is no time for weakness, madam,' he said roughly. 'I have sent runners to find out which road they are taking. My curricle is outside, if you will allow me to drive you, we should be able to catch up with them before nightfall.'

His brusque tone steadied her. She could send a message to the stables for her own carriage, but that would take half an hour at the very least, and by that time who knew where they might be?

'Of course,' she said. 'You are right. There is no time to lose. I will fetch my cloak and bonnet.'

'Good girl. I shall wait for you outside. I told my people where to find me, if there was any news.'

Phyllida ran back up the stairs. She must keep her mind upon the task of finding Ellen. Questions about why Richard should be going to so much trouble could wait.

Minutes later she was heading out of the door, tying her cloak strings as she went. Richard was standing beside his curricle, talking to a soberly dressed man in a plain brown frockcoat. With a nod he dismissed the man and turned to hand Phyllida into the curricle.

'They were taking the London Road,' he said shortly. 'We can ask after them at the turnpikes.' He added, after a brief hesitation, 'I have not brought Collins, I thought you would prefer that we should travel alone.'

'Yes, thank you. The fewer people who know of this the better.'

They set off at a cracking pace. Phyllida clung on to the side of the curricle at first, until she grew accustomed to the speed.

'Tell me,' she said then. 'Who was that man?'

'One of those I hired to keep watch over Ellen. I apologise, I know I had no right to do so, but I wanted only to keep her safe. You cannot know how much I regret I did not prevent that damnable wager from ever taking place.'

Her hand fluttered. She said shortly, 'All that matters now is that we find them.'

Phyllida's worries about losing track of their quarry soon eased. At every turnpike the keeper recalled seeing the travelling carriage occupied by a fashionably dressed gentleman and a beautiful young lady in a pale-blue walking dress.

'At least we can be confident they are not heading to Gretna,' remarked Richard, setting his team in motion again after quizzing the pike keeper at Bathford.

'Nor London,' said Phyllida as they set off towards Melksham.

'No.' He frowned. 'That surprised me, for they might be expected to hide in town for weeks, certainly until they could persuade someone to marry them.'

'Perhaps this...this gentleman, whoever he is, has no thoughts of m-marriage.'

'From what I know of your stepdaughter I would not expect her to settle for anything less,' he retorted. 'What exactly did she say in her letter?'

Phyllida clasped her hands together hard and tried to stop her voice from shaking. 'That the task of protecting her was too much to ask of me. That she w-wanted to relieve me of the burden. I s-suppose she thinks a husband is the answer.'

Richard gave a crack of laughter. 'Heaven help the husband!'

Phyllida racked her brains, trying to think back for any clue, any sign she had missed that would have told her what Ellen was planning. With a gasp she clutched at his arm. 'Richard! She was talking to your great-aunt about a special licence. That means they only have to hide out somewhere for a week!'

'They would still have to convince a priest that she is of age. And even then the marriage would be illegal.'

'But the damage will have been done.' Phyllida bit her lip. 'She will be ruined. Oh, who can have persuaded her to embark upon this outrageous scheme? I would like to think it is a young man who truly loves Ellen, but I very much fear it is someone who has designs upon her fortune.'

'Someone like me, perhaps?'

She said quietly, 'I no longer think you want Ellen for her fortune.' It was true. His concern for Ellen argued that he cared a great deal for her. Her hands were locked together so tightly it was almost painful. 'My biggest worry is that it might be Sir Charles Urmston.'

'Urmston left Bath yesterday morning,' he told her. 'Let me put your mind at rest on one point, Phyllida. Whoever it may be, if he does not make Ellen happy then he shall answer to me. She shall not be tied to him, even if I have to make her a widow to prevent it.'

So there it was. Even through her anxiety for Ellen she could feel her heart breaking.

They continued in silence, until they reached the village of Atford, where the road forked. Richard pulled up outside the church. Phyllida looked at the diverging roads and beat her fist upon her skirts in frustration.

'Which way now?'

There was an ancient sitting on the low wall of the church grounds and Richard hailed him. A few moments' conversation elicited the information that a travelling carriage, heavily laden and travelling at speed, had driven through the village a short while earlier, on the Devizes road. As they set off again Richard glanced across at Phyllida. Her face was pale and strained and he reached out to put one hand over hers.

'Don't worry, we are closing on them.'

He felt her tremble and she said in a low voice, 'After this, sir, I c-cannot doubt your devotion to Ellen. If… if we can save her from this folly, and if she wants you, Richard, then I shall not stand in your way.'

'If she—' He broke off, requiring both hands and his concentration to control the team as they approached a bend. Once they were on the straight he declared, 'Confound it, Phyllida, what are you saying? Ellen does not look upon me as anything more than a friend. And it is certainly not Ellen I want.'

'How can you say that, when you have spent the past month pursuing her?'

'I put my name to that preposterous wager, but it did not take me long to realise I had made a mistake.' He glanced down at her. 'You have no confidence in your own charms, Phyllida!'

She sat up straight, wondering if she dare believe what she was hearing. Could he truly love her? There was no time to consider that now. They were driving into Melksham and her eyes alighted upon a dusty travelling carriage standing before a large coaching inn.

'There they are!'

Richard drew up behind the carriage and almost before they had come to a stand Phyllida jumped down and ran inside.

'Where are the occupants of that coach?' she demanded of the landlord, who was emerging from the noisy taproom. If he was surprised to be addressed so abruptly he did not show it, merely waved his hand towards a door at the far end of the corridor.

'In there, ma'am. It's a private parlour.'

With Richard hard on her heels Phyllida burst into the room, only to stop so quickly that Richard all but cannoned into her. She felt his hand on her shoulder, but whether it was to stop himself from colliding with her, or as support for the scene before them, she did not know.

Ellen, a picture in pale blue, was standing by the window and sitting in an armchair beside her was Lady Hune.

'You see,' declared Ellen, smiling, 'I told you they would come.'

Obedient to the pressure of the hand on her shoulder, Phyllida moved into the room. She heard Richard close the door behind them.

'Perhaps one of you would be good enough to explain what the *devil* is going on here?' she demanded angrily.

Ellen moved towards the table at the centre of the room, waving her hands towards the food and drink that covered its surface.

'Do sit down and take some refreshment with us,' she said. 'We made sure you would be hungry after your journey. And we deliberately ordered that the coach should be left outside and not be brought into the yard, so you really couldn't miss us.'

'I think, Lady Phyllida, that we have been duped,' remarked Richard. He guided Phyllida to a chair and gently pushed her down. 'And very neatly, too.'

Ellen beamed at him.

'I knew if you saw me running away you would go to Philly.'

'Do you mean there is no elopement?' said Phyllida. 'But what of the fashionable gentleman seen at the turn-pikes?'

'One of Lady Hune's footmen,' replied Ellen. 'It is surprising how easily people can be fooled by seeing a fashionable hat and coat upon a man.'

'And may I ask where you obtained this hat and coat?' asked Richard calmly.

He was sitting beside Phyllida at the table, holding her fingers in a sustaining grasp with one hand while with the other he filled two wineglasses. She herself could think of nothing to say. For the moment, relief at finding Ellen safe and well had replaced her anger.

'We borrowed those from your room,' explained the dowager. 'I am afraid I had to coerce your valet into agreeing to help us, but I do not think he was too reluctant, for you have been going around like a bear with a sore head for the past week.'

'And so will Fritt have a sore head, when I have finished with him,' he muttered. 'How *dare* he allow himself to be embroiled in your hare-brained scheme, Sophia!'

'Oh, pray do not blame Lady Hune,' said Ellen quickly. 'This was all my idea. Ever since we returned from Shrewton Lodge I have been trying to hit upon a way to get the two of you together. I was very much afraid that Phyllida and I would go off to Tatham and you, Richard, would return to London and take up your rakish life again.'

'Ellen!'

'I beg your pardon for my plain speaking, Philly, but it is true, and Lady Hune agreed with me. As Mrs Ackroyd says, desperate times call for desperate measures, and I knew if you thought I had eloped you would both come after me. I did think of running off with Mr Tesford or Mr Fullingham, but when I suggested it to Lady Hune she thought that would not be wise.'

'After what happened with Fullingham in the Denhams' garden I am very glad you didn't,' retorted Phyllida. A sip of the wine Richard had poured for her was having its effect and she was beginning to feel a little better.

'But then I was not prepared,' argued Ellen. 'This time I would have made sure I had my hatpin ready to use, if necessary. However, then Lady Hune suggested we should make it a sham elopement.'

'I fear we have shocked you, Lady Phyllida,' said Sophia, smiling a little.

'Nothing your family does could shock me,' retorted Phyllida bitterly. 'After all you are an Arrandale, ma'am, are you not?'

'I am, and proud of it. And I think Ellen will make a wonderful addition to the family—as Richard's stepdaughter, of course.'

Phyllida's breath caught in her throat. Richard was still holding one of her hands and she felt his fingers tighten.

'Lady Phyllida has not yet agreed to marry me.'

'But she will,' replied Lady Sophia. 'The two of you have been smelling of April and May for weeks. *I* think she could do better for herself, but if she wants to ally herself to an Arrandale you are amongst the best, Richard.'

He shook his head, saying unsteadily, 'Great-Aunt Sophia, your encomium almost unmans me.'

Phyllida's lips twitched as she met his eyes and saw the lurking laughter in his own.

'Damned with faint praise, I think.'

'Exactly.' He lifted her fingers and kissed them. 'So now you know what my family think of me, will you do me the honour of accepting my hand and my heart? Will you make an honest man of me?'

The world stood still, waiting for her answer. Phyllida knew Ellen and Sophia were holding their breath and she saw the hint of a shadow in Richard's smile, as if he too was uncertain. She smiled.

'Yes, I will accept your offer, Richard. Gladly, and with all my heart.'

A collective sigh went around the room. Phyllida kept her eyes on Richard's face, saw his smile deepen, the flash of fire in his eyes, the promise of desire that set her body tingling.

He pulled her close and kissed her lips. Sophia tutted and Ellen gave a little squeal of delight, but he ignored them both, murmuring for her alone, 'I will do my best to make sure you never have cause to regret it.'

'You may wish to use this.' Sophia's voice recalled them to their situation. She was holding up a paper. 'It is a special licence. The church and parson are waiting for you across the road. And we are not twenty miles from Shrewton. Since I went to all the trouble to make the Lodge ready for visitors you might wish to use it for your honeymoon. You need not worry about Ellen, Phyllida. I shall take her back to Royal Crescent with me and send for her maid to join us—after she has packed up your trunk and sent it on to Shrewton, of course. So there is no hurry for you both to return.'

Richard gave a crack of laughter.

'You have worked it all out between you, have you not?'

'Of course,' said Ellen, twinkling. 'I said when I came to Bath that we might find Philly a husband, although I was very much afraid she would set her heart on one of the dull, worthy kind.'

Lady Hune laughed. 'There is nothing dull or worthy about Richard!' She pushed herself out of her seat. 'Now, shall we go to the church?'

The wedding passed off without incident. Lady Hune had had the forethought to bring a wedding ring, a heavy plain band that she explained had belonged to some distant ancestor and if the reverend gentleman who conducted the service had any reservations he was far too in awe of a dowager marchioness in his church to voice them. Sophia carried Ellen back to Bath immediately after the ceremony, leaving Richard and his new bride to make their way to Shrewton Lodge.

'Happy?' he asked Phyllida as they bowled out of the town in the afternoon sunshine.

'Yes, of course. But it has all happened so fast.'

'I beg your pardon,' he said quickly. 'I have rushed you, I should have waited until we could arrange a more fitting wedding.'

'No, no,' she assured him. 'I have had one wedding with all the pomp and ceremony, I do not wish for another.'

'Truly?' He reached for her hand.

'Truly.' She smiled, 'But are you happy, Richard?'

'Happier than I can say. It has all worked out so well, especially for Sophia. Ellen has helped her to overcome her sadness at Cassie's elopement, and you have fulfilled her wish that I should become a respectable married man.' He squeezed her fingers. 'And I mean to be very respectable, my love!'

Her smile could not be contained. 'Do you? Now that *will* be a challenge!'

He grinned. 'Witch!' Richard returned both hands to the reins as he said cheerfully, 'Ellen will live with us, of course. Sophia is already hinting that she will come to London to help with her come-out next year. I hope you will not object to that?'

'No, no, not in the least! Oh, dear, I fear I should have thought of all these things before I married you.'

'How could you? When we set out this morning you had no idea that we were to be married. I hope you will not regret it, Phyllida. I shall do everything in my power to make you happy, I promise you.'

'I believe you will,' she murmured. She tucked her hand in his arm and rested her head on his shoulder. 'But life will be very different for you, too, my love.'

'I am looking forward to it,' he said. 'Marriage to you will go a long way to restoring my family's name.'

'I will help you to achieve that in any way I can.' She paused. 'What of Arrandale?'

'Until I have proof that Wolf is dead I must continue to maintain the house for his return. I am sorry to say it will limit my own funds, but we shall get by, with a little prudent management.'

'Of course we shall. And my money will help.'

'Ah, I had forgotten about that!'

'You do not sound very pleased.'

'I am not. Everyone will say I married you for your money.'

'Let them. You did not give it a thought, did you?'

'No, Sophia mentioned it, but—' Swearing under his

breath, Richard brought the curricle to a halt and turned to face her. He grabbed her shoulders. 'Do you not realise that you have married me without making any provision, any settlement to protect yourself?'

'How could I?' she said, turning his earlier words back upon him. 'When I set out this morning I did not know we were to be married.' She smiled and put one hand up to his cheek. 'I am content, my love. It is a measure of how much I trust you.'

Her fingers slipped around his neck and she gently pulled his head down until their lips met in a deep, lingering kiss that only ended when a mail coach rattled past and they heard the catcalls and whistles from the passengers.

They broke apart, Richard cursing under his breath as Phyllida hid her face in his shoulder.

'I beg your pardon.' His arm tightened protectively about her. 'I am a devil to expose you to such ribaldry—'

'No, no.' She raised her head, her countenance alight with laughter. 'I am not at all upset, I assure you. Was it so very bad?'

He grinned at her. 'Quite scandalous, my love.'

As they set off again she said thoughtfully, 'Well, I think it is possibly the most outrageous thing I have ever done in my life, but I suppose I shall have to get used to it, now I am an Arrandale.'

'Not at all. I intend that we shall be the very model of respectability.'

'What, all the time?'

Greatly daring, she placed her hand on his thigh and her heart raced when she heard his growled response.

'That might be a little too much to expect.'

Laughing, she settled down beside him for the drive to

Shrewton Lodge, where it was clear they were expected. The housekeeper was at the door to welcome them.

'We have no butler here, sir, Mr Croft having gone back to Bath with Lady Hune, but I think Hinton and I can manage.'

'I have no doubt of it,' replied Richard. 'You have always done a magnificent job in the past when I have come here to stay. You always spoil me.'

'Now give over, Master Richard,' protested Mrs Hinton, clearly pleased. 'We will do our best, as you well know. And I believe your groom and valet, and my lady's maid, will be joining you here before the day's out.'

'That is so,' agreed Richard. 'Which bedchamber have you prepared for us?'

'Lady Hune instructed that the Blue room should be prepared for you—'

'Then we shall go there directly and, er, rest.' He took Phyllida's hand and led her up the stairs.

'Richard we cannot disappear immediately!' hissed Phyllida, as soon as the housekeeper was out of earshot.

'Oh, yes, we can.' His grip on her hand tightened and he led her through the corridors to a large room that smelled of beeswax and lemons. 'The Hintons have clearly been busy here.'

Phyllida dropped her bonnet on a chair and moved towards the large canopied bed, running her hands over the hangings, rich blue silk embroidered with silver thread.

'It is quite beautiful.'

'No, *you* are beautiful.' Richard put his hands on her shoulders and turned her to face him. 'I saw it that very first time I danced with you at Almack's. I *do* remember it, I assure you.'

She shook her head.

'No, I was too shy and awkward.'

'At first, perhaps, but you were such a graceful dancer, and you have a goodness and sweetness of temper that give you an inner beauty.' He put his fingers under her chin and gently eased it up so she was obliged to meet his eyes. 'Since then you have gained in confidence. You now have elegance and poise, too. You are quite, quite perfect.'

He kissed her then, his blood stirring when she put her arms around his neck and returned his embrace, tangling her tongue with his own. He was aware of the change as her body pressed against him and she drove her hands through his hair, holding him to her. Impatience overcame them both, their kisses grew more heated and they began to scrabble at each other's clothes, tearing at buttons, strings and ribbons, shrugging off sleeves, shirts, gowns while continuing to share those frantic, excited kisses that set the body aflame.

At last they broke apart and Phyllida stared at Richard's naked torso, her mouth drying at the sight of the sculpted contours, the wide shoulders and narrowing waist, all she could see since the rest of his delicious body was still encased in buckskin breeches. She reached out for him, wanting to run her fingers through the dark smattering of hair that covered his chest but he caught her hand and spun her around.

'No,' he growled. 'Not until we have you out of those damned stays. '

She laughed then, a warm, guttural sound that was strange to her own ears. It sounded so...so confident, so powerful. She felt a slow vibration through her body as he pulled out the ribbons from the corset that confined her. He went slowly, drawing the ribbon out of each eyelet with infinite care, his fingers brushing against the fine linen shift beneath as he gradually released her from her cage of whalebone. Her skin tingled, she ached to be free, to turn and press herself against his body but he was intent on unlacing her completely. Unable to bear the wait, she gave a little sigh of exasperation.

'Can you not go any faster?'

'I could.' His mouth descended to her shoulder and he gave it a little nip. 'But there is no hurry.'

Her body told her differently, but she forced herself to keep still, felt the desire pooling in her belly, the growing ache between her thighs. She put back her head and moaned softly as he continued to unlace her while his mouth trailed a line of kisses down her neck. Then the stays were gone, but now his arms imprisoned her. His hands came around to cup her breasts, only the thin shift remained between their hot bodies. He pushed her forward slightly and she put out her hands to support herself on the bed.

'Stay there.'

Dazed, languorous with desire she remained there, staring at the patterned bedcover. She heard the soft scuffle as Richard shed his boots and buckskins and then he came close and removed her shift in one smooth movement. She almost swooned with excitement as she felt his naked body on her back, skin on skin. His hands came around her again, caressing her breasts, thumbs circling the dark peaks until they swelled and hardened while he pressed himself against her buttocks. He was kissing her neck, nipping and sucking, drawing from her soft moans of excitement. He moved one hand down, caressed her waist, smoothed over her hips and then his fingers slid between the soft curls at the apex of her thighs, seeking out her hot, aching core.

She gasped as her body responded.

'Richard—'

'Hush,' he murmured the word against her neck as he continued to kiss her, sending little darts of pleasure deep into her body.

'But I want to, to pleasure you, too.'

'And you shall, but this is for you. Trust me.'

I do!

She was leaning further over the bed while his fingers drove into her, teasing, drawing up the desire that flamed inside. It was rippling out from her core, she was no longer in control. Her hips pushed back towards him. Instinctively she was offering herself to him while all the time those tantalising fingers worked their magic. She felt herself opening, aching, and then as his fingers drew back he entered her, gently but inexorably filling her. She gave a joyful cry, then gasped as his fingers continued to play her, one hand circling and caressing her breast while the other stroked and teased to a frenzy the sensitive nub between her thighs.

She was crying out now, every measured thrust Richard made carrying her higher. She was flying, soaring. Unable to take him in her arms her body gripped him and they moved together in perfect harmony until the moment when his hands slid to her hips and he held her firm. She gave a tiny cry of triumph as he spent himself within her.

Exhausted, they crawled into the bed and Richard pulled the covers over them.

'Oh, I did not *know...*' she breathed as he took her into his arms. 'I would never have thought it could be so, so wonderful. Thank you.'

He laughed softy against her hair. 'It has never been like that for me before.' He sought her lips and kissed her. 'It must be because we are joined in love.'

'Is that it?' She cupped his cheek, gazing into the

face that was now so dear to her. She felt sated, joyously happy and she could not help teasing him. 'Do you think you can be happy then, as a respectable, married man?'

His eyes narrowed.

'We may look respectable to the rest of the world, madam wife, but here in the bedchamber I think we will be quite scandalous!'

The look he gave her sent the desire curling up inside her once more and she shivered with delicious anticipation.

She said innocently, 'But I thought you had reformed, sir.'

With a growl he reached out and pulled her to him and Phyllida gave herself up to the pleasurable task of discovering just how wrong she was.

* * * * *

TEMPTATION OF A
GOVERNESS

*To Kathryn, my lovely editor
and all the team at Richmond, without whom these books
would never happen.*

Chapter One

The April sun shone down brightly on the low-slung racing curricle as it bowled through the lanes and Alex Arrandale felt the winter gloom lifting from his spirits. A gloom that had settled and remained with him since he had heard of the shipwreck that had taken the life of his brother James and made him, Alex, the eighth Earl of Davenport. He had neither expected nor wanted the succession. James was only two years his senior and, at thirty, everyone had thought there was plenty of time for him and his countess to produce an heir. That was why the couple had set out on their sea journey, sailing south to warmer climes that the doctors advised might help improve Margaret's health and allow her to conceive and carry a boy child full-term. The couple already had a healthy little girl, but a series of miscarriages had left the countess very worn down.

They had never reached the Mediterranean, a storm off Gibraltar in October had run their ship aground and all lives had been lost. The news had reached Alex several weeks later and the depth of his grief had been profound. Even now, six months on, he still wore a black cravat as a sign of his loss. In all other aspects of his life his friends found him unchanged. He had spent the winter as he always did, at a succession of house parties where hunting, gambling and flirting were the order of the day. Only his closest friend saw anything amiss in his frantic pleasure-seeking.

'Everyone thinks it is because you do not care,' Mr Gervase Wollerton told him, in a moment of uncharacteristic perception. 'I think you care too much.'

Perhaps that was so, thought Alex as he slowed and turned his high-bred team of match greys through the gates leading to Chantreys, but he had been earl for a while now and it was time he made a few changes.

The drive curved between trees that were not yet in full leaf and sunlight dappled the track. Alex slowed, conscious that there might be holes and ruts after the winter. He was just emerging from the woods when he spotted a figure sitting on a fallen tree, not far from the side of the road. It was a young woman with a sketchbook. She had cast aside her bonnet and her red hair glinted with gold in the sunlight. He knew her immediately. He had not seen her for years but the red hair was unmistakable. It was Diana Grensham, sister of the drowned countess and governess to her only child and the other Arrandale waif who had been taken into the late earl's household. She was so engrossed in her work that she did not even notice his arrival. Alex drew his team to a halt and regarded her for a long moment, taking in the dainty figure clad in a serviceable gown of green and yellow and with her wild red hair gleaming about her head like a halo.

'Good afternoon, Miss Grensham.'

She looked up, regarding him with a clear, steady gaze. Her eyes, he noted, were unusual, nut brown but flecked with green and while she was no beauty her countenance was lively and her full mouth had an upward tilt, as if a smile was never far away.

'Afternoon?' Her voice was soft, musical and held a hint of laughter. 'Heavens, is it so late already?'

'You are not surprised to see me?'

She closed her sketchbook and rose to her feet.

'I knew you would come at some point, my lord,' she told him. 'It would have been better if you had given us notice, but I am sure Mrs Wallace will be able to find some refreshment suitable for you. If you would care to drive round to the stables I will go and tell her.'

She took a few halting, uneven steps and he called out to her.

'Let me take you to the house. Stark, get down and hand the lady into the curricle.'

She stopped and turned, saying with a challenge in her voice, 'Because I am a cripple?'

'No,' he replied mildly. 'Because I want to talk to you.'

She handed her sketch book and pencils to the groom and climbed easily into the seat unaided, affording Alex a glimpse of embroidered white stockings beneath her skirts. He could not recall ever being told why she limped, but there was clearly no deformity in those shapely ankles, or in the dainty feet encased in the neat but serviceable boots.

When she would have taken her sketching things back Alex stopped her.

'Stark can carry them to the house. It is a fine day, let us drive around the park before we go in. I want to talk to you about the children.' Without waiting for her assent he set the greys in motion. 'I hope you do not mind?'

'Do I have any choice?'

'I thought it might be easier to talk out here than in the house.'

'You are probably right,' she told him. 'You are a favourite with the girls and they will want you to themselves as soon as they know you are arrived.' She added thoughtfully, 'Although Meggie might demand to know why you have not been to see them before this.'

'I have been very busy.'

'Too busy to comfort your niece?' When he did not reply she continued. 'She and Florence were left to our joint care, my lord.'

'You do not need to remind me.' He flicked his whip over the greys' heads. What could he say? He knew it was contemptible, but looking back and considering his brother's death, he knew that he had been unable to face anyone's grief save his own. He was a renowned sportsman, a hard rider, deadly with sword and pistol and a pugilist of no mean order, yet he had shied away from visiting James's young daughter and witnessing her distress. He had told himself that her aunt was the best person to comfort little Meggie. Diana had been governess for four years to both James's daughter and little Florence Arrandale, a cousin whose own mother had died in childbirth and whose father had left the country under suspicious circumstances. James had taken the child in as a companion for Meggie and the two girls had been brought up almost as sisters. It was assumed that Florence's father was no longer alive and James had provided for her in his will, including consigning her to his brother's care. At eight years old, both girls would be missing James and his wife, the only parents they had ever known. Alex featured in their lives as a favourite uncle, visiting occasionally to bring treats and play with them for an hour or two before returning to his own hedonistic life. He might be their guardian now, but what did he know about bringing up children, or comforting them? It was no defence and deep inside he knew it, but it was easy to push aside such tiny pinpricks to his conscience.

'At least you corresponded with me,' Diana went on. 'I should be grateful you did not leave that to your man of business.'

'James's wife was your sister, your sorrow was equal to my own and I wanted to send my condolences.'

A black-bordered letter with a few trite sentences. How cold and hard that must have appeared to her.

Her hand came up, as if to ward off a blow. 'Yes, thank you.'

It occurred to Alex that she shared his dislike of overt emotion, so he did not pursue the matter, merely asked after the girls.

'They seem happy enough, but they miss their mama and papa. I know Florence is only a cousin, but her grief is equal to Meggie's, I assure you.'

He said with real regret, 'I am very sorry that I did not come to visit them sooner.'

'Well, you are here now, and they will be very glad to see you. What is it you wanted to discuss with me?'

'I was thinking that the girls might like to go to school.'

She paused, then said slowly, 'You are aware that the girls' education is my responsibility? Your brother was very clear about that.'

'Of course, but that does not mean I cannot take an interest.'

'No, indeed. But I do not think school would be right for them. Especially not at present, so soon after their loss.'

'Very well, but they might prefer another house, where there are less painful memories.'

'They are very happy here, my lord. It has always been their home.'

He felt the first stirrings of irritation. He would have to admit why he wanted them to move out.

'But it is now *my* house, Miss Grensham, and I wish to use it.'

'Well, there is nothing stopping you,' she replied. 'In fact, the girls would be delighted to see more of you.'

'That is not the point. I wish to bring friends here, and it would not be…appropriate for there to be children in the house.'

'What do you mean?'

He gave an impatient sigh. 'Do I need to spell it out to you? I am a bachelor.'

He kept his eyes on the road ahead but he was very aware of her enquiring scrutiny and found it disconcerting.

She said slowly, 'Am I to understand that you and your guests might act in an, an unseemly way?'

'It is a possibility.' His mind ranged quickly over his friends. 'More than a possibility.'

'It is certainly to your credit that you wish to protect the children from such scenes,' she told him, 'but I think in that case it would be better for you to hold your parties elsewhere. The Davenport estates comprise several excellent properties.'

'I am well aware of that,' he ground out. 'But I want Chantreys.'

He kept his eyes on the road but felt her clear, enquiring gaze upon his face.

'And why is it so important to have this house?'

Because it is where he and James had spent most of their childhood. Where they had been happiest. Alex knew that if he said as much she would turn the argument against him and appeal to his better nature to allow the girls to stay. And he had long ago buried his better nature well out of reach. He set his jaw.

'Miss Grensham, perhaps you are not aware of the pressures that are brought to bear on the head of any family to marry and provide an heir. Old family friends, relatives I have never even heard of all think they have the perfect right to interfere in my life.' His lip curled. 'It is assumed that I shall find a wife before the year is out. My intention is to show the world that I will not be coerced into marriage. I want to hold the biggest, most scandalous party of my career here at Chantreys. It is close enough to town for me to invite the *ton* to see just how disreputable an Arrandale I am and to put paid once and for all to their infernal matchmaking!'

There, he thought grimly. That should do it. But when he glanced at the dainty figure beside him she was displaying no sign of shock and outrage. Instead she had the nerve to laugh at him.

'That is the most ridiculous thing I have ever heard and I shall certainly not remove the girls from Chantreys merely to allow you to indulge such selfishness.'

He brought the curricle to a stand and swung round to face her. He held his anger in check as he said with dangerous calm, 'Miss Grensham, have you forgotten that I am now the earl? These properties are mine, to do with as I will.'

She met his eyes steadily, in no wise troubled by his impatient tone.

'I think *you* have forgotten, my lord, that you promised the girls might remain at Chantreys.' Her smile did nothing to improve his temper. 'You wrote to me, do you remember?'

'Yes, I remember.'

He forced out the words, recalling the letter he had received from Diana Grensham shortly after the news of the shipwreck, asking his intentions regarding his brother's wards. He remembered his own grief-racked reply, assuring her that Chantreys would be the girls' home for as long as she thought it necessary. The terms of the will had been quite specific. He and Diana Grensham were joint guardians of Meggie and Florence, but James had added a rider that Diana was to have sole charge of their education, being the person most fit and proper for that responsibility.

'I have kept your letter very safe, sir.'

'The devil you have!'

His hands tightened on the reins and the horses sidled nervously.

'Perhaps we should move on,' she said in a kindly voice that made him grind his teeth. 'There is a chill in the air and I should not like your team to come to any harm.'

Diana folded her hands in her lap as the earl set off again. She resisted the temptation to cling to the sides of the curricle, so noted a Corinthian as Alex Arrandale was unlikely to overturn her. Not physically, that was, but she could not deny that sitting beside him was causing no little disturbance to her spirits. Her conscience was already pricking her for the way she had questioned his reason for offering to take her up. It had been a civil invitation and she had responded childishly, doing the very thing she hated most, drawing attention to her infirmity. Her only excuse was that his arrival had caught her unawares. Suddenly she was confronted by a man she had only previously seen from a distance, a sportsman renowned for his strength and prowess. To look around and see him sitting in his low-slung curricle, easily holding in check those spirited greys, had thrown her own shortcomings into strong relief. She had no doubt that when he saw her take those first, hobbling steps towards the house that he had looked upon her with pity, if not disdain.

Not that he had said as much and she berated herself for being over-sensitive. It was a relief to turn her thoughts to the future of Meggie and Florence. She felt on much safer ground there but even so, to oppose the new earl at their very first meeting was not an auspicious beginning to their acquaintance. It could not be helped, the well-being of her charges was paramount. The new Lord Davenport had shown himself to be selfish and insensitive, but that was the case with most rich and powerful noblemen so it did not surprise her. What she had not expected was the attraction she felt towards the new earl. It was so strong it was almost physical and it shocked her. Whenever he had visited his brother in the past she had made sure she remained in the schoolroom, sending the children downstairs with their nurse to join the family. James and Margaret had been more than happy to include Diana in any family party, but they knew how much she hated her deformity and respected her wish for privacy when guests were present.

The late earl and his wife had been doting parents and, apart from short visits to other Davenport properties, the children had spent their lives at Chantreys. Diana had become their governess four years' ago. She had been just eighteen and declared that she did not want to be presented, hating the thought of being paraded around Court and all the required parties, to be gawped at and pitied because she could not walk gracefully. Her parents had been relieved, not only to be spared the cost of a court presentation but also the embarrassment of having to show off their 'poor little cripple'.

She had met Alex at James and Margaret's wedding, of course, but a vigorous young man just entering Oxford had given no more than a cursory glance to the eleven-year-old sister of his brother's bride. Since then Diana had kept out of his way, but she had followed his career and knew his reputation as a fashionable sporting gentleman devoted to the pursuit of pleasure. He was a perfect example of the notorious Arrandale family and nothing like his staid and respectable older brother. Now, sitting beside him in the curricle, she was very aware of the size and power of the man. His shoulders were so broad it was impossible not to bump against him as the vehicle swayed on the uneven carriageway, and he was not even wearing a many-caped greatcoat to add to their width, merely a close-fitting coat that was moulded to his athletic body with barely a crease. His hands, encased in soft kid gloves, guided the team with the ease of a master and the buckskins and top boots he wore could not mask the strength in those long legs.

It was not that he was handsome, she mused, considering the matter. His features were too austere and rugged, the nose slightly crooked, possibly from a blow, and there were tiny scars across his left eyebrow and his chin that were doubtless from some duel. His dark-brown hair was untidy, ruffled by the wind rather than by the hand of a master, and beneath his black brows his eyes, when they rested on her, were hard as slate.

No, thought Diana, as he brought the team to a plunging halt at the main door, he could not be called a handsome man, yet she found him disturbing. Possibly because he was now the earl, and technically her employer, even if her late brother-in-law's will gave her joint guardianship of Meggie and Florence. There was no doubt he could make life difficult for her, if he so wished. She would have to tread carefully.

'Can you get down?' he asked her. 'I cannot leave the horses.'

'Of course.' She jumped out. 'Take them to the stables and I will fetch Meggie and Florence to the drawing room.'

She thought he might argue and want to continue their discussion indoors but to her relief he drove off without a word and she limped up the steps into the house.

Word of the new earl's arrival had preceded her, thanks to his lordship's groom and she found Mrs Wallace bustling through the hall. She stopped as Diana came in and beamed at her.

'Ah, Miss Grensham, I have taken the liberty of putting cake and lemonade in the drawing room, and Fingle is even now gone to draw off some ale, since we know that Mr Alex—Lord Davenport, I should say!—is quite partial to a tankard of home-brewed.'

'Thank you, Mrs Wallace. I will go up to the children.'

'They are with Nurse now,' said the housekeeper, chuckling. 'They was all for dashing out to meet his lordship, so excited were they to hear he was come, but I sent them back upstairs to have their hands and faces washed.'

Smiling, Diana made her way to the top floor, where she found her two charges submitting reluctantly to Nurse's ministrations.

'Diana, Diana, Uncle Alex is come!' cried Meggie, running to meet her.

'I know, and once you and Florence are ready I shall take you to the drawing room.' Diana smiled down at Meggie, thinking how much she looked like her mother, with her fair hair and deep-brown eyes. Would Alex see it and take comfort, as she did? A tug on her gown brought her attention to her other little charge. Florence was as dark as Meggie was fair but no less lively, her grey eyes positively twinkling now.

'Can we still call him Uncle Alex, even if he is now the earl?'

'Of course we can,' declared Meggie. 'He is still *my* uncle, and you have always called him Uncle Alex. Nothing has changed, has it, Diana?'

Diana merely smiled, but as she accompanied her charges to the drawing room she was very much afraid that everything was about to change.

The new Lord Davenport was already in the drawing room when they went in, standing with one arm resting on the mantelshelf and gazing moodily into the empty hearth. At the sound of the children's voices the sombre look fled, he smiled and dropped down on to the sofa, inviting the children to join him. They raced across the room, greeting him with a hug and a kiss upon the cheek. Diana walked forward more slowly, surprised at the change in Alex from autocrat to friendly, approachable uncle. The girls settled themselves on either side of him, chattering non-stop, and she heard Meggie asking him why he had stayed away for so long.

'I have had a great deal of business to attend,' he told her. 'But it was remiss of me not to come and see you, and I beg your pardon.'

'Diana said you would be busy,' said Florence. 'She said you would also be very sad, because Papa Davenport was your brother.'

'Did you weep?' Meggie asked him. 'Florence and I wept when we were told that Mama and Papa had drowned. And Diana did, too.'

'No, I did not weep,' he said gravely. 'But I was very sad.'

'Diana hugged us and that made us feel better,' said Meggie. 'It is a pity you were not here, Uncle Alex, because she could have hugged you, too.'

Diana smothered a laugh with a fit of coughing and turned away, knowing her cheeks would be pink with embarrassment. She might consider the new earl selfish and insensitive, but she was grateful to him for adroitly changing the subject.

'I think it is time we had some of this delicious cake that Mrs Wallace has made,' he declared. 'Perhaps one of you young ladies would cut a slice for me?'

Recovering, Diana moved towards the table to help the girls serve the refreshments. She was relieved that the gentleman showed no signs of wishing to quarrel in front of the girls and she was content to remain silent while he talked to them about how they spent their days and what they had learned in the schoolroom. The children were bright and as eager to learn as Diana was to teach them and she was very happy, once they had finished their refreshments, for Meggie and Florence to take the earl up to the schoolroom and show him their work. Diana remained below. It would do him no harm to enjoy the company of his wards for a while, so she took her tambour frame into the morning room to await their return.

Lord Davenport came in alone some time later and she could not resist a teasing question.

'Have they exhausted you?'

'By no means, but Nurse reminded them that Judd would be waiting in the stable to give them their riding lesson and even I could not compete with that treat.'

'No, they love their ponies and I can trust Judd to look after them.'

'You can indeed. He threw me up on my first pony and is devoted to the family.'

His good mood encouraged her to touch on their earlier discussions.

'You see how happy they are here, my lord.'

Immediately the shutters came down.

'They might be as happy elsewhere.'

'In time, perhaps, but not yet.' She felt at a disadvantage with him standing over her so she put aside her sewing and rose. 'They are content during the day, but they are still not sleeping well. They have suffered bad dreams and even nightmares since they learned of the shipwreck. Chantreys is their home; they know it and love it. It would be cruel to uproot them now.'

'I am informed there are very good schools, where they might mix with children of their own age and rank.'

'They have that here,' she replied. 'They have friends amongst several of the local families and the servants here all go out of their way to look after them. They do not want for company.'

'But perhaps a broader education might be beneficial. A school would provide masters in all subjects.'

'Perhaps, but the very best masters are to be found in London and living here we have access to them. There is also much to be learned from the entertainments to be found in town. Their education will not be found lacking, I assure you.'

Alex felt the frown descending. It was a novel experience to have anyone oppose his will.

'Do you maintain that you can teach the girls everything they require?' he demanded.

'I do. I will not be moved, my lord. Meggie and Florence will remain here.'

There was a calm assurance in her tone that caught him on the raw. Did she think to defy him?

He said softly, 'What would you wager upon my having you and the children out of the house by the end of the summer?'

That determined little chin lifted defiantly.

'I never wager upon certainties, my lord, you will not do it—unless you mean to evict us bodily?'

She met his eyes steadily and he realised she had called his bluff. He would not do anything to hurt the girls, but neither would he capitulate that easily.

'No, I intend that you shall go willingly.'

'What you *intend*, Lord Davenport, and what will happen are two very different things.'

His temper flared at her calm defiance.

'This was always a good marriage for your sister,' he threw at her. 'My brother took her despite her lack of fortune. I suppose he kept you on out of charity.'

It was a low blow, unworthy of a gentleman, and Alex

regretted the words as soon as they were uttered, but surprisingly she was not crushed by his comment, instead she drew herself up and her eyes flashed with anger.

'He kept me on because I am an excellent governess!'

Admiration stirred. She was only a slip of a girl, why, she barely came up to his shoulder but she was not afraid to meet his steely glance with one equally determined. There was also a glint of mischief in her eyes when she continued.

'Margaret was always the beauty, but I had the brains.'

He laughed at that.

'Very well, Miss Grensham, we will agree—for the moment!—that you are a suitable governess for Meggie and Florence, but this is *not* a suitable house for them, you must see that. There is only the one staircase, and the building is so small that every time the children left the schoolroom my guests would be bumping into them. It will not do, the girls must leave. You may have the pick of my other properties.'

'I do not want any of your other properties.'

Alex bent a long, considering look upon Diana. Most people found his stare unnerving, but she merely replied with quiet determination, 'If you insist, then I shall oppose you, sir.'

Anger stirred again. Did she dare to set up her will against his?

'You would be ill advised to cross swords with me, Miss Grensham.'

'I have no wish to cross swords with you, Lord Davenport, but I will not move the children, and since I have your letter, you cannot make me.' She added, with deliberate provocation, 'Unless you wish to fight me through the courts?'

* * *

When Alex drove away from Chantreys the spring day was ending and the clear sky left an unpleasant chill. He had failed in his quest and was in no very amiable temper. As the younger son of an earl, with a sharp mind and excellent physique, he was accustomed to succeeding in everything he attempted. His godfather, an East India merchant, had left him a considerable fortune, which had given Alex the independence to pursue his own interests once he had left Oxford. He had thus arrived in town endowed with excellent connections, good birth and considerable wealth, all the attributes he required to do very much as he pleased. He was not used to failure and it irked him.

He could easily purchase another property close to London and leave Diana and the children to live at Chantreys. He knew that this would be the most reasonable course of action, but when he thought of Diana Grensham he did not *feel* reasonable. Her opposition had woken something in him, some dormant spirit that wanted to engage her in battle. He never enjoyed losing and he certainly had no intention of being beaten by a slip of a girl with hair the colour of autumn leaves.

Chapter Two

Alex was still mulling over his defeat as he drove into town and his mood was not improved by the knowledge that he had promised to attend Almack's that night. The Dowager Marchioness of Hune had written to tell him she was helping to launch a young friend into the *ton* and asked for his support. Lady Hune was his great-aunt and one of the few Arrandale relatives who was not pressing him to marry. Also, he was fond of her in a careless sort of way and he had agreed to look in. Well, he would not go back on his word, even if it meant entering the notorious Marriage Mart.

After a solitary dinner he walked the short distance to King Street, where his mission was soon accomplished. Miss Ellen Tatham was a lively beauty so it was no hardship to stand up with her and once he had done his duty he made his escape and rewarded himself with a visit to a discreet little house off Piccadilly, where he could be sure of more congenial company.

The house was owned by Lady Frances Betsford, a widow and the youngest daughter of an impoverished peer. Despite being an accredited beauty, she had been unable to do better than a mere baronet for a husband. However he had died within twelve months of the ceremony and left his widow with a comfortable competence. She had lived in some style in town for the past five years, moving in all but the highest circles, tolerated by the ladies and sought out by their husbands. Her name had been linked with several prominent society figures in the past and most recently it had been coupled with the new Earl of Davenport.

Alex had known Frances for years. There had been a brief liaison, when he had first arrived in town, and she was keen now to get him back in her bed. Alex was well aware that her renewed interest in him stemmed from his accession to the peerage. That did not overly concern him, he knew his world and viewed it with a cynical eye. Lady Frances wanted to be a countess and she was not ineligible. Her birth was good, she was beautiful, intelligent and no *ingénue* who would bore him within weeks. That was a definite advantage, he thought as he walked into her crowded drawing room. He watched her as she leaned over Sir Sydney Dunford's shoulder to advise him on his discard and realised just how little he cared if she shared her favours with other gentlemen. That, too, he thought, was in her favour. Theirs would be a civilised arrangement with no messy emotions to get in the way.

A tall, elegant figure clad in Bath coating and stockinette pantaloons broke away from the crowd and greeted Alex with a languid wave.

'Well, Alex, have you fixed the summer party for Chantreys?'

'I'm afraid not, Gervase.'

'Pity,' replied Mr Wollerton, shaking his head. 'Lady Frances will be disappointed.'

'That can't be helped—' Alex broke off as the lady in question approached, hands held out and a smile on her carmined lips.

'My lord, I had quite given you up.'

He saluted her fingers.

'I told you I should be late, Frances.'

She gave a soft laugh and slipped her hand through his arm.

'So you did. Come along and join us. What will you play, Loo? Ombre? Commerce? Or shall we play at piquet, just you and I?'

He looked down into her beautiful smiling face. After Diana Grensham's obstinate refusal to agree to his plans, the warm invitation in those cerulean eyes was balm to his battered spirits. What could be better than an hour or two spent in such agreeable company? It would help put the unsatisfactory visit to Chantreys from his mind.

'Piquet,' he decided.

Her smile grew. She moved closer and murmured for his ears only, 'And afterwards?'

Her full breasts were almost brushing his waistcoat and he could smell her sweet, heady perfume enveloping him. She was voluptuous, desirable and knew how to please a man. The invitation was very tempting, but there was a restlessness in his spirits tonight and he was reluctant to commit himself. He gave an inward shrug. It was very likely that in an hour or so he might feel differently.

He smiled. 'Let us begin with piquet and see what happens.'

* * *

Alex's restless mood did not abate and even Lady Frances's charms could not detain him. Soon after midnight he made his way back to his rented house in Half Moon Street. Piccadilly was busy, as always. Carriages rumbled past him and the flagway was bustling, mostly with gentlemen going to or from some evening entertainment. One or two females were on the streets, gaudily dressed and clearly offering their services to any man with a few coins in his pocket and time to spare. One of the women approached Alex but he waved her away. As she turned and flounced off the flaring light from a flambeau picked out the red glow in her hair. It was garishly unnatural, nothing like Diana Grensham's glorious autumn tints, that thick auburn hair and her eyes the colour of fresh hazelnuts. A man might gaze upon her for ever without growing tired of the view.

A *frisson* of alarm ran through Alex and he gave himself a shake. By heaven, what was wrong with him tonight? Diana Grensham was not his type at all, she was stubborn, opinionated and what had James been thinking of, to give her sole charge of the children's education?

The answer of course was that she was not an Arrandale, a family renowned for loose living. James had been the exception, a steady, sober young man who took his responsibilities seriously.

'Confound it, so, too, do I!' declared Alex furiously as he turned into Half Moon Street. No sooner had he uttered the words aloud than Diana's reprimand came to mind and he stopped, a wry smile tugging at his mouth. How could he say that when he planned to set the *ton* by the ears with an extravagant ball to which he would invite all the very worst rakes and reprobates of society?

Yes, it would be selfish but the spirit of devilry appealed to him and it would show all those top-lofty dowds that he would not be bullied into settling down. He would take a wife when he was ready and not before. He reached his door and trod up the steps, the smile fading as quickly as it had come. That did not solve the problem of the girls, though. He could not hold such a party at Chantreys while they were in residence.

'It would do the children no harm to live elsewhere,' he muttered, handing his hat and gloves to a sleepy servant and taking the stairs two at a time. 'In fact, it would be good for them and she should be made to see that.'

His man jumped up in surprise as Alex burst into the bedchamber.

'My lord, I wasn't expecting you so early—'

'Never mind that, Lincoln. Do I have any engagements on the morrow?'

'Why, no, my lord, nothing apart from your tailor.'

'Well, he can wait.' Alex shrugged off his coat and handed it over. 'As soon as it is light send a message to the stables. I want my curricle at the door by nine tomorrow morning.'

Alex once again felt his spirits lifting as he drove his team towards Chantreys. The house had always been the favourite of his childhood and now, as he regarded the east front, bathed in the bright spring sunshine, he was struck anew by its beauty. Completed soon after the Restoration, the walls were of dressed chalk enhanced with decorative Bath stone at the corners and around the windows. It was small but perfectly proportioned, topped with a steep-pitched roof surmounted by a balustraded platform above which rose the elegant tall chimneys. It was a work of art in its own right and would make an excellent setting for the paintings and sculptures he had acquired over the past few years. It was also perfect for the kind of intimate parties he intended to hold here for his close friends.

It was nearing midday by the time Alex pulled up at the door. He left his groom to take the equipage to the stables and walked to the open door, where the butler was waiting to greet him.

'Miss Grensham and the children are on the west lawn.' Fingle took Alex's hat and gloves and carefully placed them upon a side table. 'Would you like me to announce you, my lord?'

'No, no, I will find them.'

Alex strode across the entrance hall and made his way through the drawing room from where the long windows gave direct access to the gardens. There was no sign of anyone on the terrace or parterre, but the sound of childish voices and laughter led him through a gate in the high hedge between the formal gardens and the extensive lawns that led down to a large ornamental lake with the park and woods beyond.

A lively game of battledore and shuttlecock was in progress with Meggie and Florence ranged against Diana. They were all so engrossed in their game that at first they did not see him and he was able to watch them at their sport. The little girls dashed back and forth, laughing and shouting with delight as they patted the shuttlecock back to Diana, who rarely missed a shot. Alex kept his eyes fixed on Diana and it took him a moment to realise what was different about her. As she ran and turned, covering the ground, there was no sign of that ugly dragging step he had noted the previous day. Meggie sent the shuttlecock sailing high into the air and Diana leapt up to reach it.

'Bravo, Miss Grensham!' he called out appreciatively. 'A fine return.'

'Uncle Alex!'

The girls raced towards him. Diana, he noted, lowered her racquet and watched him, her manner reserved. Unsurprising, he thought, considering their encounter yesterday, but there was nothing to be gained by recalling that, so he greeted her cheerfully.

'Taking advantage of the good weather, Miss Grensham?'

She relaxed slightly and warily returned his smile.

'It is a reward to Meggie and Florence for their hard work in the schoolroom this morning.'

'Must we go in now?' asked Florence, clearly reluctant.

Alex shook his head.

'You need stand on no ceremony with me. I have interrupted your game.'

'We are not doing very well,' Meggie confided. 'Diana is so much better than us.'

'Well, let us see if we can even things up a little,' said Alex, spying a fourth racquet lying on a nearby rug. 'What do you say, Miss Grensham, you and Florence against Meggie and myself?'

The girls squealed with delight but Diana shook her head at him. 'You did not come here today to play games with us, my lord.'

A few unruly red locks had escaped from their pins and he wanted to reach out and tuck a stray curl behind her ear. He would very much like to play games with her, if they were alone… The thought seared him, sending the hot blood pulsing through his body and he had to struggle to concentrate. They had been talking of battledore, not flirtation.

'The honour of the Arrandales is at stake,' he declared, fighting down his baser instincts.

He stripped off his coat, revealing an exquisitely embroidered waistcoat, more suited to Bond Street than a country garden, but he did not care for that. 'Fetch me a racquet, Meggie!'

A fast and furious thirty minutes ensued. Diana, Alex noted, was at first a little shy of having a gentleman present. She was favouring her left leg and limping badly but Alex ignored it, giving no quarter in his returns. To his satisfaction her competitive spirit soon won through and as she lost herself in the game, running and straining to reach every shot he sent her way he saw no signs of the ungainly limp that affected her walk. The game only ended when Fingle appeared with a tray of refreshments for them all and a gentle reminder that Cook was even now preparing nuncheon for the schoolroom party.

'Then tell Cook to set another place for me,' declared Alex. 'That is, if Miss Grensham has no objections?'

The girls immediately voiced their approval of the idea and Diana spread her hands.

'It will be nursery fare,' she warned him.

'Then Fingle shall look out a decent claret to sustain me,' declared Alex, nodding at the butler.

Fingle bowed and went off to inform Cook of the change. Alex took the tankard of ale from the tray and sat down upon the blanket while Diana poured lemonade for Meggie and Florence. He watched the rise and fall of her breast beneath the low-cut neckline of her gown and again felt that stir of attraction. He dragged his eyes away. This was no part of his plan.

'Is this how you spend every day?' he asked her.

'Whenever the weather permits. Fresh air and exercise are very beneficial to growing bodies.'

And those already full grown.

Diana was unable to stop her eyes travelling over the earl's muscular form as he lounged on the rug, his long legs, encased in their pantaloons and Hessians, stretched out before him. She knew he was considered a Corinthian, a man of fashion but also a sportsman, and it was not difficult to believe it when one observed those powerful thighs, or the broad shoulders, deep chest and flat stomach, accentuated by his close-fitting waistcoat.

Having served the girls, she picked up her own glass of lemonade and made her way to the only free space upon the rug, acutely aware of the awkward, dragging step caused by her shortened left leg. It was not very pronounced and had never prevented her from excelling at the more energetic games she had played as a child with her sister and cousins, but she could never forget it when she was in company. She could never walk with that smooth gliding elegance that was required of young ladies. Her mother had developed a habit of averting her eyes whenever Diana limped into a room.

When her sister had suggested that Diana should become governess to little Lady Margaret and Miss Florence, Diana had accepted readily. All talk of a court presentation and a London Season ended and Diana saw the relief in her mother's face when she knew she would be spared the embarrassment of introducing her crippled daughter to society.

'You look very serious, Miss Grensham.' The earl's voice jerked her out of her reverie. 'Have I said anything amiss?'

'No, not at all.' She pushed away the unwelcome memories. 'You asked how we spend our days here. We are always up by seven-thirty and after breakfast we work at our lessons. Then, in the afternoon, there are more lessons or if the weather is fine we might walk, or play games out of doors. Our days are very full, the girls are learning to play the harpsichord, plus all the accomplishments necessary for young ladies, such as sewing, singing and dancing, but at eight years old I think there is time enough for that.'

'I am not questioning your skill as a governess, Miss Grensham.'

Diana noted that Meggie and Florence had grown tired of sitting down and were playing battledore again, there was no one to overhear them.

'No?' she challenged him. 'Yesterday you suggested I might have been given the post because I was a poor relation.'

And a cripple.

Diana did not voice the words but they were there, all the same.

'I beg your pardon for that.' He sat up. 'Why *did* you take the post?'

'I have always been interested in book learning,' she replied, avoiding his eyes. 'As Meggie's aunt, I was able to be so much more than a mere governess.' She explained, to fill the silence. 'You know how James and Margaret liked to travel, and then there were the house parties to attend and visits they were obliged to make. The children could spend most of their time here, in familiar surroundings, and when their parents were away I was always here with them.' She plucked at her skirts. 'In the event, it was fortunate. When the news came, that Margaret and James were drowned, I could comfort the girls.'

Alex recognised the pain shadowing her eyes. He was not the only one to have lost a sibling when that ship was smashed against the rocks off the Spanish coast.

'And who comforted *you*, Diana?'

He was not sure if she shuddered or if it was merely a shake of the head, but she did not answer him.

'We had best go in now.' She scrambled to her feet and shook out her skirts. 'Meggie, Florence, bring the racquets, if you please, we must put them away safely. Fingle will send someone to bring in the rug and the tray, my lord, so do, pray, go on ahead with the girls, I will follow in a moment.'

Alex said nothing, but as he accompanied the children into the house he suspected that she did not wish him to see her walking with that dragging step.

The schoolroom was on the top floor, as it had been during his own childhood, but it was barely recognisable. It was no longer dark and austere. The walls were painted white and covered with prints and drawings, many of them clearly the work of childish hands. The girls carried the racquets to the corner cupboard and he strode ahead to open it for them. As he did so his eyes fell upon an object in one corner and with a laugh he pulled out a small cricket bat.

'I remember this,' he declared. 'Old Wilshire, the estate carpenter, made it.' He grinned down at Meggie. 'Your father and I used it when we were here.'

'We still use it, Uncle Alex,' said Florence, coming up. 'Diana taught us how to play.'

'Well, well,' he said, grinning. 'Then you must show me just how good you are.'

'Perhaps another day,' put in Diana, following them into the room. 'This afternoon we have work to do.'

'Then I shall join you, if I may!'

If anyone had told Alex that he would enjoy spending the day with two eight-year-old girls, eating bread and butter in the schoolroom, listening to them reading their books and joining them for games of dominoes and spillikins he would have laughed at the idea, but when Nurse came in to take Meggie and Florence off for their dinner he was surprised to see that it was nearly five o'clock. The day had the charm of novelty, of course, and it was undoubtedly helped by Diana's presence. She was a lively companion and clearly very proud of her charges. Alex took his leave of the girls, almost as sorry as they were that there had been no time to try out the old cricket bat and promising that they should do so on his next visit.

'Thank you,' said Diana as she accompanied him down the stairs. 'It was very kind of you to give up your day for Meggie and Florence.'

'Kind?' he repeated, surprised. 'I am not renowned for being *kind*, Miss Grensham! No, I enjoyed myself, else I should not have stayed so long. They are delightful children, although I should not want charge of them every day, as you do. Do you ever have time to yourself?'

'Why, yes. Nurse takes care of the children now, leaving me free until about eight, when I go up to wish them goodnight.' She paused as they reached the entrance hall. 'Would you care to step into the drawing room, my lord, while you wait for your carriage?'

'Oh, I am not going yet.'

'But you will wish to be back in town in time for dinner.'

'I thought I might dine here. If you have no objection?'

He watched her dark lashes sweep down, shielding her thoughts as she said politely, 'It is your house, my lord.'

His lips twitched.

'Be honest, you are wishing me in Hades.'

She flushed at that, but shook her head.

'I apprehend that you wish to discuss the children's future.'

'Pray do not show hackle, Miss Grensham. We have had a pleasant day and I thought it would be useful for us to become better acquainted. As you reminded me, we are both guardians of Meggie and Florence.'

'Yes, of course. Then if you will excuse me, I will go and find Fingle and tell him to lay another place...'

She hurried away upon the words and Alex went into the drawing room. So far so good. Diana had thawed a little and he had no doubt now that he could achieve his object in coming to Chantreys: they could have a reasoned and logical discussion about moving the girls to one or other of his properties. Upon reflection he did not think Davenport House would be suitable, it was in the far north and the climate was rather harsh, but there was the estate in Lincolnshire, or the manor house north of Oxford. They both had large grounds where Miss Grensham could exercise her charges to her heart's content.

Chantreys was too perfect to be wasted upon children. Its light rooms would show off his growing art collection to advantage. It was the smallest of the properties he had inherited and it had plenty of snug little bedrooms well suited to late-night assignations, yet it was also close enough to London to invite parties down for an evening.

A shade of unease possessed him. Was he being self-ish, to move the children out of Chantreys? He could hardly continue his bachelor lifestyle here with the children in residence. His father would not have worried about such things, but then his parents had rarely considered their children, leaving them to be brought up by a small army of nannies, nurses and tutors in some distant wing of whatever house they were occupying at the time. Chantreys was different, there was no convenient wing in which to shut the children away, but even so the earl and his countess had contrived to avoid too much contact, spending most of their time in London and driving down to Chantreys only occasionally to visit their offspring. Alex had quickly learned not to reach out for Mama, lest he make her gown grubby, or to speak unless Papa addressed him. He had learned to keep his emotions in check, to keep everyone at bay except James. And now even James was gone.

Alex paced the floor, disturbed by his memories. The drawing room suddenly felt close and confined and he walked to the French windows and threw them open. He stood there, breathing in the fresh air. To one side he could see the empty lawns, stretching beyond the formal gardens. He had enjoyed playing outside today. It reminded him of those far-off days when he and James had been left to amuse themselves, playing cricket on that very same grass. Only there had been no warm and loving governess like Diana Grensham to look after them, to join in with their games so energetically that her hair escaped from its pins and bounced around her shoulders like a fiery cloud. His eyes narrowed, as if he might better recall the image she had presented, her hair curling wildly about her head, breast heaving from the exertion, eyes bright and sparkling. It was clear the children adored her and she was devoted to them. Well, let her argue her case again over dinner. Perhaps this time he would listen.

The door opened and he turned, expecting to see Diana there, but instead it was Fingle.

'Miss Grensham sent me to tell you that dinner would be served in an hour, my lord, and to see if you required anything in the meantime.'

'Yes, I require her company.'

The butler was an old and trusted retainer and at these words he bent a fatherly smile upon his master in a way that made Alex feel about ten years old.

'Miss Grensham has gone to her room to change for dinner, my lord. I am sure she will be downstairs again just as soon as she is ready.'

Alex kept his lips firmly closed, fighting against the impulse to demand that she hurry up. That would sound petulant in the extreme. He had set out that morning with the intention of holding a reasoned discussion with Diana. To order her to attend him would immediately put up her back. She was not a servant to be commanded. He curbed his impatience to see her again and asked Fingle to bring him some brandy.

Diana made her way to the drawing room shortly before the dinner hour. As she walked in the earl gave her a frowning look.

'Are you still in mourning?'

She glanced down at her lavender silk.

'No, my lord. This is my best evening gown.'

She could have added that it was the *only* evening gown. She had never needed more. When she had first joined the late earl's household she had always been invited to join the family for dinner, whenever they were in residence at Chantreys, but one never knew how many guests would be present, and Diana preferred not to be subjected to the stares and pitying looks of strangers. After a while the invitations had stopped.

'It looks very much like mourning,' he told her.

'One might say the same of your cravat, my lord.'

For a long moment they regarded one another, before the earl looked away and walked to the sideboard.

'Sit down, Miss Grensham. Can I get you a glass of claret, perhaps. Or Madeira?'

'A little wine, thank you.' She moved to a chair opposite the one he had been occupying, glad that he was pouring the claret and not watching her limp across the room. 'What is it you wish to discuss with me, sir?'

'You are very direct.' He handed her a glass and returned to his chair. 'I have already told you, I thought we should become better acquainted. You were always absent whenever I visited the house in the past.'

'Then the earl and countess would be present. I was not required.'

He stared at her over the rim of his glass.

'Were you avoiding me?'

She was surprised that his question did not offend. She replied, equally blunt, 'I was avoiding everyone.'

'Because you limp,' he said. 'What happened?'

'A broken thigh bone, when I was very young.' She paused to taste her wine. 'The doctor set it badly, and although others were brought in they could not undo his incompetence. I was left with my left leg shorter than the right. It does not prevent me from doing anything I wish, but it looks ungainly and makes people uncomfortable. They do not wish to see deformity in the drawing room.'

'Have you ever considered that if you were to be in so-ciety more, people would become accustomed to your…' he paused '…your deformity?'

'Perhaps, but I go on very well as I am. The children no longer regard it.'

He held her eyes.

'But you must take them out and about. Does that not make people uncomfortable?'

'Oh, no,' she said quietly. 'I attract no attention at all in the street. Governesses are of no consequence, you see.'

Fingle came in to announce dinner and Lord Daven-port rose.

'Shall we go in?'

He was holding out his arm to her. Diana hesitated, tempted to tell him such courtesy was unnecessary, but he would know that. Silently she slipped her fingers on to his sleeve. It was impossible not to feel the hard mus-cle beneath the soft wool of his coat. He exuded strength and power, and she felt a tiny tremor of excitement at his proximity.

'Oh.'

Diana stopped as they entered the dining room. Two places were set at the table, facing each other across the width rather than at either end.

'I told Fingle to set it thus,' remarked her companion. 'I thought it would be an advantage not to be peering the length of the table and shouting at one another.'

He guided Diana to her seat and held her chair. She sank down, suddenly nervous. She had never dined alone with a man before. *We are here on business*, she told her-self sternly. But when the earl took his seat opposite and smiled at her it felt strangely intimate, even though the daylight was still streaming into the room.

The earl's unexpected presence at dinner had certainly put Cook on her mettle and Diana decided there could be no complaint on the number and variety of dishes that appeared on the table. If the earl was not satisfied with the ragout of lamb and tender young carrots and turnips then there was a cheese pie or a fricassee of eggs and a dessert made with some of Cook's preciously hoarded quince jelly.

For many months Diana's meals had been taken alone or with the children and at first she was a little nervous to be in company, but the earl was determined to please and be pleased. He was an excellent host, ensuring that she had her choice of every dish on the table and keeping her wine glass filled. He was at pains to draw her out and she was surprised how easy it was to converse with him. By the time the meal was over she was quite relaxed in his company.

'I had best leave you to your brandy,' she said, when the clock chimed the hour.

'No, please. Stay and talk to me.'

She chuckled. 'We have talked throughout dinner.'

'But not about the children.'

She was disappointed. They had been getting on famously, and now they would argue again. She knew it. He signalled to Fingle to refill her wine glass and she did not object. She would not, of course, drink brandy, or port, or even Madeira after dinner. That would be foolish and could lead to her becoming inebriated, but a little more wine might stiffen her resolve when dealing with the earl.

Alex signalled to the servants to leave the room. He had enjoyed dinner, surprisingly so. He had decided at the outset that he would spare no efforts to charm Diana, but in fact it had been no effort at all. Her education had been thorough and she was an avid reader. Although she lived confined he learned that she corresponded with several long-standing friends and no one had ever cancelled the late earl's subscription to the London newspapers, so she was well informed and eager to learn. Their discussions ranged from politics to art and philosophy, and if he introduced a subject of which she knew little, her questions and comments were intelligent and interesting. He made sure the wine flowed freely, and as he encouraged her to talk and express her opinions she began to relax, to blossom. Whenever some particular subject caught her interest she would become animated, waving her hands, challenging his views and not afraid to put her own. The one topic they had not touched upon was the children and their removal to another property, but it would soon be time for him to leave, and since that was the reason for his being here, he must make the attempt.

As Fingle shepherded the footmen from the room Alex refilled his glass and sat back, regarding the petite figure sitting opposite him. She would never be a beauty. No coiffeuse would tame that red hair without resorting heavily to the use of pomade, her mouth was too wide and as for those freckles sprinkled liberally across her pert little nose and cheeks, any female with pretensions to fashion would have concealed them with a little powder. Having decided the freckles were a blemish, Alex found himself looking at them again. They did have a certain charm, he conceded. In fact, some men might find them quite attractive...

Diana's voice cut into his thoughts.

'No doubt you wish we still lived in your great-grandfather's time.'

With an effort he forced his mind back to the discussion.

'The fourth earl?' His brows rose. 'What has he to do with anything?'

'By all accounts he was a tyrant,' she told him cheerfully. 'He cleared whole villages to create the park and the views we now enjoy from the house.' She shook her head, saying disapprovingly, 'Positively feudal.'

'He provided a whole new village for his people.'

'Yes, because he needed to keep them close to work on his estate.'

'You are deliberately seeing the worst of my family.'

She laughed at that. 'The worst? Moving a few dozen villagers is nothing to the debauched and dissolute manner with which the Arrandales have conducted themselves over the years.'

Alex reined in his temper. Who was she to criticise his kin?

'The Arrandales are no worse than many other families,' he snapped. 'I would not contemplate displacing a whole village, but I *would* move two little girls! It is not as though I am throwing you on the streets. You may have the pick of my properties, if you wish I will even buy you a new house.'

'I do not want a new house,' she retorted. 'My sister thought it best for the children to be settled in one place and I agree with her.'

'I am not advocating that they should be constantly moving from house to house, Miss Grensham, merely asking that you settle them somewhere else.'

Alex reached across to refill her glass. By heaven, but she was stubborn! He noticed that his own glass was empty. He might as well refill that, too. He had forgotten that the brandy in the cellars here was very fine indeed.

She sipped her wine before replying.

'No, my lord. Chantreys is an eminently suitable house for the children. Its proximity to London means that when they need dancing and singing masters we will be able to command the very best.'

There was the faintest suggestion of unsteadiness in her voice. His glance flickered over the half-empty wine glass. Was she intoxicated? He had intended that she should be at ease with him, but perhaps in the enjoyment of the dinner he had allowed her too much wine. After all, she was not used to society and possibly might not be used to wine-drinking either. He pushed his chair back.

'It is time I left,' he said abruptly.

She blinked at him, her eyes wide. 'But we have not finished our discussion, nor have I finished my wine.'

'I think you have had quite enough,' he muttered, walking round and putting his hand on her chair. 'Come along.'

With a tiny shrug of her shoulders she rose. She looked perfectly steady but he was taking no chances. He pulled her hand on to his sleeve and walked her out of the dining room. As they crossed the hall he barked out an order to a hovering footman.

'Ask Mrs Wallace to make tea and bring it into the drawing room, immediately.'

'Oh, are you staying for tea?' said Diana. 'That will be de—delightful.'

He felt the weight of her as she leaned into him. He had intended to leave her, but perhaps he should stay and make sure she drank something other than wine. She continued to chatter as he guided her into the drawing room and eased her off his arm and on to a sofa.

'Chantreys is most, most excellently situated,' she told

him. 'We are close enough to London to visit the art galleries, and the famous Shakespeare Gallery in Pall Mall. Do you know it, my lord?'

'It is not somewhere I have visited as yet,' he replied, moving away.

'Then you should do so,' she said seriously. 'It has illustrations of Shakespeare's plays, commissioned from the finest artists.'

He watched her as she rose and began to walk about the room, idly running her hand along the chair backs.

'There is nothing to say you could not live further from town,' he said, 'You could bring the children to stay in London from time to time. Money is no object—'

'This is not about money, my lord.' She stopped and turned, fixing him with those large, hazel eyes. 'Chantreys has always been their home, they know it and love it. It would be cruel to uproot them now.'

The entrance of Fingle with the tea tray gave Alex time to consider her words and to admit to himself, grudgingly, that she was right. How could he even think of moving the girls at such a time? He could buy a house, or rent one. It might not be as perfect as Chantreys but there must be something suitable for entertaining. For some reason he found it difficult to concentrate on the matter. Or on anything very much. Perhaps it was not only Diana who had been drinking a little too freely.

When they were alone again he said, 'Come, take a cup of tea.'

'I do not think I want anything just yet.' She wandered over to the open window and gave a loud sigh. 'Is it not the most beautiful view from here?'

He crossed the room to stand behind her, but it was not the rolling acres of parkland that he was thinking about, it was the way the westering sun set her red hair aflame. Without thinking he reached out to touch it, but quickly snatched his hand back when she turned suddenly to face him. She was glaring at him, the light of battle in her eyes.

'Do you know what the problem is, my lord Davenport? You are spoiled. You have never had to struggle, to fight for anything. Is it any wonder if you are dissolute and irresponsible? Whatever you desire you only have to click your fingers.' She held up her hand, frowning in concentration as she tried to fit the action to the words. After a moment she gave up and turned her rather misty gaze upon him once more. 'You only have to click your fingers and your wish is granted, your wealth has always bought everything you want.' She stabbed at his chest with her fingers. 'Well, you shall not buy *me*.'

His eyes narrowed. 'Don't do that.'

'Why not?' She looked up, a challenging gleam in her eyes. 'Are you afraid I might sully your exquisite tailoring? Or do you fear I shall disturb the perfection of your cravat?'

Her fingers began to slide up over the embroidered waistcoat, but before she had reached the black linen neckcloth he clamped his hand over hers.

The effect was shocking.

A bolt of desire shot through Alex. It was no longer an annoying little governess standing before him, rather a creature of fire, a flame-haired siren who tantalised his senses. Her eyes widened, as if she was aware of the effect she was having. Hardly surprising since he was still holding her fingers against his chest, where she must feel the drumming of his heart. His free hand slid around her neck and cupped the back of her head. He almost expected those flaming locks to burn him but her hair was cool as silk against his palm. She made no move to resist and gently he drew her closer. As he lowered his head to kiss her he saw her eyelids flutter. Soaring elation overwhelmed him. His mouth came down upon hers in a bruising kiss.

Diana's senses swooped and spun. He teased her lips apart, his tongue flickering, demanding access and she could not deny him. She knew she should be outraged but instead she was exultant, revelling in the taste and smell of him, an exciting mixture of wine and spices plus something unfamiliar but very male. Her bones turned to water but it did not matter, because he was holding her so close, his arms strong as iron bands. Her hand was still trapped against his chest and she struggled to move and slip it around his neck, to push her fingers through the thick dark hair that curled over his collar.

She had never been in a man's arms before, no man had ever so much as kissed her cheek, but she felt no fear, only a fierce, primal pleasure when Alex's teeth grazed her lip before his tongue was once more dipping and diving into her. She gave a small moan of pleasure before returning his kiss and when she felt him withdrawing she clung tighter, instinctively pressing her body against his, wanting to prolong the hot, intimate embrace.

The blood was pounding through her veins, her senses were swimming, but she was aware that his arms were no longer around her, he was easing himself away, gently but inexorably. The frantic, heated kisses came to an end.

Dragging in a breath, Diana put her hands behind her, thankful to find the window frame was within reach. She leaned against it, trying to work out just what had happened. Alex was staring at her, frowning from beneath those heavy brows, his deep chest rising and falling with every ragged breath.

'I beg your pardon,' he muttered, his voice unsteady.

Her body cried out in agony at the distance between them. They were leaning against opposite sides of the window frame, only inches apart, but it was too much. She dug her fingers into the wood at her back to stop herself from cupping her breasts, which felt so full and hard they ached. She shook her head.

'I do not—' she began, when she could command her voice. 'That is, I have never—'

'No, you haven't, have you?'

A wry smile curved his mouth and Diana felt embarrassment replace the heat of passion. She should move away but her legs would not support her. There was a throbbing ache between her thighs, so intense that she wanted to throw herself at Alex, instinct telling her that only he could assuage it.

He stepped sideways, away from her and into the room.

'Let us blame it on the wine and think no more about it,' he said, walking to the door. 'I must go now.'

Diana did not want him to leave. She tried to drag her reeling thoughts into some kind of order.

'What—what about the children?'

He stopped at the door and bent another frowning look at her.

'I do not think either of us is in the mood for more discussion, Miss Grensham. I bid you goodnight.'

He was gone. Diana closed her eyes, breathing deeply and leaning heavily against the window frame at her back. She was not sure if she was most in danger of fainting or bursting into tears. Perhaps the earl was right, it was the wine. She had certainly taken more than usual, and she had felt very relaxed by the time dinner was over. Relaxed enough to tell Alex that she thought him a rich, spoiled nobleman for whom money could buy everything.

Her hands crept up to her cheeks. She had told him he could not buy her and he had punished her by showing that he did not need riches to reduce her to a trembling, incoherent wreck. He had done that with nothing more than a kiss.

She heard a soft scratching at the door and Fingle came in. Diana turned away quickly, pretending to look out at the gardens, deep in shadow now and with the moon rising in the distance.

'I beg your pardon, Miss Grensham. I heard his lordship leave and thought—but you haven't touched the tea. Would you like me to ask Mrs Wallace to put the kettle on again?'

'No, thank you, Fingle. I, um, I am going up to say goodnight to the children and then I think I shall retire.'

'Very well then, miss, shall I take the tray away?'

'Yes, please do.' She remained in the shadows and watched him depart with the untouched tray. No, she thought wretchedly, it was not tea that her body craved this evening.

'What in the name of all that's wonderful were you about?' Alex demanded of himself as he drove through the darkened lanes.

The cool night air had cleared his brain sufficiently for him to think straight again. The brandy had momentarily clouded his judgement. Thin redheads had never appealed to him and neither did headstrong, opinionated women. Diana was a lady, and his sister-in-law, to boot. It had been reprehensible of him to ply her with drink. True, she had annoyed him when she had called him irresponsible. Who was she to criticise him, to accuse him of trying to buy her? He had merely offered her the pick of any of his houses. By heaven, many a man would not even have given her a choice in the matter.

His mouth tightened. If he hadn't written her that letter assuring her she could stay at Chantreys, then perhaps he might now have ordered her and the children to leave, but he could not in honour do so. And he was not without honour, however dissolute she might think him. He gave a little grunt of frustration, knowing he had not acted honourably this evening. Her responses had been passionate but inexpert. Why, he would wager on it that she had never been kissed before. He recalled her look when he had put her away from him, her eyes huge and dark, regarding him with a mixture of wonder and apprehension.

It was not his habit to pursue innocent virgins and she was most surely an innocent. A veritable Sleeping Beauty, whose passion he had awakened with a kiss. His mouth twisted. But he was no Prince Charming. He had been on the town long enough to know what happened to men of experience who married innocent young women. They were bored within a month and within two they had set up a mistress, leaving a wife distraught at the desertion.

His hands jerked on the reins at the thought and he was obliged to give his attention to the greys, who objected strongly to his unaccustomed treatment. No, he thought, when the team was once more running smoothly, he had no intention of entering into such a marriage. He had determined to marry for convenience, a woman who understood what was required, who would make no demands upon him emotionally.

His mind wandered back to the memory of Diana, chin up, eyes challenging. He recalled the sudden stirring of interest, a flicker that had become irresistible when he had caught her fingers. He had only meant to prevent her from committing an indiscretion, but with her tiny hand clasped against his heart he had felt an irresistible urge to pull her into his arms. She had felt it, too, that connection between them. He had read it in her eyes, along with an invitation that he had accepted far too readily.

So there was another reason to remove Diana Grensham from Chantreys. She was governess to his wards and could not risk the loss of reputation that would result from an affair. And for himself, he would not want that on his conscience. Diana Grensham was no drab from the stews, willing to indulge in a quick tumble. When he had kissed her he had recognised her passionate nature and it had drawn a response from him. He knew that these attractions were never long lasting, but Diana was not experienced in flirtations—what if she were to develop a *tendre* for him?

He reached the outskirts of London and bowled through the town, his mind made up. Whichever way one looked at it, the best thing would be for Diana and the children to remove from Chantreys and preferably a good distance from London, well out of harm's way. The problem was how to achieve it? The devil of it was that so far Diana had proved surprisingly stubborn. She was determined not to capitulate. His jaw tightened. Well, he could be stubborn, too. This was no longer about the children, it was a battle of wills, and he was not about to lose.

Chapter Three

The following day brought word from Chantreys, the letter arriving at Alex's lodgings just as he was about to set off for Jackson's Boxing Academy. With a faint sense of satisfaction he broke the seal. Perhaps his lapse yesterday had not been such a bad thing. Diana was probably so mortified that she wanted nothing more than to remove as far away from him as possible.

His hopes were short lived. The missive was brief and to the point. Miss Grensham sent her compliments—*hah!*—and wrote to inform him that she had decided the children should remain at Chantreys for the next year at least.

'*She* has decided!' he exclaimed, resisting with an effort the temptation to crush the paper between his hands. He forced himself to continue reading to the end.

> *Miss Grensham therefore considers further discussion of the children's future would be of little benefit. However, if Lord Davenport wishes to call upon the children a message to Chantreys ahead of his visit would be appreciated, in order*

that Lady Margret and Miss Florence might be ready to receive him.

Alex swore explosively. Nothing would persuade him to make an appointment to visit his own property! He threw the letter on the table, snatched up his hat and gloves and set off for Bond Street.

Striding through the crowds brought some relief and after an hour in Jackson's Boxing Academy, sparring with the great man himself, he was able to view Diana's letter more dispassionately.

She had made it clear that she did not wish to move from Chantreys, but it was equally obvious that she was reluctant to meet with him again after their last encounter. That was the reason she wished for prior warning of his visits to the house, so that when he called she could arrange for Nurse to bring the children downstairs. For a moment he recalled that impromptu game of battledore upon the lawn and felt a tinge of regret that they would not do it again. But that could not be helped. She must be persuaded that it would be better for her and the girls if they moved out of Chantreys altogether. If only he could think of a way to do it.

A week later Alex was still no nearer solving the dilemma and such was his distraction that he almost walked past Gervase Wollerton in Jermyn Street without a word.

'By Jove, Alex, I don't know when I last saw you looking so blue-devilled,' observed his friend, when Alex had stopped and begged his pardon. 'Something amiss? I was going to look in at White's, but if you want to talk…'

'No, I don't,' said Alex. 'I am on my way to see Lady Frances, if you want to give me your arm.'

Mr Wollerton lifted his eyeglass and surveyed Alex.

'Thing is,' he said slowly, 'not sure I can do that, my friend. Not with you in that coat. In fact, if it wasn't growing dark, I would hesitate to acknowledge you.'

Alex's lips twitched.

'Gammon,' he said rudely. 'Have you been listening to Brummell again, Gervase? What is it this time, are the buttons too large, is my coat not plain enough for the Beau's taste?'

'No, no,' Mr Wollerton assured him. 'It ain't the buttons and the coat's plain enough. It's the cut. Shouldn't be surprised if you can shrug yourself into it.'

'Of course I can shrug myself into it.' Impatiently Alex took his arm and urged him on. 'I am happy to follow Brummell's lead when it comes to clean linen and simple, dark coats, but I'm damned if I'll spend hours each morning letting my man dress me.'

'Which is why the Beau will never be seen in the street with you, dear boy.'

Alex gave a bark of laughter. 'I shall live without that privilege.'

'I think you will have to,' murmured his friend. 'But at least you have come out of the sullens.'

'I was not in the sullens,' Alex objected, preparing to cross Piccadilly. 'Are you coming with me to see Frances, or would you rather retrace your steps and go to White's?'

'Happy to call upon Lady Frances.' Mr Wollerton coughed delicately. 'If I won't be *de trop*?'

'Good God, no. What makes you think that?'

Wollerton gave a slight shrug.

'You seem to be getting mighty close, taking her out to Chantreys and all that.'

Alex frowned.

'I haven't taken her to Chantreys.'

'Well, she has seen it at all events.'

'What? How can she have done so?'

'She drove out to view the place recently, heard her telling Anglesey about it at the assembly last night.'

'The devil she did.'

Gervase brushed a speck of fluff from his sleeve as he said, 'I think she aspires to be your countess, old friend.'

Alex scowled. 'I thought I had made it very plain I am not yet in the market for a wife.'

'So you are not meeting her tête-à-tête tonight?' asked Wollerton, looking relieved.

'Great heavens, no. She has invited all the world and his wife.'

Mr Wollerton protested mildly, 'The world might turn up, but not so sure about the *wives*. Not the high sticklers, at any rate.'

'Thank God for that,' muttered Alex. 'That's one of the main reasons I go there, to get away from the single females and their mamas on the hunt for every eligible bachelor. This Season has been particularly grim, having been obliged to escort Lady Hune and her protégée to just the sort of parties that I most abhor.' He quickened his pace. 'Come along, it's starting to rain.'

Lady Frances's soirées were comfortable affairs where one could expect good conversation and excellent refreshments. The company was predominantly male but at least a man could relax and enjoy himself without falling prey to a matchmaker. Alex and Gervase stepped indoors before the rain had sullied their coats and since they were familiar with the house they went directly to the card room set up in one of the spacious salons. Their hostess appeared in the doorway as they approached and held out her hands to Alex, smiling.

'Welcome, my lord, and to you, Mr Wollerton. You are set upon cards, I see. What will it be for you this evening?'

'Whist,' said Alex. 'If you and Wollerton will join me.'

He noted the little flicker of surprise and wondered if Frances wanted to keep him to herself. If Gervase's observations were correct, Frances had aspirations Alex had no intention of fulfilling for a long time yet. It was reassuring to see her smile without any hint of disappointment.

'Of course,' she said smoothly. She looked about her. 'We will need a fourth… Sir Charles, you are free? Do join us for a rubber of whist.'

Alex had no great opinion of Sir Charles Urmston and when they moved to an empty table he chose to sit opposite Gervase, leaving Lady Frances to partner Urmston. As they made themselves comfortable Alex glanced up and surprised a look pass between Urmston and the lady. It was fleeting, but there was an intimacy that made him wonder if they were more than friends.

The first rubber went to Frances and Urmston. Alex threw down his cards.

'I beg your pardon, Gervase. I was not concentrating.' He glanced at Lady Frances. 'You did not tell me you had seen Chantreys. When was this, ma'am? When did you go there?'

Her eyes widened but her smile did not falter.

'I did not exactly *go there*, my lord. I was on my way to Upminster to visit friends and I glimpsed it from the road.'

'You must have driven a long way around the perimeter,' he said sardonically. 'As far as I am aware there is only one spot where you have a clear view of the house.'

'I was curious to see the place that holds such happy memories for you, Alexander.' Her fingers touched his arm. 'I am now in a rage to visit Chantreys in the summer.'

'That will not be possible. My wards will be in residence.'

She looked up at him, her finely arched brows rising.

'But you were looking forward to holding a party there for all your friends.'

'*You* were looking forward to it, Frances.' His glance was mocking. 'As I recall the idea of a ball to shock the *ton* was yours.'

The lady brushed this aside with a smile.

'Nevertheless, my lord, I thought you had decided to send the children to school.'

'The decision is not solely mine to make.' The admission rubbed at his pride. 'Miss Grensham is also their guardian and she is against the idea.' He continued, deciding it would be best to get the whole thing over with. 'She is also against moving from Chantreys for the next twelve months at least.'

'And have you no say in the matter?' murmured Urmston, unwrapping a new pack of cards.

'We discussed it,' said Alex shortly.

Lady Frances put her hand on his arm. 'My dear Alexander, you should have left her in no doubt of your wishes in this matter. I thought we were agreed that the girls would be better off at school.'

'Unfortunately when it comes to the girls' education, my brother decreed that the final decision should belong to Miss Grensham, as the...er..."most fit and proper person to attend to it".'

Gervase laughed. 'James certainly had your measure, then, my friend!'

'It seems odd that she will not give up the place,' murmured Sir Charles. 'I believe the ladies generally find your charms persuasive.'

Alex felt his lip curling in derision. 'It is my money and my title that they find persuasive.'

Lady Frances tensed and Alex wondered if she thought the barb was directed at her.

'You are probably right, old boy.' Wollerton nodded, enjoying his wine and oblivious to the tension around the table. 'Not that you ain't charming when you want to be,' he added hastily. 'It's just that most likely you didn't think it necessary to charm a servant.'

'Miss Grensham is not a servant,' retorted Alex, unaccountably annoyed. 'She is the children's guardian.'

'But that does not give her the right to monopolise your property,' objected Lady Frances.

Alex might agree, but something compelled him to put Diana's point of view. 'She considers Chantreys the most suitable place for the children at the present time.'

Sir Charles was about to deal, but he hesitated as if a thought had struck him.

'Perhaps, my lord, you should demonstrate that the lady is not a…er…*fit and proper person* to have responsibility for your wards.' He sat back, smiling in a way that made Alex dislike him even more. 'How difficult can it be?' he drawled. 'Wollerton here says you have charm, when you wish to use it. Seduce the wench and send her packing.'

'Miss Grensham is no *wench*, Urmston,' Alex retorted coldly. 'She is a lady.'

'But Sir Charles has a point,' remarked Lady Frances, her tone smooth and reasonable. 'Perhaps not seduction,' she said quickly, observing Alex's frown. 'But if some gentleman were to take her fancy, if she wanted to *marry*, she might be more willing to compromise over the little girls' education. And consider the advantage to the lady; she could exchange the drudgery of being a governess for a much more respectable station. She would be a married woman and have a man to protect her.'

Alex watched Urmston deal out the cards, but his mind was on Frances's words.

'That might be possible,' he said slowly. 'If she were to marry she could no longer look after the girls. And why not school rather than another governess? My brother's will provided Miss Grensham with a handsome sum, so she would not be a penniless bride.'

And she was not unattractive, if one liked dainty, red-headed women, he thought, regarding Lady Frances's voluptuous form.

'Yes,' he mused. 'It might just work. I know several fellows in want of a wife.'

'Well, there you are then,' murmured Sir Charles. He finished giving out the cards and turned over the last one. 'Hearts,' he declared. 'Hearts are trumps.'

The second meeting with Lord Davenport had left Diana angry and unsettled. She was appalled at her own behaviour in encouraging the earl to kiss her; just the thought of it sent a shiver running through her. She was even more appalled to realise how much she wanted him to do it again. Quite reprehensible! Clearly in future he must not call unannounced. She decided, therefore, that she would write to him, telling him as much. The letter was written and despatched before she broke her fast the following morning, but even before it could have reached its destination she was regretting the rash impulse. Her tone had not been at all conciliatory and she was sure the earl would take offence. However, when the timorous side of her nature suggested that she should write again and apologise her spirit rebelled strongly. Lord Davenport must acknowledge that he was as much to blame for the lapse in decorum.

Why should he? He is an Arrandale, after all.

The thought came unbidden and Diana was obliged to acknowledge the truth of it. Even the late earl, for all his staid and respectable nature, had possessed the famed Arrandale arrogance. They went their own way, convinced of their superiority, and she had no reason to think Alex Arrandale was any different from the rest of his family.

The thought remained with her for the next few days, contributing to her mood of restless anxiety. It became so bad that one evening, after saying goodnight to the children she did not go immediately downstairs but instead went to the schoolroom, walking around and idly touching the familiar objects.

Was she being unreasonable to keep the children at Chantreys? It was perfectly understandable that the new earl would wish to make use of his properties and since he was an Arrandale, she was in no doubt that any party he brought to Chantreys would be far from respectable. The society pages of the newspapers she read often mentioned his name in connection with the more notorious of society's hostesses. She had a shrewd idea that he considered Chantreys would be the perfect place to bring his latest flirt.

That he refused to do so with the children in residence showed he had some sense of honour, but Meggie and Florence were not his children and it was clear he saw them as an inconvenience. She had learned a great deal about the family since becoming governess to the late earl's children. James and Alex had been brought up to want for nothing, an army of servants to obey their every whim, but their parents had been shadowy figures with little time to spare for their offspring. Margaret had always said it was a blessing James had turned out as respectable as he had done, but was it any wonder if his younger brother had grown up to consider nothing but his own pleasure? No, Diana was sure he would not give up the fight to remove her and the girls from Chantreys.

Well, perhaps she would write to him again and suggest a compromise. She would offer to take Meggie and Florence away for a few months. The earl had offered her the use of any of his other properties, or perhaps they might remove to the coast. A spell of sea bathing might prove beneficial, as long as Meggie and Florence knew they could return to their home afterwards.

'It is certainly worth pursuing,' she murmured as she blew out her candle that night. But her encounter with the new earl of Davenport had roused her spirit and she was reluctant to capitulate too easily. No, she thought as she settled down to sleep. She would not write immediately. It would do the new earl no harm to savour his defeat for a little longer. However, a little over a week after the earl's visit, a letter arrived from him that sent all thoughts of compromise from her head.

Chapter Four

'How *dare* he?'

Diana screwed the paper into a ball and threw it into the corner. She paced about the morning room, hands clenched and muttering angrily, thankful that she was alone and could allow her temper full rein. The letter had been waiting for her when she returned from a walk with the girls and, recognising the seal, she had sent the children off with Nurse as soon as they had all removed their muddy boots and outdoor clothes.

She had braced herself for the earl's response to her letter, expecting at best a suggestion for another house where they might reside, or at worst an angry condemnation of her presumption in opposing his will, even an ultimatum, but not this missive couched in the politest terms, telling her that he intended to bring a party of friends to the house and was giving her a month's notice of the visit, that she and the children might be prepared.

'How very considerate of you, my lord!'

Her words echoed around the morning room, but although her indignation remained, her anger was cooling. She picked up the paper and smoothed it out, then she sat down on a chair to read it again.

Perhaps he expected her to panic at the thought of his visit, to demand that he find another home for his wards immediately, but what if she did not do so? She nibbled her finger. He might be selfish and hedonistic but she did not believe he would hold a truly outrageous party while Meggie and Florence were living in the house. Diana made a quick mental survey of the building. The nursery and schoolroom were on the top floor, there would be no reason for visitors to venture so far. The children would not be able to have the run of the house, as they did now, but it would be May, so they would be able to spend much more time out of doors. She glanced at the clock. There was no time now to reply, but once she had concluded the children's lessons she would compose a letter to the earl. A polite note that would leave him in no doubt that she would not allow the children to be chased out of their home.

The cavalcade of carriages rattled through the park and swept around the curling drive that snaked towards the front door of Chantreys. Alex was leading the way in his curricle, with Lady Frances beside him. As he drew his team to a halt she placed her hand upon his leg, saying with a laugh,

'My dear Alexander, it is quite, quite charming!'

He had to admit it was looking particularly well in the late-spring sunshine, a perfectly proportioned little confection of a building. Rather than ruin the aesthetics by extending the house itself, successive generations had added two pavilions to flank the house and provide extra accommodation.

Alex glanced upwards. The rooms under the eaves had once been the servants' quarters but his parents had moved the staff outside into one of the pavilions and converted the whole top floor into a nursery. He wondered if Diana and the children were looking out for their arrival. Or perhaps they were waiting just inside the wide door, which was now thrown open as the servants came spilling out to welcome Lord Davenport and his guests.

Alex jumped down and walked around to help Lady Frances alight. He led her past the row of wooden-faced servants and into the hall, cool and light with its pale marble floor and white-painted walls. He paused there, waiting for the rest of the guests to follow them inside. It was a small party, only six guests, as many as the house could hold without opening up the south pavilion to accommodate them. Gervase Wollerton was the last to come in, looking about him in appreciation.

'You are right, Alex,' he declared, 'it is a very pretty place. Is this where you plan to put the Canova, opposite the stairs? The plainness of that wall would be the perfect foil for it.'

'Yes, but not while the children are in residence,' murmured Lady Frances. 'One dreads to think of what might happen to such a precious statue with little ones running riot through the house.'

'Quite,' replied Alex. He beckoned to a hovering servant. 'And talking of children, where are the girls, Christopher?'

The footman gave a little bow. 'Miss Grensham begs that you will advise her what time you would like your wards sent to the drawing room.'

Alex felt a hand on his arm and heard Lady Frances softly laughing beside him.

'Dear me, I hope you will allow us time to change out of our travelling clothes and rest awhile, my lord.'

'If you wish it,' he replied, 'although I had thought this an easy distance from town.'

'It is, of course,' she returned smoothly. 'But I should like to refresh myself and look my best when I meet your wards.'

'Then I shall hand you over to Mrs Wallace.' He beckoned to the housekeeper, who was hovering expectantly. His glance swept over the guests now assembled in the hall. 'She will show you to your rooms while Fingle and Christopher deal with your baggage. If you will excuse me.'

With a brief smile he left them and ran up the stairs two at a time, a pleasurable anticipation speeding his steps as he made his way to the schoolroom. He opened the door on a particularly domestic scene. A sofa had been placed beneath one of the windows and Diana was sitting there with Meggie and Florence on each side of her while she read to them from a large, leather-bound book.

At his entrance all three rose, the young girls' faces breaking into smiles of delight, while Diana's conscious look and sudden blush told him she had not forgotten their last meeting. Neither had he, Alex thought ruefully as he stifled a sudden rush of desire at the memory of that one, sizzling kiss.

'Uncle Alex!' Margaret ran forward and he scooped her up in his arms, laughing.

'Yes, I am here, Meggie.' He hugged his niece, then set her down and turned to greet Florence, who had followed more slowly. That gave him a few moments to compose himself before he looked up and acknowledged Diana with a friendly nod. 'Miss Grensham.'

She dropped a slight curtsy to him.

'Lord Davenport.'

He surprised a slight, puzzled look in her eyes.

'Is anything amiss?'

'Your neckcloth…you are no longer in mourning?'

He put his hand up to the froth of white linen at his throat.

'I shall always mourn my brother, but I decided it was time for a change.' He wanted to say more, but the words would not come. All he could think of was how her simple cream gown enhanced her flame-red hair, which was pulled back from her face into a knot, almost tamed, save for a few silky curls that had escaped and now kissed the back of her neck. His eyes regarded that neck, noting the elegant way it rose from the folds of the muslin fichu covering her shoulders. Demure as a nun. Was that for his benefit?

'Look, Uncle Alex, we have new gowns.' Meggie was pulling at his sleeve. 'Diana ordered them. Do we not look well?'

'As fine as fivepence,' he told the girls as they twirled before him.

'They are ready to meet your guests, my lord, as soon as you wish me to send them downstairs.'

'I wish you to *bring* them downstairs, Miss Grensham.'

'There is no need for me—'

There is every need,' he interrupted her. 'You are as much their guardian as I am. In fact, more so,' he added, 'since you are in charge of their education.'

A mischievous gleam put to flight the rather anxious look he had seen in her eyes.

'I think that rankles with you, my Lord Davenport.'

Alex's lips twitched.

'I am not deceived by your demure tone, Miss Grensham,' he growled. 'You revel in your superiority in this matter.'

'That would be ignoble of me, sir.'

She was smiling, clearly more comfortable when they were teasing one another. As was he.

'It would indeed,' he replied gravely. He glanced down at his dusty boots. 'I beg your pardon for appearing in all my dirt. I wanted to come up immediately to see the girls.'

The faint blush was on her cheek again but she spoke calmly enough.

'Not at all, Lord Davenport, your eagerness to see your charges does you credit.'

Diana hoped he could not see how he discomposed her. From the moment she had heard his booted tread outside the door her heart had been racing. She would have liked to say it was from anger, or indignation, but she had to acknowledge the *frisson* of pleasure that ran through her at the thought of seeing the earl again. And when he had appeared, she had thought for an instant how much less severe he looked, but that might have been merely the fact that he was no longer wearing the black neckcloth, which had certainly heightened the glowering effect of his heavy black brows. Really, she must be desperate for adult companionship if she had been looking forward to this visit! That is what she told herself, but in her heart she suspected it was specifically Lord Davenport's company she enjoyed. The verbal sparring. The kiss.

No!

As the children took their visitor to the table to show him their drawings she busied herself with gathering up the books and slates and putting them away. The kiss had nothing to do with it. That was a mistake, the result of too much wine, nothing else. She had been alone too long at Chantreys. Since the death of her sister and brother-in-law she had shut herself away too much with the children. That was all.

'I must go and change.' The earl's voice broke into her thoughts. Diana turned to see that he was moving towards the door. 'You will bring the children to join us after dinner, Miss Grensham.'

Diana would have preferred to send the girls downstairs with Nurse, but there was something in the earl's tone that told her he would brook no defiance. She would not argue. At least not in front of her charges.

'As you wish, my lord.'

The hard look he gave her suggested he was surprised by her meek acquiescence, but after regarding her silently for a long moment he gave a little nod and was gone. The girls ran about, chattering excitedly. For Meggie and Florence the hours could not pass quickly enough but it was quite the opposite for Diana, who could almost wish for a disaster to save her from the forthcoming ordeal.

At the appointed hour Diana accompanied her charges to the drawing room. There were seven persons awaiting her, three ladies and four gentlemen, including Lord Davenport. He had a voluptuous blonde at his side but it was not the lady's striking beauty that drew Diana's attention, it was the fact that she was standing rather closer to the earl than was necessary and had one hand resting possessively on his sleeve.

Resolutely Diana turned to the other two ladies in the room. The younger one was Miss Prentiss, a single lady with all the poise and confidence Diana lacked. She also had a rather strident voice and a harsh laugh that grated upon the ear. Her companion was considerably older. The young lady addressed her as Mrs Peters, not her mother then, but Diana guessed she was here to act as chaperon.

So, thought Diana, she had been right about the earl, he would observe the proprieties while the children were at Chantreys. Considerably relieved, she turned to consider the gentlemen. They were all of a similar age and all fashionably dressed, but it was Lord Davenport who caught and held her gaze.

She was surprised. With his broad deep chest and craggy features she had not thought the earl would look so well in the plain dark coat and pale pantaloons that Mr Brummell had made *de rigueur* for evening wear, but she saw now that it enhanced his powerful frame and the lithe, athletic grace of his movements as he walked towards her. Hastily she looked away and forced herself to concentrate upon Meggie and Florence.

Diana had prepared them well. They accompanied Lord Davenport around the room while she followed, hoping that everyone would be so charmed with the little girls with their pretty dresses and glossy ringlets that they would not notice the ungainly creature in the lavender gown following them with her awkward, dragging step. Any thoughts she had of retiring unheeded to a corner disappeared when the earl took her arm and led her forward. She was puzzled when he introduced her as his sister-in-law but she recalled their conversation, when she had told him that governesses were of no consequence and she realised, with something very like gratitude, that he was endeavouring to give her some standing amongst his guests.

That thought and the earl's presence steadied Diana

as the introductions continued. The guests showed little interest, although she felt their stares upon her as she crossed the room. As always when amongst strangers Diana was painfully aware of her shortened leg and found herself limping even more. She was relieved, however, when the introductions were over and she could at last sit down upon a vacant sofa and watch the proceedings. The girls were received kindly, no one petting them so much as the blonde, whom Diana now knew to be Lady Frances Betsford. However, the novelty of having children in the room soon palled and Diana called them back to sit with her while the ladies exhibited their skill upon the harpsichord. When Lady Frances was begged to take her turn at the harpsichord she modestly declined at first, but when the earl added his entreaties she capitulated.

'Very well,' she said, casting a melting look up at him. 'But only if you will sing a duet with me.'

The suggestion was met with such approval that Diana knew it was not the first time they had performed together. She folded her hands in her lap and fought down the uncharitable hope that Lady Frances might prove inept and tone deaf.

As if in punishment for her ungraciousness Diana knew Lady Frances would excel as soon as she began to play. The earl stood behind the lady, his rich baritone harmonising with her voice in a love song that they had clearly sung together before. Diana looked down, surprised to see that her hands were tightly clasped and she made a conscious effort to relax. It should not matter at all to her that they were so at ease with one another.

When the duet was over she applauded and praised the performance to Meggie and Florence, who were clapping enthusiastically.

'You enjoyed that, did you, brats?' The earl was smiling as he came away from the harpsichord with Lady Frances on his arm.

'We did, very much,' exclaimed Florence. 'Will you sing again for us, sir?'

He laughed and shook his head.

'Perhaps later. We must let the others have their turn.'

'Diana is teaching us to play,' Meggie announced. 'And she plays for us to sing and dance, as well.'

'Does she?' Lady Frances was smiling, but Diana thought there was more speculation than warmth in those blue eyes as they rested upon her. 'Perhaps you would like to play for us this evening, Miss Grensham.'

Quickly Diana disclaimed any desire to perform but the lady persisted, finally turning to the earl.

'Alexander, my dear, will you support me? Insist that she plays for us.'

Diana froze and struggled to utter a protest from a throat that had suddenly dried.

'I assure you, my lord, I—'

'I will do nothing of the sort, Frances,' the earl said, as if she had not spoken. 'Miss Grensham shall play for us when and if she chooses to do so.'

Lady Frances was not pleased with his response and an awkward silence descended.

'I wish I could play well enough to take a turn.' Meggie sighed, oblivious. 'Or I could dance for you!'

Her comment broke the icy restraint. The earl reached out and patted her hair, saying, 'I have no doubt you could, but it is your bedtime now.' He added, when her face fell, 'You may dance for us another night, brat.'

'Mayhap Miss Grensham will help you to prepare a little concert for our next visit,' purred Lady Frances. 'Then we may see the accomplishments you have learned.'

Diana's spirits swooped in dismay at the thought of another party at Chantreys.

'Good idea.' Lord Davenport agreed absently, but it was clear his thoughts were elsewhere. 'Off you go now. Miss Grensham shall take you upstairs.'

Diana rose and encouraged the children to make their curtsies before she led them away. She was aware of the earl's unsmiling gaze as they passed him.

'Goodnight, my lord.'

'You will come back, Miss Grensham, once you have settled the children.'

She inclined her head, acknowledging that he had spoken, but she said nothing. She had endured enough for this evening. She would not return.

Alex wandered about the room, a word here, a smile there, but the evening dragged intolerably. When Diana did not appear after an hour he realised she would not be coming back. He was not surprised, she had not wanted to appear in the first place, but at least she should be proud of her charges. Their manners and deportment were a credit to her teaching.

'My lord, you are not listening to me.'

Lady Frances shook her head at him as he quickly begged pardon.

'I was merely saying that I cannot wait for this evening to be over, so I may have you to myself.' She moved closer, smoothing her fingers over the lapel of his coat. 'You could come to my room, Alexander, or...'

He had a fleeting memory of Diana in his arms, her little hand pressed to his chest and his heart thundering against it. Madness. To be forgotten. He stepped away from Frances, out of reach.

'I do not think that would be wise.' She looked at him with a mixture of surprise and disappointment and he sought to explain. 'I would not have any hint of impropriety attached to this visit.'

'Nor I.' She added softly, 'But I can be very discreet.'

'I am sure you can, Frances, nevertheless we will have to restrain ourselves while we are at Chantreys.'

Anger flashed in her eyes, almost instantly replaced with a smile.

'As you wish, Alexander. But I shall not lock my door. Oh, and I have had my maid's truckle bed moved into the dressing room. She is a *very* heavy sleeper.'

With another alluring smile she moved off and Alex watched her walk away. Every sway of her hips was an invitation but, strangely, he was not tempted to follow. He castigated himself as a fool. What difference did it make that the girls and their governess were lying abed on the top floor? They need never know what was going on below, yet he could not be easy. He signalled to Fingle to bring him another brandy. Hell and confound it, he was developing a conscience. The sooner he moved the children to another house the better.

Diana sat on the edge of her bed, slowly dragging the brush through her hair. So that was the first evening over. Mrs Wallace was disappointed that Lord Davenport and his guests were staying for no more than a se'ennight, but Diana wished he was staying only half that time. The freedom she and the children had enjoyed at the house was severely curtailed and she could only pray that the weather would remain fine and she would be able to take the children out of doors for a good part of every day.

The next morning, at least, her prayers were answered and she sent a message to the stables to have the old curricle brought to the door. She was just making her way down the stairs when the earl came out from the dining room. At the sight of her in her walking dress he looked seriously displeased.

'Why are you not joining us for breakfast?'

'I broke my fast with Meggie and Florence,' she replied evenly. 'I am now taking them out for an airing.'

'Yes, Uncle Alex,' piped up Meggie. 'Diana is taking us out in the curricle.'

'Oh? And who is driving?'

'I am.' Diana's chin went up. 'The late earl had perfect confidence in my ability to handle the ribbons.'

'Did he?'

The speculative look in his eyes roused Diana's spirit.

'You need not worry, my lord, Meggie and Florence will be perfectly safe with me.'

She shepherded her charges out of the house, but to her annoyance the earl strolled out after them and nodded to the old groom who was standing at the horses' heads.

'Well, at least you will have Judd with you in case you have trouble,' he said. 'That relieves my mind.'

The old groom chuckled. 'Now then, my lord, you've no reason to worry about Miss Grensham handlin' the ribbons. Besides, I'd be hard pressed to do anythin' from that rear seat.'

Diana was grateful for Judd's support, but she maintained her silence as she helped the children into the curricle. The girls were excited, regarding a drive in the antiquated vehicle as a high treat. Diana had just finished tucking the rug around their legs when Florence invited the earl to join them.

'Don't be silly,' said Meggie. 'There wouldn't be room for all of us.'

'No indeed.' Diana saw an opportunity for retaliation and turned to the earl, fixing him with a bright smile. 'Perhaps Lord Davenport would like to take you out today?' She glanced at the two elderly horses harnessed to the pole. 'Salt and Pepper are not quite such a, a *bang-up* team as you are used to, sir, but I am sure you will be able to manage them.'

A sudden bout of coughing affected the old groom. Diana and the earl ignored it.

'Thank you, Miss Grensham, I am sure I should, but I would not deny you the pleasure.'

The look in Lord Davenport's eyes promised retribution, but Diana met it with a bland smile before she limped around to take her place beside the girls. She knew him to be an excellent whip, but the temptation to tease him had been irresistible. Would he make her suffer for it? She thought not. He might be arrogant and selfish, but he had a sense of the ridiculous and she had seen the gleam of humour in his eyes on more than one occasion. She bade the girls to hold on as she flicked her whip over the horses' ears, relieved she did not make a mull of it with the earl's critical eyes upon her.

Alex watched them drive off in grand style, an appreciative grin tugging at his mouth. So she still had spirit enough to make fun of him. She drove well, too, he noted, although he wondered if she would have set off at such a smart pace if he had not been watching. He found himself wondering how well she would handle his racing curricle with its fast-paced greys.

The smile died and he turned and went back into the house. Not that he would ever know. The less he and Diana Grensham saw of one another the better. In fact, the sooner she was away from Chantreys the better. Not that he wished her any harm, far from it, but she was a thorn in his side where the children were concerned. What she needed was something to think of other than the children. A husband, perhaps, as Frances had suggested. Well, there were three single gentlemen at Chantreys, excluding himself, so perhaps one of them would take her fancy. Not Gervase, of course, he was a confirmed bachelor, but Hamilton and Avery were perfectly eligible. He had made it clear to them that his sister-in-law had funds. Not a fortune, perhaps, but an easy competence. Enough to tempt a gentleman of modest means, so he was not unhopeful that one of them would make a play for her.

Chapter Five

The old curricle was no longer smart, and the horses definitely not fast goers, but Diana enjoyed tooling it through the lanes surrounding Chantreys. By the time they returned to the park the sun was at its height in the cloudless blue sky. The day was very warm and Diana wished that it were possible to drive to the secret lake. Of course it wasn't really secret, but it was hidden deep amongst the trees on the south side of the park with only a narrow, little-used path leading to it. No time to walk back there today either, Diana decided. The children had been out of doors all morning and once they had had nuncheon they would spend the afternoon in the schoolroom, at their lessons. She hoped to avoid Lord Davenport for the rest of the day, but although he did not come in person to the top floor, he did send a message requesting her to accompany the children to the drawing room after dinner.

Diana was not deceived. It was not a request but a command and one she could not ignore, however much she disliked the idea of going into company. To her relief no one paid her much heed when she entered the drawing room. She was allowed to retire to a corner while the guests made a fuss of the children and, apart from a nod when she came in, the earl did not speak to her. She was a little disappointed when he did not repeat his request that she return to the drawing room once the children had retired. Not that she wished to return, of course, but she was piqued that he did not ask her.

Rain pattered against the window of Diana's bedchamber as she dressed the next morning. The weather was responsible for her dullness of spirits, she decided, eyeing the leaden sky. That and the frustration of having a house full of visitors. She kept the children in the schoolroom after breakfast, but the lessons did not go smoothly, for the girls were fractious and disinclined to sit still. However, by the afternoon the weather had improved sufficiently for Diana to take them out of doors.

After walking in the park they went into the formal gardens, where they were soon joined by Lord Davenport and one of his guests, a Mr Avery. The girls ran to the earl, delighted to see 'Uncle Alex'.

'Well, brats, are you destroying my flower garden?' he demanded, observing the plants they were clutching in their hands.

'Of course not.' Meggie giggled. 'These are wild flowers and leaves from the park. We are going to take them upstairs to paint them.'

'Really? Avery here is quite a botanist,' the earl remarked, drawing his guest forward.

The young man coloured slightly and disclaimed.

'I wouldn't say that, I have a mild interest in flora, that is all.'

'I was about to show him around the garden but I think you would be a much better guide, Miss Grensham,' the earl continued, all affability. He held out his hands to Meggie and Florence. 'Come along, girls, I believe Cook has made some gingerbread so let us go to the kitchens and see if it is ready yet!'

Diana was so surprised by his actions that she could think of nothing to say. Mr Avery gave a little laugh.

'It appears Lord Davenport is more interested in cake than flowers, Miss Grensham. I hope you do not object to showing me about the gardens?'

'N-no, not at all,' she stammered.

'I fear Lord Davenport has exaggerated my knowledge,' he confided, offering her his arm. 'I have only a mild interest in botany, as I told the earl when he mentioned it just now, but he immediately insisted upon bringing me out to look at the roses. He must be very proud of them.'

Diana blinked. As far as she could remember the earl had never shown the least interest in the rose garden, but she could hardly say so. Perhaps he wished to spend a little time with his wards, she thought as she set off along the gravelled path with her companion. If that was the case, who was she to prevent it?

Mr Avery was in no hurry to quit Diana's company and it was late in the afternoon when she finally caught up with Meggie and Florence, who told her triumphantly that Uncle Alex had agreed to play a game of cricket with them. Diana accompanied the girls to the lawns, where she found the earl had already brought the small bat down from the schoolroom. Everyone else had come out to watch and some of the gentlemen had even been persuaded to join in. When Mr Wollerton asked Diana if she was going to play she quickly made her excuses and limped back into the house. The thought of hobbling around in front of an audience was too mortifying to be considered.

Diana looked longingly out of the window as she took the children downstairs after dinner. If it were not for the visitors she would have left the girls in Nurse's care and taken an evening stroll through the park, but such luxuries were at an end, at least until she and the girls had Chantreys to themselves again.

'Ah, here come your little charges, my lord,' Lady Frances called out as Diana followed the girls into the drawing room. 'Good evening Lady Margaret, Miss Arrandale.'

Meggie and Florence ran across the drawing room to join the party gathered about the harpsichord and Diana tried not to resent the fact that Lady Frances had ignored her in her greeting. She was a governess, little more than a servant and of no interest to Lord Davenport's guests.

As if to prove her wrong, Mr Wollerton and Mr Avery acknowledged her entrance with a bow, and Mr Hamilton stopped to talk to her for a few moments. She answered him briefly before she excused herself and limped across to a distant sofa where she could enjoy the music and her own company until it was time to take the children upstairs again.

Her solitude did not last long. As Miss Prentiss took her turn at the harpsichord Lord Davenport broke away from the group. Diana felt her pulse quicken as he approached her.

'I trust you enjoyed your time in the gardens, Miss Grensham.'

'Thank you, yes. The girls spent a happy hour sketching the flowers we collected.'

'I was referring to your walk with Mr Avery.'

'That was very pleasant.'

'But you could not be persuaded to play cricket.'

She shook her head. 'You did not need me, my lord.'

'It is not a question of need, Diana. I thought you enjoyed the game.' When she did not respond he gestured towards the group gathered around the harpsichord. 'Will you not join us? Meggie tells me you sing very prettily.'

She bit her lip.

'I would rather not sing in company, my lord. Not amongst strangers.'

'If you spent more time with my guests they would not be strangers.'

She inclined her head.

'True, but they go on very well without me and I prefer to sit here quietly.' She was aware of his disapproval and added quickly, 'This is the only evening gown I possess, I would not wish to draw attention to the fact.'

They would despise me.

She did not say the words but he would understand. It would be cruel of him to insist and he was not cruel. At least, she hoped she was not wrong in her judgement of him. After a tense moment he gave a little nod and walked away. Diana let her breath go, slowly. Another ordeal averted, at least for the moment.

'Look, Diana, Uncle Alex is waving at us!'

The two girls were standing at the schoolroom window, their noses pressed against the glass. At Florence's excited exclamation Diana glanced out at the drive below where Lord Davenport was mounted upon his powerful chestnut hunter, waiting for the rest of his guests to ride round from the stables to join him. A day's riding, Nurse had explained when she came upstairs from the servants' hall that morning. Everyone was going and Fingle had been told not to expect them back until dinnertime.

'So we have the house to ourselves for the whole day,' murmured Diana, relieved. The children might run up and down stairs as much as they wished and she need not fear bumping into Lord Davenport. Or any of the other gentleman, who seemed to have a knack of being present whenever she ventured into the library or the garden or the morning room. Diana thought that if she were vain and had an inflated notion of her own worth, she might suspect that they were lying in wait for her.

Florence sighed. 'I *wish* we were going riding with them.'

'Uncle Alex likes to travel hard and fast,' said Meggie, ever practical. 'Our little ponies would not be able to keep up.'

'Quite true,' agreed Diana, smiling. 'But that does not mean we cannot take a little ride of our own in the park. And after that we will go to the drawing room for a singing lesson. What do you say?'

After a full day's riding Diana expected the house party to be a little subdued, but when she entered the drawing room with Meggie and Florence that evening they discovered that the floor had been cleared for dancing.

'Ah, Miss Grensham, you are just in time!' Mr Wollerton greeted her cheerfully. 'You see we are about to dance.'

'Oh, and may we join in?' asked Meggie eagerly. 'Uncle Alex, please say we can join in.'

'Of course,' he declared. His hard eyes glinted as they rested upon Diana. 'In fact, I insist upon it!'

She had been quelling the familiar tingle of nerves she always felt when she saw the earl, but his words turned the flutter into full-blown panic. Meggie gave a little squeal and Florence clapped her hands in excitement as they ran off and Diana found herself abandoned. The earl came a little closer.

'Miss Grensham, you will dance, too.'

'N-no. That is, I—'

'Of course she will not, Alexander,' said Lady Frances, coming up. 'It is unkind of you to ask her when you know she has an infirmity.'

'I know nothing of the sort,' he declared repressively.

Diana's face flamed and she quickly moved away before anything more could be said. She walked across to the harpsichord, feeling the drag of her left leg even more acutely than usual.

'Oh, do you not mind playing?' asked Mrs Peters, who was standing beside the instrument. 'I have to say I dearly love to dance, but one should not deny the young people their sport.' Her eyes dropped, as if she could look beneath Diana's lavender skirts to the scarred limb beneath. 'However, if you are sure…'

'Perfectly, ma'am.'

Diana sat down and began to play, concentrating upon the music. Her fingers flew over the keys as she rattled off a succession of familiar dance tunes. Lady Frances's comments were forgotten and as her confidence grew, Diana felt herself equal to anyone. The room became full of laughter and movement. When Diana would have stopped and taken the children away there were cries of protest.

Meggie and Florence were clearly enjoying themselves and Diana gave in to the entreaties to play for one more dance. At the end of it Fingle came in with the tea tray and Diana called the girls to her, surprised to find herself almost regretting her decision to make her escape. She was bidding them say goodnight to everyone when she heard Nurse's cheerful voice at the door.

'Come along, Lady Margaret, Miss Florence. His lordship has asked me to put you to bed tonight, so that Miss Grensham can stay and take tea.'

'Oh, no—that is, I do not—'

'Pray do not be shy, my dear,' Mrs Peters interrupted Diana's floundering denial. 'We should be delighted to have you join us. Mr Wollerton, would you be kind enough to set another chair for Miss Grensham here, by me? She may help me by handing round the teacups.'

It was no longer her decision. Diana saw that it would be impossible to withdraw without seeming impolite. She sent a look towards the earl, who was standing a little apart from the rest, but his response was merely an unsmiling nod.

'B-by J-Jove Miss Grensham I thought you p-played extremely well,' exclaimed Mr Hamilton, when she handed him a cup of tea.

'Miss Grensham does play well, Hamilton,' the earl called across the room. 'I believe she sings, too, and I know you have a fine voice, sir. Perhaps the two of you will entertain us with a duet.'

'D-delighted to do so, my lord.' Mr Hamilton beamed. 'What do you say, Miss Grensham, shall we look for a song to suit us?'

'Perhaps another time, sir.' Diana went back to her chair, but before she could sit down Mrs Peters gave her a cup to carry to Lord Davenport. She approached him, frowning.

'You flatter me, my lord,' she said quietly. 'I sing only with the children.'

'It was not my intention to flatter you,' he returned. 'It was Meggie who told me how well you sing. And having heard your performance upon the harpsichord I am in no doubt that you are very musical.'

'Why should that surprise you? Do you think your brother would have entrusted the children's education to me if I had been lacking in any of the accomplishments?'

'No, you told me as much at our first meeting.' He took the proffered tea. 'You are an oddity, Miss Grensham, you puzzle me.'

'Why, because I am not afraid of you, my lord?'

He looked disconcerted and Diana felt a little shot of satisfaction.

'Is that what you think I want?'

'I think it is what you *expect*,' she replied, emboldened by her success in shaking him out of his complaisance. 'The rich and powerful Lord Davenport rarely meets with opposition, in any form.'

'That is hardly my fault.'

'No, but it is not good for your character, sir. It makes you think you can ride roughshod over everyone.'

She had gone far enough. The earl was frowning but for once she had the upper hand. It was a heady feeling. She waited, ready, nay, eager to continue the argument but Lady Frances interrupted them, laying a proprietorial hand upon the earl's arm.

'Alexander, are you not going to join us? Everyone is wondering what you are saying to poor Miss Grensham. I vow you look so thunderous I am in a quake.'

'If anything it should be poor Lord Davenport,' he replied with a wry grin.

'Really?'

Lady Frances did not sound very pleased, but Diana barely noticed. The earl had not taken his eyes from her and their glinting look acknowledged that she had won that encounter. A thrill of triumph ran through her, an elation that was not dimmed even when Lady Frances removed the cup and saucer from the earl and thrust it back at Diana before leading him away.

Diana regarded the half-empty cup in her hands. There was no doubting that Lady Frances considered her little more than a servant, but tonight she did not feel intimidated. She took her seat again beside Mrs Peters and listened to the conversation as it ebbed and flowed around her. A lively discussion developed between Mr Hamilton and Lady Frances about a scandalous play they had both seen recently. When Miss Prentiss asked about its content Mr Hamilton began to describe the play to her in all its salacious detail. Lady Frances tapped his arm with her fan.

'Have a care, sir, you will embarrass the governess.'

'I am not so easily shocked,' Diana responded, in no way discomposed. 'And I confess I have a fondness for the theatre.'

'I doubt you have had much opportunity to indulge in such pleasures,' remarked Mrs Peters.

'Not recently, but when my sister was alive I accompanied her regularly to the theatre.'

'Improving works, no doubt,' put in Lady Frances, the faintest curl to her lip.

'Not always. The performances varied enormously but I was always looking out for those that might be suitable for the children.' Diana's smile grew when she saw the surprise upon the faces turned towards her. 'The theatre can be very educational,' she informed them. 'I am a great believer in introducing children to the theatre at an early age. I took them to town to see one of Shakespeare's comedies, although I think they preferred the ballet that was staged between the performances, and of course the pantomime. They could talk of little else for days afterwards.'

The earl had come closer as she was speaking and now he said gruffly, 'You dragged the children to Drury Lane and back? I would have thought any benefit they might have gained would have been wiped out by their fatigue.'

'And so it would, my lord. That is why we put up in an hotel for the night. The girls thought it a high treat, I can tell you, and we were back at Chantreys before noon the following day.' She added with a hint of laughter in her voice, 'That is one of the advantages of being placed so near the capital.'

He regarded her through narrowed eyes.

'*Touché,* Miss Grensham, you have made your point.'

The earl spoke so quietly only Diana heard him. She looked away immediately, but she knew he would not miss the little smile of triumph that played about her mouth.

'Well, I must say, I have never heard of such a thing before,' declared Lady Frances. 'A governess taking her charges to the theatre. Quite, quite *novel.*'

Diana was still revelling in her victory over the earl and she was not at all daunted by the gentle malice in the lady's tone.

'You must remember, ma'am, that I am Lady Margaret's aunt and guardian to both girls. I also know my sister thought such visits could be beneficial.'

'Well, I wish *I* had had such a governess as you, Miss Grensham,' put in Miss Prentiss with her braying laugh. 'It sounds all high days and holidays for the children.'

'Not at all. They work very diligently most of the time.'

'But, forgive me...' Lady Frances approached, the icy glitter in her blue eyes at variance with her honeyed tones '...you are very young to have responsibility for Lady Margaret and Miss Arrandale. Surely you cannot teach them *everything* they need. Lord Davenport will tell you that an accomplished young lady requires more than mere book learning. A good school would surely be the best solution for them, there they would have masters to teach them.'

For herself, Diana might have shrunk away from the lady's patronising tone, but she was here as guardian to two little girls and that gave her the confidence to disagree.

'I beg to differ, Lady Frances, but the very best masters are all in London.' Diana's eyes flickered again to the earl. 'That is why I shall keep the children here at Chantreys, that they may have access to them.'

Anger flashed across the lady's face but Mr Hamilton was already moving the conversation on and Diana sat back in her chair, content to return to the role of passive listener. She had made her point, won the argument and she felt a small but satisfying sense of triumph.

The party broke up soon after as the exertions of the day caught up with everyone. Miss Prentiss was openly yawning and declared her intention to retire. Diana decided that she, too, had had enough and made her escape. Lord Davenport reached the door before her and held it open.

'I know your game, Miss Grensham,' he murmured as she passed him. 'You think your arguments in favour of remaining at Chantreys are convincing, but do not think you have won, madam. I am still determined that you will leave here. But I am also determined that the move will be in no wise detrimental to Meggie and Florence.'

She stopped.

'What makes you think you know what is best for them?' she challenged him. 'You have absolutely no experience of children.'

'Of course I have. I...' He paused and she waited. His hard eyes gleamed and she saw the smile tugging at one corner of his mouth. 'I was one, once, you know.'

For the life of her Diana could not hold back a gurgle of laughter, quickly stifled.

'I find that very hard to believe, my lord,' she murmured as she whisked herself out of the room and ran up the stairs, still chuckling.

Chapter Six

Diana could not sleep, her head, her whole body was buzzing with excitement. She was unused to conversing so much with adults and she had to admit she had enjoyed it, even the barbed comments of Lady Frances had not wounded her. It had still been something of an ordeal, not only because she felt awkward and ungainly every time she walked, but she had been painfully aware of the earl's presence. He had made little effort to include her in the conversation and when they had spoken it had only been to disagree. And yet… He had not patronised her and there had been a sizzle of excitement at being able to talk and debate with him as an equal.

She paced her bedroom floor, so full of pent-up energy that she felt she might burst. It was frustrating to have so many people in the house. Before, on the rare occasions when she could not sleep, she had wandered the rooms at will, but now she was afraid even to potter in the schoolroom for fear that the creaking floorboards would disturb the guests sleeping below.

The day had been unseasonably warm and her room was hot and airless. She threw open the window and leaned on the sill. A full moon was riding high above the park and gardens, bathing everything in a silvery-blue light. Everything was still, like a painted stage, waiting for the actors to make it their own. Suddenly Diana knew what she wanted to do. Five minutes later she was creeping down the back stairs, a dark woollen cloak covering her nightgown.

It was no good, after tossing and turning for what seemed like half the night Alex threw off the bedcovers and sat up. He pushed back the hangings and blinked a little as the moonlight flooded over him. He was wide awake and restless. He recalled Frances's invitation. He could still go to her room, he knew she would welcome him whatever time of the night he should arrive, but the idea did not appeal. He lay back down and put his hands behind his head, wondering why it was that he suddenly found the widow less attractive.

There was no doubt that Lady Frances Betsford was beautiful, clever and accomplished and she wanted to be a countess. Why should she not? She was the daughter of a peer and would fill the role well, he had no doubt. The fact that she had had several lovers over the years had never worried Alex, yet now he was aware of a growing reluctance to make her an offer.

Why should that be, when Frances was so perfectly suited to the position? He knew it behoved him to marry at some point and beget an heir but he would not do so when society said he should, hence his intention to hold such an outrageous party that he would shock his world. But one day he must make his choice and why not Frances? He ran over all the things he required in a wife. Until recently he would have said that birth, breeding and beauty were sufficient, but now he knew he wanted something more. Just when he had changed his mind he knew not, but now he was convinced that there must be affection, too. His wife should love him for himself, not for his title.

'You are aiming too high,' he told himself, staring up at the inky black shadows above him. 'There is not such a woman in England. Go back to your original plan. Find an agreeable beauty for your consort. Someone who will not cut up your peace.'

With a sigh he slid off the bed and went to the window. The still, night-time scene beckoned him. Acres of land and no one out there to enjoy it. He resisted at first, but the insidious little voice in his head kept asking, why not? The full moon made it light enough to see and a walk might clear his head. Ten minutes later he was dressed and striding across the open park.

It did not take Diana long to reach the woods. She took a slightly circuitous route through the gardens, following a little-used path in the shadow of the high hedges, in case some other sleepless soul might be looking out of their window. Once she reached the park she headed for the thick belt of trees that stretched off to the east of the house, finally joining with the extensive woodland that bordered the estate. The branches overhead were not yet in full leaf and the moonlight filtered through, dappling the ground and giving ample light for her to see her way. At last the trees thinned and she could see the glassy surface of the lake ahead of her. She stopped, listening. The distant scream of a fox did not worry her, or the mournful cry of an owl. The lake was black and still, smooth as glass with the moon reflected perfectly at its centre. Nothing stirred. She was quite alone.

The rising ground and thick woods that surrounded the water had trapped the warmth of the day and Diana did not hesitate. She slipped off her cloak and night-gown and ran, naked, to the edge of the lake. She had been here many times before over the years and knew that this southern end of the lake was the deepest. That was the reason a small wooden landing stage had been built here. She took a breath, ran out along the jetty and jumped into the water.

The shock of the cold water forced a little cry from her lips before she sank down into the still depths of the lake. Silky fronds of weeds brushed her ankles and she felt the bottom beneath her feet. It was soft and muddy, but firm enough for her to push upwards again, arms above her head as she surfaced, turning up her laughing, gasping face to the moon before slipping back beneath the water. For the first time in a week she felt perfectly free.

Alex walked briskly and soon the house was out of sight. He began to relax, remembering the times he and James had spent here as boys. Only two years had separated him and his brother and they had been close in those far-off days. They had moved in different circles at school, but had always spent their holidays together at Chantreys. There was plenty to amuse them, the woods for hunting and climbing and they could swim or fish in the lake. By the time James went to Oxford, Alex's interests lay in more physical pursuits. James married early and settled down to his responsibilities, while the inheritance from his godfather allowed Alex to live in town and indulge his interest in sports and his taste for collecting beautiful works of art.

Over the past few years they had led very different

lives, but the news of James's death had affected Alex profoundly. Outwardly he had gone on much as before, but his grief at the loss of his brother was deep and sincere. It was only now, six months after he had first heard the news, that Alex could remember their shared childhood without too much pain. Walking alone through the still, moonlit landscape, Alex found he could at last take comfort from the memories of the happy times he and James had spent at Chantreys.

A wall of trees rose before him, dark and shadowed, and he knew he had reached the edge of the park. He should turn back, but rather than retrace his steps he struck off at an angle, deciding to prolong the walk a little longer and return by the path that ran past the lake. His eyes soon grew accustomed to the gloomy shadows of the woods. Nothing was stirring and there was silence save for the occasional call of some night creature and his own soft footsteps. A glint of silver sparkled through the trees. He was nearing the lake's edge.

At that moment he heard simultaneously a cry and a splash and he emerged from the trees to see the mirrored surface of the lake shattered. As he watched he saw one white arm emerge from the water, scattering diamond droplets. Another arm followed, then, briefly, a head and shoulders, then there was gasp and the body disappeared again beneath the water.

'What the—?'

Alex ran towards the lake, stripping off his coat as he went.

That brief glimpse of a shapely arm had been sufficient to tell him the figure was a female, but as the naked torso rose up, gleaming silver in the moonlight, he had had a perfect view of the creature's face and had recognised her instantly. Diana. He reached the landing and it was the work of a moment to remove his boots and dive cleanly into the water. Immediately he struck out for the place where she had disappeared.

Diana's feet touched the weed-cushioned bottom of the lake and she remained there for a moment, enjoying the sensation of weightlessness, but as she made to rise again she was buffeted by something large and powerful that forced the air from her lungs. In a panic she struggled as childhood fears of monsters and serpents invaded her imagination. She was gripped by strong arms and hauled upwards. As she emerged from the water, coughing and spluttering, she heard a deep voice commanding her to keep still.

'Don't struggle, I've got you,'

'Let me go!' She tried to prise herself free. 'Let me go,' she cried again, 'I don't need rescuing. I can *swim*!'

The vice-like grip eased, just a little, and she turned to face her assailant. She knew who it was, of course. There could be no mistaking that harsh voice, but it was still a shock to find herself only inches away from Lord Davenport, his white shirt clinging to his shoulders and gleaming like pewter in the moonlight. He gave a sudden toss of his head, to fling his wet hair from his eyes.

'Then prove it,' he said grimly. 'Get yourself out of the water. Now.'

Diana needed no second bidding. She struck out for the bank, heading for the spot where she had left her clothes. She felt angry and foolish at being caught out by the earl, that he should have come upon her naked, but it was impossible to swim in a gown. However, she felt sure she could acquit the earl of any amorous intentions towards her. Clearly he had thought she was drowning and when he had discovered that was not the case he had sounded quite furious.

Diana did not attempt to pull herself on to the jetty but found a spot on the bank where the plants were at their tallest and scrambled up between them, hoping they would give her some modicum of protection while she hurriedly donned her nightgown without making any attempt to dry herself.

'What the devil do you think you are doing out here at this time of night?'

The voice behind her told Diana that the earl had also reached the bank. The brusque tone also informed her that he was not a whit less angry. Well, that was hardly her fault. She had not asked him to spy upon her!

'I might ask you the same question,' she countered, swinging around to face him.

He was in the act of pulling off his wet shirt and her mind went blank. She was distracted by the sight of his naked body and could not drag her eyes away. The muscles in his powerful chest rippled as he drew the wet linen over his head, his ribcage expanded, throwing into sharp relief the narrow waist and flat stomach. There was a faint shadowing of dark hair covering his chest and descending downwards until it disappeared beneath the waistline of his breeches. She dare not allow her gaze to drop lower, for the material covering his legs clung so tightly it left little to the imagination. Quickly she turned away and picked up her cloth, rubbing her hair with hands that were not quite steady.

'I could not sleep,' he answered curtly. 'But I had no intention of taking a midnight swim!'

No, well, a midnight stroll would be enough for him,

thought Diana bitterly. He walked, nay strode, with a lithe, effortless grace. *He* did not hobble in an unsightly fashion whenever he put one foot before the other.

'I did not ask you to rescue me.'

'How was I to know that? I saw you struggling in the water and thought, with your leg—'

'Water is the one place where my leg does *not* bother me!' Diana bit her lip. She had not meant to say that. She hated any reference to her lameness. With a sigh she spread her cloak on the ground and sat down upon it. 'Swimming is one of the few things I can do well.'

'I know that now.'

His voice had softened. There was even faint amusement in his tone. She tried to ignore him, pulling her hair over one shoulder and catching it in the towel. Too late, of course, her nightgown was already sodden where it had touched her wet body and the added water dripping from her hair made little difference.

The earl went to retrieve his own clothes from the jetty.

'Here.' He held out his coat to her. 'Put this on.'

She shook her head. 'Thank you, I am not cold.'

'Not yet, but you will be. I would not wish you to catch a chill.' He dropped the jacket around her shoulders and she fought down a childish urge to shrug it off. It was a chivalrous gesture and she would be churlish to refuse.

Alex gestured towards the cloak. 'May I?'

Diana moved over, which he took for assent and threw himself down beside her. The flimsy nightgown clung to her curves, but thankfully with his jacket about her shoulders he could no longer see the swell of her breasts, nor the faint outline of dark nipples through the damp cotton. He could not forget the sight of her cutting strongly through the water as they swam to the lake's edge. He had deliberately stayed behind her, ostensibly to make sure she did not get into difficulties, but there was no doubting the pleasure of watching her naked body as she emerged from the water. It was a brief view, for she was quickly hidden by the tall grasses, but it was enough. She was petite but perfectly proportioned and scrambled effortlessly on to the bank. He noted that her shapely legs showed no sign of deformity and her soft white body looked like marble in the moonlight, very like the Canova he wanted to bring to Chantreys. But Diana was no cool statue, she was alive and hot-blooded. Hot-tempered, too, he thought as he watched her rub her hair with quick, angry movements.

'I beg your pardon,' he said peaceably. 'I see now that you can swim very well. Where did you acquire such an accomplishment?'

He thought she might ignore him or snap his nose off, but she answered quietly.

'When I was young we lived near a river and Margaret and I often used to play there. Andrews, our old groom, taught us both to swim.' A sudden smile flitted across her features. 'He said it was in case we were taken up by the press gang, we would be able to jump overboard and swim ashore.'

'A wise man,' he said gravely and saw her shoulders lift in a tiny shrug.

'He knew swimming was something I could do as well as Margaret. I am no cripple in the water.'

She threw her hair back so that it tumbled down over her shoulders, the thick tresses hanging sleek and black against his jacket. She held out the towel.

'Would you like to dry yourself with this?'

'Thank you, no,' he told her. 'It is a warm night, my skin will dry naturally.'

He saw the corners of her mouth lift again.

'I would not wish to be the cause of *you* catching a chill, my lord.'

It was not a chill that she was causing him, he thought ruefully as his pulse quickened and the hot blood began to course through his veins. She was still rubbing at her hair with the towel. The nightgown was long, but with her arms lifted it barely covered her knees. He had an excellent view of her lower limbs and shapely ankles. He frowned slightly, looking hard at her dainty feet.

Diana felt his eyes upon her. The anger had evaporated and she was acutely aware that they were alone. She reached down to pull at the hem of her nightgown, but his hand shot out and caught her wrist.

'Wait.'

Suddenly the night air was no longer balmy. It was hard and sharp as crystal. Diana swallowed as the earl reached out and ran his free hand over her left foot.

'Where was the break in your leg?'

She should protest, pull away, but she could not do so. In alarm she realised that she did not *want* to do so. It was not just the iron grip on her wrist that immobilised her, the gentle touch of his fingers was equally compelling. She felt tense, fragile as spun sugar that would shatter at the slightest movement. She managed to run her tongue around her lips and answer him.

'J-just above the knee.'

His hand moved slowly up her leg. His touch was light as a feather but it left a burning trail on her skin and provoked an ache deep inside, an ache that brought back the memory of the punishing kiss he had bestowed upon her. The gentle fingers grazed over her skin in a tantalising caress. She did not move when he gently pushed her nightgown aside to reveal the jagged scar on her thigh. She trembled when his fingers touched the puckered skin where the gash had been badly stitched together. Even now she remembered the surgeon's words as she had slipped in and out of consciousness.

'A messy fracture and badly dealt with, but we can repair the damage and the leg will be as good as new, but she will need to work at it...'

Weeks of pain while the doctors argued over her, before her parents dismissed them all and consigned Diana to the nursery where she had been cosseted and pampered. Her old nurse had no truck with modern methods, with making children put weight on a limb if it hurt them.

The earl's fingers continued to move over her thigh, pressing lightly on the tell-tale bump beside the scar, on the outer edge of her thigh just above the knee joint.

'Is this the break?'

'Y-yes.'

He lifted his hand away and Diana felt the cool air on the spot where his fingers had been. Only then did she realise how her flesh had heated beneath his touch. He shifted and knelt before her, taking her feet in his hands and studying them intently. His thumbs moved slowly over the skin in an idle caress that left her breathless.

'There is no discernible difference in length,' he said at last.

'It...' She swallowed, her voice sounding strained and hoarse. 'It is very slight. An inch or so.'

'Not even that. The limb is strong, I have seen how

you run and jump. Do you never try to walk normally?
Perhaps the muscles need to be worked.'

'I cannot do so.'

'Who told you that?' He frowned, looking down at her
feet, still cradled in his warm grasp. 'You have let such
a little thing ruin your life, Diana.'

No! It was an anguished cry inside her head. It was
not a little thing. How could he understand? How could
he know the humiliation of being referred to as the little
lame girl, of having her parents constantly apologising
for her appearance. Her mother shaking her head and
smiling sadly while she told everyone, 'It was an accident, you see. So tragic.'

Diana shivered. She must shut out those memories
and she must be practical. She did not want sympathy,
especially from this man.

'I have the life I want,' she said briskly. She pulled
her feet free and began to wipe them with the towel.
They were perfectly dry, but she needed to rub away
the memory of his touch, it disturbed her too much. 'We
should go.'

Without a word he reached out and picked up her
stockings and shoes, placing them beside her before moving away to put on his own boots. When they were both
ready he held out his hand and pulled her to her feet. She
shrugged off his coat and gave it to him.

'I have my cloak,' she explained as she wrapped herself in its voluminous folds.

It was a relief when the earl donned his coat and she
was no longer obliged to see his naked chest. None of
the statues she had seen at the British Museum had prepared her for the sheer beauty and power of a real, flesh-
and-blood male. She wanted to stare at him, to reach out

and touch the bare skin, to feel the steely strength beneath. Diana thought how fortunate it was that the path was barely wide enough for one person. He would have offered her his arm and she really did not think she dare walk that close to him. He picked up his wet shirt and stuffed it into his pocket as they turned to leave the lake, then he reached out and took her hand. Immediately she hung back.

'I can walk unaided—'

'The moon has moved on, the path is not so well defined now. I do not want you tripping over a tree root.' He ignored her protest and tightened his grip. 'Come along, I will lead the way.'

Alex moved carefully through the darkness. Diana's little hand was secure in his grasp and it felt so right there, so perfectly at home. She followed him silently, uncomplaining and he made a conscious effort to slow his own pace so that she need not run to keep up. When they came to the edge of the woods she stopped him.

'I would rather use the path I followed to get here,' she said. 'The one over there. Through the trees.'

'Afraid of being seen with me, Diana?'

'Of course I am. There would be talk, if we were seen walking in the moonlight together.'

'But it is your natural *milieu*, is it not? You are named after the goddess of the moon.'

'Do not mock me, my lord.'

'I don't.' He pulled her closer, imprisoning her with one arm while the fingers of his free hand tilted up her chin. 'There must be some magic in the moonlight. Your limp has quite disappeared.'

She gazed up at him. In the gloom her eyes were huge

and luminous and as dark as the lake they had left behind them.

'You, um, you were walking ahead of me, 'tis merely that you have not noticed it.'

'I notice everything about you,' he muttered.

Their faces were only inches apart and his body screamed at him to capture those lips that were parted so invitingly. His arm tightened. Was it her heart thundering against his chest, or his own tumultuous pulse? His fingers released her chin but only so they could trace the line of her jaw. Alex cupped her face and ran his thumb gently across her bottom lip. Her eyelids fluttered and his spirit blazed with the knowledge that she was not immune to him.

Her lips parted even before they met his own, her face turning up, straining to reach him and when they did kiss Alex felt it like a spark on dry tinder, an explosion of light and heat roared through his body. She trembled and leaned into him, her body surrendering, moulding with his as his arms slid around her back. His tongue darted, tasting, exploring, tangling with hers for a brief moment before she drew back, breaking off the kiss with a tiny sob.

'Ah, please, don't!'

Diana put her hands against his chest to push him away and he released her immediately.

'This is not right,' she said, averting her face so that he might not see her distress.

'It feels very right to me.' He had not intended it to sound like a light-hearted quip, but he was struggling for control. 'Diana.'

He reached out to touch her and she flinched away.

'Perhaps it would be best if we made our separate ways back to the house, my lord—'

That he could not allow. Who knew what perils she might meet walking in the dark woods at night.

And what of the peril of being in your company?

He thrust the thought aside. There was no danger. His body was under control now.

Diana turned towards the woodland path, only to stop with a gasp as the earl caught her arm.

'Oh, no,' he said roughly. 'If you think I will let you wander about the grounds at night without an escort, you are very far off.'

'There is no need for you to come with me. I know my way.'

She knew she must be rational, even when she wanted so very much to throw caution to the winds and hurl herself back into his arms. His grip on her arm loosened, but only so he could slide his hand down and take her fingers again. How could something feel so comforting and so dangerous at one and the same time?

'I am sure you do,' he said, 'but I shall not rest until I have seen you safely back in the house.'

He set off and she was obliged to go with him, since he would not release her hand. In truth, she was glad of his support, for she stumbled occasionally over a stone or a tree root. The moon was low in the sky by the time they crossed the short stretch of open ground and slipped through the door into the kitchen garden. The path was narrow and Diana's skirts brushed against the plants lining the way, herbs in the first flush of new spring growth. Their delicate fragrances rose up to meet her: angelica and lovage, sage, thyme and rosemary. It filled her head with thoughts of fairy dells and magical meetings.

Ill met by moonlight...

With the house now in sight her fears of being alone with the earl were beginning to recede. She could even smile at the analogy. She was no Titania and he was certainly no fairy king, although the effect he had upon her defied her comprehension.

'I went out by the servants' door, over there,' she whispered when they reached a junction in the paths. 'I left my bedroom candle in the lower hall.'

He led her down the steps and into the house. Only then did he let her go and she felt achingly bereft. While the earl locked the door behind them Diana lit her candle from the single lamp burning on the wall. She had not realised just how much she was trembling until she tried to hold the wick steady in the burning flame. The passage ahead of her was in darkness and she waited until the earl was ready before setting off, holding her candle aloft so that he might see his way on the stairs. He walked close behind her and her spine tingled at the knowledge.

They soon emerged in the main entrance hall. No lamps burned there, but the darkness was alleviated by the faint moonlight streaming in through the windows and from the fanlight above the door. The earl touched her arm and the tingle ran up to her shoulder.

'Go on upstairs. I left by the front door, so I must lock it again. Do not worry,' he added, when she hesitated. 'There is sufficient light for me here to see my way.'

Diana hesitated.

'Sir, what happens in the morning, when we meet again?'

'What would you like to happen?'

Her mouth went dry.

'N-nothing,' she said at last. 'I would prefer to forget everything that has occurred tonight.'

For a moment he did not answer her. He reached out and touched her cheek.

'Is that truly what you want?'

Of course not! I would like you to take me to your bed and in the morning to declare your undying love for me, but I am not that much of a fool.

The words screamed in her head, but only the last one taunted her. Fool.

'Yes. Truly.'

She managed the words with admirable calm. His hand fell and he gave a little bow.

'Then it shall be as you wish,' he said lightly. 'It is forgotten.'

Without another word Diana slipped away, being careful to avoid the creaking stairs and floorboards. By the time she reached her bedchamber on the top floor she felt as if she had climbed a mountain, her heart hammering against her ribs and her breath ragged and painful. She climbed into bed and huddled beneath the bedcovers.

Tears were very close but she would not let them fall. Indeed, why should she be unhappy? She had enjoyed swimming in the lake, it had been invigorating, liberating and she had done nothing wrong. True, the earl's arrival had shocked her, but he had not really been angry with her. She shivered when she recalled the sight of him when he had first climbed out of the water. He had positively glistened in the moonlight, the damp shirt moulding to his form like a silver skin.

She remembered how he had examined her ankles and the shivering grew more intense until she could feel it deep inside her, but it was not unpleasant. She was already curled into a ball and her hands slid down her calves, wondering why his touch should cause such strange and unfamiliar sensations. He had said he could see no difference in her legs. He could not understand why she should limp so badly, and as he had led her away from the lake it was as if he had cured her simply by the force of his will. Not so, of course, but it had been less noticeable, just as it was when she played outdoor games with the children, running and jumping and forgetting the heavy, awkward drag of that left leg.

She had followed him silently to the very edge of the woods, lost in a moonlight world where nothing mattered save the fact that they were together. Even when he had taken her in his arms she had not resisted, even though he had seemed to envelop her in his huge, dark and powerful presence. It was only when she started to drown in his kiss that she realised her danger, Her treacherous body had responded to him, crying out for his touch, his kiss. She had never wanted him to stop, but some deeply ingrained sense of self-preservation had made her bring that kiss to an end. He had awoken a deeply buried longing within her, a yearning that she now realised had been building up during the long lonely years since her come-out. Years of self-imposed exile.

It had taken every ounce of determination to resist him, to beg him to stop and it had not been thoughts of impropriety that had made her do so, nor fear for her reputation. It was the knowledge, deep and instinctive, that if she allowed that kiss to continue she would crumble, as she had done before but this time, in this mystical moonlight world, there would be no escape. She would be lost, consumed by forces she could not control. She would give herself, body and soul, to a man who did not love her.

The tears scalded her lids as they squeezed themselves

out and soaked her pillow. She was a governess, and a good one. If she gave herself to Lord Davenport, if she became his lover, even for one night, she would forfeit her position, most certainly lose her self-esteem and she suspected that the aching loneliness she felt now would be infinitely worse once she had tasted the happiness that he could give her. The tears flowed in earnest and she was racked by deep, wrenching sobs, but at least now she knew why she was so unhappy.

She was crying for what could never be.

Alex shot the bolts on the main door as quietly as he could and made his way up to his room. The house was silent, the staircase empty and grey in the faint moonlight that shone in through the windows, but in his mind he could see Diana ahead of him, her dark cloak billowing like smoke as she ran up the stairs. He could still remember the feel of her hand in his, the delicate, fragile fingers clinging to him as he led her back through the woods. His mouth twisted into a wry smile. She was aptly named, Diana, goddess of the moon. She had bewitched him. When he reached the landing he had to steel himself not to continue up to the top floor in search of her. She would not thank him for following, and in the morning he would regret it. Diana was not the perfect, comfortable wife he envisaged for himself, she was far too opinionated and would cut up his peace most dreadfully.

Yes, he thought as he turned and made his way to his bedchamber. In the morning he would see this night's work for what it was, a moment of moonlight madness.

Chapter Seven

By morning Diana had shed all her tears and was able to face the day philosophically. Lord Davenport and his guests were remaining at Chantreys for another two days and she must face them all. She trusted the earl not to tell anyone of their midnight encounter and therefore the best thing to do would be to act as if it had not happened. Indeed, the episode felt very much like a dream so it should not be difficult to pretend that is all it had been.

She decided to take the girls out for a morning walk. They met no one on the stairs, voices from the dining room suggesting that some people were still breaking their fast, but it was not until they were in the park that Diana realised how tense she had been, how nervous of seeing the earl.

An hour strolling through the park with Meggie and Florence did much to calm her and Diana thought herself quite composed as they returned to the house, until a footman relayed Lord Davenport's message that she and the children were to present themselves in the hall at noon, when they would all be setting off to picnic at nearby Saxon Hill.

Meggie and Florence were with her when Fingle broke the news and they were so excited at the prospect that Diana had not the heart to refuse them. She tried to make her own excuses but she discovered that the earl had anticipated that. Fingle smiled at her in a kindly fashion and told her that Lord Davenport had specifically requested that she should accompany them.

'I think his lordship feels he owes you a little treat, miss, for all the inconvenience you have suffered during his visit.'

'Oh, no, no...' she began, flustered, but the butler interrupted her with a chuckle.

'No, it's been a pleasure to have the house so full, hasn't it?' Fingle remarked, his faded eyes twinkling. 'I tried to say as much to his lordship but he would have it that you and the young ladies must attend.' Diana looked at him in dismay, but the old retainer took her silence for joyous astonishment and his smile only grew wider. 'It's no wonder if you cannot find the words, miss. Now, you and the young ladies had best go upstairs and get yourselves ready, you won't want to keep his lordship waiting.'

Shortly after twelve the picnic party set off. Any apprehension Diana had of awkwardness between herself and the earl was soon allayed. He spoke to her only to suggest the girls should travel with him in his curricle, leaving Diana to ride in one of the two open carriages with the rest of the guests. Lady Frances elected to travel with Mr Wollerton and Mr Hamilton while Miss Prentiss begged Diana to accompany her in the second carriage with Mr Avery.

'Mrs Peters has the headache and is not coming with us,' explained Miss Prentiss, adding with an arch look, 'We will have to chaperon each other, Miss Grensham.'

The earl had sent his servants on ahead to lay out an array of rugs and cushions beneath a cluster of large and spreading trees, so when the party arrived at Saxon Hill all they had to do was to make themselves comfortable in the shade and enjoy the refreshments that had been provided. It was not a long walk from the carriages, but Diana felt the earl's frowning glance as she limped towards the picnic site. It made every step a struggle and she stopped at the first rug and called to Meggie and Florence to join her.

'Oh, do pray let them sit with me,' cried Lady Frances, holding out her hands to the girls. 'I do so wish to become better acquainted with Lord Davenport's little wards.'

Meggie and Florence glanced uncertainly at Diana, but having received permission they ran off to sit beside Lady Frances. Miss Prentiss came up, saying gaily, 'Let us sit down here together, Miss Grensham, and the gentlemen shall wait upon us.'

'Yes, sit down, Miss Grensham,' murmured the earl as he passed her. 'This is your treat, remember.'

'But perhaps I should be with the girls—'

'You need not be anxious about Meggie and Florence. I am sure I can be trusted to look after them.'

He walked off and threw himself down beside Lady Frances. Diana was aware of a stab of something very like jealousy. She quelled it quickly and looked away. The other gentlemen had joined them and Miss Prentiss gave her loud, braying laugh.

'Three gentlemen and two ladies, Miss Grensham, I vow we should think ourselves very fortunate!'

It was an effort, but Diana forced herself to relax and join in the conversation. With the sun shining and everyone determined to be pleased, the time passed quickly. Diana was surprised to discover that she really was enjoying herself as they dined on dainty pastries and cakes washed down by wine, ale or lemonade. She glanced across only once to where the girls were sitting. The earl was reclining at his ease and Lady Frances was tempting Meggie and Florence with the choicest delicacies from the hamper. Diana quickly looked away. Lord Davenport had told her he would look after the girls, so she determined not to give them another thought. As the earl had said, this was her treat, she should enjoy it.

Alex watched Lady Frances as she cooed and petted the children, who giggled and chattered away as they helped themselves to the fancy cakes and sweetmeats Cook had prepared for their delectation. He would not look at Diana, even when he heard her laugh at something one of the other fellows had said. He realised how rarely she had laughed during this visit, so different from when he had called at Chantreys and they had played battledore and shuttlecock. Then they had both laughed almost constantly.

He heard Eliza Prentiss express a desire to pick a posy of spring flowers and from the corner of his eye saw the gentlemen scramble to their feet. Miss Prentiss skipped off across the grass with two of the gentlemen in attendance, but Hamilton paused.

'M-Miss Grensham, will you n-not come with us?'

Alex felt rather than saw Diana shrink away and he was aware of a ripple of irritation. Was she so ashamed to have people see her limping, or did she think her leg would prevent her from keeping up with the others? He had seen her playing games with the children, he knew it was not the case, but she did not believe it and that was what mattered.

Hamilton ran off and Alex scowled. The fellow should have tried harder to persuade her. He felt a light touch on his arm and looked up to find Lady Frances on her feet beside him.

'I am taking Margaret and Florence to collect flowers, too. Will you come with us, my lord?'

He shook his head and made his excuses.

Instantly Frances was hesitating.

'Well, perhaps the sun *is* a little hot…'

But Meggie would not hear of it. She and Florence were exhilarated by the attention they had received and they now jumped around Lady Frances, begging her to go with them. Alex grinned.

'You will get no peace if you do not go, Frances.'

Her smile became even more fixed and Alex bit back a laugh to see the spoiled beauty at a loss. He was well aware that her interest in the children was tepid, but it would do her no harm to exert herself a little more on their behalf.

'Off you go now,' he murmured wickedly. 'I will watch you from here.'

He did so, too, until they were some distance away, then he sat up and turned to Diana.

'You did not wish to join them?'

She shook her head. 'I collect flowers regularly for the house, albeit from the gardens.'

'The displays in the hall and the morning room are your creation?'

'Yes, they are.'

'Another of your many accomplishments, Miss Grensham.'

'A very minor one.'

'Not so. Your arrangements show you have a good eye for colour. Do you paint, as well?'

She answered in the affirmative and he began to draw her out, describing the exhibitions he had seen at the Royal Academy and telling her of the growing collection of paintings and sculptures squeezed into his London house. He did not say he wanted to move many of them to Chantreys, where they could be displayed to advantage, he did not wish to spoil the moment by reminding her of their dispute. Instead he moved the conversation on to include literature and the theatre. Gradually she lost her reserve and began to talk freely. Her eyes lit up and she waved her hands expressively when she talked of the plays she had enjoyed, the books she had read. It was a small step from there to politics, history and the recently resumed hostilities with France.

Alex found it was no hardship to talk to Diana. She had a lively mind and the questions she posed were intelligent, taxing his memory as he tried to satisfy her thirst for knowledge and find the arguments to refute her opinions, when they differed from his own. He found himself sitting forward, dragging up long-forgotten facts, debating subjects he had not even thought of since his student days, and he was thoroughly enjoying it.

All too soon Miss Prentiss's strident voice interrupted their conversation and Alex saw that the others were returning. He glanced across at Diana, who gave him a shy little smile.

'What a pity we did not meet and talk years ago, my lord. We might have become good friends.'

Friends! His brows contracted as she turned away to greet the others and he realised with startling clarity that her life so far had been—and still was—a very lonely one.

Meggie and Florence were the last to come up and Diana noted at once their over-bright eyes and flushed cheeks.

'Margaret wanted to pick a bouquet for you, Miss Grensham.' Lady Frances put her hand on Meggie's shoulder. 'Come along, my dear, give them up before they become too crushed to be of use.'

'Thank you.' Diana jumped up and took the proffered flowers, but she rested the back of her free hand against Meggie's brow. 'You are very warm, my love.'

Meggie's bottom lip began to tremble. 'I do not feel very well.'

'Nor do I.' Florence wound her fingers in Diana's skirts.

'Then you shall both sit in the shade with me for a little while,' said Diana, leading them to the empty rug.

'La, I am quite parched,' declared Miss Prentiss, collapsing on to a pile of cushions. 'I should be very grateful for another glass of wine, Mr Avery.'

'And for me, if you please,' called Lady Frances. She glanced down at the girls. 'Poor little dears, perhaps we can tempt them with a little marzipan—'

'No.' Diana put up her hand. 'I think they have had more than enough to eat. A few sips of lemonade might help, but nothing more, unless you wish them to be ill on the homeward journey.'

Lady Frances stepped back, staring in horror at the children as if they were infectious.

'They did have rather a lot of pastries,' Alex admitted.

'Oh, nonsense!' Lady Frances tossed her head. 'They are merely hot and tired. A little rest is all that is required. Come along, my lord, we will leave them to Miss Grensham while we enjoy another glass of wine. I vow I am quite exhausted by all the exertion.'

Diana kept the children with her while the others raided the hampers for the last of the refreshments. They leaned against her, uncharacteristically quiet, and she scolded herself for not keeping more of an eye upon them. Clearly they had eaten too many sweet things and were suffering the consequences. Diana was filled with remorse. It could have been avoided if only she had warned the earl, instead of giving in to the demon jealousy and studiously ignoring him and Lady Frances.

'I am so sorry, my dears,' she muttered, cuddling both little girls. 'I shall take better care of you in future.'

Her pleasure in the day was quite destroyed, the earlier discussions with Lord Davenport forgotten. She sat quietly with Meggie and Florence and could only be glad when it was time to return to Chantreys. The girls were still looking a little pale but she hoped they would make the return journey without mishap. However, when they reached the waiting carriages Lady Frances stepped up to the earl and took his arm.

'I will travel with you in the curricle, Alexander. The

other gentlemen may travel in one of the landaus with Miss Prentiss, that will leave the final carriage for Miss Grensham and the little girls. That way they will inconvenience no one if they are unwell.'

The earl stopped.

'You would leave Miss Grensham to deal with the children alone?'

Lady Frances's finely arched brows rose.

'My dear sir, who better to look after them than their governess?'

'I will go with them,' offered Mr Wollerton. 'I have a young brother and sisters of my own, you know.'

He bent his kind smile upon Diana but she quickly shook her head.

'That is very good of you sir, but there is no need—'

'No, none.' The earl stepped forward. 'Gervase, you will go with Lady Frances in the curricle. *I* shall ride with Miss Grensham and the children.'

Diana's surprise was matched by that of Mr Wollerton, whose eyes fairly bulged in his head.

'D-drive your greys, Alex? Are you sure?'

The earl's hard eyes gleamed. 'Not up to it, Gervase?'

'Of course I am, it's just…you never let anyone drive your cattle.'

'I trust you not to ruin their mouths,' said the earl shortly. He turned to the girls. 'Now, let us get you two into the landau.'

'My lord, truly, I can manage perfectly well on my own,' said Diana as he lifted the children into the carriage.

'I have no doubt of it. Nevertheless I shall come with you.'

He held out his hand and silently Diana allowed him to help her into the landau. The carriages pulled away.

The earl watched Mr Wollerton set the spirited greys in motion then he turned back to look at his travelling companions.

'Now, Miss Grensham, how shall we best divert ourselves on the journey home?'

There was no doubt that the hazy cloud covering the sky robbed the sun of much of its heat and made the drive much more comfortable for the girls, but Diana could not fault the earl's good humour as he sang children's songs with Meggie and Florence and entertained them with riddles and stories from his own childhood. At one point he surprised the thoughtful look in Diana's eyes and gave a rueful smile.

'You have a very low opinion of me as a guardian, do you not?'

'No, no,' she disclaimed quickly, then admitted with a twinkle, 'You have risen in my estimation enormously this past half-hour! Seriously, I am very grateful for your presence. You have left me with quite nothing to do.'

'You will have plenty to do if either of them is unwell,' he muttered. 'I doubt I will be of much help to you in that situation.'

She laughed. 'I do not fear that happening now. They may feel a little uncomfortable but they both look much brighter. Is that not so, Florence? Do you feel a little better now?'

The little girl looked up at her with a doleful stare.

'I still have a belly-ache, but I do not think I am going to be *sick*.'

'Nor me,' put in Meggie. She was sitting beside the earl with her hand tucked snugly into his. 'So, Uncle Alex, will you tell us again how you and Papa stole the plum pudding and ate it all in one go, and how you were both *disgustingly* ill afterwards?'

Diana met Alex's eyes and could not prevent herself from laughing.

By the time they arrived at Chantreys Diana had never felt so much in charity with the earl. Alex, she thought, recalling how he had invited her to use his name. He handed Diana out and then helped the girls down.

'Until dinnertime, then,' he said as she took their hands and prepared to carry them off to the nursery floor.

Diana shook her head.

'I beg you will excuse us. We have had enough excitement for today, I think. We shall spend a quiet evening upstairs.'

As she turned away he caught her arm.

'I will excuse Meggie and Florence, but you will join us after dinner.'

Startled, her eyes flew to his face. Immediately he released her and stepped back.

'That, of course, is an invitation, not an order.'

'Of course,' Diana said quietly.

She led the children into the house and handed the little posy Meggie had picked for her to Mrs Wallace to put in water. Then she took the girls upstairs. There was nothing she wanted more than to go down to the drawing room and see Alex again. To discuss the children, talk over the events of the day, continue their earlier discussions, but she knew it was impossible. Every time she saw Alex she was drawn a little further into the net. If she came to look upon him as a friend the pain would be so much worse when he went away again. And go away he would. His world was a bright, colourful one full of beauty and balls and, and *people*. Hers was the life of a recluse.

To go into society, to be laughed at, mocked, pitied—it would destroy her just as surely as the quiet domesticity of her existence would destroy Alex. And if they could not be friends, then what? Lovers? She shivered. It might amuse him to make her his mistress, but she knew enough of the world to be sure that when the new Lord Davenport married, his choice would not be an insignificant little cripple but an accomplished society beauty. Someone like Lady Frances Betsford. Diana prayed he would not choose Frances. She detected a coldness beneath that beautiful exterior. Alex deserved someone who would love him, someone who would love Meggie and Florence, too, and make them a part of their family.

And she would no longer be needed.

Suddenly the leaden weight inside her was almost too heavy to carry. Diana stumbled. Florence and Meggie looked at her in alarm.

'I beg your pardon,' she murmured, trying to smile. 'I am more tired than I thought. Thank goodness I have you two big girls to help me.'

Somehow she managed to get them up the last few stairs to the top floor where Nurse was waiting for them.

'Well, well, my dearies, have you enjoyed yourselves?'

'I have the belly-ache,' Meggie informed her.

'Is that right, Lady Margaret? Well, that's no surprise. I am sure you are both so stuffed full of good things that you will not want your dinner tonight, is that not so, Miss Grensham?' Nurse's keen old eyes narrowed. 'And you look as if you are about to drop, miss, if you don't mind my saying.' She did not wait for Diana to reply but held her hands out to the children. 'Now, miss, you leave the little

ones to me and you go and lie down upon your bed before
you fall down. Blessed if I's ever seen you so pale afore.'

'I think I will go to bed,' said Diana. 'I informed his
lordship that the children would not be going downstairs
this evening.'

'I should think not,' Nurse agreed. 'Why, they will
never sleep tonight if they has any more excitement. I
shall give them a light supper and then put them to bed.
Never you fret, miss, Nurse'll look after them, and you,
too, my dear.'

The old servant's kindness was almost too much to
bear. With a little nod Diana escaped to her room where
she curled up on her bed and lay, unmoving, as the sun
travelled across the floor and the day slid silently into
night.

She was not coming. Above the chatter of the drawing room Alex heard the tinkling chimes of the ormolu
clock on the mantelshelf. Dinner had been over for more
than an hour and there was no sign of Diana. He prowled
restlessly about the room, refusing to play cards and only
pretending to pay attention when Lady Frances moved to
the harpsichord and played a series of Italian songs with
flawless precision. A dozen times during the long hours
of the evening he almost sent word to the top floor with
a message that Miss Grensham was to come downstairs,
and when at last the party broke up and everyone made
their way up to their bedchambers he was tempted to go
and find her, to assure himself that she was not ill. But
he did not.

He could not fool himself into thinking she had been
taken ill and in need of him. Nurse lived up on the top
floor and she had ruled the nursery since he and James

had been young. Alex did not doubt that she was more than capable of looking after Diana and the children. He had to face facts. Diana had not come downstairs because she did not wish to do so.

Chapter Eight

The light pouring into the bedroom woke Diana. It was a glorious clear dawn and the rising sun reflected off the gilded plasterwork around the edge of the ceiling. She lay quietly, allowing herself to wake up slowly. One more day and the house party would be gone. Alex would be gone. She would have the house to herself again. She was relieved, but she was also aware of a vague feeling of depression. There was no doubt she had enjoyed some aspects of having adults in the house, in spite of Lady Frances's barbed comments and the uncomfortable feelings that the earl aroused in her. She had especially enjoyed the conversation. Not only with the earl, yesterday, although that had been exceptional, but in the drawing room each evening. She had spent most of the time listening but occasionally she had expressed her views, even though they must have thought her horridly unworldly. She would miss the conversation.

'But not so very much,' she said aloud as she scrambled out of bed. 'It will be a relief to be able to go where I want, when I want. In the meantime, life must go on and I must pick fresh flowers for the morning room.'

* * *

'Why did you not come downstairs last night?'

Diana jumped. She was in the rose garden, cutting the early blooms, and had not heard the earl approaching. Nerves made her clumsy and she winced as a thorn pricked her thumb. She replied without turning, 'I was fatigued, sir.'

'You are bleeding.' He reached out to take her hand and she was obliged to face him. He was too close, his presence too powerful and with an undignified squeak she pulled her hand away.

'I can deal with this!'

'Then do so,' he retorted irritably. 'Else you will have blood on your gown.'

She hesitated, uncertain. He was right, she had no wish to stain her cream-muslin gown. In desperation she put her thumb to her mouth.

A powerful wave of sheer lust surged through Alex. Did she not know how provocative she looked, standing there with that half-frightened, half-defiant look in her eyes and her thumb between those cherry-red lips? The children's presence in the house had damped his ardour for Lady Frances but it was doing nothing to quench his desire for Diana. He dragged a handkerchief from his pocket.

'Here, bind it up with this.'

'Thank you, but I think it has stopped.' She removed her thumb from her mouth and inspected it. 'Yes. It was only a little wound. Nothing serious.'

Her attempt at a smile made him want to take her in his arms. He harrumphed and stuffed the handkerchief back in his pocket.

'What are you doing out here so early?'

She waved at the basket on the ground beside her.

'The flowers in the morning room need replacing.'

'Do we not have gardeners for that? Or Mrs Wallace could do it.'

'Mrs Wallace is busy enough with a house full of guests.' She selected another rose to cut. 'I *could* ask the gardeners to fetch the flowers for me, but they do not know exactly what is required. It is not a chore,' she added quickly, anticipating his next objection. 'I enjoy arranging the flowers in the house. It is a task I have done ever since I came to Chantreys. Margaret…' She paused, as if struck with a momentary pain at the mention of her sister. 'Margaret never liked the task and was happy to let me do it.'

He watched her carefully snip off two more yellow blooms and lay them gently in the basket.

'What was the real reason you did not come to the drawing room last night?'

Diana's hand hovered over another rose while she decided on her answer.

Tell the truth and shame the devil, Diana.

She said quietly, 'The picnic was ordeal enough.'

'Ordeal? Was anyone unkind to you?'

'No.'

'Was the company not to your taste? I thought you enjoyed yourself.'

'I did, for the most part.' She put the final rose and her scissors in the basket and picked it up.

'So what was it you did *not* like?'

'I—' a heartbeat's pause '—I do not like being gawped at.'

She turned to make her way back through the rose garden towards the north front, where a solid wooden door gave access directly to the staircase hall. Alex fell into step beside her.

'I do not understand you.'

She waved a hand towards her skirts, saying impatiently, 'My leg. This horrid halting step.'

'I did not even notice.'

'You may be sure your guests did. And it is even worse indoors. I am aware of it every time I enter the drawing room.'

'Perhaps they did notice it, when they met you for the first time. By now I wager they do not even think of it.'

She felt the hot tears pricking at her eyes.

'You are very kind, my lord, but—'

'Kind! Why should I be kind?'

His response was so typical of the man she was beginning to know that she was surprised into a laugh, but answered bitterly, 'True. It is much more likely that you brought your friends here to laugh and ridicule me, so that I will give up all claim to Chantreys.'

With an oath Alex caught her arm and swung her round to face him.

'Do you truly think I would do anything so base?'

It was not his glare or his angry words that caused her to blush and look away, but her own shame at suggesting he might do such a thing.

She said quietly, 'No, I do not think it, my lord. I beg your pardon.'

'You are back to calling me "my lord"? I thought we were past that.'

When she did not reply he put a finger under her chin and forced her to look up at him.

'I do not deny I want you and the children out of this house, but I told you at the outset that you would go willingly. Proudly,' he added. 'With your head held high.' His eyes narrowed, they bored into her as he said slowly, 'I do not see you as a cripple, Diana Grensham. I see you as an opponent worthy of my mettle. This will be a battle of wits, madam.'

Diana swallowed. He must be joking her, but there was no mockery in his hard eyes. It was a serious challenge, one adult to another. Equals. The thought was strangely uplifting. She replied cautiously, 'I have told you I have no intention of leaving Chantreys, Lord Davenport.'

'And I have every intention of changing your mind.'

His finger was no longer holding up her chin, she was meeting his gaze of her own accord and she did not feel at a disadvantage.

'How?' she asked, intrigued.

'That is my affair.' He released her and they began to walk on towards the house.

'But you promise the girls will not be distressed?'

'You have my word. By the end of the summer you will be agreeing with me that their best interests would be served by moving them elsewhere.'

She considered that.

'I do not see how that will happen, unless you trick me with some magic potion?'

'Something like that.'

She chuckled. 'Like Titania and Oberon in Shakespeare's play.'

'That ended very happily for everyone concerned.'

'So it did' she replied cordially. 'But that, Lord Davenport, was a play, a fairy tale.' They had reached the north front. Diana ran up the three steps to the door but stopped on the top one and turned to face him. For once she was looking down upon him. 'I think you will find real life will not work out quite so well for you.'

She held her ground, maintaining her smile even when she saw the disturbing glint in his eyes. He mounted the steps towards her and for one fearful moment she thought he was going to kiss her. Again.

She held her basket of roses before her like a shield with one hand while she reached behind with the other, scrabbling to find the door handle. She was trapped on the steps, the only escape was through the door and she could not open it! The menacing glint in the earl's hard grey eyes deepened and changed to unholy amusement as he observed her panic. He was on the top step now, towering over her, only the flimsy wicker basket was keeping them apart. Her pulse fluttered erratically and her heart was hammering so hard it threatened to unbalance her. A moment ago she had felt so strong and in control, but he had turned the tables on her. Nervously she ran her tongue over her lips and prayed that her knees would not give way. She was at his mercy as he leaned closer, a dangerous smile curving his lips.

'Allow me,' he murmured, his mouth so close she could feel his breath on her cheek. Her whole body froze.

He reached behind her and she heard the soft click as he opened the door.

'After you, Miss Grensham.'

If she had fallen from a tree she could not have felt more winded. He was *not* going to kiss her. She was *not* going to faint. Indignation rushed in. He had been teasing her, toying with her. She gave a little huff of anger but the gleam was still in those hard eyes and she knew it would be unsafe to remain. In fact, it would be positively hazardous. Without another word she turned and fled.

* * *

Alex watched Diana run off into the house. What a strange, jumbled mixture of parts she was. Shy and reserved, reclusive even, but he had experienced for himself her passionate nature. She was mentor and instructress to Meggie and Florence while little more than a child herself. She was not afraid to stand up to him, yet she was so painfully conscious of her slight impediment that she shunned company.

He shook his head as he went in and closed the door behind him. What had possessed him to invite her to engage him in a battle of wits over where the children should live? He should have told her instead to prepare to move out. Teasing her like that was only prolonging the inevitable but, confound it, he could not bear to see that wounded look in her eyes. It did not matter. When the time came, she would leave Chantreys and he would be able to get on with his life.

Diana ran directly into the morning room and quickly closed the door. She leaned against it, feeling much more weak and breathless than one would expect from such a short spell of exertion. It was Alex, of course. He was the cause of this heady, excited feeling. She did not believe that he deliberately set out to flirt with her, yet how else could she explain that wicked gleam in his eye, or the provocative things he had said to her? Perhaps he thought she knew how to play those games, but flirting was something she had never learned. No one had ever tried to flirt with her before, men were more inclined to avoid her, or turn away in embarrassment.

As soon as she thought her legs would move again she walked to the table where there was a pretty jug waiting to be ornamented with the roses she had cut. She began to trim the stem of each butter-yellow bloom and place it in the jug. She had to admit that Alex had never exhibited any embarrassment in her presence. Perhaps he was telling the truth when he said he did not notice her disfigurement. She had to admit she forgot it herself, when she was playing with the children, or in the company of good friends whom she had known for years.

She had even forgotten it in the earl's presence, more than once. Just now, for example, when he had called her an opponent worthy of his mettle. That was pure foolishness, of course. Alex was merely being kind. She slowly added another rose to the jug. He had said on more than one occasion that he was not renowned for being kind. But if not kind, what had he meant? She shook her head. The man was an enigma, she could not make him out at all. Yet there was no doubting that he made her forget that she was a cripple, that she had one leg shorter than the other.

But had she? It occurred to her that she had never questioned it before. Diana put down her scissors and placed her hands on the table top. She consciously adjusted her weight until it was spread evenly between both her feet. She was so used to favouring her left leg, keeping the weight from it when walking or standing, that she felt the strain immediately in her calf muscles, but both heels *were* on the floor. Perhaps the difference was not so great, after all...

'Oh! I beg your pardon.'

Diana swung around at the sound of the soft voice, blushing as if she had been caught doing something reprehensible.

'Do come in, Lady Frances. I was just replacing the flowers in here.'

'Pray, do not let me keep you from your work.' Lady Frances moved forward, the skirts of her pale-blue riding habit billowing slightly as she glided into the room. 'Lord Davenport is taking me driving this morning. He is gone to fetch the curricle but there is such a chill wind sprung up I thought I would wait here by the window until he brings it to the door.'

'Oh, yes, yes, of course.' Diana trimmed the final few roses and added them to the arrangement before placing it carefully in the centre of the table.

'How pretty,' remarked Lady Frances, in the same patronising tone she used for the children. 'I am sure the earl appreciates your efforts here, Miss Grensham. Alexander is a great lover of all things beautiful. He has acquired quite a collection of works of art, did you know?'

'Yes, I had heard that.'

'He is considered something of a connoisseur, I believe.' She sighed. 'Dear Alexander, he is quite intolerant of anything that is less than perfect. He has the most exacting standards, I vow I am almost afraid to go out in this wind lest it should pull my curls out of place.'

'I like blustery days,' replied Diana, adding with a smile, 'which is fortunate, since we have so many of them.'

'Ah, but you have the advantage of me, Miss Grensham.' Lady Frances replied in silky accents. 'The appearance of a governess is of little importance, is it? Ah—here is the earl now. I must go!'

She swept out of the room, leaving only silence and the faint trace of her heavy, cloying perfume in the room. Slowly Diana gathered up the abandoned leaves and trimmings from the roses and placed them back in her basket. She heard the thud of the main door and went over to the window. Alex's curricle was standing on the drive with Stark the groom holding the heads of the restive greys while Alex helped Lady Frances to climb up.

There was no doubt they made a handsome couple, Alex so large and rugged, the perfect foil for the lady's fair beauty. The final vestiges of the morning's happiness drained from Diana's spirit. Even if she could rid herself of that hateful, limping gait she would still be small, thin and freckled. No pretensions to beauty at all.

With something like a sigh she picked up her basket and limped slowly from the room, her left leg dragging more heavily than ever.

Chapter Nine

A day spent with Meggie and Florence restored Diana's cheerful spirits. Knowing the visitors would be leaving in the morning engendered a holiday mood in the schoolroom. The wind showed no sign of abating and by the afternoon the rain had set in, so they kept to the top floor all day, venturing downstairs only to join the house party for an hour after dinner. The girls were by now quite at home with their guests and when Mrs Peters invited them to come and sit with her they ran off happily, leaving Diana to retire to her customary sofa on the far side of the room. She was a little apprehensive when she saw the earl approaching, which he noted immediately.

'Lay those ruffled feathers, Diana, I have not come to quarrel with you.'

'That will indeed be a novelty,' she replied, unable to resist.

He grinned. 'Witch. I merely came to say that if you were planning to bring the children to London again you need not put up at an hotel. I have rooms enough for you all at Half Moon Street.'

'Th-thank you,' stuttered Diana, surprised. 'I—'

'It is a bachelor establishment, but if you bring Nurse, or your maid, I am sure they will be able to make everything comfortable enough for you.'

'I do not have a maid,' she said, distracted. 'At least, not one that could be spared to come to London. Jenny, the head housemaid, does all I need.' She added, her encounter with Lady Frances not yet forgotten, 'My appearance is of little importance.'

He frowned, accentuating the ragged scar across one dark brow.

'Why the deuce should you think that? Meggie and Florence have no mother to guide them. You must set them an example, Diana. How will they learn to run their household if they have no experience of such matters?'

'Surely there is time for that later?' she responded, nettled. 'From your wife, perhaps.'

He said irritably, 'It may have escaped your notice that I have no wife.'

'Not yet, but—'

'You will appoint a maid, madam, with immediate effect. Take this Jane, or whatever her name is, if she suits you, and bring in another housemaid.'

'But—'

'See to it, Diana, or I shall do so.'

His tone and his look were implacable and Diana eyed him resentfully. His frown disappeared as suddenly as it had come and he laughed.

'I know, you think me overbearing and autocratic, do you not? But it is not only the girls' comfort I am thinking of. You are a lady, Diana, not a servant.'

His swift change disconcerted her but before she could say anything they were interrupted by calls for music.

'It is our last night here and we should dance with the

little girls,' declared Lady Frances. 'And Miss Grensham can play for us again, since she does not dance.'

'Oh, but Diana *does* dance.' Meggie's young voice floated across the room. 'Very well, too. She never limps *then*.'

Diana's faced flamed. Alex was looking at her and she quickly excused herself, hurrying away to take her place at the harpsichord before anyone could press her to dance.

The carriages were at the door, the trunks and bags had all been loaded and now it was time for the guests to take their leave. Diana stood in one corner of the hall with Meggie and Florence while everyone bustled to and fro. Mr Hamilton dashed upstairs in search of Mrs Peters's lost gloves, Miss Prentiss tied and re-tied the strings of her cloak and no one seemed in any hurry to quit the house. Lady Frances came across to take her leave, acknowledging Diana with no more than a nod, but bending to say goodbye to the children.

'Your uncle has promised that we shall come to Chantreys again very soon,' she said, giving Meggie and Florence her dazzling smile. 'Then you will dance for me, will you not?'

'I am sure they will not disappoint you, Frances,' said the earl, coming up. He turned to Diana. 'When I come again the party will be much larger, the south pavilion must be opened up to accommodate my guests.'

'I am sure Mrs Wallace will take care of that, my lord.'

'And the orangery must be cleared. Meggie and Florence will need somewhere to show off their dancing skills. And, of course, we must have a ball.'

'A ball!'

'Why, yes, Miss Grensham.' Lady Frances straightened and sent a smiling glance towards Lord Davenport. 'Why should you be so surprised? It is time the new earl was seen by the local society, especially if we—if *he* is to spend more time at Chantreys.'

Diana had no doubt that the slip was deliberate. Her eyes shifted to Alex's face, but it was inscrutable. Lady Frances, however, was looking like a cat that had lapped up a bowl full of cream as she took the earl's arm.

'Of course, Alexander, for such a large party you will be needing a hostess.'

'I do not see that.'

'Oh, my dear sir, how can you be such a tease? You must have a hostess to look after your guests.'

The lady gave a soft, sultry laugh and threw a coy glance at him. Diana was aware of a very reprehensible feeling of satisfaction when the earl appeared unaffected by these blandishments, but his next words surprised her.

'Then Miss Grensham shall do it,' he declared.

'No!'

Diana's dismay was matched, if not surpassed, by that of Lady Frances. Her smile disappeared and her eyes positively snapped with displeasure. Alex, however, continued as if nothing was amiss.

'Since Diana will be here with the children she might as well make herself useful.'

Diana gave an uncertain laugh. 'How gallantly expressed, my lord.'

There was a glint of humour, but no remorse in his hard grey eyes when they rested upon her.

'You have lived at Chantreys for years. Clearly you are the best person to oversee the preparations for my visit.

I also need a list of all the local families to be invited to the ball. Do you think the task too much for you?'

'Not that part of it, but I have no wish to be your hostess.'

'You are in effect the mistress of this house. By your own admission you do not wish to leave. It seems only fitting that you should fill the role. Unless you would prefer me to put one of my other properties at your disposal?'

So that was it, he was trying to oust her from Chantreys. Well, he should see that she would not be moved. Head up, she smiled, aware that her charges were listening intently to the exchange.

'Having promised Meggie and Florence the pleasure of another visit from you, I could not deprive them of it now, my lord.'

There was a flicker of appreciation in his eyes but he merely nodded and began to pull on his gloves.

'I will send you word of the dates for my next visit as soon as it is decided. I shall also have the invitations for the ball printed. How many people do you think we can get in the orangery, a hundred, two?'

'When the late earl held a ball there we had every family in the neighbourhood plus guests from London, so over a hundred.'

'Ah, so you *have* done this before.'

'I helped my sister with the arrangements, but your brother's secretary, Mr Timothy, took care of most of the work.'

'Then he shall do so again. He has been making his way around all the estates for the past few months, refreshing the inventories for me, but I shall write and ask him to come to Chantreys to help you.'

Lady Frances shifted impatiently at his side.

'My lord, everyone else has gone to the carriages.'

'Yes, yes, one moment, I have yet to say goodbye to my wards.' He bent to accept a kiss and a hug from Florence and Meggie, and as he straightened he addressed Diana again.

'I shall leave all to you. Write to me, tell me what you need. It shall be done.'

With a final nod he turned and went out with Lady Frances on his arm. Diana and the girls followed and stood on the drive, waving until the carriages were lost from sight.

'When do you think they will be back?' asked Florence. 'How long will we have to learn a dance for them?'

'And will we have new dresses?' asked Meggie, skipping back to the house beside Diana. 'Oh, and shall we be allowed to go to the ball? When Alice Frederick's parents held a ball last year Alice said she was allowed to sit at the top of the stairs and watch the dancing.'

'But there are no stairs in the orangery,' Florence pointed out. 'And there is no minstrels' gallery either. Squire Huddleston has a minstrels' gallery at the Manor, and that is where the musicians sit to play. Where will they sit in the orangery, Diana? And what about—'

'Peace, peace!' Diana laughed, stopping and throwing up her hands. 'I have no answers for you. We must wait until Lord Davenport decides upon a date—indeed, by the time he reaches London he may have thought better of the whole idea!'

And I really, truly hope he does, she thought in silent desperation.

'So you have set the date for the Chantreys ball.' Gervase Wollerton ushered Alex into the box he had secured at the King's Theatre. 'Your grand ball will take place on the ninth of September.'

'Correct,' said Alex. 'I would have preferred it to be earlier, but I was obliged to delay when I learned that peace with Bonaparte is at an end. Lady Hune believes her granddaughter is trapped in France. It was inevitable that the Treaty of Amiens would not hold and she had written to Lady Cassandra, urging her and her husband to return to England, but it would seem they remained just a little too long.'

'Dashed unfortunate. I believe there are a number of families caught up in that way. How is Lady Hune taking it?'

'You know my great-aunt, Gervase, she faces it with her usual sangfroid, but she is anxious and I want to be nearby to support her,' replied Alex. 'Having agreed to sponsor Miss Tatham in her first Season, Lady Hune is committed to remaining in town, but she would want to stay in any case, since if there is news it will reach here first.'

'Then let us pray there is some news, and soon, my friend,' said Gervase with unusual gravity. 'When do you intend to go to Chantreys?'

'Two weeks before the ball. I will be taking a party of guests with me, including you, Gervase.'

'And will your wards be in residence?'

'They will indeed,' Alex replied grimly, thinking of the letter he had received that very morning.

'So Miss Grensham hasn't panicked at the thought of the house being overrun with your louche friends.'

'On the contrary, Miss Grensham has informed me that the children are looking forward to it. They are preparing a theatrical performance for us.'

Gervase laughed, but quickly turned it to a cough when Alex glared at him.

'I think she has your measure, Alex,' he said, keeping his eyeglass fixed upon the dancers who were now coming on to the stage. 'You are too fond of your wards to want to corrupt them. And she knows your guests won't be that disreputable. After all you are holding a ball to introduce yourself to the local society.'

'I am well aware of that,' replied Alex impatiently. 'I thought when I suggested the ball, the idea of acting as my hostess would have been enough to make her vacate Chantreys, for a few months at least.'

Mr Wollerton tore his eyes away from the stage long enough to cast a reproachful look at Alex.

'I have seen your guest list—it is hardly the sort of party we discussed holding there, old friend.'

'I am well aware of that fact, too!' Alex scowled. 'Dash it, Gervase, I had to invite my more respectable acquaintances. I can't take a crowd of rakes and lightskirts to Chantreys while Diana and the children are there.'

His scowl deepened. If he was honest with himself, the society of his more outrageous friends held little appeal for him these days. He would not have invited Lady Frances if he had not as good as promised her she should attend. However, she was entertaining company and would add a little leaven to the respectable party he had put together.

As the orchestra struck up for the opening melody he turned his eyes to the stage, wondering what had possessed him to arrange such an event. He could easily have found another property for his parties and his precious art collection, instead he had committed himself to what could only be a very tedious two weeks. The answer was clear, of course. He had told Diana he would persuade her to leave Chantreys of her own free will and he was not about to back down, not when the protagonist was a slip of a girl who showed no deference at all for his title or his social standing.

The dancers tripped on to the stage. Beside him Gervase raised his eyeglass to inspect them, but Alex was too lost in his own thoughts to give them more than a cursory glance. He had always been impatient of the sycophants who bowed and scraped and agreed with his every utterance, but Diana should show him some respect. He was after all several years her senior, as well as being a great deal more worldly-wise.

He shifted in his chair. It wasn't that he was conceited, puffed up in his own esteem, but it had become a matter of pride. Even as the thought formed he felt a grin tugging at his mouth. He had to admit he enjoyed pitting his wits against Diana. He wrote to her in the most high-handed manner regarding the arrangements for the house party and she always answered him graciously. She made no demur at his rapid and frequent changes to the guest list for the ball, and his outrageously flippant suggestion that she should invite the Prince of Wales was firmly but politely declined on the grounds that to have such an august personage at Chantreys would run the risk of at least two of his neighbours being carried off by apoplexy and seriously overpower the sensibilities of several local matrons.

'I am surprised you didn't invite Lady Hune and her young protégée,' remarked Mr Wollerton, when the dancers had finished their first performance.

'The marchioness has agreed to bring Miss Tatham to

the ball, but they will stay only a couple of nights.' Alex grinned. 'Dash it, Gervase, I hope the two weeks ain't going to be *that* respectable. Besides, I am still hopeful of finding a husband for Diana and do not want my great-aunt's débutante getting in the way.'

'Your attempts to palm Miss Grensham off on Avery or Hamilton didn't work last time,' said Wollerton frankly. 'I had thought one of them might take a fancy to her, for she is sensible enough and passably good-looking, if one discounts the freckles.'

'Some men would think the freckles quite charming,' replied Alex, unaccountably rallying to Diana's defence. 'But I have to admit that she didn't appear to advantage. Her gowns were too plain and several seasons out of date.' His lips twitched. 'I have done something about that. I am confident she will be more fashionably dressed when you next see her.'

In a mood of devilry he had sought out the town's most notorious modiste and sent her to Chantreys, complete with enough silks and muslins to clothe the whole of the *ton* and instructions to supply Miss Grensham with all the dresses she would need to fulfil her duties as his hostess.

Madame Francot was famous for producing outrageously daring gowns for society's most dashing matrons and she also ranked amongst her customers many of the most successful courtesans in London. Since she made no secret of the fact and was herself always dressed in the most flamboyant style, Alex had expected Diana to turn her away at the door and write him a furious letter full of righteous indignation. Instead he had received a politely worded missive, thanking him for his thoughtfulness and informing him that not only was *madame* supplying her with the most delightful gowns, she had also conjured several very pretty dresses for Florence and Meggie, as well as providing some very useful lessons in dressmaking skills for them.

He said now, 'The next time you see Miss Grensham I hope she will be dressed in the very latest fashion. We shall see then if we can't find someone to take her to wife and get her out of the way. I have invited several fellows who might just do the trick.'

'D'you know, Alex, I am beginning to think this trip to Chantreys will prove devilish dull.'

'I know, but it can't be helped. This party will be comprised only of those I can rely upon to behave themselves.'

'What, no straw damsels?' asked Mr Wollerton, a note of regret in his voice. 'No opera dancers?'

'I'd have thought you get enough of your dancers here,' retorted Alex, grinning in spite of himself. 'Why, have you taken a fancy to one of the little beauties currently parading her wares before us?'

He raised his quizzing glass and ran his eye over the line of dancers performing on the stage, their diaphanous skirts scandalously short.

'Certainly not,' retorted Mr Wollerton, affronted. 'I'll have you know we are watching a celebrated French ballet troupe. They have performed at the Paris Opera and are noted for their artistic interpretation.'

Alex gave a crack of laughter. 'Looking at the audience, I doubt many of them are here to admire the artistic interpretation.'

'These young ladies are extremely talented,' said his friend, spoiling the effect by adding, 'and extremely expensive.'

'Are they, now?' murmured Alex. He watched two of

the female dancers leap and twirl across the stage, his mind racing.

'Yes, they are,' affirmed Wollerton. 'As you would know if you ever bothered to come backstage with me.'

'Well, Gervase, you have convinced me.' Alex grinned. 'When the performance ends tonight I *will* come backstage with you!'

'Diana, Diana, there is a carriage coming towards the house!'

Meggie's excited voice brought Diana and Florence to the schoolroom window to see an elegant travelling chaise bowling along the drive.

'Could it be Madame Francot with our dresses?' asked Florence, her nose pressed against the glass.

'Not unless she has employed an army to finish them all in so short a time,' remarked Diana.

She smiled at the memory of the exuberant little Frenchwoman who had arrived at Chantreys with her entourage just over a week ago. Lord Davenport had given the lady quite the wrong idea of the kind of clothes required—quite deliberately, Diana suspected—but once they had resolved the misunderstanding Diana found Madame Francot most obliging. *Madame* was also enchanted by Meggie and Florence, said they reminded her of her own darling grandchildren and went out of her way to produce the most delightful sketches of gowns that would suit them. Diana had to check the voluble modiste only a couple of times for her rather colourful language and after that they proceeded very well indeed.

Madame had stayed two nights, entertained Diana with tales of her flight from France during the Terror, taught the children a little French as well as the secret of attaching a flounced hem to a gown, and left Chantreys in a cloud of perfumed silks and the promise to return *tout de suite* with all the gowns, cloaks, habits and dresses made up as they discussed.

Surely not even the indomitable Madame Francot would produce everything in so short a time? thought Diana as she ran down the stairs. A female voice talking rapidly in French floated up to her from the hall and she thought for a moment that she was wrong, but when she descended the last few stairs she found herself confronted by two young women she had never seen before in her life. They were both very pretty, very petite and wearing high-waisted walking-out dresses of the latest fashion. Fingle was goggling at them and when Diana arrived he cast an agonised appeal in her direction.

Before Diana could speak one of the young ladies came tripping over to her, taking off her bonnet and shaking out her golden curls as she said in her pretty, musical voice with a strong French accent, 'Ah, you must be Mademoiselle Grensham. Milord told us all about you and the *jolies filles*.'

'Did he?' said Diana warily.

'Mais oui.' The girl gave her a dazzling smile. 'He sent us 'ere to teach your leetle girls to dance!'

Chapter Ten

Diana blinked.

'Are you…' she paused, then continued slowly '…are you, perhaps, opera dancers?'

The second young lady approached. She was as dark as her companion was fair, but equally pretty.

'*Non, non, mademoiselle.* We are from ze Ballet de l'Opéra de Paris. They 'ave only the finest dancers in ze world, *je vous assure.* Monsieur Reynard, he brought us to *Londres* where Milord Davenport, he saw us perform, and he…er…*il a organisé avec* Monsieur Reynard that we should be…er…' She waved her little hands and looked to her companion for assistance.

'Zat we should come 'ere for two weeks to 'elp you with ze ballet your leetle girls are to perform.'

'*Bon.*' The brunette smiled and made a deep and graceful curtsy to Diana. 'I am Chantal, *à votre service, mademoiselle.*'

'*Et moi*—Suzanne.' The blonde twirled about, as if to demonstrate her ability.

How dare he?

The two girls stood before Diana, smiling expectantly. She bit her lip. It was not their fault. Alex had sent them on purpose to outrage her. So far she had managed to turn to advantage his every attempt to put her out of countenance, but opera dancers!

I see you as an opponent worthy of my mettle.

Diana heard his words as clearly as if Alex was standing at her shoulder and it calmed her. She must not react in anger, that was what Alex expected. She took a deep, steadying breath and coolly invited Chantal and Suzanne to accompany her to the drawing room, where Fingle would bring them refreshments. They went before her, exclaiming at the view from the window, the pretty furnishings, the paintings on the wall.

'Thank you. Will you not sit down, ladies?'

As they made themselves comfortable she observed them. They were very young, not yet twenty, she suspected, and brimming with friendly good humour. One could not dislike them, there was no malice in their attitude, they were genuinely happy to be at Chantreys and seemed unaware of Alex's motive in sending them here. She waited until Fingle had brought in wines and sweetmeats before questioning them. She decided it would be easier if the conversation was conducted in French, then they could have no excuse for thinking she did not understand them.

'Lord Davenport sent you here to teach his wards to dance, is that not so?'

'But, yes, *mademoiselle*. He says they are to perform for his guests at the party he is arranging.'

'Are you well acquainted with Lord Davenport?' she asked them. 'The truth, if you please.'

'He came backstage, with his friend, Monsieur Wollerton.' Chantal's big brown eyes looked at her with not a hint of guile. 'Monsieur Reynard, he is very strict about the gentlemen he allows to visit us after the performance.'

'No doubt they have to be very rich.'

'Certainly, *mademoiselle*.'

'And Lord Davenport is exceedingly rich,' Diana continued. 'He is able to…er…pay Monsieur Reynard very well for your services.'

'But, yes, of a certainty. It is not at all convenient for us to leave the ballet at such a time, but milord, he was very exact about the dancers he required.'

'Ah.' Diana felt an inordinate amount of relief. 'So you are not…'

'We are not his lovers,' finished Suzanne with a frankness Diana wished she could emulate.

Suzanne clapped her hands and gave a little trill of laughter. 'I wish it might be so, *mademoiselle*, but, no. Milord Davenport, he comes to watch us dance, yes, but he has been backstage but rarely and he has never taken any of us for his mistress.' She looked at her companion and they sighed in unison. 'It is a great pity, for he is very 'andsome, do you not think?'

'No, I do not,' retorted Diana, rattled. 'His countenance is too rugged and his nose is not straight.'

'But he is so very big, *mademoiselle*,' murmured Chantal dreamily. 'Such a strong, shapely body. And when he smiles…'

Yes, well, Diana did not want to think about that. She rose abruptly.

'Very well. If Lord Davenport has gone to the trouble of sending you here then we must make use of you. I shall have rooms prepared for you immediately. And I shall take you upstairs to meet the children. It will be beneficial for you to converse with them in French, I think. They know enough now to follow you and it will improve their ability considerably. Now, shall we go?'

Lincoln delivered Diana's next letter to Alex when he brought up his hot water a few mornings later. The missive had been sitting on a silver tray in the hall and the valet recognised the neat, sloping writing. He had become familiar with it over the past few months and was intrigued to see its effect upon his master. So far the lady's correspondence had elicited a variety of responses. Sometimes the earl would burst out laughing as he scanned the lines, other times he would scowl and mutter ominously under his breath.

With his face devoid of all emotion, Lincoln handed the letter to Lord Davenport and then busied himself at the washstand. He heard a bark of laughter. That augured well.

'The little minx.'

Lincoln turned, a look of innocent enquiry upon his face.

'My lord?'

But the earl was in no mood to expand upon his utterance.

'Nothing.'

He waved Lincoln away, declaring he would shave himself. This was nothing unusual, but the valet would have dearly liked to remain a little longer in the bedchamber and try if he could see just what it was that Miss Grensham had written. However, his master had put the letter under his reading book and was even now preparing to get out of bed. Lincoln tenderly draped the folded towel over the rail and took his leave.

'So she is delighted with my choice of dancing teachers, is she?'

Alex brushed the soap liberally over his face and picked up the razor. He had really thought that Diana would take one look at those two little charmers and send them packing. Instead, her letter informed him that Meggie and Florence were not only enjoying the ballet steps they were learning, but they were also becoming most proficient in the French language. His eyes narrowed. He would wager Diana's first reaction was not as sanguine as her letter implied.

He had been most careful in his choice of dancers. Reynard had assured him that Chantal and Suzanne had been strictly reared and that he looked after them like his own daughters. Alex was not so sure about that, but he had interviewed them both and satisfied himself that they could be trusted to behave well during their stay at Chantreys. Indeed, if they wished to earn the enormous sum he had agreed with Reynard, they would make sure there was no hint of impropriety attached to their visit. Perhaps he should take a trip down there, just to make sure.

The idea took root. There was also his secretary to consider. He had sent John Timothy to Chantreys to deal with arrangements for the forthcoming ball, but it would do no harm for him to go and see for himself just how things were progressing. He cast his mind over his engagements. His great-aunt was bearing up well, despite her worries over her granddaughter's incarceration in France, and he need not dance attendance upon her and her protégée every day. Lady Frances would expect him to attend her party that evening, but he could send his apologies for that. No one would wonder at it if he wished to assure himself that everything at Chantreys was in readiness for his guests.

His ablutions complete, Alex dried his face and considered the matter. He was honest enough to admit that none of these points was the real reason he wanted to drive into Essex. It had cost him no little effort to keep away from Chantreys these past weeks and with every letter he received from Diana the temptation grew. He wanted to see her, to talk to her. He wanted to know what she really thought of Madame Francot and if she was truly pleased to have the dancers at Chantreys or if she was merely trying to pay him back in kind.

She haunted his thoughts, with her stubborn refusal to move out, her continuous opposition to his plan to find her and the children a new home. And why had he challenged her in that foolish way? He enjoyed teasing her, but there was little enjoyment in remaining in London, unable to see for himself just how she was reacting to his taunts. A smile tugged at his mouth. Her countenance was so expressive, he could read it like a book. That is what he missed. Her letters amused him, but it was not the same as a face-to-face confrontation. His duties to his great-aunt had filled most of his summer, but even when he had got away from town for a short time the horse-racing had failed to divert him.

With sudden decision he threw down the towel and set the bell pealing for Lincoln. Within minutes a message had been sent to the stables to prepare his curricle and he was changing his town dress for something more suited to a drive into the country.

* * *

'My lord, this is a pleasant surprise. Miss Grensham and the young ladies are in the orangery, taking a dancing lesson.'

There was a twinkle in the butler's eyes as he welcomed Alex into the house.

As if the old man had detected a blossoming romance, thought Alex in alarm.

'I have come to see my secretary.' Alex stripped off his gloves and put them on the hall table beside his hat. 'Is Timothy in the office?'

His cold tone had its effect. Immediately Fingle became the perfect butler, inclining his head a little as he answered in the affirmative. Good, thought Alex, as he strode away. He didn't want anyone getting the wrong idea about his visit here today. Diana was co-guardian of his wards. He would have to see her in that capacity, naturally, but he had no interest in her as a woman. She was small, thin, freckled and confrontational. A nuisance. She had no place in his hedonistic, well-ordered life. None at all.

His business with John Timothy was soon concluded. Arrangements for his visit were well in hand, the south pavilion was cleaned out and all the rooms made fit for guests while the orangery roof had been repaired and extra staff from the village would be recruited in time for the arrival of the earl and his guests in two weeks' time.

'I have ordered a covering over the path from the house to the orangery, my lord, just in case the weather should be inclement for the ball.'

'Good idea.' Alex nodded absently, wondering how

Diana would react when she saw him. Would she be pleased, or would she rip up at him for his high-handed behaviour?

'Miss Grensham thought of it, my lord,' said John Timothy, tidying the papers on his desk. 'She is an excellent manager, if I may say so.' He smiled. 'She really has left me very little to do.'

'I had hoped your being here would take some of the work from her shoulders, John.'

'And I have, my lord, but she had most of it organised before I even arrived. She knew exactly what was required and how to obtain it. I suppose it comes from living in the house for several years, she is well acquainted with all the local tradespeople. Very efficient, she is, but in no way *managing*, if you know what I mean, sir. It has been a pleasure to work with her.'

'I am glad you have got on so well.' Alex was a little taken aback by this fulsome praise from his usually laconic secretary. He spent a few more minutes discussing business before going off to find Diana.

The orangery was situated at some distance from the house itself, behind the south pavilion. It was a large structure, its southern wall consisting entirely of glass and was built originally to house and protect citrus fruits during the winter. It had been enlarged considerably during the early years of the last century in an unsuccessful attempt to cultivate the highly fashionable pineapple, but the very size of the building had made it impossible to heat successfully. Since then the building had returned to its original function, with a few pieces of furniture added so that guests might take their ease on sunny days, and on rare occasions it was used as a ballroom.

As Alex followed the path to the south front of the orangery he saw that the long windows had been opened and sounds of much merriment and childish laughter drifted out to him, overlaid by the melodic sounds of a pianoforte. He remembered Diana writing to tell him that she had asked John Timothy to hire an instrument for the musicians to use at the ball. Perhaps she thought he would baulk at the expense. Perhaps that was her way of paying him back in some measure. Well, let her think that. He had been considering replacing the old harpsichord at Chantreys with a more fashionable keyboard, so if she thought to upset him with her extravagance she would be disappointed.

Alex entered by the side door that led into a small anteroom. It was filled with the odd pieces of furniture that had somehow accumulated in the orangery over the years. They had obviously been moved in preparation for the ball and were swathed in new holland covers. He smiled. That would be Diana's doing, no one else would have thought it worthwhile to protect the old sofa that had been relegated to the orangery in his father's day. He slipped quietly into the main room and stood for a moment, enjoying the scene. The orangery had been emptied of all but a few decorative citrus trees in their pots. The walls were freshly painted and the candle sconces had been polished until they shone. The hired pianoforte stood in one corner of the dais at the far end and a woman he had not seen before was playing a lively tune that echoed around the large room, but Alex paid scant heed to the music or the pianist, for it was the little group in the centre of the dais who held his attention. The two French girls, his wards and Diana were all dressed in gowns of gossamer-thin white muslin that stopped well short of the ankle.

He was immediately aware that of the three ladies, Diana's ankles were by far the most shapely. Meggie and Florence were sitting on the edge of the dais with their backs to him, watching as the two dancers helped Diana to rise on tiptoe. There was a great deal of giggling and laughter as she wobbled and collapsed and tried again, encouraged by her companions. On her last attempt she achieved a very creditable attitude.

Alex could not help himself.

'Well done,' he declared, coming forward.

The lady playing the piano stopped suddenly and everyone turned to see who had spoken. Their differing reactions caused him no little amusement. His wards shrieked joyfully and ran towards him while the two French dancers followed, beaming. Only Diana held back, her hands creeping to her cheeks as if trying to cover up the deep blush that had risen to her face. His amusement grew. She would find it difficult to rip up at him now, at least until her confusion had died away.

'Ah, milord Davenport, welcome, you are just what we need!' The blonde, whom he remembered was called Suzanne, clapped her hands in delight and gestured him to join them. 'We are teaching Mademoiselle Grensham to stand *sur le demi-pointe*, as we do now in ze ballet. Come, come, milord, we need you to play the part of the great Monsieur Vestris.'

'But I am no dancer,' protested Alex, laughing as he stepped on to the dais.

'*Tiens*, we do not need you to *dance*,' explained the brunette, with an impatient toss of her head. 'Only to 'elp the lady to balance.'

Diana gave a little gasp.

'No, Chantal, we were not seriously trying to—I do not think—'

'Stand 'ere, milord,' Chantal commanded him, ignoring Diana's breathless protest. 'You must be behind *mademoiselle* and place your hands *comme ça. Bon.*'

Alex was aware of Diana's alarm but she made no further demur as he took his place behind her. No, she wouldn't, he thought, not with Meggie and Florence watching, and the two dancers acting as if there was nothing the least unusual in what was happening. He guessed Diana and he were thinking the same thing at that moment, to get this over with and move on with the least possible fuss.

Smiling to show he thought there was nothing amiss, Alex allowed Chantal to take his hands and place them on Diana. Immediately his throat dried and he lost all desire to smile. Her waist was so tiny his fingers almost spanned it. He could feel the soft flesh of her body through the thin layer of fine muslin. With a jolt he realised she was not wearing stays. Of course, he should have known it the moment he saw those diaphanous gowns, they would not be able to dance so freely if they were restricted by stiff linen and whalebone.

It had become very hot and his neckcloth felt far too tight, but he dared not lift a finger to loosen it. He kept silent as the dancers encouraged Diana to rise on tiptoe again. He supported her lightly, but he could feel the smooth curve of her waist as it narrowed beneath her rib-cage and his fingers rested on the hard bone of her hips. He wanted to tighten his hold, to pull her close, feel that soft body yield against his own. The mere thought of it sent a jolt of pure lust through him and he struggled to suppress it as everyone applauded Diana's graceful rise.

'Very good, *mademoiselle*. You are *très naturelle*.'

Diana came down off her toes, Alex removed his hands and she quickly stepped away him.

'Thank you, Suzanne, but I think you flatter me.'

He heard the slight tremble in her voice and saw her shoulders pull back, as if she was trying to regain her composure.

'That is enough for today,' she continued. 'We should return to the house and change. I have asked Mrs Wallace to prepare a light nuncheon for everyone in the dining room.'

Her voice was much firmer but she was taking all her weight on her right leg, the left foot lifting very slightly. He had not noticed her doing that when he came in. When she was not aware of his presence.

'You will eat with us, will you not, Uncle Alex?' said Meggie, coming up.

'Yes, of course.' His own voice was a little less sure than usual. He cleared his throat. 'You had best run on ahead and make sure Fingle has laid a place for me.'

Laughing and chattering, Meggie and Florence set off with the dancers while Diana moved towards the pianoforte where the unknown lady had risen and was packing away her sheet music.

'Mrs Appleton, thank you for playing for us again today. I am most grateful.' She cast a fleeting glance towards Alex but did not meet his eyes. 'Do you know Lord Davenport, ma'am? He is the girls' guardian. Mrs Appleton lives in the village, my lord, and kindly agreed to play for us.'

Alex murmured a polite response, his attention still

distracted by the memory of Diana's waist beneath his hands. Mrs Appleton blushed and murmured something incoherent, clearly discomposed to be facing an earl and when Diana invited her to remain for nuncheon she accepted with a few more disjointed sentences, then hurried away to the house.

Diana realised her mistake as soon as Mrs Appleton had left the orangery. She should have accompanied the lady back to the house rather than remain alone with Alex. Why was it that whenever he was near her wits disappeared? He did not look to be best pleased and was no doubt going to rip up at her for something. She eyed him resentfully.

'I do wish you would give me notice of when you intend to call at Chantreys, my lord.'

His frowning look disappeared.

'But it is my house, Diana. Besides, if you had known I was coming you might have cancelled your dancing lesson.'

'I would certainly not have been dressed thus,' she replied frankly, colouring a little. 'I did not expect to have an audience.'

'Evidently.' He grinned. 'Pray do not feel embarrassed on my account. Shall we go back to the house?'

He held out his arm and Diana placed her fingers upon it. Her body was still thrumming with the memory of his hands on her waist. He had behaved with perfect propriety, his hold had been light, impersonal, just enough to support her, but it had sent excitement fizzing through her blood. Suzanne and Chantal had been perfectly at ease, they saw nothing wrong in being so lightly clad and having a gentleman stand so close, but they were dancers and accustomed to such things. She could only hope her face had not been as red as a beetroot!

'So,' said the earl, 'will our guests have the pleasure of seeing you dance with Meggie and Florence?'

'Heavens, no. I would not dream of—that is, I was merely...' She tailed off, wondering miserably how she could explain to him that when she saw them all dancing so freely, not restricted by a corset, she was eager to experience it for herself. And then Chantal had offered to lend her one of her gowns and there had seemed no harm in it... 'I did not intend for anyone to see me dancing.'

'I am not just anyone.'

'Quite true,' she replied with false sweetness. 'I have no doubt you are quite accustomed to consorting with dancers and are not at all shocked by their scanty dress.'

'Oh, I have seen dancers much more scantily clad,' he replied cheerfully.

Diana bit her lip. He was laughing at her. She wanted to laugh, too, and to retort, but she knew it would be unwise to challenge him further. She must maintain a dignified silence until they reached the house. Instead of thinking of Alex and his teasing ways she would concentrate upon walking, as she had been doing for the past few weeks, trying not to favour the left leg, but to put each heel to the floor with equal weight and prevent the halting, dragging step that has become such a habit.

They entered the hall just as Suzanne and Chantal came skipping down the stairs, their dance dresses replaced by demure muslin gowns. They informed her that the 'leetle girls' had gone upstairs with Nurse to be made tidy in readiness for their nuncheon.

Diana nodded. 'Thank you. If you would all like to go

into the dining room I will fetch Meggie and Florence and join you shortly.'

'What,' Alex murmured wickedly as she released his arm, 'you would leave me alone with these charming young creatures? Is that wise?'

'I shall have to trust you to behave yourself.' Diana stepped over to the dining-room door and threw it open, adding with a mischievous smile, 'And in case you forget yourself, my lord, we have Mrs Appleton and Mr Timothy here to keep you in order.'

When their repast was finished the party broke up. Mr Timothy offered to drive Mrs Appleton back to the village while Chantal and Suzanne took the girls off to the gardens. Diana was about to leave the room when Alex stopped her.

'I thought we might go through the guest list for the ball.'

'I sent you the full list last week, my lord.'

'But you will have had more replies to the invitations since then.'

Bowing to the inevitable, Diana led him to a small room that had been furnished as a study. She pulled a large ledger from the desk. Alex walked over to the window, which gave a good view of the flower gardens.

'My wards appear to be on the best of terms with the *mademoiselles*.'

'I told you as much in my letter, sir.'

'I thought you wrote that merely to punish me for my impudence in sending them here.'

Diana laughed. 'I confess I was at first nonplussed that you should do so, but they assured me they are not opera dancers, but respectable members of the French ballet.'

She added shrewdly, 'I also suspect they are being paid very well.'

'True, but you have promised my guests theatricals and I would not have them disappointed.'

'Meggie and Florence are learning a ballad to sing and they have a very pretty dance to perform. They will not let you down.'

Alex turned from the window. 'And what will you be doing?'

'Me? Why nothing. I am merely their governess.'

'You are my hostess,' he reminded her. 'And while I think of it, I hope you now have sufficient new gowns for the occasion?'

Diana thought of the cupboards and the linen press in her room, all full to overflowing.

'More than sufficient, sir, as Madame Francot's bills will attest. There is only the ballgown yet to be delivered. *Madame* was dissatisfied with the colour and had to order more material.'

'And are they very daring? Madame Francot is renowned for her dashy dresses.'

She saw the teasing light in his eyes and it was an effort not to reply in kind, but that was a slippery slope. It was better to keep him at a distance, to keep her dignity.

'I think you will find they are appropriate to the occasion.'

He was smiling at her and, oh, how she wanted to give in, to confess how much she had enjoyed looking at the silks and muslins with the modiste, who had insisted she choose gowns for all occasions, for dancing, walking, riding or merely looking elegant. Very much like a débutante preparing for her first Season. At least she assumed that is how it must feel, although she had never been in that position herself. If only she could tell Alex, but it was not possible. He might laugh at her. Worse, he might pity her. Quickly she thrust the open ledger at him.

'Here is the list of everyone invited to the ball, my lord, and you will see there is a mark against those who have accepted. There are very few replies still outstanding.'

She sat down in the window while Alex took a seat at the desk and perused the list. It gave her an opportunity to look at him, to observe the unruly dark hair that fell forward as he leaned over the page. Chantal and Suzanne had said they thought him handsome. She did not consider him so, but she was forced to admit there was something attractive about him. Perhaps it was a combination of his strong, rugged features, the mobile mouth that would curve suddenly into a smile and those slate-grey eyes that could pierce her soul.

She dragged her eyes away and realised she had almost let out a sigh. If she *had* been a débutante, young and naïve, she might have pined for his good opinion, tried to win his regard, but she was a woman of two-and-twenty, governess and guardian to two young girls. Such dreams were pointless. Alex knew her flaws, he had seen the ugly scar on her leg and he found her small and unattractive. She could not possibly compare with all the beautiful ladies he knew. Beauties like Frances Betsford.

Diana felt a sudden chill and rubbed her arms. He had seen her naked when she had climbed from the lake and now he had seen her dressed in the short skirts of a dancer. If it had been possible to enflame him then one of those scenarios should have done the trick, but they had not. On both occasions he had acted with humour, with kindness, but never with passion.

No? Then what about the kisses?

She fixed her eyes on the far horizon. The first time had been the result of much wine. It was well known that men could not control themselves when they had been drinking. It was a lowering thought that a man could only find her attractive if he was drunk. She thought of that second, searing embrace in the moonlight. He had broken away as soon as she had resisted. Very commendable, but it clearly showed he only thought of her as a passing fancy.

'Hmm?' Alex looked up. 'Did you say something, Diana?'

'N-no.' She shook her head. 'I said nothing. I beg your pardon if I disturbed you.'

'It does not matter, I have finished with this.' He closed the book. 'So, you have everything arranged. Is there anything you need me to do?'

'I do not think so. The ball is organised, the musicians engaged, Mrs Wallace is already turning out all the guest rooms. Mr Timothy is on hand to help with any last-minute crises.'

'And you have allocated the rooms?'

She nodded. 'As you instructed.' She threw off the last shreds of melancholy and allowed herself a small smile. 'You have nothing to do but to arrive with your guests, my lord.'

'Excellent. John Timothy told me you managed everything very well.'

'Yes, in spite of your attempts to throw me into a panic.'

'You gave me my own again on every occasion.'

'I shall take that as a compliment, my lord.'

'Yes, do so!' He hesitated, looking as if he would like

to say more, but after a moment he seemed to change his mind. He pushed himself out of his chair. 'I must go.'

'Yes.'

Diana wished she could find some way to keep him there longer, but what good would that achieve, save to delay the inevitable parting? She rose. 'Will you find Meggie and Florence? They will be unhappy if you leave without saying goodbye.'

'Yes, I'll find them. I hope all this planning will mean you are able to enjoy yourself once the guests arrive.'

'Of course, although you must understand that I will not neglect the girls.'

'I would not expect you to do so, but Nurse is perfectly capable of looking after them while you fulfil your duties as my hostess.'

'I trust I shall not disappoint you, sir.' She said, unable to resist, 'But tell me the truth! Did you suggest this whole thing—the house party, the ball and the idea of my being your hostess—was it all done in the hope I should take fright and remove from Chantreys?'

'Do you think me capable of such a thing?'

'Why, yes,' she said frankly. 'I do.'

He smiled.

'I said you were a worthy opponent, Diana. Very well.' He shrugged. 'I admit that was my intention, to intimidate you with the idea of a large party and a ball. It was reprehensible of me and I beg your pardon.'

She chuckled. 'But it is a large and *respectable* party, sir. I do not think that is quite your usual style.'

'No, it is not.' He grimaced. 'I admit I was caught out there, but having committed to it I cannot go back. And, do you know the strangest thing of all? I find myself quite looking forward to it now.'

'I am delighted to hear that.'

A smile spread through her and burst forth as she held her hand out to him. All restraint was forgotten, so much so that she did not recognise the warning signs, did not hold back as he pulled her closer, into his arms. It seemed the most natural thing in the world to accept his kiss, to close her eyes and forget everything except the warm, enveloping embrace.

When at last he raised his head she remained in his arms, her head thrown back against his shoulder, eyes half-closed while he stared down at her. It took a few moments for Diana to bring his face into focus and when she did the warm contentment that had wrapped around her was stripped away. She gathered her strength and pushed herself out of his arms, turning away that he might not see the hurt and disappointment in her eyes.

'Diana, I beg your pardon—'

She put up a hand. 'Please, do not say anything. I realise you had no intention of kissing me.'

'No. I forgot myself.'

The knife in her heart twisted.

'I quite understand.' Her voice was calm, controlled. She gripped her hands together. She could do this if she did not look at him. 'Please leave me now, sir. You have a long drive back to town.'

'Yes. Diana, I—'

His voice was harsh. What right had he to be angry with her? He had already admitted he was at fault. She whipped up her own indignation to protect herself.

She said coldly, 'There is no need to explain your reprehensible behaviour, my lord. Just leave me, if you please.'

Diana stood with her back to him, tense, head held

high, straining her ears for any sound behind her. At last there was the faintest noise, like a sigh, then a firm step, the opening of the door, the soft click as it closed. He was gone.

She kept her eyes fixed on the window but all she saw was the look she had seen in Alex's eyes when he had raised his head from that kiss. Bewilderment. Consternation. Horror.

Chapter Eleven

It was just over a week until Alex was due to take his party to Chantreys. He had not had any word from Diana since that last, calamitous visit. He had tried to write and apologise for his behaviour, but every attempt ended with the paper being torn to shreds. How could he explain what had happened when he did not understand it himself? When she had smiled up at him his response had been pure instinct. He had taken the hand she was holding out to him and drawn her into his arms as if they had done it a hundred times before. Afterwards she had been so calm about it, so understanding, but she must now think him a hardened rake who would take every opportunity to steal a kiss.

His lip curled in bitter self-derision. Perhaps that is what he was. He had grown so accustomed to being courted by every woman he met, perhaps Diana's resistance had attracted him. What a courtcard he must be, if he must pursue a woman simply because she did not pursue him!

London was white-hot, baking in the August sun, and Alex did not want to venture out but he could no longer put off a visit to his tailor, or to his bootmaker. It was just past noon and he was crossing Piccadilly when he saw Diana and her charges emerging from one of the shops. For one wild, foolish moment he thought he had conjured her from his imagination, because she was constantly in his thoughts these days.

She looked very fetching in a new sage-green pelisse and with a chip-straw bonnet fixed over her glossy red curls. He recalled her comment that no one noticed governesses. No one would think of her as a governess today, several gentlemen turned their heads to take another look as they passed her. She was busy handing a neatly wrapped parcel to her footman and did not see Alex until he called out to her.

She looked around. There was no mistaking the dismay in her face. Meggie and Florence immediately ran up, holding up their purchases for Alex to admire. Diana let them chatter on for a few moments before she shushed them and drew them back to her side.

'Good day to you, Lord Davenport,' she greeted him without meeting his eyes. 'We have come to town to do a little shopping. Madame Francot's new clothes made it necessary to buy matching gloves and slippers and all kinds of little extras.'

He glanced at the shop behind them.

'And books?'

His teasing question brought only the ghost of a smile.

'One cannot come to town without visiting Hatchards, my lord.'

'Where do you go next?'

'I am not quite sure.' She glanced back at the footman. 'There are more purchases to make, but poor Christopher has about as much as he can carry already.'

'I have a suggestion,' said Alex. 'Let Christopher take your parcels to the carriage while I take you all to Gunter's tea shop for ices.'

The idea found instant approval with Meggie and Florence and he was pleased to see that Diana's hesitation was very brief before she nodded her agreement and dispatched her footman, with orders that he was to meet them later in Berkeley Square. Piccadilly was particularly crowded and it was impossible for them all to walk together. Diana invited Alex to lead the way and he found himself with Florence at his side. She slipped her little hand into his.

'Is this not quite delightful, Uncle Alex?'

'Yes, delightful,' murmured Alex.

He spotted George Brummel strolling in the centre of a group of fashionably dressed gentlemen on the other side of the road. One of their number was Gervase Wollerton and Alex touched his hat to him, hiding his grin as the rest of the party glanced across the road, several of them raising their quizzing glasses to stare at the sight of the noted Corinthian hand in hand with a chattering child. That would give them something to talk of in the club today, he thought and he had no doubt that Gervase would quiz him mercilessly when they met up at Feversham House later that evening. Surprisingly, Alex found he did not care.

There was no opportunity to talk until they were seated in Gunter's and the girls were enjoying their ices. Diana had declined the treat, but had been persuaded to take a cup of coffee. Alex waited until they had all been served before he spoke.

'Do you go back to Chantreys tonight?'

'No, we are booked into an hotel.'

'I told you to come and stay in Half Moon Street.'

'That was very kind of you, my lord, but I did not think it wise.'

She kept her eyes lowered and it did not need the faint flush on her cheek to tell him why she had not brought the children to his town house. She did not trust him.

'Diana is taking us to the theatre!' announced Meggie.

'We are going to see *The Frozen Mountain,*' Diana hurried to explain. 'I have studied it thoroughly and taken advice from acquaintances who have already seen it. I am content that it is quite suitable for young minds. And there is a ballet, too, which they will enjoy.'

She gave him a bright smile, but it was a professional one, it did not warm her eyes. She had put him at a distance.

And that was what he wanted, Alex told himself, nettled. The woman was a confounded nuisance, she distracted him, made him act out of character. And she was standing in the way of all his plans. The best thing would be to marry her off, give her something to think about apart from the children. They could then be moved off with a new governess to another house, or sent to school. That way everyone would be happy. A movement at the window caught his eye.

'Ah, Christopher has arrived,' said Diana, looking up. She pushed away her empty cup. 'And in excellent time, as we are ready to go.'

When they emerged into the sunshine Diana gathered the girls to her.

'Meggie, Florence, thank Lord Davenport for his kindness and we will be on our way.'

'Have you more shopping to do? I could come with you,' offered Alex.

'Thank you, my lord, but we have taken up more than enough of your time today. Your way lies towards Piccadilly and we have a few purchases to make in New Bond Street. We shall look forward to seeing you at Chantreys next week.'

Alex watched, silenced as she walked away, Meggie and Florence on either side. She had dismissed him and with such confidence that he had been quite unable to argue. He felt a reluctant admiration for Miss Diana Grensham, who was proving to be a very worthy opponent. His eyes narrowed as he watched the little group disappear around a corner. Diana's awkward, halting step had almost completely disappeared.

Alex turned and made his way back to Piccadilly. The day was almost gone and he had much to do before this evening, when he was promised to join his friends at the Fevershams' rout, but the thought of a riotous evening of cards and drinking was surprisingly unappealing. He thought he would much prefer to watch an innocuous play at Drury Lane.

Chantreys was alive with activity. The guests were due at any time and Diana was as apprehensive as her wards were excited at the thought of having so many visitors. Not that it showed when she and the girls made their way to the drawing room shortly before the dinner hour. She had left Fingle and Mrs Wallace to greet the earl and his party and deal with the bustle and confusion of settling everyone into their rooms. She had continued with the girls' lessons in the schoolroom, but ever since she had heard the first scrunch of wheels on the gravelled drive she had been expecting a curt summons. It had not come and she took the girls downstairs at the appointed hour, steeling herself to appear calm and composed as she entered the room.

She was wearing one of her new evening gowns, a moss-green silk that Madam Francot had said would enhance her beautiful eyes. Diana had dismissed her words as mere flattery, but when she tried on the gown she was surprised to see that her eyes did look larger, brighter and it brought out the tiny green flecks in them. It gave her confidence. She might never be beautiful, but in this gown she did not look *dull*.

Diana breathed slowly, steadily and forced herself not to drag her left leg as she led the girls forward. Alex had called her a worthy opponent and worthy opponents did not cower or walk with a halting step, not if they could do anything about it.

A memory flickered. She was a child, crying, while across the room Mama and the doctor were locked in fierce debate.

'Madam, the child must try to put her weight on the leg. It will hurt at first, of course, but if she *persists*—'

'It is no good. She is a cripple and we must face the fact. Good day to you. Your services are no longer required. Send in your bill...'

And Diana had been left to her own devices, favouring the left leg, allowing the muscles to waste, accepting the fact that she would always walk with a limp. Until Alex had questioned it.

The earl appeared, imposing, breathtaking in his dark coat and white linen. His rugged countenance was impassive. Had he noticed the effort she was making to walk normally? Did he care? It would appear not, she thought as he gave her a little bow. His frowning gaze rested on her neck.

'Is that the only jewellery you have?'

'It is.' She put her hand up to the single string of pearls clasped around her throat. 'Are they not suitable?'

'Oh, eminently.'

His attention was claimed by the children and she observed how his hard look softened at their effusive greeting. She might have told him that governesses had little need of trinkets but he was already taking the girls off to meet his guests. He indicated by a look that Diana should accompany them.

The introductions began. Diana recognised some guests from the first house party, including Mr Wollerton, whose friendly greeting she returned with a grateful smile, but there were still a dozen faces she did not know. Exchanging greetings with so many strangers was a struggle for one who had spent the past few years avoiding society but everyone was very polite. It was clear that Alex had already informed them all of her position at Chantreys as the girls' governess and guardian and no one questioned her right to be hostess, although when Alex led her past Lady Frances Diana felt those blue eyes boring into her like daggers of ice.

When dinner was announced Nurse came downstairs to collect the children, leaving Diana free to join her guests. It needed every spare leaf inserted into the table to accommodate all the diners and as she took her place Diana felt very alone, for she and Alex had the full length of the table between them. Her glance moved to Lady Frances, who was sitting on Alex's right. If he had appointed Frances as his hostess then she would have been sitting here, as far away from the host as it was possible to be.

Diana concentrated on her duty, making sure those around her had everything they required. At one point she looked up to find Alex was watching her. He raised his glass and her chin went up. What did it matter if he wanted Lady Frances by his side? It was nothing to her. She smiled and returned his salute. Alex might not admire her as a woman, but he did consider her a worthy opponent.

Throughout dinner Alex cast frequent glances down the table. Diana was conversing quite happily with her guests, whereas the company around him seemed dull and lacklustre. Even Frances's barbed wit failed to amuse him. At the appropriate moment Diana rose and invited the ladies to follow her into the drawing room, leaving the gentlemen to enjoy a glass of brandy. The conversation moved on to politics and gambling and, inevitably, women. Sir Charles Urmston leaned forward to address his host.

'I understand you wish your guests to act with decorum this week, Davenport.'

'Discretion was the word I used,' replied Alex coolly. 'I expect my guests to behave with discretion while they are under my roof. I hope Lady Frances made that clear to you?'

He had not been pleased when Frances had told him this morning that her cousin Simonstone could not come and she had invited Urmston to take his place. However, at that point it was too late to do much about it. He signalled to Fingle to charge the glasses again and sat back, his brow slightly furrowed.

'She did, my lord, and I must say I was a little surprised.' Urmston gave the superior smile that never failed

to grate upon Alex's nerves. 'Your wards are quite delightful, my lord, but I had not thought you the sort to turn
prudish.' He stopped, raising his head as though some
shocking thought had struck him. 'You ain't taken to religion, have you, Davenport?'

'No, of course he hasn't,' exclaimed Wollerton, laughing. 'He's just trying to protect his wards from corrupt-
ing influences such as yourself, Urmston!'

A ripple of laughter went around the table and the conversation moved on, but Alex found himself regarding
Urmston with growing dislike. Why had Frances invited
him? Did she think he hadn't heard the rumours about
the two of them? Surely she knew Urmston was not the
sort of bachelor Alex wanted to foist upon Diana. Simonstone now, the cousin who was meant to have come, he
was a different proposition. A respectable fellow of independent means, very much like Avery and Hamilton.
Dull dogs, all of them, but any one of them could be re-
lied upon to make a good husband for Diana. That was
why he had invited them to Chantreys.

Alex's gaze strayed back to Urmston. Most likely
Frances was trying to make him jealous by flaunting
Urmston before him and in his own house, too. Alex's
mouth thinned. Such tactics would not work with him.
Quite the opposite, in fact.

The decanters were empty and Alex decided not to
send for more. Instead he suggested they should join the
ladies. As they all rose and moved towards the door, Sir
Charles waited for Alex and fell in beside him.

'You know, that governess of yours is a taking little
thing, Davenport. I'd be happy to give her a tumble, if
you want her discredited.'

Alex stopped. The others were already crossing the hall and he detained Urmston in the now-empty dining room, closing the door upon them.

'I never wanted her discredited, as you put it,' he said in icy tones. 'Let me tell you now, Urmston, that I should take it very badly if anyone were to seduce Miss Grensham. Very badly indeed.' He met and held the older man's gaze. 'I hope we understand one another.'

For an instant he saw a flash of something in those hooded eyes. Anger, dislike, he could not be sure, then it was gone and Sir Charles was smiling and spreading his hands.

'Why, of course, Davenport, I was just trying to be of assistance.'

'I think I can do without your assistance in this matter, Urmston.' Alex opened the door. 'Shall we go?'

Diana tried to keep the conversation lively and interesting, but it was clear that the ladies were not enamoured of their own company, for when the gentlemen came in the atmosphere changed immediately. Only Mrs Peters appeared not to be affected and continued to rattle on inconsequentially to whoever would listen to her. One of the gentlemen suggested music and the ladies were delighted to oblige.

'It is a pity you do not have a pianoforte, my lord,' remarked Lady Cranbury, a dashing matron with roguish eyes. 'It is all the rage now, you know.'

'I am aware,' returned Alex. 'I intend to install one here before the year is out.'

'The children will like that,' observed Diana. 'Our neighbours, the Fredericks, have one and they have been allowed to try it.'

'And who will teach them?' asked Lady Frances. 'Are you trained upon the pianoforte, Miss Grensham?'

'We have one in the orangery,' said Diana. 'A Broadwood, hired in readiness for the ball. I have been practising upon that. And if the children show an aptitude then I shall hire a music master from London to drive out and give them lessons. That is one of the advantages of living near town.'

'Point taken, Diana,' murmured Alex as he passed her chair.

She smiled. *Point won*, she thought.

She went off to bring the children down to spend an hour in the drawing room, but conscious of her role as hostess she arranged for Nurse to collect them and put them to bed. She knew Alex would not allow her to slip away early this time. They were like two cats, she thought, as the evening wore on. They prowled around each other, perfectly polite but wary.

Or perhaps it was just her imagination. She was so conscious of Alex, his voice, whenever he was speaking and where he was in the room. He might not be thinking of her at all.

Towards the end of the evening as the guests began to retire, Alex crossed the room to stand over Diana, who was sitting a little apart.

'You are very quiet. Are you tired?'

'No, sir, I was thinking of the ball. I would like to move some paintings to the orangery, to brighten the walls. Would you object? They would mainly be from the servants' passages and the top floor. I would not leave conspicuous gaps that your guests would see, I promise you.'

'You may move what you please, Diana, you know that. You are mistress here.'

'Thank you, then I shall begin to make a list of the pictures I need.'

'And your first day is over. I hope it was not too much of an ordeal?'

'No, thank you. Your guests are all very kind.'

Everyone had treated her with courtesy and she had soon begun to relax and enjoy herself. Even Lady Frances, dazzling in a daringly low-cut gown and with a collar of diamonds and sapphires around her neck, had not daunted her.

'Your step is much improved.'

She blinked. 'I thought you had not noticed.' She could not read his look, but was heartened by the fact that he had seen the change. 'I have been practising. Working the muscles, as you suggested.' She was glad of the candlelight to hide her blush as she recalled the circumstances of that conversation. 'When I concentrate I find I limp hardly at all.'

'I am glad I was of some use to you. Even if I could not save you from drowning.'

His tone made her cheeks burn even more.

'And you are not regretting your decision to stay?' he continued. 'Even if I decide to hold parties such as this frequently?'

The teasing note was back in his voice. She could cope with that so much better than when he was being serious.

'I have told you, my lord, Meggie and Florence will remain here for at least the next year, whatever you choose to do. They are at home here, they feel safe and comfortable. And talking of drowning has reminded me of another reason to remain at Chantreys.' She rose. 'I want to teach them to swim this summer. You said yourself it was a useful attribute.'

With a slight curtsy and a mischievous smile she said goodnight to the remaining guests and made her escape.

'So, the little hostess has gone to bed.' Frances stood at his shoulder. 'Should we do the same, Alexander?'

'Of course, but not together.'

'Oh, my dear, are we still preserving your little foible about respectability?'

Her laugh was soft, smoky, and once he would have found it seductive, but he had heard her use it too often and with too many men. He turned to face her. The last few remaining guests were gathered at the far side of the room. There was no one to overhear them.

'No, I mean that our little flirtation is at an end. It should not come as a surprise, we have seen so little of each other recently.'

'You have been busy with your plans for the party,' she replied. 'And then you have been running around after Lady Hune and her heiress.'

'True, but we could have found time to see one another, had we so wished.' He said gently, 'A little light-hearted flirtation, Frances, that is what we agreed.'

'At first, perhaps—'

'I hope you won't pretend to be heartbroken,' he continued, a hint of steel entering his voice. 'You may not have been able to get me into your bed recently, but I know there have been plenty of others.'

She stared at him, biting her lip. Anger was smouldering in her eyes and he wondered what it cost her not to rip up at him. After a moment she lifted her white shoulders in a shrug and gave a small, rueful smile.

'Why should it end? If we still amuse one another—'

'It is over, Frances.'

She touched the jewels at her throat. 'Is that what you were trying to tell me with this?'

'I think perhaps it was.'

'Then why did you not say so, when you gave it to me?'

'Then I had not quite decided. We might have gone on a little longer, if you had not invited Urmston to join us here.' His eyes narrowed. 'A mistake, my dear, to bring your lover here.'

She did not deny it, he noticed.

'Sir Charles and I have been...friends...for many years.'

'Then he will be able to console you now our liaison is at an end.'

The smile grew and she moved closer.

'I may yet change your mind.'

'I doubt it.' Alex stood his ground. Her perfume filled his senses, but it did not move him. He saw her beauty for what it was: a thin veneer over an ice-cold heart. Eventually she realised he was not going to succumb to her charms and she moved away, giving him one final, regretful smile before she left the room.

It was a novel experience for Diana, to leave the children with Nurse and go downstairs to break her fast with the guests. Alex was right, Nurse was more than capable of looking after Meggie and Florence, and Jenny, who had been promoted to be her full-time maid, was the eldest of a large family and was only too pleased to add the care of the two young ladies to her duties.

Without exception everyone attended morning worship on Sunday. As hostess, Alex demanded that Diana should enter the church with him, but she insisted that they should have Meggie and Florence walking between them. The rest of their guests filed in behind and Diana knew that her neighbours were watching everything with the liveliest curiosity. The invitations to the Chantreys ball had all been accepted, no one would miss the opportunity to attend such a grand event. She was grateful to receive an encouraging nod from Squire Huddleston's lady and smiles from Mr and Mrs Frederick, kindly people who had often deplored Diana's solitary existence at Chantreys, and as everyone went out into the sunshine after the service Diana knew there were many introductions to be made before she could return to the house.

Strangely Diana was undaunted by the prospect. She kept her head high as she left the church, concentrating upon her steps, not scurrying away to the carriage but walking slowly, putting equal weight on each foot. Her left leg ached with the effort but her reward was in her smooth, almost gliding progress. And the smile she received from Alex.

The first week passed uneventfully and much more agreeably than Diana had envisaged. Even Lady Frances showed her no more disdain than she displayed for the rest of the party. It was clear that with the exception of Sir Charles Urmston, Lady Frances found the company at Chantreys beneath her. Diana had seen the pair exchanging looks full of mockery and deplored their ill manners, but she said nothing. They were the earl's friends, not hers. Alex himself proved to be an affable host, there was little ceremony and the guests were left to amuse themselves as they wished. If Diana could fault the earl it was that he was very eager she should not be left out, even though she would have happily remained in the background. He asked her to assist Mr Johnson in seeking out a particular book from the library, encouraged Mr Avery to accompany her when everyone strolled in the gardens and he even persuaded her to play the harpsichord for Sir Sydney Dunford when he entertained them with a song in the evenings.

It was all very enjoyable, but Diana wondered why Alex should be putting himself out for her, when he still maintained he wanted her and the children to leave Chantreys. She watched him as he moved about the drawing room each evening after dinner, laughing and talking with his guests. She had the strangest feeling that she had known him all her life and yet it was not true, she knew almost nothing of him. When she saw Mr Wollerton sitting a little apart from the rest one evening she took the opportunity to join him. Wine and brandy were available as well as tea and she knew the gentleman had been imbibing freely, so she felt confident he would answer her questions. They spoke idly for a few minutes and then she plucked up her courage.

'Mr Wollerton, you know Lord Davenport better than anyone here, I think. Will you tell me something of his life, how he lived before he became earl?'

Mr Wollerton looked a little hesitant.

'I would have thought you would know most of it, being his sister, so to speak.'

'We have been in company together very rarely,' she explained. 'I was still in the schoolroom when Margaret married his brother and after that, when he visited Chantreys, my duties as a governess kept me in the schoolroom.'

It was not the whole truth, but the gentleman did not question it.

'You knew him at school, I think,' she prompted him. 'Was he a scholar or a sportsman?'

He considered the matter as he settled himself more comfortably in his chair. As Diana had hoped, having been well fed and supplied with ample quantities of drink, Mr Wollerton was in an expansive mood.

'Oh, a sportsman, most definitely,' he said at last. 'But he always had a taste for the arts.'

'I know,' she said wryly. 'He wants to house his collection at Chantreys.'

'Ah, yes.' Mr Wollerton coughed and looked a little embarrassed.

Diana laughed, begged pardon for discomfiting him and gently drew him out to talk of Alex's schooldays. She built up a picture of a lively, vigorous young man but with a serious side, one that few people but his closest friends ever saw. She did not doubt that Gervase Wollerton was a good friend and a loyal one, too. He showed a reluctance to talk about the wild young Alexander Arrandale, who had burst upon the *ton* with a fortune in his pocket and no responsibilities.

'Was he a typical Arrandale?' she asked him. 'I have only heard about the family from my sister. She told me that James was the exception, quiet and studious and nothing like his wayward brother, with his sports and gambling and women.'

She realised Mr Wollerton was looking uneasy.

'Should I not have mentioned it? It is the truth though, is it not? You may tell me, sir, for I am not easily shocked, I assure you.'

'Well, yes, Alex was very wild when he first came to

town, but nothing serious, you understand. He did not run through his fortune, like many young hotheads might do. He used his money to develop his sporting prowess and to indulge his passion for art. He likes collecting beautiful objects.'

'And beautiful women, Mr Wollerton. Is London littered with broken hearts?'

'No, no, not at all—Alex ain't like that,' he said quickly. 'There are females aplenty on the hunt for a husband, London is full of 'em. But Alex is a great gun and he is not one to raise false hopes. Believe me, his liaisons have always been with females who understand what he is offering them. And he's very generous, too, he always makes sure they have some pretty but expensive gift when it's time to part. Diamonds and the like. That's what the ladies seem to like most, jewellery!' He stopped, then added ruefully, 'By George, Miss Grensham, I should not be telling you all this, I beg your pardon.'

'No need, Mr Wollerton. I am glad to learn so much about the earl.' She laughed. 'And you have my word I shall not tell him you have, um, opened the budget!'

Across the room Alex watched them with growing irritation. What the deuce was Gervase saying to keep Diana at his side for so long? And laughing so freely. She had not appeared so much at ease with any of the other fellows. He straightened in his chair. Do not say that Diana was forming a partiality for Gervase! Everyone knew Wollerton was a confirmed bachelor.

An unpleasant doubt shook him. There was no denying Diana looked very well in the new gowns Madame Francot had made for her. Last night's creation in teal-coloured silk had enhanced the flames in her red hair, while the green silk she was wearing now made her eyes shine so that he was reminded of the seasons, of hazelnuts and spring moss. His eyes fell on the pearls around her neck. They were very fine, but she needed something warmer on that fine skin of hers.

He was aware of a sudden change in the conversation. Lord and Lady Goodge were preparing to retire. Alex walked to the door with them and called to the footman dozing in the hall to light their bedroom candle. When he returned to the drawing room he wandered across and stopped beside Diana's chair. She was laughing at something Gervase had said to her and when she turned her face towards Alex it was still alight with mischief, her eyes dancing. His breath caught in his throat at the beautiful picture she presented.

'Go away. Alex, can you not see that Miss Grensham and I are enjoying a tête-à-tête?'

For once Alex was not in the least amused by his friend's humorous quip. His scowl deepened.

'Miss Grensham—' he stressed her name '—must not neglect her duties as hostess.'

Her brows rose but she responded mildly enough.

'No, of course not. The party is breaking up, I must go and speak to Mrs Peters again before she goes to bed. If you gentlemen will excuse me…'

Gervase jumped to his feet as she walked away.

'You are rather cross-grained tonight, old friend,' he observed, his eyes on Diana's retreating form. 'If I did not know better, Alex, I would think you were jealous.'

'Jealous? What rot!' Alex gave a short laugh as he walked away, but he was uncomfortably aware of his friend's thoughtful gaze following him across the room.

Chapter Twelve

Another day, another new gown. Diana felt the smile building inside her. She had never before had so many new clothes. There was no doubt it lifted one's spirits to have so many to choose from. Or perhaps it was just to have so much adult company. She hummed quietly to herself as she allowed Jenny to help her into the embroidered lemon muslin. The girl had also proved herself adept at dressing hair, and when Diana went downstairs her wayward tresses had been tamed and confined upon her head by a wide yellow ribbon. She felt fresh and cool, which was an advantage when the day was promising to be very humid.

It was so warm that Diana ordered all the windows in the reception rooms to be opened and had cushions, chairs and rugs placed out of doors in the shade of the trees on the lawn so that everyone might wander freely out of doors. It proved a popular idea and by noon most of the party were gathered under the trees, sitting or reclining as their mood dictated.

Alex strode out to join them.

'Fingle is bringing refreshments for us.'

'Oh, well d-done, my lord,' stammered Mr Hamilton. 'That is just what is required.'

'Pray do not thank me, Hamilton. Our hostess arranged it.'

'Then Miss Grensham has our undying gratitude,' declared Sir Charles Urmston. He directed a little bow at Diana, but there was mockery in the gesture and she chose to ignore it. He was lounging very close to Lady Frances, who murmured something that made him smile. Diana could not help wondering if that was the reason Alex did not sit down beside the lady.

'Is that John Timothy going off?' remarked Mr Wollerton, observing a solitary figure riding away from the house.

Alex threw himself down upon a spare rug. 'Yes. He is gone to town to fetch something for me.'

'Poor man, to be obliged to ride out today, when it is so very warm,' declared Miss Prentiss, fanning herself vigorously.

'Yes, indeed,' agreed Mrs Peters, closing her book. 'I vow it is a day for doing nothing at all.'

'I do not think Miss Grensham would agree with you,' murmured Alex. 'Did I not see you in the grounds with Meggie and Florence before breakfast this morning?'

'Why, yes.' Diana nodded. 'I thought it would be wise to take them out early, before the day became too hot.'

'Dear little girls,' murmured Lady Frances with an insincere smile. 'And what are they doing now?'

'Giving Nurse a headache, I shouldn't wonder,' murmured Alex.

Diana chuckled, but shook her head at him.

'Nothing of the kind. My maid is looking after them and when I left they were engaged in painting pictures for her. When that is done I expect they will take up their sewing. Jenny is an excellent needlewoman and is helping them to make clothes for their dolls.'

'How admirably well organised you are.' Alex stretched out and put his hands behind his head. 'You think of everything, Diana.'

Diana started slightly at his use of her name in company, yet there was no reason why he should not do so. They were brother- and sister-in-law. She was his hostess. Yet she was aware of the knowing glances that passed between some of the guests and the cold stare Lady Frances bestowed upon her. Diana was thankful she was wearing her rose-green spencer or she would have shivered at the iciness of that look.

Fingle provided a welcome diversion when he led out a small procession of servants with various jugs of wine, ale and lemonade, plates piled with tiny baked fancies, plus a large and colourful bowl of fruit. She was gratified by the exclamations of delight, the little crows of pleasure from the ladies as they picked out a delicate pastry, the satisfied sighs of the gentlemen as they quaffed the cool ale or sipped a glass of wine.

When everyone had been served the servants withdrew, leaving the remainder of the food and drink on a small table placed beneath one sturdy tree. Conversation became desultory as everyone relaxed, enjoying the food and drink. Only Diana remained alert, observing her guests closely and getting up to hand round more cakes or refresh the glasses when necessary.

Sir Sydney Dunford beamed up at her as he held out his wine glass for refilling. 'As Davenport says, you think of everything, ma'am.'

'I suppose one in your position must be organised,' observed Lady Frances, her voice dripping with insincere sweetness.

'I am afraid I do not understand you, ma'am.'

'You will not wish to be moving around any more than you have to, not when each step is such a struggle for you.' Too late did Diana realise she had walked into a trap. The honeyed words continued. 'Your poor leg. A childhood accident, I believe. Although I fancy you do not limp as badly as you did in May, Miss Grensham.' Lady Frances looked pointedly at Diana's skirts. 'Has the doctor suggested a metal brace for your leg, perhaps?'

The air was charged with embarrassment. Diana heard someone gasp. Mrs Peters, she suspected.

Miss Prentiss stifled a giggle. 'Lady Frances—!'

Those blue eyes widened. 'What have I said? I beg your pardon, Miss Grensham, but we have all been getting along so famously, I thought there could be no harm in mentioning it. Not when we are all such good friends now.'

Diana felt her left leg stiffening, the heel beginning to lift. She must concentrate upon standing straight. These barbs could only hurt her if she let them in. Alex, she noted, had not moved. He was still lying on the rug, his eyes closed. She supposed it was possible he was asleep...

'Oh, my dear...' Lady Frances put her hands to her cheeks in mock horror '...have I offended you? I would not for the world have drawn attention to your little—in-firmity if I had realised it would upset you.'

Diana kept her head up and gave a smile every bit as false as Lady Frances's. 'No, indeed, why should I be of-fended? I am very happy to tell you that there have been no doctors involved in my recovery, merely my own hard work and persistence.'

'Indeed, Diana works harder than anyone I know.' Alex scrambled up. 'More wine, anyone?'

So he had not been sleeping. But he had not rushed to her defence, either. Had he enjoyed her humiliation?

Having her affliction brought to everyone's attention? She felt a sudden surge of anger. She had misjudged him.

Dismayed at the prickling of tears in her throat, Diana moved over to the table full of food and tried to look busy, pointlessly moving things around. Even there she could not escape, for Lady Frances followed her and murmured in a low voice.

'Oh, my dear, I *do* beg your pardon. I am mortified to have embarrassed you, but indeed, *indeed* we are all very pleased to see you walking so well. It must have been very disagreeable for you to appear in public with such an ungainly step. Alexander was very aware of it—'

Diana's hands stilled. 'The earl mentioned it to you?'

Lady Frances looked coy.

'We are very close, you see. And he is so keen to find you a husband.'

'I beg your pardon?'

'My dear, have you not seen how he has gone out of his way to present you in a good light to the gentlemen he has invited here? Of course it will be much easier now there is no longer that ungainly walk to worry about.'

Diana stared at her. There was malice in those sky-blue eyes, but her words made sense. Alex had been throwing her in the way of the bachelors in the party. She moved back towards the main group, forcing a smile.

'If you will all excuse me, there is something I must attend to.'

Alex watched Diana hurry away. She was favouring her left leg again. Not as much as before, but he noticed it. She was making an effort, he thought, but she was distracted. He looked suspiciously at Frances.

'What did you say to her? I thought you were going over to make peace.'

'I did.' Frances smiled at him, all innocence. 'I even begged her pardon for mentioning that ugly walk of hers. I am sure Diana and I will be very good friends now.'

Diana went quickly into the house, but she was only halfway up the stairs when she slowed and finally came to a halt. The children were in the schoolroom, all the doors and windows there would be open to allow in what little air there was. She needed to be alone, to think, and she did not want the children to see her distress. She went back downstairs, but going through the empty rooms she realised that none of them was really private, she might be disturbed at any moment. The orangery. No one would question her going there. She slipped out of the house and made her way along the winding path, relieved that there was no one in sight, not even a servant.

Why should Lady Frances launch an attack upon her now and why did Alex say nothing to defend her? Close upon that question came another—why should he? They were combatants, after all. Perhaps it was his plan to humiliate her, to force her to remove from Chantreys. She had not thought that of him. She had thought him...honourable. A bitter laugh caught in her throat. Alex was no knight in shining armour, prepared to fight for her honour and shield her from every unfavourable wind.

But he could be and I wish he was.

The thought caught her unawares and a wave of longing crashed over her, so strong that she actually stumbled. Diana rubbed her temples, feeling the beginnings of a headache. It was the weather, it was hot and sultry, no wonder she was feeling low. She forced her mind to concentrate upon the forthcoming ball. It was Wednesday already and she had done little yet to prepare the orangery for the ball on Friday. Tomorrow evening Meggie and Florence would perform there and in the morning a team of men were coming to fit a canopy over this very path, to shelter the guests as they made their way from the house to the orangery. She was glad they were not there now to see her dashing an angry tear from her cheek.

The orangery was empty but stiflingly hot. The few potted plants that had been placed around the walls were wilting from the heat and Diana made a mental note to have them watered. She went from window to window, throwing them wide. The curtains she had ordered had been put up, hanging over the pillars between each window in soft folds of butter-coloured muslin, but even with all the windows open there was no wind to stir them.

'I thought I might find you here.'

Alex was walking on to the terrace. Diana turned and went back inside.

'Please go back to your guests, my lord. There is nothing for you to do here.'

'You are right,' he said, following her into the room. 'The walls are too bare.'

So they were to ignore what had occurred in the garden. Very well.

'I do not want to move the paintings from the house until the last minute,' she replied. 'The heat in here might damage them.'

'Have you chosen the ones you want?'

'I have. I will give you a list for approval.'

'I have already said you may do as you wish.'

Diana turned away from him. She began to rearrange

the curtains—it was an idle, useless occupation but it meant she did not have to look at him.

'I am very sorry if Lady Frances upset you.'

She felt the tears pressing against her eyelids and fought them back by summoning up her anger.

'Why should you be sorry? Perhaps you think her animosity will make me wish to quit Chantreys.'

'No, of course not—'

She rounded on him.

'Oh, do not lie to me, my lord. You want this place to show off your works of art and to hold your, your riotous parties. You find this sedate gathering all very boring, you and Lady Frances and Sir Charles Urmston, yawning behind your hands at the decorous conversation. Nothing like your usual racy style, is it, my lord?'

'Nonsense! And stop calling me my lord.'

'Well, that is what you are, is it not? Lord of all you survey. Except me, of course. And Chantreys. That irks you, does it not, that your brother's will gives me the right to remain here?'

'No! 'Pon my honour, Diana, I will not force you from this house, I have already told you that.'

'Oh? And what of your plans to m-marry me off?' she threw at him. 'Can you deny you invited Mr Hamilton, Mr Avery and the other single gentlemen in the hope that I might fall in love with one of them?'

He glowered at her. 'Who told you that?'

'How I learned of it is not important. It is perfectly obvious that that is what you have been doing.'

'Was it Frances? She was making mischief, Diana.'

'Oh, I am well aware of it. She wishes to humiliate me, that is very clear.' She brushed a rogue tear from her cheek. 'And since you do not stop her I can only conclude you are happy for her to do so.'

'You are wrong.'

'Hah!'

She went to turn away but he grabbed her arm.

'You think I should have jumped to your defence when she suggested you had fitted a brace to your leg?' He shook his head. 'You are wrong, Diana. I believe your family—even my brother—defended you far too much, with the result that you have come to see yourself as some ugly, deformed creature. Can you not see now that it is not true? It is time you took your place in society, Diana, you do not need to remain hidden away. And as for Lady Frances, you did not need me to defend you. You answered her very well for yourself.'

'Yes, well—' she snatched her arm free '—I have grown up having to look after myself.'

'You have grown up hiding away from the world!'

Suddenly she could stand no more. If he did not leave her soon she would dissolve into tears and she could not bear to show so much weakness before him. She threw up her arms.

'Just go away!' she shouted. 'Leave me alone, *Lord* Davenport. I do not need you. I do not need *anyone*!'

'Diana, stop!'

His words followed her as she dashed out of the orangery and away through the gardens.

She ignored his call. She had lost her temper and needed to be alone with her misery and her anger until she was once more in control. Tears of rage and frustration streamed down her face. She could not go back to the house looking like this, the children would want to know what had upset her. She ran through the gardens and across the grass, away from the house and the guests. She would seek shelter in the woods.

Alex strode quickly after Diana, swearing softly when she veered from the path and headed for the trees. He should catch her, make her see that he had not intended for her to be hurt. Frances had been deliberately provoking, but Diana's response had been perfectly judged. She had not crumbled but had replied with her head held high. Even while he was supposedly lying at his ease he had noted that. It had been an effort not to jump in, but he was well aware of the dangers of publicly defending Diana. Frances was already smarting from his rejection. If he gave her reason to think Diana was the cause, she was quite capable of spreading rumours and lies that would be even more injurious than her barbed remarks today.

Diana disappeared from view and he stopped. He exhaled, long and slow, thinking of their guests lounging at their ease on the lawn. She was clearly not going back to them, so he must do so. Later, when she had recovered a little, he would talk to her. Explain.

As the afternoon wore on the clouds that had been building on the horizon moved in, a thick grey canopy that blotted out the sun and covered Chantreys in an ominous shade. Alex ushered his guests indoors to amuse themselves in the library or the drawing room while the thunder began to roll around the house. Frances and Sir Charles Urmston had disappeared but Alex gave it no more than a thought. Frances was no longer his concern.

When the rain started Alex moved restlessly from room to room. There was no sign of Diana, but it was possible that she had slipped up to the schoolroom. He was making his way upstairs to find out when he saw Diana's maid on the landing and stopped her to ask if Miss Grensham had come in.

'No, sir.' A loud thunderclap made the girl jump and look nervously towards the window. 'She said earlier that she was going to the orangery. I 'spect she's sheltering in there.'

Alex dismissed her and stood for a moment, irresolute. A lightning flash, followed by an even louder crash of thunder, decided him. He turned and ran swiftly back down the stairs.

The heavy rain was lashed by a gusting wind and Alex was drenched within moments of leaving the house. He gave a hiss of frustration when he saw the orangery was just as he had left it hours earlier, the windows thrown wide and long folds of yellow muslin billowing out into the rain. He began to run. He should have thought to send someone out to make sure it was closed up. But if Diana wasn't here, where was she? His heart went cold at the thought of her being out of doors in this storm.

Then, through the deepening gloom, he spotted a bedraggled figure in the first of the windows, pulling it closed. Alex reached the terrace and leaped in through the next window, dragging it shut behind him. Diana hurried past him and in silence they secured the rest. The storm was overhead now, an almost continuous roar of thunder while the rain lashed at the glass and rattled the window frames. A flicker of lightning flashed in through the glass and caught Diana in its brilliant glare. She was drenched to the skin, her hair plastered to her head and the skirts of her thin gown clinging to every curve. Alex's relief at knowing she was safe was so strong it confounded him, rocked him off balance and found expression in a sudden outburst of anger.

'What the hell do you think you were doing, leaving this place open to the elements?' He waved one hand. 'The new curtains are sodden and the floor is awash!'

Compared to his furious outburst her voice was low, controlled.

'It is a pity and I am very sorry for it, but we can wash the muslin and hang it out to dry once the storm has passed. And the stone floor will not suffer from a little water. I am sure everything will be in order for Meggie and Florence's little performance tomorrow evening. I have checked the Broadwood, it is well away from the windows and not harmed.'

'No thanks to you!' he raged at her. 'Of all the irresponsible acts, to go off and leave the place unattended.'

'*You* were here when I left, my lord,' she retorted angrily. 'I do not think you can put all the blame upon me.'

Alex was being unjust and he knew it, but he could not stop. Such was the raw emotion blazing through him he was almost shaking with it.

'I am only thankful you had not brought my paintings out here! Heaven knows what damage might have been caused by your thoughtlessness.'

She threw up her head, raking him with her angry glare.

'Yes, that is all you care about, isn't it, your precious works of art. Inanimate objects, but they are more important to you than any living, breathing creature!'

'Now you are being ridiculous.'

'Am I? You want to fill Chantreys with your paintings and statues, to make it a display case for beautiful things rather than a home for real people, with all their flaws and imperfections.'

She was standing very close, eyes glittering and her breast heaving. The air between them was so charged with emotion it was tangible. He could taste it, feel it. Alex clenched his fists to stop himself reaching for her, whether to shake her or kiss her he did not know.

Diana felt the first stirrings of alarm. She had allowed her temper to get the better of her, she had lashed out, wanting to wound Alex, and judging by his thunderous countenance she had succeeded. But it was not only murder she read in his fierce gaze, there was something else. A look, a primal gleam that she had seen there before. It burned into her, set her pulse racing and threatened to overwhelm her. She felt as if they were balanced on the edge of a precipice, one false step and they would plunge into some unimaginable peril. Surprise and apprehension flickered over Alex's countenance, gone in an instant, but she knew without a doubt that he too realised the danger of the situation. They must draw back. Somehow she dragged her eyes away and tried to speak calmly.

'I hope there will be no lasting damage. I came back as soon as the rain started.'

'Not soon enough,' he barked at her.

There was no placating him. Diana had the nonsensical notion that she had disturbed a slumbering dragon and she had no strength left to defend herself. She must get away. Quickly.

'No,' she agreed, determined not to antagonise him further. 'We had best get back to the house.'

She had stopped fighting him. Alex was aware of an irrational disappointment.

He said sharply, 'Do not be so foolish. You cannot go out in this weather.'

'But we are already wet through.'

'Only an idiot would go out in an electrical storm.' As if to reinforce his point, the air shuddered with another roar of thunder. In the accompanying flash of light he saw the dejected slump of Diana's shoulders. He had never seen her so defeated and it tore at his heart. He took her arm and said more gently, 'Come into the other room. We need to dry you off a little.'

The shadows were deeper in the anteroom, but at least its small windows faced away from the storm. Alex dragged the protective cover from one of the chairs.

'Here, use this. Not the finest linen, perhaps, but better than nothing.'

Diana took the cloth and wiped her face. The urgency that had consumed her when she saw the orangery windows standing wide had evaporated, now she felt cold and miserable. The day had been a disaster, the rapport that had been building between herself and Alex had gone. She had made him angry and shown herself quite ungrateful for all he had done for her. She felt as if she had lost a friend. Her only friend.

Alex had shed his coat and was vigorously rubbing his hair, but he stopped when he saw that she was watching him.

'Come, you need to dry yourself.' He took the cloth from Diana's nerveless fingers and dragged it over her hair, removing the worst of the wet. He briefly rested a hand on her shoulder. 'That spencer of yours has soaked up water like a sponge. It needs to come off.'

She reached up, but her fingers were shaking too much to do anything more than fumble uselessly with the buttons.

'Tsk. Here, let me.' He pushed her hands aside and

dragged the sodden velvet from her shoulders. The sleeves were tight and had to be tugged off, but at last the spencer was discarded and he rubbed her bare arms with the cloth. Even through the coarse linen he could feel the chill of her skin. He gave an exasperated sigh, covering his anxiety with irritation.

'How could you be so foolish?' he muttered. 'If you catch a chill you would be well served.' He threw aside the sodden cloth and dragged off another chair cover which he arranged over her shoulders. 'You should have gone indoors as soon as the rain started.'

'I know it,' said Diana quietly. 'I am sorry—'

'Ah, don't!' He stopped her, exclaiming as if the words had been forced from him. 'You must not be sorry, Diana. Never sorry.'

She looked up, her misery forgotten when she saw the blaze in his eyes. Lightning flickered warningly. They were frozen in a moment of tense silence and Diana knew with sudden, frightening certainty that they were still on the edge of the precipice. She had not stepped back and had no intention of doing so.

There was an explosion of thunder as they crashed together. Diana raised her face and Alex covered it with kisses, finally finding her lips. They parted eagerly beneath the onslaught and his tongue explored her, plundered her senses, possessed her. She pushed herself against him, with only instinct to guide her responses. The kiss became more frenzied, the cloth slipped from her shoulders but she did not need it, she was burning and barely aware of the damp muslin that clung to her body.

His arms tightened. He lifted her as if she weighed nothing at all and laid her gently upon the sofa. Her loose wet hair pressed against her back and Diana trembled slightly. Alex paused, raising his head, and even in the dim light she could see the question in his eyes. Fearful he would leave her Diana threw her arms about his neck, dragging his head down towards her. He obliged her with another searing kiss. She clutched at his shoulders, wanting him, needing him to continue his assault of her senses. Excitement rippled through her body, she moved restlessly beneath him, sighing as his hands began to explore her, tearing at her gown. When he uncovered her breasts she gasped at his touch, but made no attempt to stop him when he trailed a line of kisses down her throat. Her hands drove through his hair, feeling its silky strength as his lips travelled lightly over her skin. She arched towards him, offering up to him her full, aching breasts. He cupped one with his hand, his thumb circling, teasing while his mouth covered the other and his tongue began to flicker over its hard nub, drawing a response from deep within. A yearning hunger was unfurling inside. Her body was heavy with it, her skin so sensitive that she was aware of his every touch and impatient for more.

Her skirts were bunched around her hips and Diana felt his free hand moving over them and down to the juncture of her thighs where his fingers stroked and caressed and finally slid inside her. Urgent desire shot through her, heating her blood, making her moan with the exquisite craving that his touch unleashed. She did not understand it, only the need to go on, to finish this. She reached for him and, obedient to her touch on his face, Alex gave up pleasuring her breast and returned to kiss her lips, the sweep and thrust of his tongue matching the movements of his fingers deep inside her and rousing her to a frenzy. Somehow amidst the fury of their embrace he had unfastened his breeches and she exulted in the feel of his skin upon hers. He was hard against her, she should have been frightened but instead it only heightened her own need, even as the insistent rhythms of his tongue and his fingers carried her almost beyond reason.

She groaned into his mouth, her hips moving, pushing against his hand as new sensations took hold, rippling and growing, filling her like floodwaters rising against a dam. He eased himself over her and she slid her hands over his smooth, firm buttocks, urging him on, knowing there was more he could give her. She cried out as he entered her, not with pain but joy. He pushed into her again and again, up to the hilt. Her body tightened around him, she wanted this to go on for ever, but even as the thought formed she felt herself unravelling, bucking and writhing as the dam broke and she was carried away on a wave of heady, intolerably sweet sensations. She screamed, shuddered and clung to Alex, falling, drowning in sweet sensuous pleasure even as he gave a shout and a final, urgent thrust before collapsing against her, his own passion quite spent.

Chapter Thirteen

The storm was moving away, the lightning had all but ceased and the thunder was nothing more than an occasional, distant mutter. Alex shifted his weight to one side but kept his arms about Diana. In truth he never wanted to let her go. He felt dazed, confused and battered by the feelings that had raged through him. His anxiety for Diana's safety had thrown him off balance and he had hidden his confusion beneath a veneer of anger, but even that had been no proof against the wave of emotion that swept over him when she stood before him looking so lost and vulnerable. At first he had wanted only to protect her, but having her so close roused a strong desire to possess her. He had not intended to kiss her, he had wanted to turn away but his body had suddenly become a separate entity, answering only to the siren call of the woman before him. The woman who was now in his arms. The virgin he had deflowered.

That was not his way. What madness had come over him? He had not felt so out of control since his schooldays, when the love of his life, the stepmother of one of his school friends, had initiated him into the pleasures of the flesh. She had been much older than he and her protestations of love had been false and short-lived. Alex had soon been cast aside and he had never let himself grow so fond of any woman since. Looking back, he recognised that she had seduced *him*, taken advantage of his innocence.

And was that not what he had done now to Diana? She had been very willing, but he was the experienced one, he should have shown restraint. He closed his eyes, angered by his weakness, and yet he could not feel any real regret at what had occurred, it had been so natural, so right and it was as much as he could do not to roll her over and take her all over again. And again. To make her his own.

To make her his countess. The thought came suddenly, shockingly, but he knew now that was what he wanted. Not some barren, sterile, comfortable marriage of convenience, but to spend his life with this tempestuous, spirited woman who would infuriate and enchant him by turns.

What of Diana, what would she want? A sudden chill ran through him. He had always said he would not be coerced into wedlock so why should she, just because he had taken advantage of her? She had grown and blossomed since that first spring meeting. Alex felt a certain pride that he had somehow been instrumental in her transformation, but despite what they had just done he had no right to claim her as his bride. She might not wish to be tied down when she had only recently discovered her own strength. He buried his face in her wet hair and breathed in the unique scent of her. He had likened her to Sleeping Beauty, but just because he had awakened her did not mean they would live happily ever after. She needed to live in the world a little, to choose her own partner, whoever that might be. He would not rush her into a decision, she must be allowed to consider her position and that would take time, more time than they had now. With a long sigh he gathered her to him for one last kiss.

'We must go, sweetheart. We will be missed.'

He helped Diana to her feet then bent to scoop up the holland cover from the floor and place it once more around her shoulders.

'I would this were the finest cashmere,' he told her. 'But it must suffice. At least it will cover the ravages I have wrought upon the neck of your gown.' He ran one gentle finger along her cheek. 'You must go to your room now. If anyone sees you, tell them you were caught in the storm and took shelter in here, but with luck everyone will be changing for dinner.'

'And you?'

Her eyes were still starry and luminous from their lovemaking and he could not resist taking another kiss.

'I shall slip around the house as if I were coming in from the stables.' He smiled. 'Have no fear, Diana, I shall protect your reputation. No one need ever know of this.'

'Alex, we must talk—'

'I know, sweetheart, but there is no time now for all that must be said. If we are both late for dinner it will give rise to the sort of speculation we wish to avoid.'

The warm, beloved feeling that had enveloped Diana evaporated when Alex moved away. She wanted to remain beside him for much longer, to explore these new and delicious feelings. Was it love? She thought so, but how could she tell? Diana felt bemused, stunned by her own behaviour. He was right, of course, she must get back to the house and change, but there was so much unsaid, implied but never put into words. It was on the tip of her tongue to ask Alex if he loved her but she held it back.

She was afraid he might lie.

It was still raining when she ran back to the house, but only a light drizzle. The storm had spent itself and there were signs of a clear sky spreading from the west, promising a fine evening. Jenny was waiting for her in the bedchamber, and burst into relieved chatter when Diana came in.

'So there you are miss, I was beginning to be that worried about you! I guessed you'd stay in the orangery until the rain stopped.'

'Unfortunately I went for a walk and I was in the woods when the storm broke.' Diana was surprised that her voice was so normal after all that had occurred. 'I ran back to the orangery to wait for it to pass.'

'Very wise, mistress, I've heard stories before now of animals and people being struck down in an electrical storm.' The maid shook her head. 'La, but your gown is all ruined. That's the trouble with these very fine muslins, they're that flimsy they don't stand no wear at all. You should've put on an old dimity gown if you was going to be working in the orangery.'

'I should indeed, Jenny.'

'I've filled a tub for you, miss, in the dressing room. The water might be getting a bit cool now but I'm sure you will feel better for a bath—'

As the maid came forward to help her mistress undress, Diana held out the wet spencer that she had carried back with her. 'Take this away, if you please, Jenny, it is dripping all over the carpets. Take it down to Mrs Wallace and see if this can be dried and restored. Quickly now.'

While the maid hurried away Diana drew off her gown, trying not to think about how the bodice came to be torn. She inspected the muslin skirts and her petticoats for evidence of her wanton behaviour in the orangery, but thankfully there were no telltale signs, so her secret was safe, for a little longer.

Her spirits swung between euphoria and despair, soaring when she thought of the way Alex had kissed her and swooping when she considered how reckless she had been, giving herself to a man in such a wild, abandoned manner with no thought for the future. She summoned up every vestige of courage to fight down her fears. Alex felt the same, she knew it, her very bones told her that he loved her. But what if she was wrong?

Jenny had looked out her moss-green gown and Diana put it on, allowing the maid to pin up her hair and thread a matching green ribbon through the curls which were damp and heavy about her head. Just before the appointed hour she made her way downstairs, but as she was about to enter the drawing room she heard Alex's voice from across the hall.

'Ah, well timed, Diana. If you could spare me a moment, there is something I wish to discuss with you.'

The sight of him, calm and immaculate in an evening coat of deep-blue superfine, almost turned her bones to water. She suddenly felt very shy.

'It—it is almost time for dinner, sir. I—'

'I am aware, but it will not take long.'

He was standing by the study door and after the briefest hesitation she preceded him into the room and heard the door shut behind them. Diana wondered if he intended to sweep her into his arms and knew a moment's disappointment when he moved away from her towards the desk. She stifled her regret and faced him with a calm that matched his own, but his first words came as a surprise.

'I am glad you are wearing green tonight.' He picked up a small leather case from the desk. 'I thought these might go well with it.'

Her brows went up when he opened the box and she saw the cluster of emeralds nestled against the velvet lining.

'Oh, how lovely.' She reached out to touch one finger to the gems. The set comprised a necklace and earrings of fine, dark emeralds in a heavy gold setting. 'You would lend these to me?'

'No, I am *giving* them to you, since you appear to have no ornaments of your own.'

'No.' She kept her eyes on the jewel case, fascinated by the sparks of green fire that flew from the gems as they caught the light. 'I have never purchased anything for myself.'

'Best not to wear jewels or too much finery, Diana my dear. You must not draw attention to yourself.'

Mama's voice, kind but firm, echoed in her head. Diana sighed. She had never questioned it, until now.

She said, 'Margaret left me her personal jewellery in her will, but of course she was carrying it with her when, when the ship went down.'

'I beg your pardon, I did not mean to distress you with that memory.'

She shook her head and gave him a faint smile.

'You did not, sir. But, are you sure you wish to give these to me?'

'Of course.'

'May I wear them now, tonight?'

He smiled at her eagerness.

'Of course, that is why I am glad you are wearing that gown. Turn around now and let me fix the necklace for you.'

Diana removed her pearls and stood very still while Alex fastened the emerald necklace about her throat. The stones rested heavily on her collarbones, but she was even more aware of Alex's fingers at the back of her neck, brushing her skin and sending little darts of fire through her blood. She breathed deeply and slowly, resisting the urge to lean back against him. She closed her eyes for a moment, imagining herself turning and pulling his head down until their lips met in another sizzling, explosive kiss.

'There, it is done. Here, take the drops for your ears and put them on.'

Her eyes flew open. She could no longer feel his touch on her skin and she wanted to cry out, but instead she forced her reluctant feet to move away from him. She walked to the mirror and slipped the emerald drops in her ears. As Diana stepped back to look at herself the evening sun chose that moment to blaze between the dispersing rainclouds and she was caught in a shaft of golden light that enhanced the red-gold tints in her damp hair and made the green silk of her gown glow richly. It set the emeralds on fire, but they sparkled no more brightly than her eyes, which positively shone with happiness. She stared at her reflection in wonder.

I look beautiful.

She put her hands to her cheeks, shocked by the revelation. Margaret had always been the pretty one, Diana was the red-haired little cripple, to be hidden away, despised and pitied. But no longer. Alex had neither despised nor pitied her this afternoon. He had *worshipped* her! A huge smile burst from her as she turned back to Alex.

'Thank you so much.'

He looked slightly nonplussed at her gratitude.

'John Timothy collected the emeralds for me from the London today. They were in the family vault and you are…family. James would have given them to Margaret, but he told me once that she did not like emeralds.'

'No, she never wore green, she thought it an unlucky colour.'

But avoiding the colour had not saved her from drowning. Diana gave a little shiver.

Alex saw the shadows of sadness flitting across Diana's face and he longed to cross the short distance between them and take her in his arms, but he was very much afraid if he did so he would not be able to let her go until he had kissed her so thoroughly that she would be obliged to go upstairs again to tidy her hair, and possibly her gown.

There was no doubt that the emeralds were a good choice, they enhanced the creaminess of her skin and brought out those tantalising green flecks in her eyes. He had thought her quite splendid when she was angry, but now, glowing with happiness, she looked truly magnificent. If there hadn't been a room full of guests waiting for them he might well have ravished her again, here, over the desk…

He turned away so that she might not see how she affected him. He thought of the bachelors he had invited to stay. He had made it clear to them that Diana would be a good match. Well, he had vowed she might choose her own husband, but he knew now he would not promote anyone but himself for that role! Alex cleared his throat. Perhaps he was wrong to wait until they had time to discuss the matter. He should tell her now, make her an offer.

'We had best go to the drawing room,' said Diana. 'Fingle will be announcing dinner very soon.'

He closed his eyes. As he was thinking of marriage, so she talked of dinner. Clearly this was not the moment to propose. He dropped the pearls into the empty jewel case.

'I will send this up to your room later.' He went to the door. 'Shall we join our guests?'

Diana walked beside Alex across the hall, matching her step with his. She could walk with barely a hint of drag now and every day it became a little easier. And it was all Alex's doing. He had called her a worthy opponent and encouraged her to believe in herself.

She was well aware that he had sent the dancers to her in a spirit of mischief but they had been very useful, not only teaching the girls to dance but they had shown her exercises to stretch her leg muscles even more than she had already done over the past weeks, convincing her that she would walk normally if only she continued to apply herself.

Even sending the outrageous Madame Francot to Chantreys had proved a success, for she had not attempted to dress Diana in gowns unsuitable for a respectable hostess, instead she had provided her with fashionable gowns in colours and styles that made the most of her slender figure and unusual colouring.

It had all given her confidence. The confidence to face a house full of guests. To stand up for herself. What advantages had come her way through tangling with the new Lord Davenport! She could not stop her thoughts going back to their encounter in the orangery. It seemed to her that their coming together had been inevitable. Her body tingled with excitement at the very thought of it and although it had been irresponsible, even foolhardy, she could not regret it. She had never before felt anything quite so glorious or exhilarating. It was the sort of feeling poets wrote about, or artists captured with their brushes and oils, but she had never expected to have such an experience. A chuckle escaped her and Alex glanced down.

'Now what has amused you?'

She clasped his arm, saying impulsively, 'Oh, Alex, I have so much to thank you for—'

He stopped her.

'Hush now, we must perform for our guests.' He lowered his head to murmur in her ear as the footman threw open the drawing-room door. 'We must talk tonight, once everyone has retired.'

Uncertainty returned. Alex had made her no promises, she had asked for none, but perhaps what had been for her a momentous occurrence had meant very little to him. After all, he was an experienced man of the world. He had had many lovers.

Almost everyone else was gathered in the drawing room when they went in. Mr Wollerton was standing close to the door and turned immediately to greet them.

'Ah, our host and hostess at last.' He put up his glass. 'New coat, Davenport? I like the cut, Weston's, I would wager.' He stepped closer. 'I would have said you were trying to outshine Brummell, but I see you have the Davenport arms on the buttons, and the Beau would not like that. Simplicity is his style, y'know.'

'He might like it more if he was an earl,' drawled Alex. 'The buttons were made for my father. James never wore them, but I thought they would look well on the coat...'

Not by the flicker of an eyelid did Diana show her dismay when Alex walked away with his friend. He was right, they had their duties to perform, but being in company brought home to her the fact that things could never be the same again. She was no longer a maid. She had given herself to Alex wholeheartedly, thrown herself at him. She could not even claim that he had seduced her, she had been quite aware of what would happen if they kissed. Had she not recognised the edge of the precipice? But in that moment of passion the feelings had been so strong, so overwhelming, that it had been impossible to deny them. The world would not see that as any defence, of course. *She* might not regret giving herself to Alex, but in the eyes of society, she was ruined.

Dinner taxed Diana to the utmost. Without Alex by her side she felt vulnerable, as if everyone could see how she had changed. She expected disapproving looks and cold stares but her reception was the same as always and that made her feel deceitful. Mrs Peters exclaimed at her misfortune in getting caught in the rain and Diana could not deny it, since her hair was still damp, but it was generally assumed that she had been soaked running back to the house from the orangery and she said nothing to contradict it.

Alex kept his distance. Not by a word or a look did he show that anything had changed between them. Her head told her he was being discreet, but that did not satisfy her heart. Then, when she returned to the drawing room after seeing Meggie and Florence to bed, Alex looked up and smiled at her, and everything was well again.

Lady Frances touched her arm. 'Do come and sit with me for a while, Miss Grensham.'

Before Diana knew what was happening Frances was leading her across the room.

'I vow I have not had the opportunity to tell you how much I admire your new gowns. You must tell me, who is your modiste?'

She guided Diana to a sofa at some distance from the harpsichord, where Miss Prentiss was playing a lively sonata.

'Ah, dear Madame Francot,' Frances exclaimed, when Diana had replied. 'Did Alexander send her to you? I told him she is a genius with a needle, and her creations can transform the most unpromising of subjects.' She put her hands to her face. 'La, pray do not take that amiss, my dear, I did not mean—that is, what I intended to say is that your colouring must be quite…*daunting* when it comes to purchasing new clothes.'

Diana was still basking in the memory of Alex's smile and the barb missed its mark.

'Red hair and freckles? I believe it is.' She laughed. 'However, *madame* was quite delighted with the challenge of finding fabrics and styles that were a little less *ordinary* than those suitable for her usual clientele.'

The blue eyes snapped and Diana was pleased to think she had given the lady a taste of her own medicine. She would have risen but Lady Frances put a hand on her arm to stay her.

'There is something about you today, Miss Grensham, a certain air,' she hissed. 'I hope you do not think that these new gowns of yours will entice the earl. He is far too much of a connoisseur to be taken in by a few pretty clothes—' She broke off, her eyes narrowing. 'Or am I wrong…is that glow because he has already seduced you?'

Diana felt her cheeks burn under Frances's close scrutiny. The fingers on her arm tightened.

'Oh, my poor child, I am so sorry for you.'

'There is no reason to pity me,' Diana flashed back, but the knowing little smile about Frances's mouth unnerved her. One hand lifted towards the emeralds and she quickly pulled it back, but Frances had seen the movement and her smile grew.

'No? I think it was not only Madame Francot who saw you as a challenge. And who can blame the earl? After all you are here, living in his house, he would have to be made of stone to ignore what was so clearly on offer, however flawed.'

'You go too far, madam!'

Diana rose to her feet, but Lady Frances had not finished with her.

'Would you deny he gave you those emeralds, my dear? How very like him to ease his conscience with such a gesture.'

Without another word Diana turned and walked away. It was not true. It could not be so. These were stones from the family vault, not trinkets for some lightskirt. But the doubt remained. She continued to do her duty, a word here, a smile there, but at length she found a few moments when she was alone and could stop and survey the room. Lady Frances was on the far side, moving towards the harpsichord. She was almost gliding across the floor, her hips swaying in a provocative fashion that attracted almost every male eye. Diana glanced at Alex.

He was turned away, talking to Lady Goodge, or else she had no doubt that he, too, would have been unable resist watching Lady Frances. Diana fingered the necklace. How could she have forgotten what Mr Wollerton had told her, that his friend was always generous when ending his affairs? She had a sudden urge to laugh. An affair? Their brief coupling could not even be graced with the term.

The rain had quite gone, but it had cleared the air and there was a deliciously cool breeze coming in through the open windows. Everyone was gathered about the harpsichord, where Lady Frances was entertaining them all with a lively French ditty and Diana took the opportunity to slip outside. The moon was rising, not yet full but sufficient to illuminate the landscape in shades from bluegrey to black. Diana fanned herself gently as she gazed out over the scene and breathed in the heady scents that wafted across from the flower gardens.

A slight movement caught her attention.

'No, do not run away.' Alex stepped out on to the terrace. She could hear the smile in his voice when he spoke. 'I have not been near you all evening and I cannot bear the deprivation a moment longer.'

He was standing so close that her breast was almost touching his waistcoat and she felt her body responding to him, aching to move and bridge the tiny gap between them.

'Alex, I c-cannot, I do not want—'

He put his finger beneath her chin, turning her face up to receive his kiss and she was lost. All reason disappeared as her senses reeled again and his lips demanded her surrender. She melted against him, hands clasping at his coat, her body pressing against him, exulting in the hard, raw masculinity he exuded.

'Will you tell me now that you do not want me?' he murmured, his mouth close to her ear, rousing the slumbering desire deep inside.

'No.' She sighed, resting her cheek against his coat and feeling the thud of his heart through the soft wool. 'I want you too much, I fear.'

A laugh rumbled in his chest and his arms tightened around her.

'You do not know how much that pleases me. But what is this?' His hands slid to her arms and he held her away from him, looking intently into her face. 'What has upset you, Diana?'

She had not thought he would notice her sigh but she knew she must answer him.

'My, my leg, sir. The scar—does it not repel you?'

He looked at her silently for a long moment, then he lifted her hand and pressed her palm against his face.

'Does the scar on my brow repel *you*, my dear, or the one on my chin?'

'No, of course not, they make you what you are.'

He smiled. 'Exactly so.'

He kissed her again, sending the aching desire spiralling through her body. She wished they were alone in the house and they could spend the night sating their lust, but the ripple of applause from the drawing room recalled her to her duty. Reluctantly she broke off the kiss.

'Alex, our guests. We must go in.'

She turned away, but he pulled her close until she could feel his solid chest pressing against her back.

'Must we?'

He nibbled gently at her ear and she almost purred

with the pleasure of it. His hands slid over her breasts. They hardened beneath his palms, straining for his touch. How easy it would be to give in, but the soft sound of voices in the drawing room tugged at her conscience. It was an effort to free herself but she forced herself to ignore the urgent call of her body and stepped out of reach.

'We must,' she said. 'We will be missed.'

Alex observed the flushed cheeks, the eyes dark and liquid with desire, and his heart soared. He wanted to carry her off into the gardens and make love to her all over again and devil take the world, but it would not do. She put a hand up to straighten her bodice and gave a little self-conscious laugh.

'I would not give them cause for gossip, sir.'

'Let them gossip all they want,' he said recklessly. 'I would shout it to the world. Diana—'

He reached for her but she evaded him.

'No more, my lord. I must go in. It is growing late and some of our guests might be wishing to retire. It would look odd if neither of us was there to wish them goodnight.'

He watched her turn and walk away, the light setting her hair aflame as she stepped into the drawing room. By heaven, she was beautiful! He had come out to find her with the intention of making her a formal offer of marriage, but all coherent thought had fled when he had seen her standing in the moonlight.

Later. He had promised they would talk when everyone else had gone to bed. There would be no fear of interruption then, he would lay his heart at her feet and ask her if she could love him. Perhaps tomorrow he might send Timothy to London again to bring the rest of the jewels from the vault. There might be a ring there that Diana would like to wear as a token of their betrothal. He sat down on the low stone balustrade that edged the terrace, deciding to give her a few more moments before he followed her indoors. A chance for his body to cool down.

Lady Frances was still at the harpsichord when Diana came in from the terrace, but now she was performing a duet with Mr Hamilton. Diana noted that the gentleman sang in a strong tenor voice without any sign of the stutter that affected his speech. No one had noticed Diana's absence, they were all chattering and laughing and there was a lively air in the room, aided she suspected by the wine that had been flowing all evening.

In one corner Lord Goodge was dozing in a chair while his wife chattered away to Mrs Peters and in another Mr Wollerton and Sir Charles Urmston reclined at their ease, the glasses on the small table between them filled with an amber liquid she suspected was the earl's best brandy. Sir Charles caught Diana's eye and called out to her.

'Miss Grensham, we were just talking of you.'

She smiled politely and moved closer.

'Wollerton and I were discussing tomorrow night's little entertainment. The earl was telling us about it earlier—I believe his wards are to dance for us.'

'Why, yes, in the orangery,' she replied, mildly surprised at his interest. 'They will perform there after dinner tomorrow evening.'

'Excellent news,' declared Sir Charles. 'You know of course, that little Florence is a relative of mine? Yes, her poor mama was my cousin.' He shook his head. 'Bad business, that, killed by her own husband, don't you know.'

'I understood nothing was ever proven,' Diana replied cautiously.

'No, no, of course not, and since nothing has been heard of Florence's father we must suppose he is dead, and we should not speak ill of him, but these Arrandales, you know...' He let the words hang suggestively, but when he saw her frown he laughed suddenly. 'Enough of such sad talk. I wanted to say how glad I am to see the child so happy.'

'Ah, very good. Capital,' murmured Mr Wollerton, smiling blearily. 'They are both dear little souls.'

'I must say I have seen a great change in Davenport, too, these past few months, Miss Grensham,' Sir Charles told her. 'Why, he is becoming positively domestic. Never known him take an interest in children before. In fact, it wasn't so long ago he was wishing his wards in Hades, do you remember, Wollerton?'

'Eh?' Mr Wollerton looked as if he had been nodding off to sleep, but he sat up when Sir Charles addressed him and blinked owlishly. 'Oh, yes, yes. Wanted them out of Chantreys.' He reached for his brandy. 'No mention of it now, though.'

'No, completely changed,' agreed Sir Charles. He laughed. 'Do you remember how it was, Wollerton, that night we were at cards with Davenport? He was completely blue-devilled at not being able to do as he wished at Chantreys.' He gave Diana a conspiratorial wink. 'Back then he was looking for all sorts of ways to persuade you to take the children away.'

'Indeed.' Diana kept her smile in place, but it was a struggle. She did not wish to hear this.

'Why, yes,' put in Mr Wollerton, his eyelids drooping. 'He was all for moving you out at all costs.'

'Yes, he was most put out that you were to be given the last word when it came to the children. He said the late earl considered you a more fit and proper person to look after them,' explained Sir Charles. 'Was that not it, sir?'

'Aye, 'twas,' muttered Mr Wollerton.

Sir Charles rubbed his chin. 'Now what was it Davenport said that night? Something devilish amusing—'

His companion gave a laugh that ended with a hiccup. 'I'll tell you what it was, Urmston. He said, "Seduce the wench and send her packing." That was it.'

Sir Charles started and cast a horrified look at Diana.

'No, no, sir. You must have that wrong,' he said quickly. 'I am sure he would never—Miss Grensham, take no notice of Wollerton, he is foxed—'

'No, no,' continued that gentleman with the dogged determination of the very drunk, 'I remember distinctly. Those were his words—or somebody's—'

Sir Charles jumped up.

'Nonsense old fellow, you must be dreaming. Do excuse me, Miss Grensham, I think I should take Wollerton off to bed now. Pray ignore his ramblings, it is all nonsense, nonsense.'

'Yes, yes, of course.' Diana stood back as Sir Charles dragged Wollerton from his chair and helped him away.

Diana could never remember how she got through the rest of the evening. The final hour dragged and while she kept her smile in place, inside her rage was building. How could she have been such a fool? Of course she had never meant anything to Alex. With his wealth and position he could choose from amongst the most beautiful women in society, and everyone agreed he was a connoisseur in these matters. He had merely been amusing himself with her. Worse, it had all been an act, a charade to remove her and the children from Chantreys. Even the guests he had invited to this house party were undoubtedly part of his plan. Bachelors to try to win her hand and if that failed and he had to seduce her, the likes of Lord and Lady Goodge were the more respectable of Alex's acquaintances, invited so that the outrage and condemnation at her disgrace would be all the greater. No wonder Alex was not concerned about gossip, he *wanted* her ruin to be known. Diana felt quite sick.

She wanted to retire, to go to her bedchamber and cry her eyes out, but she forced herself to remain until the last of the party had gone. She and Alex were alone, save for the footman who was silently and methodically closing the long windows.

Diana clasped her hands together tightly.

'May we go to your study, my lord? I would like to speak to you privately.'

Silently he followed her across the hall. Candles still burned in the branched stick on the study desk, although one was guttering badly and Alex went across to trim the wick. Diana watched him, remembering those same hands on her body, caressing her. The thought only deepened her agony.

'There, that's better.' Alex turned towards her, that glinting smile in his eyes. 'Now, do you really wish to speak to me or—'

He reached out for her, but she batted his hands away, saying angrily, *'Seduce the wench and send her packing.'*

If any proof were needed that the gentlemen had been telling her the truth she had it now. Alex's hands fell, his brows snapped together.

'Where the devil did you hear that?'

'Mr Wollerton told me.'

'Gervase? What the deuce was he about, to be saying such a thing?'

'Do you deny it? Do you deny that you were planning ways to get me out of Chantreys?'

'You know I cannot deny that, but I said you would go of your own accord.'

'So you tried to marry me off!'

Alex looked perplexed. He pushed a hand through his hair.

'At first that was my intention, yes, but—'

Diana cut him short. 'Oh, despicable, despicable man! And when that failed you—you—' She dashed a hand across her eyes. 'How *dare* you ruin me, just to get your own way?'

'What? Diana, it was not like that—'

'When were you planning to denounce me, on Friday, at the ball perhaps?'

'No!' He caught her shoulders.

'Let go of me!' She shook him off, backing away as she put her hands to the back of her neck and fumbled with the clasp of the emerald necklace. 'No doubt you think I should be grateful for your...your *gift*!'

'No I do not want your gratitude, you little hothead, I want you to listen to me. Those emeralds have nothing to do with what happened between us.' Alex kept his hands at his sides, fists clenched as if to stop himself from reaching out for her again.

'There is no excuse for what happened in the orangery,' he told her. 'I mean to atone for it by marrying you.'

Diana was already in a towering rage and this little speech only heightened her indignation. Her eyes flashed.

'La, thank you my lord, I am *vastly* obliged to you

for your kind offer but I have no wish to, to sacrifice myself just to ease your conscience!' At last the clasp on the necklace was undone. 'I have money of my own and would infinitely prefer to live with my, my *disgrace* rather than be your wife!'

With jerky, unsteady hands she dragged the necklace from her throat, slipped off the earrings and hurled everything at Alex before running from the room.

The slam of the door resounded around the study before the air settled over Alex in a tense, prickly silence. He stared down at the floor. The earrings winked up at him from the boards and the emerald necklace was draped across one foot like an elegant but old-fashioned shoe buckle.

'You fool,' he muttered bitterly. 'You crass and utter fool.'

Chapter Fourteen

Diana spent a tearful, sleepless night going over the events of the previous day, allowing herself to remember how it had felt to be in Alex's arms, to enjoy the memory of his caresses before the pain of knowing how little it had meant to him was too much to be borne. He had planned it, after he had tried and failed to find a husband for her. Indeed, his attempts in that quarter had been laughable. As if she could ever fall in love with Mr Hamilton just because he liked music or Mr Avery, because they shared a mild interest in gardening. Or any of the other single gentlemen he had brought to Chantreys. None of them had sparked her interest, nor had any of them shown a preference for her.

It was impossible not to think of Alex's kindness to her. The way he had given her the courage to work on that irregular, halting walk, to believe that she could conquer it. But before she could feel too grateful towards him she reminded herself that it had all been in an effort to make her more attractive to the bachelors he paraded before her.

And failing that, he had fallen back on the original plan. *Seduce the wench and send her packing.*

The long night wore on. Diana stirred restlessly in her bed. She could not deny she had enjoyed challenging the earl, rebutting his attempts to shock her. It had become a game, but that had all ended yesterday, and not merely because he had seduced her like the practised rake he was.

No, it had ended when she realised how much she loved him.

When at last the grey dawn broke Diana summoned a sleepy Jenny to help her dress. She was determined to get through the day, to see Meggie and Florence perform this evening, but after that she would pack her bags and quit Chantreys. A sigh filled her. She had grown to love Meggie and Florence as if they were her own and leaving them would be agony, but there was no alternative. She was ruined and she could not allow her scandal to touch them. She would admit herself beaten.

A party of pleasure to Upminster had been arranged and everyone was gathered for an early breakfast, which gave Diana the opportunity to make her apologies. There was work to be done in the orangery and Meggie and Florence wished to practise their dance. She made her announcement calmly, not looking at Alex who was at the head of the table. He said nothing, for which she was grateful, even though it showed how little he wanted her company. She thought miserably that it proved his offer to marry her had come from his head, not his heart.

The guests expressed their disappointment that she would not be joining them, Mrs Peters even offering to remain behind and help her with her preparations, but Diana was adamant that they should all go off and enjoy themselves. She slipped away from the breakfast table while Alex was caught up in conversation with Lord Goodge and made her way to the schoolroom, where she remained until the last of the carriages had driven away. Only then did she venture downstairs again. There was much to be done and she hoped fervently that being busy would keep her thoughts away from her own troubles for the rest of the day.

The orangery was looking splendid: Mrs Wallace had worked miracles with the muslin curtains overnight. They had been washed, dried and pressed and were now in place again, softening the lines of the long windows. The pictures Diana had chosen had been carried across and it did not take her long to decide where they should be displayed. Then she turned her attention to the chairs and tables that needed to be arranged so that everyone would have a good view of the dais. A few benches were placed around the walls of the anteroom but everything else was banished to an empty barn, including the old sofa, where she had given herself to Alex. She could not bear to have that reminder of her ruin and disgrace on display.

Mrs Appleton was accompanying the girls' performance that evening and she had been invited to Chantreys for dinner, but Diana had sent a carriage to bring her to Chantreys for an hour at noon to play for the girls' rehearsal. Their dance had been choreographed by Chantal and Suzanne, and as the little girls skipped, jumped and twirled about the stage Diana wished the two dancers could be present to see how well it looked. Indeed, she wished they could have been there to take her place at the side of the stage, from where she would introduce the ballad Meggie and Florence were to sing and narrate the little story they had made up to accompany their dance.

'Too late now,' she told herself as the last notes died away and the girls moved to the front of the dais to make their curtsies to an imaginary audience. 'But tonight I will perform my last duty as hostess here. I shall not stay for the ball.'

As if conjured by her words, a footman came hurrying into the orangery to inform her that Madame Francot had arrived.

'Ah, she has brought your ballgown ready for tomorrow,' cried Florence, clapping her hands. Diana wondered if she should tell the children now that she would be leaving before the ball but she did not have the courage.

'How exciting,' declared Mrs Appleton, misreading Diana's hesitation. 'Pray, Miss Grensham, go on up to the house and see your modiste. I can easily run through the music again with the young ladies and then escort them to the schoolroom before I make my way home. You have been so good as to put a carriage at my disposal today, so I am only too happy to do anything I can to help you.'

In the face of such kindness Diana had not the heart to argue. She found Madame Francot and her assistant had already been shown up to her bedchamber, where Jenny was in attendance, her face alight with excitement. A large box lay open on the floor, surrounded by a sea of tissue paper, but that was soon forgotten. Draped over the sofa was a gown of vivid red silk embroidered with gold thread at the neck and hem.

It was so lovely that Diana had to steel herself to utter the words she had been rehearsing all the way from the orangery. She dismissed her maid and then turned to face the modiste.

'Madame Francot, so good of you to come but I am afraid it is a wasted journey. I shall not now be requiring the ballgown.' When the lady's pencilled eyebrows rose alarmingly she felt compelled to explain. 'I am not going to the ball tomorrow after all. You will be paid in full, of course…'

'Tsk, that is unfortunate, *mademoiselle*,' replied the modiste. 'I shall not ask you why. I can see from your sad face that something most *catastrophique* has occurred. But tell me, if you please, if you are withdrawing for ever from the eye of the public? Are you, per'aps, to become a nun?'

Even through her misery Diana was obliged to smile. 'No, nothing like that.'

'*Bon*. Then the journey he is not wasted. *S'il vous plaît*, *mademoiselle*, to try on the gown and we will make the final adjustments.'

In vain did Diana argue, Madame Francot stood as one not to be moved and in the end it was simpler to acquiesce.

'*Voilà,*' declared Madame Francot. '*C'est fini.*'

Diana regarded herself in the long glass. A stranger looked back at her. The face was pale, but despite her unhappiness the vivid red of the gown made her eyes sparkle like jewels and it enhanced the rich fiery glow of her hair. She had been very uncertain when *madame* had suggested the colour to her, but now she saw that the modiste had been perfectly correct, the scarlet silk became her very well. Diana felt a sigh building up inside her.

'If you cannot wear the gown tomorrow night then I am sorry for it,' declared Madame Francot, regarding her with a professional eye. 'But this gown, it is a triumph. You must keep it to wear on another occasion.'

Without waiting for a reply she turned to her assistant, rapping out her orders to pack away the needles and thread. Diana took one last look in the mirror, thinking of what might have been. Then she sent for Jenny to help her back into her day gown before she slipped away, leaving her maid to reverently pack away the gown and see Madame Francot off the premises.

Diana was descending the stairs when Alex came in, dusty from riding. She quickly turned back but his voice stopped her.

'I would appreciate a few moments of your time, Miss Grensham.'

With Christopher the footman standing wooden-faced by the front door Diana felt she could not refuse. She descended the last few steps to the hall.

'I did not expect to see you until dinner, my lord.'

'No, I left the party in Upminster and rode back ahead of them.' He strode to his study and held open the door. 'I am expecting my great-aunt and her protégée later today.'

'I am well aware of that. The arrangements for their reception are in hand.'

'I beg your pardon, I did not mean to question your ability to welcome them.'

We are talking like mere acquaintances, thought Diana as she went into the study. Polite, civil. Distant.

Excruciating.

Alex shut the door. 'Diana, about yesterday—'

'No!' That wound was too raw. 'We will not discuss it further, if you please.'

'But we must. I would not have you think that what happened in the orangery was part of any plan to remove you from Chantreys.'

'Nevertheless you have succeeded in your original

design,' she replied coldly. 'I cannot remain here. And I can no longer act as governess to Meggie and Florence.'

'*What?*'

His shock only increased her anger. She said bitterly, 'What did you expect to happen? I acted foolishly. I no longer consider myself a, a *fit and proper person* to look after the children. I will leave in the morning.'

His brow darkened. 'You cannot quit so abruptly. You are my hostess.'

'Better I go now than wait to be denounced. Lady Frances has already guessed what happened yesterday. I will not remain to be publicly humiliated.'

'No one is going to humiliate you,' he ground out. 'I will speak to Frances.'

Diana's hand fluttered.

'There is no point. What's done is done.'

He caught her fingers.

'There is a solution, Diana. Marry me. We will announce our betrothal at the ball. That would place you firmly under my protection.'

She snatched her hand away. 'To save my name? No, I thank you.'

Somehow she kept her head up. He must never know how much he had hurt her. All she had left now was her pride and she must hold on to that at all costs. She took a deep breath and pronounced with slow deliberation, 'If I loved you, my lord, then perhaps I might accept your offer. As it is I prefer to make my own way in the world.'

Diana forced herself to look steadily into the slate-grey eyes that stared at her beneath the dark and frowning brows. She tried to forget when she had seen those same eyes smouldering with passion, she thrust from her mind the memory of being held in his arms, surrendering to his kiss. Even now, if he had dragged her into his arms she knew she would crumble.

The silence stretched on. A tiny, almost unacknowledged hope flickered that he might beg her to stay, tell her that he could not live without her.

He turned away. Hope died.

'Very well.' Alex stared down at the desk, idly moving the inkwell and straightening the pens. He had spent the night preparing for the meeting, vowed he would not hurt her any more than had already done. She did not want him, did not love him. He must respect that. At least she was honest enough to admit it. She was not like all the others, who pretended to care when all they wanted was his money and his title. Even his first, disastrous love affair had been a lie. The older woman had used him because her ailing husband could not satisfy her. She had never loved him and he had soon been replaced by another, more experienced youth. No woman had ever loved him for himself, but he had thought it did not matter. After that initial schoolboy infatuation he had never allowed it to matter.

'Very well,' he said again. 'I cannot force you to remain, but I would beg you to consider the children. To leave so precipitately would cause them great distress.'

'If I leave tomorrow you will still be here for them.'

'But I am not you, Diana.' The words were wrenched from him. 'You have been everything to them since their parents died. You were their sole comfort in those first months while I—' He broke off, swallowing hard. 'I was too caught up in my own grief to spare a thought for their loss. If you go, without a word, it will break their hearts.'

And mine.

He looked up. 'At least stay until I can find another

governess to take your place. I need your help for that. You know what will suit the girls. John Timothy will draw up a list of suitable candidates and I will send them down to you for approval.' He saw the flicker of indecision in her eyes and pressed home the advantage. 'In a day or two the guests will be gone and I shall return to London. You and the girls will have Chantreys to yourself again.'

'That would give Meggie and Florence time to grow accustomed to my leaving,' she acknowledged.

Alex felt the weight lifting from his chest. He had some irrational feeling that if he could keep her at Chantreys there was a chance she might change her mind.

'And you will continue as my hostess?'

'I will stay for the girls' performance tonight, but that is all.'

'But the ball—'

'Nothing would persuade me to attend!'

Her vehemence cut him. He realised how much he had been looking forward to seeing her in all her finery, dancing with her, showing her off as his future bride. How on earth had he handled things so badly? She was close to tears and he knew he must tread carefully.

'As you wish. But tomorrow I would like Meggie and Florence to spend some time with my great-aunt and I am aware she can be quite formidable, they would be much more comfortable if you were with them. And it would be a pity for you to miss the dinner, when you went to such pains to plan it with Cook.' He went on quickly. 'You need not think that I shall impose my company upon you, or importune you any further. You may slip away directly after dinner, when everyone goes off to change. I will tell the marchioness then that you have been taken ill and ask her to stand in as hostess.'

'Yes, yes, that will do.'

Diana felt the tears pressing. If she did not get away soon they would spill over and she was determined not to show such weakness before him.

'You agree to my plan?'

Another steadying breath was required before she could speak.

'Yes, I agree. Now if you will excuse me I must get on—'

She almost ran to the door.

'Diana.' His voice halted her. She stood with her back to him, her hand grasping the door handle. 'I never meant to hurt you.'

She closed her eyes, squeezing back the hot tears. He sounded so humble that she almost believed him.

Almost.

Diana fled to the schoolroom, where she found that Jenny had taken Meggie and Florence for a walk, the girls being far too excited about their forthcoming performance to settle to any work. That gave Diana an opportunity for a little quiet reflection in her room, which did much to restore her equilibrium and make her see the sense in remaining at Chantreys, at least for the moment. Much as she would prefer a quick, clean break, it would be better for Meggie and Florence if they were prepared for her going. It would be painful for her to continue as hostess and act as if nothing had occurred, but she would do it, for their sake.

It had been agreed that Diana would take the girls to the drawing room before dinner to be introduced to the Marchioness of Hune and her protégée, Miss Ellen Tatham, but even on the top floor of the house it was impossible to avoid news of their arrival. Nurse came puffing up the stairs to announce that the marchioness was come and with such a quantity of luggage that Mrs Wallace was in despair as to where it would all go, and when Jenny arrived to help Diana and the girls to change their gowns she was clearly impressed by her ladyship's dresser.

'Miss Duffy, she is, and she has 'em all in a spin below stairs,' Jenny declared as she took a brush to Meggie's tangled curls. 'When I saw her in the hall she looked down her nose at me in *such* a way that I mistook her for the marchioness herself!'

'I believe it is often so with retainers of long standing,' Diana replied calmly, not wishing to make the girls nervous of meeting Lady Hune.

'Perhaps it is, miss,' said Jenny cheerfully. 'Now, then, Miss Grensham, what are *you* going to wear tonight? The rose-green looks very well.'

But if she wore that Diana thought someone might comment upon the fact that she was not wearing the emeralds.

'The teal,' she decided. 'I shall wear the teal and my pearls.'

The summons came soon afterwards and Diana escorted her charges to the drawing room. Alex was waiting for them and as they came in he fixed Diana with a dark, enigmatic stare.

'Davenport is worried I might frighten you all away if he is not here to protect you.'

The voice, rich with amusement, brought Diana's attention to the old lady sitting in regal state in one of the arm chairs. So this was the Dowager Marchioness of

Hune. She was dressed all in black with quantities of silver lace at her wrists and neck and held an ebony cane in one gnarled and beringed hand. Her silver hair was neatly piled about her head and the faded blue eyes were sharp, but not unkind as they surveyed Diana and her charges. Alex performed the introduction and the girls made their curtsies before moving to sit on the sofa near the dowager's chair.

Lady Hune turned to Diana. 'I believe you are the girls' governess, as well as sharing guardianship with my nephew?'

'Yes, ma'am, for the moment.'

'Why do you say that? Is there some doubt of your continuing here?'

Diana was trying to frame an answer when there was a welcome distraction. The door opened and a young lady appeared, a golden-haired vision in cream muslin sprigged with tiny blue flowers that matched the cerulean blue of her large eyes. She was, thought Diana, startled, the loveliest creature she had ever seen.

'I beg your pardon, Duffy could not remember where she had packed my Norwich shawl and in the end I have come down without it, for I did not wish to put off meeting Lord Davenport's wards.' Her pleasant voice was laced with laughter as she crossed the room. 'My goodness, but you are both so pretty, no—do not tell me, let me guess. You must be Lady Margaret, yes? And if that is so then you are Miss Florence.' Having delighted the children with her friendly manners the vision addressed Diana, who was standing a little to one side. 'And you must be the famous Miss Grensham,' she said, dipping a little curtsy. 'Lord Davenport has told me so much about you.'

'And this baggage,' declared Lady Hune with mock severity, 'this is my protégée, Miss Ellen Tatham, putting me to the blush with her lack of manners.'

'Oh, fie, ma'am, you know we stand on no ceremony with Lord Davenport,' Miss Tatham responded, casting a mischievous look at Diana. 'He is Lady Hune's great-nephew, you see, Miss Grensham, and obliged to be courteous to me and to stand up with me whenever we meet at the balls and assemblies, so we have become great friends.'

'This is your first Season, I believe?' murmured Diana, sinking down into a chair even as the vision disposed herself gracefully on the sofa next to Florence.

'Yes, and Lady Hune has been good enough to sponsor me,' replied Miss Tatham. 'It was intended that Phyllida, my stepmama, would present me, but not only was she disobliging enough to fall in love last autumn, she felt it necessary to marry *and* to set up a nursery immediately, so she has not been in any fit state to be jauntering around London. It was proposed that my Aunt Hapton would step in, but *fortunately*, Phyllida's husband is another of Lady Hune's great-nephews, so I am part of the family now, which makes it perfectly proper for her ladyship to bring me out.'

'And your stepmama?' enquired Diana, smiling at this breathless recital.

'She has presented her husband with a lusty heir,' Miss Tatham said. 'But Lady Hune thought it best to leave the doting parents to coo over their baby while we continue to enjoy ourselves.'

'Enjoy?' declared the dowager. 'If I had realised how fatiguing it would be, I should have remained in Bath and left you to your aunt's ministrations.'

Miss Tatham was not a whit cast down by the words, nor the scowl that accompanied them. She merely laughed.

'You know you love every minute of it, ma'am, and looking after me stops you from worrying yourself into a fever over Lady Cassandra.'

'Lady Hune's granddaughter,' Alex explained to Diana. 'She and her husband were in Paris when war was declared.' He turned back to the dowager. 'Is there any news of Cassie, ma'am?'

Lady Hune shook her head.

'I had one letter soon after hostilities resumed, to say they had been detained. Since then it has been difficult to discover just what has happened to them. I hope, if her cousin had indeed escaped to France…'

'Ah, the infamous Wolfgang Arrandale,' said Alex. He glanced at Diana and said, by way of explanation, 'Florence's father.'

She nodded. She knew the story, how Florence had been born as her mother lay dying and the wild young man who was her father had fled abroad, accused of murdering his wife.

Alex turned to Lady Hune and said gently, 'You are aware, ma'am, that nothing has been heard of him for years.'

'But there was a rumour he was living in France under an assumed name,' the dowager replied. 'If that is so, he might be able to help Cassandra.'

Alex gave the slightest shake of his head. 'I fear you are clutching at straws, Aunt.'

'I fear so, but I have to *try*. The boy certainly had friends in France. I have tried to contact them, but it is impossible to know if my letters ever arrived. And even if they did, there is only a small chance they would be of help to Cassandra.'

For a moment the mask slipped. The thin hand holding the cane clenched until the knuckles gleamed white and Diana saw the haunting sadness in the old lady's face, but only for a moment, then Lady Hune seemed to straighten her shoulders. 'However, there are reports that many of the English have gathered in Verdun and are enjoying themselves vastly. They have made themselves at home there with entertainments and gambling and horse-racing.'

'Yes, I have heard that.' Alex nodded. 'I believe they call it Little England. Let us hope that Cassie and her husband have found their way there.'

'Yes, let us hope that.'

The sorrowful note in the dowager's voice was not lost on Miss Tatham, who immediately jumped up.

'You must be tired from the journey, my lady. Let me take you upstairs where you may rest until it is time for dinner. I am sure Miss Grensham will excuse us.'

Miss Tatham suited actions to her words and gently led the dowager away, leaving Alex and Diana alone with the girls. The room seemed suddenly very quiet and Diana sought for something to say to break the silence.

'Miss Tatham is a lively companion for the dowager.'

''She is, but she is also very conscious of my great-aunt's age and takes great care of her,' Alex replied. 'The arrangement works exceedingly well.'

Another silence stretched. Alex felt the awkwardness and wished he could say something to ease it.

'Diana—'

'We must be getting upstairs, too.' She rose and held

out her hands to the girls. 'Meggie and Florence have to prepare for their performance tonight.'

Meggie looked up at Alex anxiously. 'Will everyone be coming to watch us?'

He smiled and ruffled her hair.

'Why, yes, I will not allow anyone to miss it. I am sure you will sing and dance delightfully.' He glanced up. 'Can the girls not make their own way to the schoolroom? We might take a walk in the garden—'

The suggestion made her shy like a nervous colt. She murmured, not looking at him, 'You promised, my lord.'

Yes, he had promised and he must keep to it. Alex went to open the door.

'Of course. Off you go then. Until dinner, Miss Grensham.'

Chapter Fifteen

There was no doubt that Lady Hune and Miss Tatham made a welcome addition to the company gathered in the drawing room before dinner. The dowager was happy to converse upon any subject, while Miss Tatham's liveliness lifted the spirits and charmed everyone, not just the gentlemen who gravitated towards her.

'Like bees around a honeypot,' observed Lady Frances, stopping beside Diana. 'Ellen Tatham has everything, she is young, handsome and endowed with a considerable fortune.'

'Indeed, she is a very fortunate young woman,' agreed Diana, looking across the room to where Alex was laughing at something Miss Tatham was saying.

The leaden weight around her heart grew heavier and she turned away, but Lady Frances followed her.

'The earl has been seeing a great deal of her in town the past few months.'

If Frances was trying to make her jealous she was missing her mark, thought Diana, and in any case it no longer mattered, since she would soon be leaving Chantreys and Alex for ever. The lady continued in a low voice.

'There is much talk in town that they will make a match of it.'

'I wish them well then,' muttered Diana.

'Yes, it is best to accept the inevitable,' murmured Frances with spurious sympathy. 'Even though you have worked so hard to minimise that ugly walk of yours, Miss Grensham, you could not compete against such a beauty.' Her contemptuous look raked Diana from head to toe. Suddenly the teal gown with the gold-silk tambouring felt no more special than a rag upon her back. 'Your transformation came too late.'

Diana remained rooted to the spot as Frances walked away. How was she to bear another full day of this?

You must. It is for the children's sake. Hide your grief and keep your head up, Diana.

Dinner was easier. Diana kept her attention fixed upon her food and entertaining those guests seated immediately around her. On her left she had Sir Charles Urmston, and although she could not like his rather unctuous courtesy, it was some comfort that he did not spend the whole time staring stupidly at Miss Tatham, which she noticed Mr Avery and Mr Hamilton were doing.

As soon as the ladies withdrew Diana excused herself and went off with Mrs Appleton to collect Meggie and Florence and take them to the orangery. She knew Alex would not allow the gentlemen to linger over the brandy tonight, so they had less than an hour to prepare.

The candles were burning brightly in the orangery by the time the earl and his guests came in. Mrs Appleton played a selection of music that blended with the chatter of the audience as everyone took their seats. Diana kept Meggie and Florence beside her, sitting quietly on a bench behind the pianoforte. From there Diana watched Alex walk in with the dowager on his arm, Mr Wollerton following with Miss Tatham and they settled themselves on the front row of seats with Alex sitting between Lady Hune and Ellen Tatham.

Once everyone was settled Diana rose to introduce the ballad Lady Margaret and Miss Florence Arrandale were to sing. She was nervous, but not overly so. It was as if she was looking down upon the scene, watching herself walk slowly to the front of the dais. The skirts of her gown caught the light, shifting from green to blue and whispering about her as she moved gracefully across the raised platform, her steps even and steady. Alex was regarding her intently, a look of approval on his face. Of pride. And why should he not? Whatever wrong he had done her, she could not deny that he had given her the courage to stand tall and face the world. A small victory and a bittersweet memory to take with her when she left Chantreys.

She stood to one side, her back to the audience as the girls sang. She smiled encouragement, mouthed the words and led the applause that followed their rendition. Then she stepped forward again. There was silence in the room, every eye was upon her, expectant, waiting. She cleared her throat and began her next little speech, inviting them to imagine a leafy glade and two fairy sprites dancing therein…

Diana took her place at the side of the dais while the music flowed and soared, filling the room. Meggie and Florence danced the routine Suzanne and Chantal had created for them, their flowing white dresses sashed with dark green and wreaths of evergreens upon their heads. They jumped and twirled and skipped about the stage quite beautifully and when it was over the audience showed its appreciation, the gentlemen clapped, the young ladies exclaimed in delight and the matrons in the audience sighed and wiped away a tear. It was done and it was a success.

'Well, that went very well, I think,' declared Mrs Appleton when Diana went over to thank her.

'Very well indeed.' Diana smiled and looked across to where Meggie and Florence were being praised and fêted by a group that included Alex and Miss Tatham. 'You will stay for refreshments, Mrs Appleton? I have asked Fingle to bring wine and cakes and lemonade for everyone.'

The room was already being rearranged into a more informal setting. Tables were brought in and servants began to circulate with their heavily laden trays.

'I must say, Miss Grensham, you have worked wonders with the little ones,' observed Mrs Appleton, packing away her music. 'When one thinks that it is not yet a year since Lady Margaret lost her parents. I am sure it has been a great comfort to the little girls that you have been here to look after them.'

'Thank you, ma'am.' Diana's restless gaze wandered over the room, quickly moving on from the sight of Alex laughing at something Ellen Tatham was saying. Had Fingle sent in enough wine? Should she ask him to bring in more lemonade, or ratafia, perhaps, for the ladies…?

'And what changes will the future bring, hmm?' continued Mrs Appleton, turning a beaming smile upon Diana. 'Are we to expect an announcement tomorrow night, my dear?'

Diana's wandering thoughts snapped back. 'An announcement, Mrs Appleton?'

'Why, yes, one cannot live in a small place like this without everyone knowing what is in the wind, my dear. The new earl paying you such distinguished attention, bringing a house party to Chantreys with you as his hostess and tomorrow, when the whole neighbourhood is gathered here, you will be standing beside him—*such* an exciting time, Miss Grensham!'

'M-Mrs Appleton, I assure you, you must not expect anything tomorrow other than the ball.'

'Now, now, there is no need to colour up.' Mrs Appleton patted her hand. 'I do not wish to spoil the moment, but just to let you know that we are all delighted at the prospect. Delighted.'

Cheeks flushed, Diana murmured her excuses and moved away. If ever anything was needed to convince her she must not appear at the ball, that was it.

'What an excellent display, Miss Grensham.' Lady Frances came up, her smile honey-sweet. 'I vow I have never seen children dance better. You were clearly born to be a governess.' Diana met her comment with a stony silence and the lady's smile widened before she turned to address the company. 'Since we are all here then should we not make the most of this beautiful instrument? Mr Hamilton, will you not join me to sing for the company?'

The idea of a musical evening was greeted enthusiastically. Mrs Appleton declared herself only too delighted to play for anyone who needed her and everyone refilled their glasses and milled about the room while those who wished to perform took their turn on the dais.

Diana could not be persuaded to join in, saying she must look after the children, although in truth Meggie and Florence were sitting at a table with Miss Tatham enjoying a treat of cake and lemonade. She wandered about the room, accepting compliments on behalf of her charges, but keeping well away from the dais. And from Alex.

When Jenny arrived at the appointed time to collect Meggie and Florence Diana had to prise them away from Miss Tatham. They parted reluctantly and only after that young lady had promised to join them for their walk the following morning.

'No, pray do not you rush off, Miss Grensham,' said Ellen, when the children were finally consigned to the maid's care. 'I would very much like you to sit with me for a little while.'

She signalled a passing footman and procured two full glasses of wine.

'I would have thought you would like a little peace and quiet after sitting with the girls for so long.'

Ellen laughed. 'They are charming, Miss Grensham— no, I shall call you Diana, and you shall call me Ellen, if you please—Meggie and Florence are delightful children and a credit to you. Lord Davenport has told me how you have been like a second mother to them. But as their governess I hope you will forgive me for spoiling them a little tonight. I promise you I did not allow them too much cake, but they are so excited I am afraid they will not wish to go to bed.'

Diana chuckled. 'I think you are right. I am sure they will not go to sleep until they have described to Nurse and Jenny their triumph this evening.'

'They performed beautifully.' Mischief danced in Miss Tatham's eyes. 'Oh, dear. I do hope it has not given them a taste for the stage. Lord Davenport was telling me he sent down a couple of opera dancers to tutor them in the steps.'

'*Ballet* dancers,' Diana corrected her, a twinkle in her own eyes. 'I was assured they were young ladies of the highest respectability.'

'And *I* am sure you would have sent them packing if they had been anything else.'

'I should, but I knew I could rely upon the earl not to do anything that might harm the children.'

Diana sipped her wine. How long ago that seemed now. She and Alex had understood one another then and she had enjoyed the game. Now it was over and very soon she would pack up and remove herself from Chantreys and the girls for ever. She shrugged off the melancholy thoughts as the atmosphere around them changed again. Lady Goodge had finished playing a fiendishly difficult piece by Mr Mozart and the room was filled with applause and excited chatter. She heard calls for the earl and Lady Frances to sing another duet and she was surprised when the lady demurred.

'I think we should invite Miss Tatham to sing with Lord Davenport,' said Lady Frances, at her most gracious.

There was no doubting Ellen's surprise. Across the small table Diana forced herself to smile and nod encouragingly and while Ellen went off to join Alex by the pianoforte, Diana moved to one side of the room where she could watch the performance. Lady Frances wandered by and paused when she reached Diana.

'Do they not make a perfect couple, Miss Grensham?' she purred. 'They are constantly together in town.' She gave a sigh and said sadly as she moved on, 'I have quite resigned myself to the match. Even *I* cannot compete with the heiress's charms.'

Not by the flicker of an eyelid did Diana respond. She kept her eyes on the duo, listening to the melodious sound their voices made together, but inside the splinter of unhappiness was working its way deeper into her heart. Ellen Tatham was indeed perfect. An ideal consort for an earl who was renowned for his love of beautiful objects. Meggie and Florence liked her, too, which augured well for their future. Diana felt the hot tears pressing. The girls would not miss her for very long, if they had Ellen Tatham to comfort them.

Gervase Wollerton was waiting when Alex led his partner from the dais.

'An excellent rendition, Miss Tatham,' he declared. 'And you, Davenport. Never heard you in better voice.'

Alex said nothing, merely standing, frowning, while Ellen Tatham accepted Gervase's compliments with a pretty grace. When she was called away Alex and Gervase were left staring at one another in silence.

'Alex, old friend—'

'Enough, Gervase. Let us forget the matter.'

'But I can't, Alex.' Gervase glanced around. Everyone else was engaged in chatter, no one was taking any notice of them. 'I cannot,' he said again. 'I have racked my brains to think how I could have been such a fool last night, to say what I did to Miss Grensham. I didn't even remember it until you tackled me about it this morning.' He shook his head. 'I cannot even blame it on the brandy, you would never allow a bad barrel in your cellars.'

Alex felt his scowl deepening. 'Urmston got you drunk and primed you with what to say. I have seen him do as much before, with other fools.'

Gervase took the insult without a flinch. He said, 'I remember sitting down with him, but I did not think I had had that much to drink.' His usually cheerful face was full of grief. 'I am more sorry that I can say. If you want satisfaction—'

'And make a bad situation even worse? No. What's done is done, Gervase. I was a fool to allow Urmston anywhere near Chantreys. Where *is* he, by the bye?'

Wollerton looked around him.

'No idea. Lady Frances is still here, so—' He broke off and cast an anguished look at Alex.

'Don't worry about offending my sensibilities in *that* quarter,' he said grimly. 'I have long suspected they are more than friends. I think they have been working together to poison Diana's mind against me—did you see the way Frances encouraged me to sing with Ellen Tatham?' He shrugged and gripped Wollerton's arm. 'Cheer up, Gervase. I do not hold you wholly responsible for what occurred. I have been a blundering fool where Miss Grensham is concerned. In fact, the blame for this whole fiasco rests squarely at my door and I must take the consequences.'

With all the confusion of chatter and singing and the servants moving between the guests to supply them with refreshments, Diana thought no one would miss her if she slipped outside. She needed a few moments to compose herself and to force back the silly tears that were never far away.

It was blessedly cool on the terrace and there were deep shadows between the blocks of light that spilled out from the long windows. She stepped into one of the shadows and wiped her eyes.

'Miss Grensham, are you quite well?'

Diana jumped as Sir Charles Urmston approached her.

'Oh, th-thank you, sir. I am very well. Suffering a little from the heat and the noise, that is all.'

'Ah.' He came closer and Diana found herself stepping back further into the shadows. 'It is very hard, is it not, when one's dreams are shattered.'

'I'm afraid I do not understand you…'

'Davenport and the heiress. An ideal match. I saw Miss Tatham in Bath last year. She was even then a piece of perfection, but so well *guarded*. At the time I thought it a little excessive, but I see now that the marchioness was keeping her for Davenport. He is her great-nephew, you know, and the Tatham fortune will enhance the Arrandale coffers.'

When Diana did not speak he continued in a reflective tone.

'Yes, one can quite see that she will suit him perfectly. Another beautiful object to add to his collection. You know, of course, that Lady Frances had hopes of being his countess. She has been so, in all but name for some time.'

'Really, Sir Charles, I do not think you should be telling me this.'

'Oh, but it is a relief to be able to speak without restraint about these matters, to talk to someone who *understands*. I have known Lady Frances for many years and I had thought, with Davenport out of the way…' He sighed. 'But she is heartbroken and she will not let me comfort her.'

Diana began to feel uneasy.

'I really think I would like to go in now—'

He caught her hand.

'Not yet. We should ease each other's pain.'

'No, I do not want—'

He dragged her into his arms. Diana struggled, but

Sir Charles was too strong, he was holding her so tightly against his body that it was difficult to breath. Panic was rising, but she had to contain it.

'Let me go!'

Her hands were against his chest but she could not push him away. She kept turning her head to avoid his lips until he grabbed her hair, forcing her head back. He was squeezing her so hard that she could not find the breath to scream.

'A kiss,' he muttered, his breath, thick with wine and spirits, was hot on her face. 'Let me show you that in the dark one man is very much like another—'

The kiss never came. Suddenly Diana was free and she staggered back, unbalanced. She heard a growl, a tussle in the darkness and the sickening thud of a punch. By the time she had recovered her balance and looked up Sir Charles was lying on the floor with Alex standing over him, fists clenched. Even in the shadows Diana could see the naked fury in his face. She gave a little gasp and, as if recalling her presence, Alex stepped back.

'Get up, Urmston,' he barked. 'Pack your things and leave my house. There is a good moon, I want you gone within the hour.'

Sir Charles scrambled to his feet and stood for a moment, rubbing his jaw.

'Very much dog in the manger, ain't you, Davenport? You don't want the lady but no one else shall have her either.' He gave a savage little laugh. 'And I thought you might appreciate my helping you out of a predicament by taking the wench off your hands.'

With a muted roar Alex advanced, but Diana grabbed his arm.

'No, please!'

Sir Charles watched them, his lip curling.

'She is right, Davenport. You would not want your guests to witness an unseemly brawl, especially the lovely Miss Tatham.'

'Get out of my sight, now, or I will mill you down again and to hell with who sees it!'

With a final, malevolent glare Sir Charles dusted himself down and lounged away. Alex turned back to Diana.

'Did he hurt you?'

'N-no. I was merely shocked, that is all.' She sank on to the balustrade restlessly clasping and unclasping her hands. Alex sat down beside her.

'Another wrong to lay at my door.'

'I will not blame you for Sir Charles's actions, my lord.'

He reached out and caught her hand, holding it in a warm, sustaining clasp.

'I blame myself for putting you in his way. Diana, I want to protect you from men such as Urmston. I want to make sure such a thing never happens again. I have wronged you and I want to put everything right. Marry me!'

Diana knew it would be so easy to lean against that strong shoulder, to give in to her heart and say yes, but she must not. She loved him, but it was not reciprocated. A vision of her life stretched ahead of her, bound to a man who had married her out of duty. Out of guilt. Such a marriage would make neither of them happy. Gently she pulled her hand free. She must end this, now and for ever.

'In my world, Lord Davenport, if a marriage cannot be a love-match at the very least it must be based upon mutual respect, affection and trust. There would be none of these things in our union and therefore it cannot go ahead.'

* * *

So that was it. His brave Diana, even after the indignity of Urmston's attentions—and he had seen how she fought against the brute—even after such a shock she was still determined to refuse him. What had she said? *If it cannot be a love-match.* Nothing could be clearer. He pushed himself to his feet.

'Very well, madam, I shall say no more on this matter.' He rose. 'But Chantreys has been your home. There is no reason why you should give up your place here.'

'There is every reason, my lord. The children need a governess who is above reproach. In all conscience I cannot claim that for myself.' She rose. 'You will instruct Mr Timothy to find another governess, if you please. As we agreed.'

'But you will remain their guardian?'

'Of course. Any communication can be dealt with by our lawyers.'

'If that is what you wish.'

'Then it is all settled.' Her voice was firm, matter of fact. 'I will fulfil my duties here tomorrow and then I shall prepare the children for my departure.'

Alex nodded. His right hand was throbbing where it had come into contact with Urmston's jaw but it was nothing to the pain of the iron band that was squeezing his chest.

'Now if you will excuse me, I will return to our guests.'

She swept past him and in through the open window, head held high and with never a backward look.

Chapter Sixteen

There was no chill to the bright September day when Diana stepped out of the house with Meggie and Florence the following morning. She had not expected Ellen Tatham to remember her promise to join them, but a message had come upstairs while the schoolroom party were breaking their fast to say Miss Tatham would be waiting for them in the rose garden.

As soon as they saw Ellen strolling amongst the roses, Meggie and Florence ran up to her and Diana tried hard not feel resentment. Miss Tatham greeted the girls with genuine pleasure and waited for Diana to join them.

'Is it not a glorious day, Miss Grensham? Shall we walk in the park?'

They set off at a brisk pace, the little girls skipping along beside them and chattering happily to their new friend. Soon they were telling her all about the secret lake and suggesting they should go exploring in the woods. Diana's heart sank. She had not been to the lake since Alex had surprised her there and she was very much afraid that the memories it evoked would prove too much for her. She feared her reluctance was apparent, for after a quick glance in her direction Ellen said she thought they should save such a treat for another day, when there was more time.

'I really think I must save my energy for the ball to-night,' she told them, smiling. 'We are to dine early, I believe, so we may all have time to change into our finery before the festivities begin.'

'Diana has promised that we may watch for a little while, so we shall be able to see you dancing,' Florence confided.

'Will you indeed?' exclaimed Ellen. 'How exciting.'

Meggie nodded solemnly. 'Jenny will take us to the orangery to watch the first dance, and then when we come back I hope we can have macaroons, and orange flummery and lemonade for our supper!'

'I am sure Mrs Wallace will be able to send up a selection of treats for you, if you are very good today,' said Diana solemnly.

'We are always good,' replied Meggie, affronted.

Ellen laughed and linked her arm with Diana's.

'What a wonderful place this is,' she declared. 'I love it here and I am sure we are going to be very good friends.'

Diana smiled and realised how much she would like to have Ellen for a friend, but it was not to be. As soon as another governess could be found to look after the children she must cut all ties with Chantreys and the Arrandale family.

They made their way back through the formal gardens, the girls running on ahead to ask the aged gardener if they might pick some flowers for the schoolroom.

'Now we are alone there is something I wanted to ask

you.' Ellen lowered her voice. 'Did Sir Charles Urmston try to molest you on the terrace last night?'

Diana flushed at the forthright question, but she found it impossible to be offended with Ellen Tatham. She decided to answer frankly.

'Yes, he did.'

'I thought as much. And Lord Davenport came to your rescue. How romantic.'

'Not at all. It, it was quite horrid.'

'I saw Urmston step out of the orangery last night and he never reappeared. Then this morning we learned that he had left Chantreys. It was put about that urgent business called him back to town, but I am not deceived. Davenport threw him out and I am very glad of it.' Ellen lowered her voice, saying confidentially, 'Sir Charles is not at all to be trusted, Diana. He tried to do me a great disservice in Bath last summer. He was part of a wicked wager to dishonour me.'

Diana stopped and stared at her in shocked dismay.

'Is that all Lord Davenport and his, his *cronies* can find to do with their time?' she exclaimed.

'Oh, Sir Charles is no friend of Davenport's,' said Ellen cheerfully. 'It was Lady Frances who invited him to Chantreys. The earl was most put out about it, he told Lady Hune as much when we arrived. Of course the dowager has said nothing to Alex about the wager, but nevertheless I know Lord Davenport dislikes Sir Charles, and I suppose seeing him trying to kiss you last night was the last straw. Did he mill him down? I do hope so, for Urmston is an odious toad and if there is any mischief to be made he will do it, you may be sure.'

'Lord Davenport was certainly very angry,' Diana admitted.

'Of course he was, to see that beast manhandling the woman he loves. I am sure he was incandescent.'

Diana stopped.

'No, no, you are quite mistaken. Lord Davenport does not care for me.' She added earnestly, 'Indeed, Miss Tatham, you must put that silly idea quite out of your head. He feels an obligation to me, but nothing more than that, I assure you.'

Ellen did not look convinced, but as the children came up at that moment with an armful of flowers she turned to them.

'Well, you have collected so many, there is nothing left for me to do,' cried Ellen. 'Shall we go indoors and find a pretty vase to display them?'

'You go on ahead,' Diana urged them. 'I think I will remain in the gardens a little longer.'

She watched them walk off and as soon as they were out of sight she slipped into the shrubbery to think about what Ellen had said.

Alex could not love her. It was not possible. It was merely Ellen's romantic nature that had made her imagine such a thing. Ellen Tatham was very young and had most likely lived a very sheltered life. She would not yet understand that a man might desire a woman physically and yet feel nothing more than a passing fancy for her.

'Miss Grensham, do I disturb you?'

Diana jumped. She had been so wrapped up in her thoughts she had not heard Mr Wollerton approach but now he was before her. She summoned up a smile.

'No, sir, not at all.'

'Good.' He turned and fell into step beside her. 'And I am glad that I have found you alone. I want to apolo-

gise for what I said the other night. It has been on my
conscience ever since.'

'About the earl wanting to ruin me?'

The gentleman winced at her frankness.

'There is no excuse for it, I was foxed in your drawing
room, Miss Grensham, and I humbly beg your pardon.
But here's the thing, I may have given the impression
that it was Alex who said those words, but do you know,
I am not sure that it wasn't Urmston's idea.'

Diana gave a bitter little laugh.

'That I can believe! But it makes little difference, Mr
Wollerton. The earl did not dismiss the idea out of hand,
did he? You need not hesitate to be frank with me, sir.
Lord Davenport told me as much himself.'

'Well, no, he did not. But I think—I *believe*, Miss
Grensham—that once Alex became acquainted with you
he quickly changed his mind about moving you out. Quite
the contrary, in fact.'

'Oh?'

'Yes, yes,' declared Mr Wollerton eagerly. 'I heard
him only yesterday, telling Lady Hune that there was no
one better suited to looking after his wards.'

'Yes, I was born to be a governess,' she muttered, recalling Lady Frances's words.

'And now Alex tells me you are determined to leave.
He is quite cut up about it and I know he blames me in
part, for repeating something that you should never have
heard.'

'But it was not totally false, was it, sir?'

'No, but I do not think it was ever Alex's intention to
resort to such measures.'

'Whatever the earl's *intentions*, Mr Wollerton, things
have come to such a pass that I cannot remain at Chant-

reys. As soon a suitable governess can be found I shall leave.'

The gentleman's cheerful countenance took on a mulish look.

'I do not think you should, Miss Grensham. I have never seen Alex in such a mood before. I think he is in lo—'

She stopped him, feeling an angry flush building inside her.

'If the earl is in a bad mood it is because for once he cannot have his own way. He, he has made it impossible for me to remain as instructress to Meggie and Florence and I can never forgive him for that!'

With a twitch of her skirts she left him and hurried back to the house.

Diana put on her teal gown to go down to the early dinner. She had considered wearing her lavender silk, which would have been more in keeping with her mood but compared to her new gowns it was very sober and old-fashioned, and with a sudden flash of spirit she knew she did not wish Alex to remember her as dowdy.

She gazed with a quiet defiance around the crowded drawing room. Alex was standing by Lady Hune's chair. Had he told her yet that she would be required to act as his hostess later this evening? Perhaps it was too much to ask of such an old lady. Lady Frances drifted into view, looking beautiful and untroubled. Perhaps Alex would ask her to stand at the door to greet his guests.

The idea woke the insidious worm of jealousy in Diana but she would not allow it to subsume her. After all, what did it matter? Soon nothing at Chantreys would be her concern, and even her involvement in the children's welfare would be reduced to correspondence between lawyers.

Across the room Alex watched Diana, so absorbed in his thoughts that he did not realise Lady Hune was addressing him until he felt her stick bang against his leg.

'I beg your pardon, ma'am, I was not attending.'

'That is quite evident,' came the sharp reply. 'I was saying that Miss Grensham looks a little distracted.'

'Perhaps she is pining,' murmured Ellen Tatham, coming to sit down beside the dowager. 'I think she is suffering from unrequited love.'

'Then more fool her,' uttered the dowager.

'Indeed, ma'am, I think perhaps it is the *object* of her affections who is the fool.' Miss Tatham carefully arranged her skirts. 'I suspect he is quite as besotted as Miss Grensham, only he has not had the wit to tell her so. I fear they will go their separate ways and both be equally miserable, all for the want of a little resolution. Do you not agree, my lord?'

Alex dragged his eyes from Diana's graceful figure and looked down to find Miss Tatham's wide, enquiring gaze fixed upon him.

'What a cork-brained idea!' he declared savagely.

There was an air of excited anticipation in the drawing room. Diana felt it but was unmoved, after all she would not be at the forthcoming ball. When anyone commented that she was quiet, or pale, or abstracted, she explained she had a headache. It was not completely untrue and would be remembered when she sent her apologies later in the evening. She spent the short time before dinner mingling with her guests but carefully avoiding the earl. The few times they had found themselves in the same group they had been studiously polite to one another. There were no shared jokes, no laughing looks. Diana found that even more painful than if he had not been there at all. She glanced at the clock. A little more than half an hour until dinner was announced. She would engage Mrs Peters and Miss Prentiss in conversation until then.

'Miss Grensham, I would like a word with you, if you please.'

Alex was at her shoulder, his face a polite mask. What could she say, in front of everyone?

'Of course.'

A smile, cool and distant as his own, and she went with him to his study. He shut the door upon them but did not speak immediately. Instead he walked to the window, then to the mantelshelf to straighten an ornament. At last he turned to face her.

'I needed to make sure you had not changed your mind. You are determined to stay away from the ball.'

'I am.'

'Then after dinner I shall ask the dowager marchioness to stand in for you.'

His words were harsh, his face unsmiling and for a moment she allowed the hurt inside her to creep to the surface.

'Mayhap you would prefer Lady Frances to take my place!'

As soon as the words were out Diana regretted them.

'I beg your pardon, I should not have said that.' She turned away, blinking rapidly. 'Of course Lady Hune is the most proper person to be your hostess. Now if you will excuse me—'

'No. Not yet.' He caught her arm. 'Why should you think I would do that? Why should I put Frances in your place?'

'Sir Charles told me—'

'Hah! I should have known Urmston would stir it up if he could. Go on, what poison did he drip in your ear?'

She shook off his hand, disturbed by the reaction his touch caused in her, the way her stomach swooped and the sudden compulsion to throw herself into his arms. She clenched her fists, digging the nails into the palms to help her keep calm.

She said, 'He told me you and Lady Frances were very close. That she had hopes of becoming your countess.'

His dismissive laugh shocked her.

'He said she loves you, my lord.'

'Frances? The only person she loves is herself.'

'How can you say that?

'Because I know the woman.'

'I thought you and she were friends.' Diana frowned a little. 'I thought, perhaps, you were even more than that.'

'Lovers?'

Diana nodded, her eyes sliding away from his piercing gaze. They stood in silence for a long moment until at last he spoke.

'I did have a brief liaison with the lady. It was when I first came to town. Frances likes novelty, but it came to nothing and we parted on good terms and we remain—remained friends. We have many acquaintances in common, you see. I admit I enjoy her parties, the company she gathers about her is interesting, there are few women, in general the men are sportsmen and gamblers and one is not constantly on the alert for the parson's mousetrap.'

He walked back to the window and stared out, his hands clasped lightly behind him.

'My reputation is bad, Diana, but that is mostly because when I came to town I would not conform to society's rules. I am not a recluse, but I have avoided those parties and assemblies where one is expected to do the pretty with a host of young ladies all on the catch for a husband. My fortune has allowed me to indulge my passion for sport and collecting those works of art that appeal to me.

'Lady Frances has been very useful, I do not deny it. She has been on hand to act as my hostess upon occasion when I have held my own parties in town and because I have had no one to please but myself those attending such parties were not the most respectable. And occasionally Frances and I appear in public together. It is convenient. She is generous with her time and I ensure she is well rewarded. I have no illusions about the lady's interest in me, it was non-existent until I became earl, but in the past months she has been trying to beguile her way back into my bed.' He swung round. 'She has not succeeded, Diana. I realised at the outset that Lady Frances is one who likes to share her favours and that is not my way. I have also come to realise that there are far too many men like Urmston in her circle. In fact, I think I have outgrown such company now.'

He came to stand before her again and Diana fought down the urge to flee. This might be the last time they would be alone together. Even when he reached out to take her hands she did not resist.

'I have been a fool, Diana. I could not see what I wanted when it was here all the time.'

'Please,' she whispered, forcing the words from her drying throat. 'You gave me your word you would not speak of it again.'

'I know, but let me beg you one more time to accept my hand in marriage, Diana. I do love you, you know.'

'No.' Tears misted her eyes, she wanted to run away from the temptation Alex was offering her, but he was holding her hands, his thumbs gently caressing the soft skin of her wrists and she could not move. She tried her best to argue, to fight him with reason. 'It is not love, my lord. It is merely lust, and having given in to it you think you need to make reparation. You do not. I would not tie you to such a bleak existence.'

'I do not see it that way. Do you not think you could love me, if you tried?'

His voice was low and coaxing. Those circling thumbs were drawing up the aching longing from deep within. Diana felt it spreading through her limbs, taking away her ability to move, to think clearly. He was so close now, towering over her. If she looked up into his face she would be lost. He released one hand and put his fingers under her chin, gently lifting it.

'Diana, my beautiful woodland goddess.'

He was lowering his head. Her eyes fixed on his lips and her own were already parting in anticipation. She remembered how his kiss had ravaged her before, how his tongue had plundered her mouth, demanding a response and she longed to respond to him again. To give herself to him again.

'I say, Alex, have you seen my—oh. I beg your pardon.'

Mr Wollerton's entrance and clumsy apology brought

Diana back to reality. It was as if a pail of icy water had been thrown over her.

Even as Alex looked up she stepped away from him. How could he love her, how could he in all honesty call her beautiful? She was small and thin and insignificant and he was an expert on beauty. It was true she no longer walked with that ugly, halting gait but the scars were still there. That long ridge on her thigh would never disappear.

His intentions were honourable but he was lying to her. It was all a trick. He had decided she should marry him to save her reputation and he knew she would not enter into a loveless marriage so he was trying to make her believe he had fallen in love with her.

All those years of discipline now came to her aid, those years when she had had to summon every ounce of pride and spirit to get her through the door, to smile as if she could not hear the whispers or see the pitying looks as she limped into a room.

'Do come in, Mr Wollerton,' she said now with admirable calm. 'Lord Davenport and I have finished our conversation and I must return to my guests.' She raised her head and fixed the earl with a clear, steady look. 'Thank you, my lord, for your kindness, but my decision has not changed.'

Chapter Seventeen

Alex watched Diana walk out of the room and close the door. Such calm, such poise did not belong to a woman labouring under strong emotions.

'Have I interrupted something? Alex?'

He realised Gervase was still in the room and staring at him.

'What? Oh, no, no. What is it you want?'

'I thought I might have left my snuffbox in here. Can't find it anywhere.'

Alex waved a hand. 'Feel free to search the room, then.'

He went back to the drawing room, pausing for a moment before going in. If Diana could refuse his proposal with such sangfroid then he must accept it with the same cool composure. It was over.

Diana sat at the foot of the dining table and ate a little from every dish with an outward appearance of enjoyment, but despite Cook's exceptional efforts, every mouthful tasted like ashes. She wanted to weep and cry and rip and tear, instead she had to smile and make polite, meaningless conversation. By the time she led the ladies out of the dining room there was no doubting that she was unwell. Several of the ladies remarked upon her pallor as they drifted into the hall, so she had the dubious comfort of knowing that when Alex announced she was too ill to attend the ball no one would doubt him.

She dawdled in the hall, pretending to straighten a stray bloom in the arrangement at the bottom of the stairs while the ladies began to make their way upstairs, but at last she knew she must go, too. As she put her foot on the first step she found Lady Frances at her side.

'My dear, you look positively *grey*. Pray, let me help you up the stairs.'

She supported Diana in what must appear to any onlooker as a friendly grasp. To Diana it felt more like the jaws of a mastiff clamped around her arm, but to throw her off would have taken effort, and Diana was too exhausted to care. There were other ladies on the stairs but no one close enough to overhear Lady Frances's soft murmur.

'Very convincing, my dear, I take it you will not be appearing again this evening.'

'No, I do not think I will.'

'So you have seen the folly of your ways? You see now what a fool you would be to stand beside Davenport and meet his guests, his neighbours. How small and insignificant you would be beside him, my dear, with all your…imperfections. Better not to put yourself through that humiliation, would you not agree?'

Diana lifted her head.

'I have nothing to be ashamed of—'

'Have you not?' Lady Frances purred out the words. 'Would you deny that you have given your silly little heart to Davenport?' Her knowing smile was a mixture of pity and contempt. 'And you have as good as told me the earl has taken more than your heart, has he not? Just as he intended.'

Diana stopped, wrenching her arm free. 'How dare you insult me.'

'Oh, I dare.' Lady Frances halted on the next step up, as if to increase Diana's humiliation by the extra height. 'What will you do about it, go crying to Davenport? He has given you little support thus far. Do you remember, my dear, when I mentioned that ugly limping gait of yours? I must say you have done very well to disguise it.'

Diana was too angry to be intimidated. She marched up the next two steps until she was eye to eye with Frances.

'I am not your dear and I remember it very well. But then, as now, there is no need for anyone to support me against...' she breathed in, allowing her rage full rein '...against the railings of a toadying mushroom with the manners of an alley cat!'

The stunned look on Frances's face was very satisfying, if Diana had been in the mood to appreciate it, but she was too shocked at her own outburst. She ran quickly up to the top floor, anxious that her fury should not betray her into any more unladylike behaviour.

Alex did not encourage the gentlemen to tarry once the ladies had departed. They drifted out of the dining room and at last Alex was alone with his thoughts. He poured himself another brandy, carried it to the window and gazed out without seeing the landscaped grounds looking their best in the late afternoon sunshine.

'Not feeling quite the thing, old boy?' Gervase appeared at his shoulder.

'I did not hear you come back in.'

'No, you was lost in your own thoughts, what? I hope

your neighbours are impressed by you putting on a ball for them.'

'I wish I had never started this whole thing,' Alex muttered. 'I should have bought another house for my treasures and my amusements and left Chantreys well alone.'

'Yes, well, it's a little late to think that now.' He coughed delicately. 'I tried to put it right with Miss Grensham. Told her it was never your plan to ruin her.'

'And did she believe you?'

'Well, no…'

Alex gave a tight little smile.

'No, she wouldn't. Not after we had—' He broke off and rubbed one hand across his eyes. 'I have ruined her life, Gervase, and she will not let me put it right. She says she won't enter into a loveless marriage.'

'Aye, but would it be?' murmured Gervase, rubbing his nose.

'Not on my part,' said Alex quickly.

'That's what we thought.'

'We?'

Gervase waved his hand. 'Figure of speech, old boy. Well, I had best go. I told my man to bring up the hot water early, before it is all taken by the ladies.' He laid a hand on Alex's shoulder. 'Cheer up, my friend. It may all yet turn out well.'

The earl's only answer to his friend was a grunt.

Upon reaching the schoolroom floor Diana went directly to her bedchamber, but the first thing that met her eye was her new evening gown, thrown over a chair with its voluminous skirts flowing out like a scarlet waterfall.

'What is that doing here?' she demanded of her maid. 'I told you it would not be required tonight.'

Jenny bobbed a nervous curtsy.

'If you please, miss, I *had* packed it away, like you said to do, but when I was downstairs Mistress Duffy came up to me and told me that I must shake it out and leave it over a chair, to prevent any creases.'

'My gowns are not the business of Lady Hune's dresser,' exclaimed Diana angrily.

'I know that, miss, but she was so insistent, and I thought she would come and see that I had done as she bade me...'

With a huff of exasperation Diana turned on her heel and walked out. She went into the schoolroom, where Meggie and Florence were working on their samplers under Nurse's indulgent eye. When they saw Diana they demanded that she come and inspect their progress. Diana's anger faded and was replaced by the aching realisation that they would not be in her care for very much longer. She sat with them for a while, wondering how best to explain that she was leaving them, but just the thought of it made her head pound even more. She decided she would broach the subject in a day or two, when all the guests had departed and they could be quiet again.

At last Nurse took the girls away but long after they had gone Diana remained alone in the schoolroom, sitting at the big table with her head in her hands.

'May I come in?'

Diana sat up.

'Oh, Miss Tatham. Yes, please do come in. Did you wish to see Meggie and Florence? They have gone to lie down on their beds for a while.'

'Well, then, I shall not disturb them.' She looked around her with lively interest. 'It is so lovely and peaceful in here, may I stay for a while, Miss Grensham? I think we are very alike and do not wish to be hours at our dressing table, preparing for a ball.'

'I, um, I am not going,' said Diana. 'I am not well.'

'Oh, dear, and here am I, chattering on, when no doubt you wish to lie down upon your bed.'

'No, no, there will be plenty of time for me to do that later,' Diana replied politely. 'Please, stay as long as you wish.'

'Thank you.'

Ellen wandered around the room, inspecting the paintings on the walls, running a finger along the spines of the books on the shelves.

'You have made this very comfortable, Miss Grensham. I never had a schoolroom, only the nursery and my lovely Matlock to look after me. I was sent away to school at an early age, you see. Papa thought it best that I should learn something of the world before my come-out. It was an excellent establishment and I learned a great deal.' She bent a mischievous smile upon Diana. 'Probably much more than Papa ever intended.'

'And now you are enjoying your first Season,' offered Diana.

'Yes, I am, very much.'

'And...' Diana traced a crack in the table top with one finger '...I expect you have any number of suitors.'

'Yes, dozens.' Ellen gave a trill of laughter. 'Does that sound very conceited? It is the truth, but it is not really anything to boast of. Most of them are attracted by my fortune.'

'And, do you have any particular favourite amongst all these suitors?'

'Oh, I find them all most diverting, in their way.'

'And, and Lord Davenport?' Diana tried to sound unconcerned. 'He clearly has the advantage of being related to Lady Hune, who is your sponsor.'

'Yes, I suppose that is true,' said Ellen, sitting down at the table. 'We have met frequently in town this Season and he was good enough to escort us to several parties. But he is an Arrandale and the family has the most shocking reputation.'

'I think Lord Davenport could be a very good husband,' Diana observed, a little wistfully.

'I believe you are right, Miss Grensham. But I have no intention of marrying for years yet and certainly not the earl.' She smiled at Diana's surprise. 'Oh, he is very charming, but he can be a little tiresome. When we met in London all he talked of was his wards and their governess.' There was a mischievous look in Ellen's eye. 'Mr Wollerton and I think he is quite enamoured of her, you know.'

Diana quickly returned her attention to the crack in the table, not knowing what to say. The schoolroom clock began to chime the hour.

'Goodness, is that the time?' Ellen jumped up. 'I must go and change. Thank you for your company, Miss Grensham.' She ran to the door and stopped to look back at Diana, who had not moved. 'Oh, and talking of Lord Davenport and the governess—I believe he is hers for the taking, if only she would put herself to the trouble of catching him.'

She was gone before the clock had chimed its final note, leaving Diana to stare at the closed door.

The sky was glorious, the final blaze of the evening sun sending streaks of red and gold through the darkening azure. Torchères had been placed around the drive and along the covered walk to the orangery, where the musicians were tuning up in readiness for the evening's festivities. The air was so calm and clear their discordant notes could even be heard floating in through the open windows of the drawing room. Alex was there alone. Most of his guests were already making their way to the orangery but he had sent a message to Lady Hune to join him here. He did not want an audience when he asked her to act as his hostess for the evening. He turned as the door opened.

'Frances.' With an effort Alex prevented himself from frowning. 'Everyone has gone to the orangery.'

'Not quite everyone, Alexander.' She came towards him, resplendent in white silk trimmed with blue and silver, the diamonds and sapphires he had given her sparkling at her throat. 'Your little *ingénue* will not come up to scratch. I believe she will cry off.'

'She is unwell,' Alex replied shortly.

'Really? I rather thought she was suffering from a guilty conscience.' When he did not reply she gave a soft laugh. 'Poor Alexander, you spend all your time in town avoiding those matchmaking mamas only to become entangled with a governess.'

'Miss Grensham is joint guardian of Meggie and Florence,' he corrected her.

'And that makes it all so much more complicated, doesn't it?' She came closer and brushed a speck from his evening coat. 'She is not of our world, my lord. She does not understand the games we play.'

He said heavily, 'I do not play games, Frances.'

'No? Then why did you invite the tedious Mr Hamilton and Mr Avery to Chantreys? Not for your own pleasure, surely. And then there was Madam Francot and the two dancers you sent here. Were you not trying to shock Miss Grensham?'

'Yes, yes, very well. I wanted her out of Chantreys,' he admitted, turning again to the window, but not taking in the pleasing view. 'But all that has changed.'

'I know it, but there is no going back, my lord. The damage is done and the question is, what happens next? Have you asked Miss Grensham to marry you?'

His shoulders lifted a fraction. 'She will not have me.'

'Well, I am glad one of you is showing some sense.' His keen ears caught the rustle of silk as she moved closer. 'You and I both know that an innocent like Diana Grensham would bore you within a month. You need a woman, my lord, someone who can amuse you without desiring your constant attendance, or throwing a tantrum every time your eye is taken by a pretty face.'

Bore him? Alex could not agree. Diana would infuriate, challenge, argue, even surprise him, but life with her would not be boring.

But she has refused you.

Frances was at his shoulder, her voice soft and seductive. 'We are not in love, Alexander, but we understand one another. You need a wife and I would like to be a countess. You know I am perfect for that role. I could run your houses, see to your…comforts and provide you with an heir. I was brought up to do that, bred for it. Your life need change very little, we would be obliged to entertain your neighbours occasionally, very much like this evening, but otherwise we might continue to enjoy ourselves as we do now. I would not complain if you wished to take your pleasures elsewhere. It would be a very civilised arrangement and no one would suffer.'

A civilised arrangement. No raging passion that would overwhelm him, none of the pain that was now tormenting him.

'Think it over, Alexander,' the soft siren voice murmured in his ear. 'Think how pleasant it would be to have a wife who wants nothing but your comfort, who will not disturb your peace with tears and arguments and will let you go your own way, whatever that may be.'

Her fingers squeezed his arm and then she was gone, he heard the soft click of the door as she went out. There was no doubt it was a tempting prospect, thought Alex. He would have to marry at some point, and this way he could go back to his old hedonistic lifestyle, knowing he had done his duty.

And in time the memory of Diana would fade.

He heard the door open again and turned to see the Dowager Marchioness of Hune coming into the room.

'Well, Nephew, you wanted to see me?'

Chapter Eighteen

It seemed to Alex that there was an endless procession of guests filing in from the anteroom. The orangery was already crowded and noisy with loud, chattering voices, but still they came. Some were acquaintances from town but many were strangers, neighbours invited here to meet the new earl.

He told himself it did not matter that Diana was not beside him to make him known to the local families, Fingle took each guest's name and announced it in a majestically sonorous tone. Most of those coming in were too awed at being met with not only an earl but a dowager marchioness to do more than make their obeisance and move on, but one or two, like Squire Huddlestone and Mrs Frederick, were emboldened to ask after Diana.

Their disappointment and concern when they heard that Miss Grensham was indisposed was clearly genuine and from their comments Alex realised that although Diana might not go into society a great deal, she had made some good friends at Chantreys. His eyes wandered around the room. With the exception of Gervase, how many of those who called themselves his friends would care if he were ill?

'Well, Nephew, have you decided whom you will honour with the first dance?'

Lady Hune's voice recalled his attention. The doors to the anteroom had been closed, his guests were all assembled and the orchestra was tuning up. He must find a partner, but he was well aware of the speculation that would arise when he made his choice.

'Perhaps it is fortunate Diana is not here to stand up with you, since you tell me you have no intention of offering for her,' said the dowager, as if reading his mind. 'Pity, though. I thought she would suit you very well.'

'Unfortunately the lady does not agree with you,' he muttered. 'I wish to goodness I did not have to do this.'

'With rank and privilege comes responsibility, Davenport.'

'You need not tell me that, ma'am.'

'So who will it be? Not Ellen. We both know my protégée is not for you so let us not raise any more conjecture there. You must find a partner, Davenport.'

Alex looked about him. Frances had moved closer and was standing with Miss Prentiss and Mrs Peters, smiling graciously at something the older lady was saying. A few steps would take him to her side. She was clearly ready and waiting for him to invite her to dance. Ready to become his countess. And why not? As she had said, they understood one another. It would be a very elegant solution. She looked across at him and her smile widened. He could see the triumph in her eyes.

An expectant hush had fallen over the room. The musicians were waiting for his signal to begin, the guests were all turned towards him.

He raised his hand.

'Davenport.'

Lady Hune's urgent tone and tap on his arm made him swing around to see that the doors of the anteroom had been thrown wide again. Framed in the opening was Diana, dressed as he had never seen her before in a scarlet ballgown that glowed in the candlelight. It was cut low across her breast and fell in soft, shimmering folds from the high waist. Her red hair was piled on her head and only one glossy ringlet had been allowed to escape, falling like a narrow tongue of flame against the cool ivory skin of her shoulder.

She wore no jewels, just a simple length of red ribbon around her throat, but as she came slowly into the room the flickering candlelight was reflected in her eyes, making them glow with sparks of emerald and amber. Those same eyes were fixed anxiously upon Alex and in the near silence that now filled the room he heard her soft, musical voice addressing him.

'Am I too late?'

It had taken all Diana's courage to come to the orangery. When she reached the anteroom and saw the doors were closed she would have run away again, but Fingle was blocking her retreat.

'Forgive my impertinence, miss, but it would be a shame to come thus far and not go in.'

There was understanding in his voice and in the smile he bestowed upon her. He was right, she had to do this. Diana turned towards the ballroom, put back her shoulders and lifted her head another inch.

The butler moved ahead of her. 'Shall I announce you?'

Diana gave a little shake of her head. Silently he threw wide the doors and, gathering up all her courage, she stepped forward in a whisper of scarlet silk. She had a sudden, vivid image of Mrs Siddons, making an entrance at Drury Lane. The room was hushed and every eye was turned towards her—or perhaps not.

Perhaps they were watching the earl putting out his hand to Lady Frances.

As Alex turned to look at Diana she took another few steps into the room.

'Am I too late?'

She prayed Fingle had not closed the doors behind her. One look, one word from Alex and she would turn and flee. Her heart was hammering against her ribs and the blood was pounding so loudly in her ears that she feared she would not hear Alex's response, but it did not need words. There was no mistaking the explosion of joy that lit his face. He came towards her, both hands reaching out, and any lingering doubts fled when she read the message in his eyes. They glowed with love and pride.

'No, you are not too late,' he murmured, smiling down at her in a way that made her spirits soar. 'Never too late, my love. My goddess.'

He pulled her closer and as he lowered his head she forgot about the crowded room and raised her face to accept his kiss. Gasps of shock and outrage rippled around the room but they were quickly replaced by laughter and a smattering of applause. Diana heard Gervase's voice calling out cheerfully, 'And about time, too!'

As Alex raised his head Diana felt her cheeks burning and turned an apologetic look towards Lady Hune, but the dowager was smiling broadly, while beside her Ellen Tatham was laughing and clapping. In fact, as Diana looked about the room everyone was beaming at her. Even Lady Frances had managed a forced smile.

Alex led Diana to the centre of the floor and signalled to the musicians to strike up.

'Do you realise that we have never yet danced together?' he remarked as guests flocked to take their places in the set. 'If you recall, I have been assured that you dance beautifully.'

He was grinning at something over her shoulder and she glanced around to see Meggie and Florence peeping in from the anteroom. Heavens, they must have followed her down the path! She turned back to find Alex regarding her seriously.

'Do you mind if we stand up for just one dance?' he asked her. 'I want the children to hear our announcement before they go off to bed.'

'Our…our announcement, my lord?'

'Why, yes.' The first notes of the dance filled the air and they saluted one another. Alex stepped up and held out his hand to her, ready to execute the first move. 'I think they should be here when I ask you to marry me, don't you?'

'Alex, you c-can't ask such a thing here, in front of all these people!'

He stopped abruptly. Immediately everyone else stopped dancing and the music died away.

'Why not?' Alex's deep voice filled the awkward silence. 'After all, you *kissed* me in front of all these people.'

A laugh caught in her throat.

'I—that is—'

He interrupted her disjointed protest. 'Are you going to refuse me?'

Another startled murmur fluttered around the room as Alex went down on one knee in the middle of the floor. He was still holding Diana's hand and he spoke with ringing clarity.

'Miss Grensham, will you do me the very great honour of becoming my wife? Will you allow me to bestow upon you my hand and my heart?' His grip on her fingers tightened. He said more quietly, 'It is a long time since I wanted you to leave Chantreys, Diana. Now I want you to be its mistress. For ever. Pray, answer truthfully, refuse me if you must, you have my word that whatever you decide, Chantreys shall remain your home, Meggie and Florence shall remain in your care, our care, for as long as you wish it.' He glanced about him. 'There are enough witnesses to my declaration that you can be sure I shall not go back on my word. On my honour.'

Once again she was the centre of attention. A few months ago she would have cringed to be in such a position. Now, she barely noticed the crowd. Only Alex, kneeling at her feet. She said slowly, 'I have never doubted your honour, my lord, but…can you really *love* me?'

She read the answer in his eyes.

'With all my heart and soul,' he said ardently. 'If you return my regard, if you love me and can agree to become my wife, you will make me the happiest man on earth.'

His image became blurred and she blinked rapidly.

'Oh, Alex, I do,' she whispered. 'I do love you, and—'

Her words were cut off as Alex jumped to his feet and dragged her into another fierce embrace. His kiss was brief but ruthless and when it was over Diana hid her face in his shoulder. It was shameful, totally outrageous to behave this way in public. What would everyone think? She felt a laugh bubbling up inside. She did not *care* what anyone thought!

'We will be married by special licence,' he murmured. 'But even that is too long to wait. As soon as everyone is gone I shall take you to bed and worship you, my goddess. But only if you wish it, Diana.'

A glow suffused her body at the thought and she could not suppress a beaming smile of happiness.

'I would like nothing more,' she whispered to him.

With a laugh Alex released her, but only to pull her hand on to his arm.

'Head up, Diana,' he murmured, smiling down at her. 'We have an announcement to make!'

* * * * *

LET'S TALK
Romance

For exclusive extracts, competitions
and special offers, find us online:

- **f** facebook.com/millsandboon
- ⊙ @millsandboonuk
- 🐦 @millsandboon

Or get in touch on 0844 844 1351*

For all the latest titles coming soon,
visit millsandboon.co.uk/nextmonth